David Andrew Westwood

ISBN 9781097900428

FICTION: General
FICTION: Historical – 20th Century

Published by

DAVIDANDREWWESTWOOD.COM
Los Angeles, California

To the casualties.

Contents

2000

A dog barked somewhere. There was always a dog barking somewhere. Up through the canyon from the coast drove a deep blue Porsche 911, followed a minute or two later by a red first-year Mustang, while from the Valley direction drove a dowdy black Honda minivan.

The Porsche's driver, a fifty-year-old man with a paunch, balding gray hair, and a double-breasted charcoal gray suit, eased himself out and edged to one side as the Mustang pulled next to him in a brief flurry of dust. A striking woman opened its door, grabbed her purse from the seat and stood. She wore a battered Levi's jacket over black jeans, but with a silk blouse and an expensive diamond necklace. Despite being two years older than him she was in far better shape, though her eyes had the thousand-yard stare of a veteran.

"Can't believe you're on time," Robbie Sobieski said to his elder sister, Sundown. "That's a first."

The two siblings watched as the minivan pulled in behind their cars. Their younger sister Charity slid out and embraced them. No observer would have guessed the two women were related. Charity's demeanor was cooler and more conservative, and she wore a stylish but low-key pantsuit in taupe and short hair; her only jewelry simple silver stud earrings.

The three turned to look at the pale blue stucco house, its two-story octagonal tower giving it a vaguely Italian look.

"Coulda used a lick of paint," Sundown said.

Robbie nodded. "They'll probably tear it down anyway. The buyer's a TV producer. Doesn't really look like a producer's house."

"Looks like a hippie house," Sundown said, with sadness in her tone. "And it was."

"'Hophead Hills'..." Charity mused, "wasn't that what you two used to call it?"

Robbie walked to the front door and unlocked it, and the three wandered through the now-empty rooms. The house smelled of dust and sandalwood incense, and he thought he could detect a tinge of garlic. Or was that just his imagination, drawing on his memory? "Take a last look," he told them. "Escrow's expected to close tomorrow."

Charity ran her hand across the kitchen countertop, now bare of any family paraphernalia for the first time in her memory. "It has no soul now."

Robbie laughed. "Charity's the resident expert on soul."

Used to ignoring him, Charity peered out of the back window across the expanse of grass, still briefly green from the winter rains. "I forgot the tree house."

Robbie snapped his fingers. "I didn't think of that. I bet it's still got junk in it. Jackson used to hang out up there, didn't he?"

No one responded to this mention of their older brother.

They walked out and down the hill to the two pepper trees and the cabin built between them. It had once been painted in an approximation of a paisley pattern, in various shades of blue with touches of violet and green. But the paint, insufficiently primered and baked by three decades of summer sun, had mostly peeled off. Colorful flakes lay like confetti at the foot of the ladder.

Sundown squinted upward. The feathery leaves of the peppers were dry and curling. "The trees don't look so hot."

"Drought," Robbie told her. "Dad wasn't watering them, I guess."

Charity clambered nimbly up the ladder and, after a moment inside, called down, "Come up! It's a time capsule!"

Robbie and Sundown hauled themselves up a little more slowly. Robbie looked and felt overdressed, and he loosened his collar and tie.

A scruffy beanbag sprawled over part of the floor, and cushions of various sizes and color took up the remainder. A small table held an ashtray, and candles slumped into puddles of tinted wax. A book of matches announced "Barney's Beanery, Hollywood." Posters sagged from the walls—a "Keep on Truckin'," with its red leached to a mottled pink, an orange and black Grateful Dead at the Shrine Auditorium dated July, 1968, a "War is Not Healthy for Children and Other Living Things," and a copy of *Desiderata* on parchment decoupaged to a wooden plaque.

"Wow," Sundown said, taking it all in. "Either dad kept this as a museum, or he just forgot it was here."

There was also, tucked into a dusty corner filled with spider webs and mouse nests, a small metal file cabinet. Sundown slid open one of its drawers, withdrew a sheet of foxed paper, and burst into tears.

"What is it?" Robbie asked.

She handed it to him. It was a form headed, "Selective Service System. 11 February 1968. Order to Report for Induction." The name typed on it was Jackson Sobieski.

I

WINTER, 1968

DAYDREAM BELIEVERS

Charity Sobieski turned right out of Topanga Elementary School's driveway and began her walk home. She wore her favorite Vera print dress with big, stylized flowers under a wool pea coat, carried a small backpack over one shoulder containing her books and transistor radio, and a Monkees lunch box.

One of the school's two huge school buses lurched past, the one that headed south toward the coast. Several of her friends yelled and waved from its windows.

The street had no sidewalks, and the girl walked carefully. All drivers, especially those who treated Topanga Canyon Boulevard as a way between the coast and the Valley, were known to take the curves here too fast, and among the dry oak leaves underfoot twinkled cubes of windshield glass from accidents.

Charity liked the mailboxes. Residents' creativity always seemed to come out in the way they presented themselves to the street—U.S. flags, confederate flags, peace signs. One had been spray-painted through paper doilies to look like lace. She had recently helped paint her family's—metallic blue with white stars. This had come about because on Taj Mahal's latest album he sang, "Gonna move up to the country, paint my mailbox blue," and she had talked her father into adding the lyric too, though she was disappointed to discover his lettering was worse than hers.

Soon the village was in sight—a few houses, a few shops, and a couple of restaurants now turning on their lights. Most of the homes hereabouts were hidden among the trees down side roads. Hers was down a lane too, but sat on a piece of property distinctly larger and more open than most.

In just a couple more minutes she was in its wide driveway, crowded with vehicles. She eased past her mother's white VW bug, her eldest brother's bright blue Pontiac GTO, her younger brother's small orange Honda motorcycle, her sister's scruffy black Corvair, and a dusty garnet Camaro Z28, so new it had temporary license plates, still ticking as it cooled. Her father was home.

In the middle distance, at the far end of the lot and down a slight slope, a warm orange glow came from the tree house.

As Charity opened the front door of the house Jackson's black lab Gilligan, wearing his usual red bandana, welcomed her with wagging tail. She was drawn to the kitchen, where her mother Maddy was cooking something fragrant, humming as she moved efficiently between counter and cupboards. Her younger brother Robbie was dipping into a box of Nilla wafers, so he probably had the munchies. Her older sister Sundown was toying with her hair and smiling as she whispered into the pale blue wall phone, its cord stretched to its limit, so she must be talking to a boyfriend. It had to be her father and older brother Jackson in the tree house. For a moment she considered joining them, but there always seemed to be tension between the two lately and she had no intention of interrupting. Besides, tonight was the final *Monkees* episode.

— · —

Father and son sat among the jumble of cushions. Candlelight flickered over the pinned-up magazine photos of the Beatles and the Doors, and a "Robert F. Kennedy—Our Next President" button stuck in the wood. They had experimented with running an extension cord to provide electric light, which was deemed ugly, and then Bret tried a small generator, which was noisy. In rare mutual agreement the family voted for the softness of the candlelight.

As the day's heat left the canyon it drew up the cooler ocean air, and the tree house, a ramshackle affair with ill-fitting windows and door, became drafty. Jackson wore a baggy-pocketed fatigue jacket, while his father wore the fleece-lined corduroy jacket he kept in his car for work.

The young man regarded his father. Bret's long hair, still slightly bleached by last summer's sun, was tangled, and his beard, redder than the hair on his head, was more unkempt than usual. "How did the shoot go?" he asked.

"Crazy, as always. Way over-budget. The execs showed up and threw a fit. The lead was drunk half the time. My best boy got zapped by a bare wire, but he's OK. Usual bullshit." Bret grabbed a baggie from the stash box, and swiftly rolled a well-proportioned joint—none of those humped-in-the-middle efforts that beginners made. He liked to boast he was one of the first to get into weed, long before the kids made it trendy. "It was a long drive from Arizona, but I got the Camaro up to a hundred a coupla times on the way back." He held out the finished joint. "Toke?"

Jackson shook his head. "No thanks." He rarely took a hit, unwilling to relinquish the clarity of his mind. When he did it was only to be polite. Instead, he lit a Camel.

The tree house filled with smoke.

Bret looked at his elder son, seeing him for the first time in almost a month. The boy was a young man now. Beard stubble, the beginnings of crow's feet at the corners of his eyes and a new crease across his forehead, and embarrassingly short hair for a Sobieski, or at least one of the West Coast Sobieskis. He lit the joint and took a long hit.

Jackson gave him a wry smile. "I got my draft notice while you were gone."

Bret choked, and for half a minute he couldn't respond. "Goddammit—they don't waste any time. When do you have to report?"

"I already did. Yesterday."

"Jeez, Jacks. When were you going to tell me?"

"I just did, dad. It can't be much of a surprise. You know how these things work."

"Yeah, yeah. I figured you were going through a phase."

"You thought I'd just grow out of it?"

"What about college? You've already started."

Jackson shrugged. "It can wait."

Bret fumed. He looked out of one of the windows at the sun setting behind the clouds stacking up over the ocean, his face reddening as he tried to control his anger. "Storm coming in."

— · —

Charity had made herself a nest of cushions in front of the TV with her troll dolls, and her dinner on a tray, when her father returned.

Bret, as he often did after being away from home for any amount of time, burst in and started to bark orders: "Robbie! Bring in the chairs before it rains. Make sure all the cars have their windows up. Sundown, when the rain's over, wash the windows, but not in the middle of the day or they'll streak. First thing in the morning is best. Charity—you need to clean up your room, or you'll be grounded."

"But dad, it's Sundown's room too, and the Monkees are on!"

Maddy touched his arm. "Let her watch it, Bret. It's the last one."

This final *Monkees* episode was titled "The Frodis Caper," and was unusual in that the boys awoke to the sounds of the Beatles' "Good Morning Good Morning," the first time anyone else's music had been used on the show. The storyline was, as always, wacky and juvenile. Glick, a wizard, is attempting to control people's minds via their television sets, which all feature an evil eye not so subtly based on the CBS logo. The Monkees discover that something called the Frodis plant has been captured when its spaceship landed on Earth, and is being used by the wizard for his nefarious plans.

"And stay off the phone, everyone," Charity added, adjusting the volume. "I may get a call from one of the band members."

Robbie laughed. "Yeah. Like they're gonna call *you*."

Charity waved her membership badge for the Monkees Club. "I'm Secretary-Treasurer for the Topanga Chapter. I could get a call any Monday night. It says so in the bylaws."

Robbie snorted. He was sitting in the corner of the room, pretending to do his homework. He would try to copy someone else's before school. "'Frodis' is a code word for grass," he muttered.

Charity glanced back at him in annoyance. "You think everything is about grass."

"No, really." He pointed to the screen. The Monkees had rescued the Frodis and returned it to its spaceship. The plant emitted a cloud of gas that mellowed out the wizard and his henchmen. "See? Everyone's stoned."

As the episode came to a close, in another break from tradition, the singer-songwriter Tim Buckley performed a solo acoustic version of his "Song to the Siren." Charity immediately fell in love with him, his song, his earnestness, and his hair like stuffing spilling out of a pillow. Then, at the closing credits, after fifty-eight episodes of which she had only missed one, she burst into tears.

— · —

Jackson roared off into the rain in his GTO. These days, he became exasperated with the rest of the family's fascination with crap like *Mod Squad* and *Hawaii 5-0*. While everyone else was repeating the goofy gag lines from *Laugh-In* he could recite the trouble spots of North and South Vietnam.

He was the only one of his family glued to the news, and he preferred to watch it with his buddies, usually at the house of his like-minded friend, Duke Samson.

Duke lived with his father, a grizzled WWII vet, in another part of Topanga. Duke was a bit of a loose cannon, and his father was even worse, known to threaten an uninvited guest with one of his many guns, and so when Jackson approached the house he announced himself loudly before coming too close.

Duke's room was plastered with a chaotic jumble of all kinds of mementos: a 48-state flag folded in a triangular frame, a U.S. Marines seal, Dodgers and Rams pennants, a shelf sagging under one of every different brand of beer bottle he had ever sampled, and an embroidered bible quotation reading, "Greater love hath no man than this, that he lay down his life for his friends. John 15:13." Next to this was pinned a small and indistinct close-up of a WWII war memorial, and its inscription reading, "When you go home, tell them of us and say / For your tomorrow, we gave our today."

Cronkite came on at ten, and they watched intently for his latest editorial on Vietnam. Tonight, he was giving his post-Tet Offensive summary.

"For it seems now more certain than ever that the bloody experience

of Vietnam is to end in a stalemate. To say that we are closer to victory today is to believe in the face of the evidence the optimists who have been wrong in the past. To say that we are mired in stalemate seems the only realistic, if unsatisfactory, conclusion."

Jackson's mouth set in a grim line. Americans had become soft. They had forgotten the importance of national defense. They thought the only important wars were over and done with, without remembering the hard-won lesson learned from them—the need for eternal vigilance. They thought America's power was a given; a permanent thing that existed without having to be maintained by strength. But he remembered his history. Before World War I the U.S. was a backwater, its army woefully undermanned. As late as Pearl Harbor America was still weak and vulnerable. He felt ashamed, sometimes, at the shallowness of his brother and sisters—even his father, who ought to know better. They dealt with what was under their noses, ignorant of the wider world and its catastrophes. Sure music and movies were fun, but they were luxuries. Luxuries bought at a high price by might and the ability—and willingness—to use it.

Duke snorted. "The North's not gonna negotiate. Cronkite's a defeatist."

"The whole country's defeatist. People are turning against the war."

Duke looked at Jackson. "It's the hippies."

Jackson knew what he meant. Hippies like his family. To change the subject, he said, "So what you going for?"

"Marines."

"Really? Tough training."

Duke grinned. He was built, as his friends loved to point out, like a brick shithouse. "I can take it. What about you?"

"I wanted to be a fighter pilot, or helicopter pilot at least, but I don't think my eyes or my math are good enough."

"Well, just stay away from gliders. My dad says they fly like a brick."

"I don't think they use gliders any more. Gliders were strictly a one-way proposition. Helicopters get 'em in and out. I was studying them. Took them a coupla decades to get the mechanics down, but the new ones are pretty slick. They can do anything."

Duke's interest was waning. "Uh-huh."

"The main rotors give the lift, but the torque would twirl the plane around without the tail rotor, which cancels it out and allows it to fly straight." He leaned forward, eager. "They used to be heavy and slow, with piston engines, but now they have turbines."

"Yeah, well, as long as they can kill VC, I could give a shit. Ready for another beer?"

— · —

Trapped inside by the rain, and unable to escape their chores, Sundown and Charity had no choice but to deal with their shared bedroom. As they cleaned up they argued, as they often did, about how their room should be decorated.

"I'm sick of the Monkees!" Sundown complained. "They're just a contrived band anyway. Just a TV gimmick. They don't even play on their own records!"

"I don't care! I like them!" She pointed to one of Sundown's many posters. "And who's that Choy guy anyway?"

"*Che!* He was a revolutionary in Argentina. He led his people to freedom!"

"But everyone has one of those on their wall. Is it a requirement or something?"

"Ha ha. And take down that Jesus picture, for God's... for Pete's sake. I don't like Him staring at me."

"I can have that up if I want to. You've got that blue Indian elephant thing."

"That's Ganesha!"

"I don't care! He's creepy!"

Charity hung the last of her dresses in her closet and pulled out a raincoat. Now her father and Jackson had vacated it, she ran outside to the tree house. Here she could be alone, and if someone else was coming she could hear them long before they arrived.

A small filing cabinet was crammed in a corner, placed there at her request, which contained pens, rolling papers, matches, spare candles, and any other supplies the family members had left behind. From one of the drawers she took a notepad and began a letter.

> *Dear Monkees,*
>
> *As secretary-bookkeeper of the Monkees Club, Topanga Chapter, I want to say how sad I am that the Monkees show is no longer going to be on TV. All my friends agree this was a great show, and there can be no reason for canceling it. I think*

you owe it to America to continue the show until you decide to stop being a band, which I hope will never happen. You are as important to pop music as the Beatles.

Charity Sobieski

After a moment's thought, she replaced the three dots over the "i's" in her name with flowers. Then, remembering something her sister taught her when she first learned to write, she scrawled on the back of the envelope

Mailman, mailman, don't be slow. Be like Elvis—go man, go!

Would the Monkees see the humor in this? She hoped so.

2

Maddy regarded herself, hands on generous hips, in the full-length mirror. The storm had dissipated and the sun was back. California light was pitilessly bright, and she would have appreciated some flattering shadows. When she was young she had been compared to Sophia Loren, though a shorter version. Now her curves were starting to fill in.

She grimaced. Along with her dismay at her realigning body she was becoming disillusioned with her life. The changing times were beginning to affect her too, to her surprise, despite being of an older generation than last year's flower children. She felt as if she were watching her family disintegrate, drift off in different directions, and far earlier than she had imagined it happening.

After twenty years of marriage, Bret was starting to get on her nerves. He was gone a great chunk of the time, and when home seemed to think reconnecting with his family involved a mixture of bullying and boasting. Robbie was an underperforming wild child, Sundown was getting rather too heavily into men, Charity seemed to need framework just as it was disappearing, and Jackson, her firstborn, wanted to go off to war.

She walked out and into the kitchen. Movement outside caught her attention. "Look at that," she said to Charity, reassured by the sight of Robbie walking down from the blue mailbox, clutching an armful of envelopes and looking intently through them. "Robbie always gets the mail. He's such a good kid."

Charity gave a derisive snort. She was more interested in her transistor radio than the exploits of her little brother. She wandered away, humming "Yummy, yummy, yummy / I've got love in my tummy."

Robbie found the envelope he was searching for and pocketed it quickly. Inside the house he handed the remainder to his mother, gave her an innocent smile, and hurried down to the tree house.

Once inside he ripped open the envelope and read the letter it contained. It was as he suspected. Palisades High School was advising his parents that he had missed several classes during the previous week. He dealt with this in the same manner as his recent report card—"Too easily distracted"—he tore the letter into indecipherable shreds and stuffed them into a pocket. Then he pulled a pad of notepaper and a pen out of the cabinet and began a letter to the attendance office.

> *To Whom It May Concern.*
>
> *Please excuse Robert Sobieski from his recent missed classes. He has been fighting bronchitis lately, and we had to keep him home. His father and I are confident he will soon make up his lessons.*
>
> *Thank you,*

He forged his mother's signature, at which he had become particularly adept,

> *Madeline Sobieski.*

— · —

Next morning, a Monday, Robbie jumped astride his little orange Honda CT90 and headed out of the driveway. The familiar sick dread filled his stomach. He loathed school and everything it stood for.

Once out of sight of the house, he pulled off the road under some trees and took a few tokes from a joint he carried in his school backpack. Then, as a muffled sensation began to press against his inner ears, the thought of school dissolved until it was a barely perceptible stain on his otherwise cheery consciousness. He popped a Life Saver in his mouth in an effort to disguise the smell and cruised on down the canyon, past the HIPPYS EAT SHIT graffito on a fence, past someone selling cheap and garish rugs, to Pacific Coast Highway. The silver ocean, empty and shimmering, stretched away in front of him, uncontaminated by crass commercialism.

Early in the day the road was filled, southeastward, with commuter traffic traveling from Malibu into Los Angeles. This was the direction he was supposed to be taking. Coast residents had no other way of getting to work, unless they wanted to drive the eight miles through Malibu Canyon or a tortuous six through Topanga. In the opposite direction, away from the city, traffic was light, and this was the way Robbie chose. In just ten minutes he was at Zuma Beach, at this time of day empty of anyone except surfers and a few pelicans gliding low over the waves in search of fish.

A sign read CLOSED FROM SUNSET TO SUNRISE, and someone had scrawled TO VALS under the word CLOSED. Robbie was used to anti-Val sentiments. Local surfers were territorial, and gave visitors from the Valley a hard time if they tried to surf here.

He looked for one surfer in particular—Jeff—and found him standing, his wetsuit hanging half off to reveal a narrow but muscular chest, chatting casually with two young women. The tide had turned, and so Jeff's morning's surfing was done.

"Hey," Robbie said, walking over.

"Oh, hey, man."

"Got anything ... for sale?"

"Yeah, Mexican. In the magic bus. Wanna check it out?"

They walked over to a VW 18-window minibus, all fat tires and flower decals with a hula girl on the dash, and climbed in the back.

Jeff peered in all directions, and then pulled a sack from inside a sleeping bag. "Here. Some seeds an' stems, but it's OK."

Robbie tried a sample. It was harsh on the throat and a mediocre high. They reached a deal. Jeff separated the bag into several four-finger lids in Baggies, to which Robbie added a little of his mother's oregano to pad out the quantity and improve the color. Then he stashed them in his backpack among the schoolbooks and comics.

Alone in the van now, Robbie gazed out at the surfers as they rinsed off under the beach shower. An intrusive thought of school tried to worm its way into his mind, and to keep it out he began a song about the open road, and freedom. The road led away from the straight world, and the freedom was his.

He pictured himself sauntering along a dusty country road toward a distant blue ridge, a battered guitar slung over one shoulder.

"I'm a rambler, I'm a traveler,
An' I can't be tied down.

I'm a lover, I'm a loner,
An' I hate this small town..."
Now it needed some kind of middle eight.
"I know you love me, babe,
But I yearn to be free.
I can't help your heartbreak,
It's the open road for me."
Maybe some chicks singing backup here:
"Though I love our ballin',
I hear the road a-callin'."
Yeah. Classic.

— · —

During recess, instead of running around with the other children, Charity sat on a bench and wrote in her journal. Her writing was loopy and precise, slanting slightly backward.

> *Robbie is such a weasel. I don't think he goes to school. I think he heads off somewhere with his stoner friends. But he puts on such a good show that no one knows what he's up to. Mommy and daddy fall for it every time.*
>
> *He used to be a good kid. He and I used to have fun together. But now he pretends to be something he's not. I bet if I could follow him I'd find him smoking weed in some cave somewhere. I don't see how he thinks he'll get away with it. Sooner or later everyone will find out what a sneak he is.*

Then, as she looked out at the oak trees ringing the playground, she impulsively began a different topic.

> *It's not true that California has no seasons, though to a visitor from upstate New York it might seem that way. California seasons, at least here in the south, are mild.*
>
> *At the beginning of the year is a kind of winter, with a short rainy season. Usually this means a couple of one-day storms off the Pacific, but the rainfall runs off the dried-out hills and mountains and along creeks that often haven't seen water for years, and floods the sewers. Topanga Creek runs at these times, flushing the year's trash out into the Pacific and giving surfers ear infections for the next few weeks.*
>
> *California's roads, dry for months and coated with a buildup*

of oil and rubber particles, turn into skating rinks. Cars slither around for the first few hours until everything's washed away and tires can grip again.

The bell rang, and she hurried inside.

— · —

Sundown pulled up in front of her friend Len Williams' house. He was waiting, his hair in an Afro with a pick stuck in its side. They were so different in appearance they could have been negatives of each other.

Len slid in next to her and said, "What's happenin'?"

Her car ground its way up Topanga Canyon Boulevard toward the ridge, the cabin filled with its clattering rear engine and transmission whine. They passed a house where workmen were pouring concrete piers on either side of the creek in front of a ramshackle house.

"Bridge?" she asked him.

"He's bought a railroad boxcar and he's planning on putting that over the creek—it's cheaper."

"What—cutting the ends off?"

"I guess."

"Weird. This place is so weird. I'm embarrassed to be from here. Why can't I live somewhere normal?"

Len looked at her. "It's not so weird."

"No? What about the guy who lives on the hill behind the Corral with a lion cub? What about the guy down PCH that's building an *ark* in his front yard?"

"Maybe he knows something we don't." Len looked out the window, smiling vaguely. "I like it here. It's different."

"It's the sticks. The boonies. Hicksville." Sundown felt a familiar exasperation wash over her. Stuck in the backwoods with her father's outsized ego, sharing a bedroom with her uptight little sister, having to sit through boring school classes, and now expected to go off to college to endure four more years of the same. "They call us 'gypsies' at school, you know."

He laughed. "Who cares? I get called a lot worse than that."

"*I* care. I don't want to be a freak. Well … not *that* kind of freak. Not a redneck freak."

"You'd hate the suburbs."

Sundown looked ahead. They had reached the upper lip of the canyon and the road now tilted down to the wide expanse of the San Fernando Valley and its myriad cities. They stretched out to the horizon, ten thousand stucco boxes blanketed in a dun haze.

She sighed. "Yeah, probably."

— · —

Once Sundown had descended the 350 feet to Woodland Hills and parked in the Taft High School lot, she and Len parted company to their respective homerooms. She only had a small coterie of friends, and none was in evidence this Monday. Despite the mass of students milling about the sidewalk and entryway, no one said "hi."

She had to pass a gaggle of half-bouffant cheerleaders, and one of them whispered something snide to her friends as she passed. Sundown whirled on her and glared. "What's your problem, helmet hair?"

She strode to classes, fuming. Perhaps when she left school her looks would be an asset and not a liability, but here they brought her the worst kinds of notice. To her classmates she was resented for drawing the attention of the best-looking boys away from them. To the female teachers, a consistently homely bunch, she was just plain resented. The male teachers, incapable of comprehending that someone might be good-looking *and* smart, pegged her as shallow. As for the boys, they were either too intimidated to ask her out—many a Saturday night passed without her having a date at all—or if they were jocks, they assumed she put out. When she wouldn't, their way of dealing with rejection was to label her "frigid" or a "lez." It didn't seem to occur to them that they might be stupid, or unattractive, or boring, and often all three combined into a triad of undesirability.

Smug. That's how her schoolmates seemed to Sundown. Satisfied with their petty, small-minded world, and happy to just feed their faces and play their silly dating games. There was a war on, and they squandered all their energies pretending it didn't exist. She couldn't wait to get out of this madhouse. But she was afraid college would be more of the same.

One of the senior boys stood at her locker. "Hey, Sunburn! How's things in hippieland?"

"Piss off, Haig."

"Now that's not very *peaceful*, is it?" he said, holding his fingers in a V sign.

She held up one middle finger and pushed him out of the way.

In her English class, the teacher, Mr. Vandevere, smiled at her. At least he treated her like an adult. She looked forward to his class largely because he, out of all of them, took her seriously. She had told him once of her dreams of becoming a model, and Vandevere had actually listened, and been supportive, though he had assured her she could become something that relied on her intellect too.

Today, Vandevere discussed the work of Herman Hesse. He knew the author's work was experiencing a resurgence in popularity with the kids, and he was trying to capitalize on this with his class. He spoke at length about Steppenwolf, Siddhartha, and the Glass Bead Game.

"Where can I get a glass bead game?" one of the footballers, a defensive lineman, asked.

Vandevere smiled indulgently. "The Glass Bead Game was an *allegory*. You'll notice, if you read it, that he describes the game in the vaguest of terms. Hesse was actually taking a poke at the Nazis. He started the book in 1931 and it was finally published—in his homeland of Switzerland only—in 1943. Now—any questions?"

Sundown raised her hand. "Sir, the characters in Hesse's book are scholars, intellectuals. But the Nazis weren't scholars—they were thugs and psychopaths."

The smile left Vandevere's face. "Nazism was confined to one or two types of German—but the whole country bought into the Nazi philosophy."

"But—"

"Homework will be an analysis of the stages of the character Knecht's life."

— · —

Finally, close to noon, Robbie left Zuma and drove five minutes farther north on Highway 1, turned right onto Morning View Drive and parked in the Malibu High School lot.

He knew he was technically trespassing, and so he hung around the lawn outside. In front of him he placed a Rider-Waite deck face down. From his mother he had absorbed the fundamentals of Tarot, and at his parents' parties during the last two years he had fleshed out his understanding by listening to their guests' readings. The colorful cards never failed to bring over curious students at breaks.

A full reading would take far too long, and too much concentration, both of which were in short supply during recess and lunchtime. To keep readings brief, Robbie limited himself to simple three-card spreads. For the girls, he always suggested *What you want from the relationship / What he wants from the relationship / Where the relationship is heading.* When his mother gave a reading like this, she might delve into more personal aspects, like *Material state / Emotional state / Spiritual state,* but he had found schoolkids either didn't care about this, or cared but didn't like to expose their interest to an audience. For these brief readings for boys and couples, he kept it simple: *Past / Present / Future.*

A lanky teenage boy wandered over, hand in hand with a girl. Robbie assessed the pair—their body English, the brands of the boy's shoes and watch, the way the girl clutched the boy's arm a little over-tightly. Well-off, probably spoilt, and insecure. Everyone knew these Malibu kids had rich and fucked-up parents.

They stopped and stared down at the cards.

"Want a reading?" Robbie asked. "No charge."

"Yeah," the boy said, pretending indifference and sitting. His girl-friend followed. "OK."

"Shuffle the cards." A 78-card deck was awkward to shuffle, so he kept that brief too. "That's fine. Now think of a question while cutting the cards. OK, now pick three and put them face down in a row."

The first card he turned over was *Lovers*, upside down—showing Adam and Eve in the Garden of Eden standing in front of some angel. The boy and girl gazed at it in fascination. He had captured his audience.

Robbie nodded sagely and said, "The Past. You've had some dishar-mony, some imbalance," this was a pretty safe bet, "but everything will be OK. This is a time for patience. Things'll soon get back to normal."

He flipped over the next card, an orange wheel full of arcane symbols sitting on the devil's backside, surrounded by mythic creatures—*Wheel of Fortune*. This always piqued people's curiosity, he knew. "Present. This shows good luck is here, a turning point in your destinies. A change for the better."

Last was *The Sun*—a naked child astride a white horse in front of a row of sunflowers, watched by the sun itself. He beamed. "Future. Success is ahead, a rebirth. Just as the sunflower turns toward the sun, so keep heading toward the positive."

Robbie summarized, striving for a simple and uplifting wrap-up. "You've been through some difficult times, but changes for the better are just around the corner. Things look good." He smiled. Then, sotto voce, he added, "You oughtta get high to celebrate."

The boy looked up, startled, and then looked around for teachers. "Got any?"

"Sure. Good stuff, too."

"How much?"

"Fifteen a lid."

The boy reached for his wallet in his school blazer. "OK."

Robbie had the baggie already folded inside a copy of *Zap Comix*.

Once the couple had wandered off, he looked around for another customer. There was time for one more, possibly two if he was lucky, before the bell rang.

Over the last few months he had come to know many of the Malibu High crowd, but today a boy he didn't recognize sauntered over. He was Latino, good-looking, and introduced himself as Hector, a senior. He sat through his reading with an indifference that Robbie put down to a limited understanding of English, and when Robbie wrapped it up with a hint about grass, Hector asked Robbie if he would drop off some to his place in the Valley later, since he had no money now. Robbie was a little uncomfortable at the thought of going to a strange address at night, but he was buzzed and greedy, and he didn't think too deeply about anything. As a clincher, the boy assured him he'd buy three lids if he liked it.

— · —

Jackson strode across the bright and open campus of Pierce College, past the rows of tall queen palms, past the many temporary buildings, past one of the aggies' plots full of artichokes, past the gym's huge HOME OF THE BRAHMAS sign.

Up the steps of the library he trotted, past the bulletin board and its flyers for Pierce's upcoming first graduation ceremony, a love-in in Will Rogers Park, a rap session about peace, and an introduction to meditation.

Inside, he sought out the latest issues of *Time* and *Newsweek*, reading their assessments of the war, their summaries of the Viet Cong's Tet Offensive earlier in the year. The press appeared, on the whole, to consider it a valiant but failed effort by the losing side, a typical all-or-nothing

Asiatic throwing away of men because life was cheap to them.

It seemed to him, though, that since the January offensive America's opinion had palpably swung against the war. The percentage of the public's confidence in its military had taken a steep dive.

But soon it was time for his first class of the day. He returned the magazines to their racks and hurried back outside. As he ran down the steps he passed a group of longhaired students, lounging and smoking.

"There goes G.I. Joe," he heard one say, "saving the world for democracy."

— · —

At lunchtime, Sundown had to run the gauntlet of the soshes again.

She had tried out for the lead in the school version of Broadway's Annie Get Your Gun, going to the extent of borrowing a long auburn wig, and her mother had modified a fringed leather jacket from her clothing boutique to look more cowgirl. Though Sundown wasn't a belter like Ethel Merman, she felt she could carry the singing, and did well at the audition with the show's most memorable tune, "You Can't Get A Man With A Gun."

Her success infuriated the soshes, who mounted a concerted campaign to have one of their own chosen. The director picked Sundown.

They were thwarted, but not defeated. They changed lines on her and gave her outdated scripts, sabotaged her costume, and generally took every opportunity to make her life difficult. But they took it too far.

On opening night they stole her prop rifle, without which Sundown felt ridiculous since the whole plot revolved around her marksmanship, and substituted a plumber's helper in its place on the prop table in the wings. Sundown refused to take this onstage, and for the entire first act used her pointed finger instead. The director was furious, and warned the clique, whose members she knew well, against any more stunts on pain of being dropped from the show. Since then they had behaved themselves, albeit in a surly and uncooperative fashion.

Len Williams looked up as she approached his table. "You'll get yourself into trouble, sitting with me."

Sundown slid her tray onto the scratched Formica and sat. "You're more likely to get into trouble being seen with me." She looked down. "At least it's fish sticks today—they can't mess them up too much."

He pointed to some long green and orange items on one of her plates. "What are those?"

"'Cheese and celery sticks,' it says. They're—"

"*Hey, Williams!*" someone yelled from across the cafeteria, "*It's watermelon day!*"

Sundown glared across at the speaker and was unsurprised to see one of the jocks with a wide grin on his beefy face. She glanced back at her friend. "Do you get that often?"

"Ignore 'em. That's what I do."

"But it sucks."

"Yeah, well, we'll be outta here soon. You going to graduation?"

"Sure. You?"

He shook his head. "Dunno. I don't feel … *connected*. Doesn't seem to apply to me."

"Yes it does! It's as much for you as anyone else! If you don't go, people like him," she jerked her head toward the boy who had yelled, "win."

Len was silent for a moment, drinking from his carton of milk. "Taft," he finally said. "We're in a high school named after the president who got jammed in the White House bathtub. Our motto should be 'you're stuck here.'"

— · —

Charity approached her homeroom teacher after school. "Miss Gleason? What are commies?"

"Why do you ask, Charity?"

"A boy said my family were commies."

"Take no notice."

"But what *are* they?"

"'Commie' is short for *communist*. Communists believe everybody has to live together and work together. They believe that everybody should be treated the same, earn the same."

Charity frowned as she tried to absorb this. "Is that so bad?"

Miss Gleason regarded her. "Would you like to leave your big house and share an apartment in town with two other families? Would you like to eat the same thing day after day, and wait in line at the stores for hours to buy it? Would you like it if your dad was told to pick up the trash for his job in future, and your mom told to plow fields on a farm?"

"No."

"People in communist countries can be put in prison without a trial. The government listens to their phone calls. And they don't have a choice, Charity. They can't move about their country like you can. They have to do what they're told, think what they're told, live where they're told."

"And they have to live in Russia?"

"And China. And now they want Vietnam."

"So why can't they have it?"

"Because then they would want the next country, and the next, like dominoes, until they wanted the United States. Someone has to stop them; say no. And that's what we're doing."

Charity thought about this on the walk home. So her brother was going to fight the Vietnamese to stop them turning Americans into communists. She didn't quite understand why this had to take place there. Why couldn't there just be armed guards around the United States' border? That would stop them, wouldn't it? And Jackson would only have to go down to San Diego, a couple of hours away, instead of wherever it was he was being sent.

— · —

That evening Robbie rode down into the twinkling lights of the San Fernando Valley.

The address was a big apartment complex—three levels around a large swimming pool filled with children and surrounded by people drinking beer. One child on a Big Wheel trundled toward the edge, fell in, and had to be pulled out, choking.

Robbie walked up some stairs and along a long balcony to the unit written on the note, and rang the bell. The door opened to reveal a bunch of tough-looking men and women with two German Shepherds. All eyed him with suspicion.

Marijuana, dark green and resinous, covered the kitchen table to a height of eighteen inches, and two of the women were weighing and bagging it.

"Is this the kid?" one asked Hector. "Let's see what you got there, longhair." He opened Robbie's bag and examined its contents. He sniffed it. "Man, is this what you hippies are sellin'?" He glared at Robbie with a malevolence that made the boy step backward.

Hector snarled, "You on our turf, kid. *We* sell at Malibu. *You,*" he reached to the back of his belt and withdrew a short-barreled gun that he poked into Robbie's chest, "stay out, or you get dead. Unnerstan'?"

The other man pinched Robbie's cheek painfully. "Thin' you're cute, huh? Cute li'l white boy sellin' shitty dope." He yanked so hard that Robbie's head was jerked sideways. "Not no more you don'!"

Robbie, realizing the enormity of his mistake, backed to the door and fumbled with the lock. Adrenaline made his surroundings super-sharp. "N-no problem. Keep it."

The man threw the bag at him, and grass spilled over Robbie's T-shirt and onto the carpet. The dogs got to their feet, alert, growling. "I don' wan' your shit, man. Go fuck yoursel'."

Robbie staggered out into the night.

"We see you again, we set the dogs on you."

It seemed as if everyone was looking at him as he slunk to his bike.

— · —

"Dad? Are we commies?"

Bret put down his fork and sighed. "Who said that, Charity?"

"Jack Henderson. At school."

"His parents own supermarkets in the Valley. To them, everyone looks like a commie."

Charity frowned. "How come?"

"The Hendersons are into making as much bread as they can. So to them, anyone whose life isn't geared around profit is suspect."

Charity's thirteen-year-old mind attempted to grasp the big picture. "But you and mom make money."

"But it's not all we care about."

— · —

When Robbie got home, which given the steepness of the road and the weakness of the Honda's engine seemed to take forever, he hurried to the bathroom.

In the mirror he saw, apart from the usual bloodshot eyes, one of his cheeks was a fiery red. He splashed it with cold water but it didn't seem to help. In the end he just had to go out to the kitchen.

His mother looked up from a recipe book. "Oh, hi, Robs. What happened to your face?"

He walked past her to the TV room. "Oh, scratched myself shaving."

"Shaving? In the evening?"

"Yeah, it's the testosterone. I have to shave twice a day."

— · —

Charity considered writing in her journal about Communism, but the subject bored her. Instead, she wrote,

> The skies in Topanga are patrolled by black and white turkey vultures, called buzzards by residents, which ride the hot air and look for prey, though it's rare to see one land. Hawks of all kinds...

She consulted her Golden Book of Birds.

> ...Red-tailed, Cooper's—are everywhere, too. Their big wings are designed for gliding and not sharp movements, and the smaller birds know this, so if they venture into the lower territories of the jays or crows they are pestered until they leave.
>
> The bushes are full of canyon wrens, tiny birds that have a descending call that sounds as if they're losing interest. The call of the scrub jays, on the other hand, is just a squawk. They are scruffy creatures that look as if they've been washed too many times. They sometimes dive on cats and pluck fur from their tails.
>
> In the spring, red-winged blackbirds show up and lurk around creeks. Only the males have the scarlet shoulder patches, and they puff them up while they sing in a liquid trill to attract the females, who have such duller plumage they look like a different species.

3

Jackson loved working on his car almost as much as driving it. He had been criticized by all three of his girlfriends so far that he cared more about it than them, and he couldn't deny it. He found women puzzling, whereas the car was predictable and did more or less what he wanted, unlike his limited experiences with dating.

His current girlfriend, Shirley, had come to understand her place in the pecking order: after the GTO. She already thought men were big children, so at first it didn't bother her. But their relationship soon passed through the early infatuation stage into a kind of romantic limbo in which Shirley attempted to insert herself between Jackson and his vehicle, sometimes succeeding, more often stuck watching him work on it and not going anywhere.

His father told him, with a reluctant admiration, that he had reached a kind of Zen state with his car, a state in which the journey—in his case the incessant repairs and improvements—was more important than the arrival at a finished machine. Jackson knew nothing about Zen, but if it kept his old man off his back it was all right in his book.

The latest upgrade was a paint job in metalflake blue, not an Earl Scheib cheapie but a full price workover, and this had wiped out his savings. He would have to put in some extra hours as a stockboy at the Henderson Market before he could afford to make any more cosmetic changes. He might as well fix the more boring stuff in the meantime—the brakes. The '64 was notorious for its inadequate drums, which were the same as the base model Tempest of which it was souped-up version, and it desperately needed something with the ability to slow it from its V8's high speeds.

His concern about money may have distracted him as he bled the brake line. At any rate, he was less than his usual meticulous self.

Once Jackson was done he walked back to the house to wash. His siblings all happened to be in the kitchen at the same time. "OK—who wants to go for a joyride?" he asked.

Robbie and Sundown glanced at each other. Joyrides with Jackson were exhilaratingly dangerous, given that he consistently flouted the speed limit on the steep local roads. And down in the Valley, along Ventura Boulevard beside the cornfields, was the locals' racetrack. Passengers soon found themselves stamping on the floor in the vain hope of finding their own set of brake pedals.

"I'll go!" Charity said.

As she and her big brother walked out to the car, he turned to her. "Where to?"

"Point Mugu!"

He suspected she just liked the name, since Mugu was just a lump of rock at the side of Pacific Coast Highway, but it was a fun forty-minute drive. "OK."

They tore out of the driveway in a fountain of gravel, drove through the town and headed down toward the ocean. The car growled in a feline way, its wide body swaying around the curves on its too-soft springs.

"It's beautiful," Charity told him. "I'm glad it's blue."

"Cops pull over more red cars than anything else," Jackson said, lighting a Camel.

Charity busied herself punching the buttons of the radio, looking for a song she liked. "Jacks ... about the war..."

"Yes?"

"Do you really have to go?"

Her brother grinned. "I'll be OK. It'll be over soon."

"But ... all the songs ... don't you think that love is what the world needs? Don't you think that we all have to learn to get along with each other?"

Jackson smiled at her. "Maybe, honey, but it only works if everybody plays the same game. Violence beats love, like rock beats scissors. Turning the other cheek just gets you two sore cheeks."

Charity did not want to believe this. She thought for a quarter-mile. "What about the car?"

"I'll put it up on blocks. Don't want Robbie driving it when he gets his license. What will you be doing when I'm gone?"

She was silent for a moment, weighing whether to let him in on her secret. "I'm writing a book."

"You are? On what?"

"It's called The Plants and Animals of Topanga Canyon."

"Flora and Fauna."

"What?"

"Plants and animals are called 'flora and fauna' in those kinds of books. Latin, I guess."

"Oh. Then I suppose I ought to change it."

"Sounds like a great idea. I want to read it when I—" His foot, pressing on the brake pedal before a sharp bend, went all the way to the floor. "Uh-oh." He slammed the gearshift down into second. Though the engine howled, the car still hurtled on toward a slowing car in front.

Charity screamed.

"Goddamn!" Jackson said through gritted teeth. He had no choice. As they approached the curve he slewed the car into the hillside to stop its forward momentum. With a long grinding sound of tearing metal it came to a stop, hissing.

Shaken, they got out and walked to examine the front fender. It was torn and dented, and the new blue paint was scoured away by sandstone and grit in long, ugly streaks that reached as far as the door.

Jackson regarded it sadly. "Looks like I'm starting again."

Charity looked about to cry. "What do we do now?"

"We need a tow somehow. I can't leave you here while I go back for one, though, and I don't want you walking along this road on your own. We'd better hope someone we know passes."

They waited, eying the passing traffic for a friendly face. Finally, it was their neighbor Cueball, on his Harley, who recognized them and pulled in behind. The man got off his bike and swaggered, bow-legged, up to them.

He, too, looked gloomily at the damaged car. "Accident?"

"Brakes gave out. Can you call in a tow for us?"

"Sure. I'll turn around. Want me take her home while you wait?"

Jackson could imagine his father saying, "You let a Hell's Angel take Charity home? Are you fucking nuts?" He looked at Cueball and said, "No, thanks. We've got some talking to do."

— · —

Now that Charity was seriously undertaking her book, she decided she really ought to research it. She wandered over to the Topanga library, which stocked a woefully limited selection of any subject, and managed to find a volume entitled Wildflowers of the Southwest, with typewritten text and poor black and white illustrations. But its disheartening lists of brooms, larkspurs, mallows, mulleins, spurges, sedges and vetches drove her back to her own, more idiosyncratic, view.

She found a chair, opened her journal and continued.

> On dry hillsides, small bushes of gray-green stalks topped
> with bunches of tiny white sunflowers are known as Califor-
> nia Everlasting. "Everlasting" because it dries well for flower
> arrangements, though it might make you hungry for break-
> fast, since it smells like maple syrup. I prefer its pioneer name,
> "Ladies' Tobacco."

— · —

Bret and Jackson left the house by the back door and walked through the twilight air, still warm from the day, to the tree house.

They climbed the steps they had built together ten years earlier, and seated themselves among the jumble of cushions. This was becoming the venue for their father-son talks, and it was time for another.

"Sorry to hear about the car," Bret said.

Jackson nodded and pulled out his cigarettes, deciding on bluntness. "I'm signing up."

Bret looked out at the sunset. The sky was luminous lavender. "Fuck. Why?"

"I want to serve my country. Like granddad."

Bret pictured his own father, veteran of Saipan. "This war's nothing like World War Two."

"Since when do soldiers get to choose?"

"It's a new world, son."

"No, dad. The same old things need defending. America. Freedom."

Bret rolled a skinny one and lit it. "Jackson, we've had this talk before. We have no business being in Indochina. We've dropped more bombs on Vietnam than during the whole of the Second World War. Seven thousand American boys killed so far; God knows how many civilians—they don't even bother to count 'em. The U.S. Army doesn't know how to fight guerrilla warfare. Its only solution is to napalm the bejeesus out of everything. This is just imperialist—"

"You supported Kennedy." Jackson had learned to interrupt his father's tirades. "He got us in there for a reason."

"Yeah," Bret said with heavy sarcasm, "'Cause of the Bay of Pigs fuckup."

"Dad, I'm an American and my country's at war. I go where it sends me."

"I thought you were playing around with this stuff. I never thought you'd actually go."

"Well, there's a good chance I will."

"Jeez, Jacks. Why can't you let someone else do it?"

"What if granddad said that? We might be part of Japan now."

"That was a d—"

"A different war, I know. But they're all the same. A man has to stand up and fight."

Bret looked at his son: bigger, fitter, and better looking than he had ever been. Just the kind the army preferred. He tried to lower his tone of voice. It didn't come naturally. "You don't have to prove your manhood to me. Or anyone."

"I'm not going because I have something to prove. I'm going because I believe in it. And my buddies feel the same. 'Sides, I'd be drafted soon anyway."

"No, you wouldn't. You're taking fifteen credits."

It was dark outside now. A few weak stars were visible. Bret pinched out the roach and placed it in one of the ashtrays the family had liberated from various places around town. This was from a Santa Monica coffee shop. "The Broken Drum—You Can't Beat It," it read around the rim.

"Shit. Go to Canada. Or take a year off, travel Europe. I'll pay. Lots o' kids—"

"I'm not a draft dodger. After the Tet Offensive our guys need all the help they can get. There's seniors from my school last year out in 'Nam now, depending on me. And I'm not a kid any more, dad."

"Listen, son—just join the Peace Corps. You'll still be serving—"

"Digging wells in Africa won't stop communists in Southeast Asia."

Bret sighed. His eyes darted around as he tried to come up with another argument and failed. "Don't mention your mechanical abilities to the Army or you'll end up a grease monkey."

Jackson thought about this. "I'd like that."

"But you could be an officer."

"No, dad—not till after college. Besides, I don't want the responsibility."

— · —

Maddy decided she had better look in on "The Stitch Witches," the boutique she had launched a year earlier in Topanga Center, to check on her assistant. The shop was open for limited hours—noon to six, Tuesday through Saturday—and she paid the girl to staff it when she didn't feel like going in, which these days was getting to be more and more often. But when she slid into the VW it wouldn't start. *"Jackson!"* she yelled out of the window. "Help me bump the bug!"

Jackson's big frame burst out of the house and up the driveway. "I can shove you down the hill," he told her, "but then it won't start again when you want to come back. It's the damn six-volt battery they used to put in these. Best to charge it for a while—can you wait half an hour?"

Maddy looked in the rearview mirror and watched her son's muscular arms attach the jumper cables. "Jacks? Are you sure about joining? We don't mind if you—"

"Start her up now. Mom, I've made up my mind. What if everyone avoided their national service? We'd be in a pretty sorry damn state."

"OK, I get that, but why you? The army's for ... well ... poor people, isn't it? To give them a chance when they get back, afterward?"

Jackson laughed.

Maddy felt her eyes sting with tears.

Jackson looked up at the hills. "Ma, it's something I gotta do. If I didn't go I'd feel like a coward for the rest of my life." He slapped the bug's roof. "Let her run for a while and you should be OK. I'm going over to Duke's. If you get stuck, give me a call there—I'll be home later." He stooped to kiss her, briefly.

She watched the big Pontiac drive away, and, leaving her car charging, she went inside to confront her husband, eyes ablaze. "Didn't you try to talk him out of it?"

Bret flinched, and then his bluster took over. "Of course I did. Offered to send him to Canada."

"Couldn't you have tried harder?"

"Maddy, I did my best. He's a man now."

"Yeah, old enough to fight, but not old enough to vote. He got into engineering school, for God's sake. He has a deferment!"

Bret grimaced. "Johnson's stepping down, and whoever gets in will wind it up over there. It may be over by the time—"

"Hah! Don't you be too sure of that. Those are just election promises—they don't mean a thing."

Sundown, sprawled on the sofa reading *Psychology Today,* overheard the last part of her parents' conversation. "Everyone's against the war now. If they don't stop it, there'll be a revolution."

Bret gave a short, disparaging laugh. "Revolution my ass. Too many people are profiting from the war. There'll be martial law first."

"There's demonstrations everywhere," Robbie said, with excitement. "The government'll have to listen to us."

His father turned on him with a sneer. "You saw how the cops put down the Selma demonstrations. Since when did governments listen?"

Charity said in a quiet voice, "That's why there's so much talk about love lately. We need it to balance all the hate."

Bret looked out the window. "Why's your car running, Maddy?"

"Flat battery again."

"I'll convert it to twelve-volt for you, like the newer ones. I'll do it this weekend." He decided to change the subject. "How's work?"

"I have a new commission," Maddy told him.

"Oh? Through the shop?"

"One of the bands with Reprise. A new group's come out from England—Sunday Joint. Their manager saw my outfits for Blue Cheer and liked them. I invited one of them out to the house—Owen Penychain, the lead guitarist. Is that OK?"

"'Course. When?"

"Saturday. You'll like him. He's loose."

Bret was immediately suspicious. "You've already met him, then?"

"Yes, the other day when I was delivering the Blood, Sweat & Tears stuff. He knows Mick Jagger. The kids'll get a kick out of him. They've never met a Limey before."

"Reprise. That's Neil Young's new label. You know he lives just down the street, right? If you run into him, invite him over. Anytime, tell him."

— · —

A scarlet Ferrari 365 GT 2+2 pulled into the driveway. It looked like some alien machine, a glimpse into the future of car design, and made even Bret's brand-new Camaro look lumpy and graceless.

A thin man with long hair in a ponytail walked down the path. He wore a tight pale yellow T-shirt with a rainbow and applique stars across it, battered bell-bottoms that were frayed at the hem, and a puka shell necklace. He looked underfed and more than a little crazy.

Maddy ran outside to greet him. "Owen! Welcome! Come in and meet my family."

"I like your place," Owen said, shaking Bret's hand. "Or should it be 'ranch'?"

Bret laughed. "It's not *that* big. So you're with Sunday Joint."

"Yeah. The name's a little play on words that doesn't work so well here. In England everyone has roast beef on Sundays. Oh well; stuck with it now."

"What's Maddy making for you?"

"Waistcoats."

"Huh?"

"Oh—*vests*, I suppose you call 'em. 'Vests' to us are underwear."

Maddy led Owen into the living room, where she had laid out some Doritos and peanuts. "Want a beer? A joint?"

"Better not smoke if we're doing business. We'll all end up wearing kilts or tutus. Beer would be great."

Robbie, Sundown and Charity would normally have dispersed to their own activities on a weekend morning, but with a visit from a real band member they stayed glued to the couch and his every word.

Bret introduced the children, and they all shook hands.

"What's England like?" Sundown asked.

Owen laughed with a peculiar braying sound. "Damp. Old-fashioned. But fun, in a fuddy-duddy sort of way. One of our concerts was fined for 'blue language.' I'd said 'bum' onstage."

Sundown had other concerns. "Is it true women don't shave their underarms there?"

Owen frowned. "Hadn't really thought about it."

Charity asked, "Have you met the queen?"

"Royalty's an expensive anachronism—useless and out of date. They all ought to be shot—bunch o' leeches. Big changes are coming to Britain—there's going to be a revolution. It's time the class system was overturned once and for all."

Robbie was stunned for a moment. "We don't have a class system here."

"No? D'you have very rich people, and very poor people?"

"Yeah."

"Well, there you go."

Bret never liked someone else being the center of attention. "Americans love royalty," he said. "We may not have it, but we're fascinated by it anyway. It's like some kind of vestigial memory of the grandeur that we left behind when we quit Europe. We don't want to be ruled by it, but we love hearing about it."

Owen made a comical gagging expression and the kids laughed. "Well, at least we're a democracy, and Queenie's just a figurehead."

In an effort to regain control, Bret asked, "Are you touring here?"

"Yeah, some West Coast gigs. Management says we'll do the East Coast some other time."

"Who does your lighting?"

"No idea. I leave all that stuff up to the producers. As long as it works, I don't care."

"Lighting's crucial," Bret said authoritatively, with a hint of reprimand. "Without it, performances are flat and one-dimensional."

Owen sized him up as a blowhard. "I'm sure you're right," he said, in way that implied the subject bored him.

Maddy asked, "How's the album doing?"

"*Ball and Socket?* Getting some airplay. Moving up the charts, but slowly."

"'Ball and Socket'?" Robbie repeated. "What does it mean?"

Owen smirked. "It's a kind of joint. So it's a little in-joke. Doesn't really matter if people get it or not."

Robbie was in awe of Owen. He'd never met an Englishman before, let alone one who'd been flown out to record and perform in the States. He had even seen Sunday Joint on TV one night, though they were introduced as "Sunday J," which was just as bad but the network apparently didn't realize. He wished there was someone he could boast to that he knew one of the members, but he doubted his classmates would believe him. "What's that effect that's on a lot of songs these days?" he asked. "The sound goes kinda swooshy."

Owen nodded. "Like on 'Itchycoo Park'? Mono flanging. It was invented by a guy named Chkiantz at Olympic. The engineer doubles a signal and then puts a time delay on one."

Robbie looked at him blankly. "Oh."

Owen noticed a guitar on the deck. "Yours, Robbie?"

"Yeah. I'm still learning. What chords d'you think I should I practice?"

"Depends on who you want to play like," Owen said.

"Hendrix."

Owen laughed. "I don't recommend starting with him. Even experts have trouble with his playing. And I don't recommend starting with leads. You have to learn the basics first. Rhythm guitar. How about Crosby, Stills, Nash? Just concentrate on D, G and A."

"OK. But what about an easy solo? What could I learn?"

"All right. How 'bout 'Satisfaction'? Here—I'll show you." He took Robbie outside and effortlessly picked out the lick up the neck. Then he sat patiently while the boy learned it.

Robbie was ecstatic. As he practiced they talked.

"So..." Robbie said, his voice low, "do you ever get ... *groupies?*"

"Hell, yes." Owen grinned. "There's all kinds. There's the kind that throw their panties up on stage. There's the kind that show up in your changing room or hotel room—somehow. God knows who they bribe to get there." He looked back at the house to make sure no one could overhear. "And then there's the plaster casters."

Robbie wasn't sure he'd heard correctly. "Plaster casters?"

"Two women who travel around making plaster molds of rock musicians' ... y'know."

Robbie was blank-faced for a moment, and then his eyes widened. "Really?"

"Really. They've got a whole collection of 'em. Signed, no less."

"Did they … ever…?"

"Me? No. But I'd be game. Mind you, I hear from guys that did it that it's hell to get all the plaster off afterward."

Robbie found this a difficult answer to follow. Eventually, he asked, "Have you met the Beatles?"

"I have, actually. We're with Decca and they're with EMI. Decca turned them down, and they've been kicking themselves ever since."

"Anyone else?"

"Of course. Small pond; a lot of fish. The Kinks, The Stones, The Who—they're all there."

"Wow. The Stones. What are they like?"

"Mick's a bit hard to get close to. Keith's like a vacuum cleaner for drugs. Brian's a bit off-kilter—very touchy. And Charlie—well, he's a pretty straight jazz drummer, and they're the best."

"So," Robbie asked, "Who's the best guitarist in Britain?"

Owen's long face looked thoughtful. "Hard to say. There's so many good 'uns. Clapton, of course. There's a new kid called Jimmy Page that I think we'll be hearing a lot of. Alvin Lee of Ten Years After is the fastest, but I'd have to say it's between Peter Green and Jeff Beck for the best."

"I don't know Lee or Beck."

"Yeah, well, Ten Years After isn't that big here, and Jeff Beck's *songs* are rubbish, it's just his *playing* that's great."

Robbie's eyes took on a faraway look as he envisioned a rainy island full of bands and mini-skirted girls, and those sentries with the big furry hats who weren't allowed to smile. "Wow. I'd love to go one day."

"Well, maybe you will."

"If I do, can I look you up?"

Owen scribbled on a piece of paper. "Here's my number. Just don't give it to anyone." He cackled again. "Just say the magic word, *Topanga*."

Robbie picked out a few more notes. "I'd like to be a session man—y'know, back up famous people on recordings."

"Sure. Pay's good, but you'll have to practice a hell of a lot."

"When are you going back?"

"Dunno yet. Up to management. We have some commitments here—touring, recording. I'm in no rush. I like the weather in California."

"When you do … can I come with you?"

"Well, now, hold on, chum. I don't know about that."

"Robbie!" Maddy called from the door, "Stop pestering our guest!"

As Owen reentered the house, Robbie put the phone number carefully into a pocket.

Sundown had been waiting for Owen's return. "So what are the girls wearing in Swinging London?"

"Mini skirts, of course, but maxis too."

"Maxis?"

"Long skirts. Seems to be either one or the other. Long hair or very short hair, too. Nothing in between."

"And the men?" Sundown persisted.

"Not the clown trousers men wear here. We get pleats in the side of our bell-bottoms, in a contrasting fabric. Sailor's shirts were big last year. Some fellas wear shirts and ties made of the same material."

Maddy made a mental note of all this.

Charity finally asked her own question. "Have you been to Penny Lane?"

Owen shook his head. "No. That's in Liverpool, up north. I'm from the south."

This struck Charity as odd. The only island she had been to was Catalina, and she envisioned Britain as slightly larger. Surely a trip to Penny Lane must take no time at all. If she lived there, she'd visit every weekend.

"Your car..." Maddy said, "Did you bring it over from England?"

"The Ferrari? No, just leased it while I'm here."

"Why, what do you drive back home?"

"World War II jeeps are popular at the moment—the English ones. Austin Champs. Some of them have Rolls Royce engines, and they're considered the best. I have one of those."

"Wow," Robbie said, entranced. "Cool."

"Of course, they leak like a sieve when it rains. And it rains a lot. I once took a girl on a first date and pulled back the top, but a big puddle had collected overnight and it soaked her to the skin. She was furious. Had to take her home."

— · —

After Owen's visit, Charity's mind was so active she again had trouble getting to sleep. Up to now Topanga had represented the world, but this glimpse into another threw her own into stark relief as just one of many.

She quite liked the queen, and was now concerned that she might be assassinated in a revolution. It wasn't the poor woman's fault that she was born into a royal family.

Charity looked over at her globe atop the bookshelf. The British Isles were so small compared to the Americas, Asia, everywhere else. They must be crowded with crazy longhaired people, driving on the wrong side of the road and trying to overthrow the government.

— · —

Robbie dreamed of being a session musician, his photo in Billboard and on the front cover of that new magazine, *Rolling Stone.* In his dream he had a blue guitar that sparkled like a drum kit. Girls broke into his dressing room, and his nights were spent in experimental sex with all of them, often several in one night.

In the morning, disappointed to be back in the real world, he stole his mother's egg cartons, and then toured the local grocery stores to glean more. He even bought two dozen eggs himself to bolster his collection. When he finally returned home, hours later, he tore down his *Tommy* poster and glued them over one of his bedroom walls, the one that faced Charity and Sundown's room, until the whole area was covered with a pattern of egg box. The following day he painted them red—it was harder than anticipated, since the surface area had quadrupled—and stood back, admiring his work. Now he had a recording studio with a wall of baffles to deaden the sound.

He grinned. Robbie Sobieski, session man.

4

The morning was cloudy. Someone played a flute somewhere—it was impossible to tell from which direction the sound came. The dew had been heavy, and Charity walked down the hill until her canvas shoes were thoroughly soaked. She looked down at the funnel spider's webs nestled in the grass, milky with moisture. Who knew there were this many? It was only the dew that made them visible. They reminded her of her grandfather's hairy ears.

She walked over the PVC pipes that led from the house to the creek, where her father had planted a few cannabis plants. The stream was usually dry, and the pipes brought the necessary irrigation water from the house, but after the recent rains his plants had perked up naturally. He would be happy.

The creek, after the recent storm, was running with murky water. She wished it would run all year. She could hear a frog but not find it. It was probably tiny. Perhaps there were salamanders—she had seen one once, all glossy orange and black—but there were none today.

Hanging from the trees were tattered remnants of last summer's wild cucumber vines, mysteriously named since its fruit was a spiky ball. There was one left now, hanging dry and brown. She picked it and carefully peeled away the spines of its outer shell to reveal a loofah-like fibrous lattice. Inside this were four fat seeds, presumably precious seeing how much effort the plant had gone into protecting them. Perhaps when they were soft they were tasty to wildlife. Now they were dense, and hard.

Bay trees grew by the creek. They liked water. Their long, dark green leaves looked ordinary until you crushed them, and then the most intense aroma stung your nose, if you were unwise enough to hold them under it. She picked a handful and placed them in her pocket. Her mother used them for cooking, and her dad said they kept the fleas out of Gilligan's doghouse. But Gilligan didn't like the smell and kicked them all out.

Sycamores liked the creek too. Their bark, as pieces flaked off, were an abstract jigsaw puzzle. She picked a few and let them drop into the water to drift lazily downstream. She wondered if they would ever reach the ocean.

Jackson was the brave and heroic one. Robbie was the wild one. Sundown was the beautiful and clever one. Which was she? What was left? She caught a glimpse of her reflection.

She was the plain one.

She touched her cheeks. Why couldn't she have been born with Sundown's cheekbones? Would they appear when she got older? Probably not. Sundown would always be the center of attention, whereas she would be lucky if anyone gave her a second glance.

What whimsical system assigned features in people's faces? What combination of luck and heredity ended up with an arrangement of eyes, nose, mouth and face shape, like her sister's, and what were the odds of getting a perfect set?

She was destined to be one of the millions of forgettables, the ones to whom nature had awarded an unremarkable set of features.

She had heard someone say that there was someone for everyone. She took that to mean that someone would fall in love with her no matter what she looked like. Would that person be ugly? Was she doomed to be married to one of the runts of the world?

A tear rolled down her cheek. Life was so unfair.

She took her journal and a ballpoint pen out of her pocket and prepared to write.

> *Wet weather sends the spiders indoors, and they come in all shapes and sizes. Most are harmless, but some, if they feel threatened, can cause trouble. By far the largest of these is the tarantula, a hairy gray ball the size of a fist, with legs. Unnerving to come across when cleaning the garage, or dismantling a tent, but often kept as pets.*

A black widow's webs are easy to identify because the spider's normal ordered pattern has been abandoned for a crazy jumble, but its venom is mild compared to the brown recluse, whose bite's effect looks like something from a zombie movie.

She looked up when she heard her father's Camaro growl into the driveway. He was back from one of his shoots. She felt a mixture of excitement and dread. He would have interesting stories, but also chores. Nevertheless, she ran up to greet him as he got out.

"Well?" she asked breathlessly. "Did you find out?"

Bret was lugging his big leather bag out of the trunk. "Find out what, hon?"

"The Monkees tour! Where are the Monkees playing?"

"I'm sorry, Charity, they're not playing in the U.S. this year."

"What? Where are they playing, then?"

"Japan and Australia, that's all."

Charity's chin trembled. "No concerts here?"

"No, hon. Sorry."

"Then can I go to—?"

"No, it's too far."

He tousled her hair and left her to walk into the house. Shortly, from inside came the sound of Steppenwolf playing "Hoochie Coochie Man," her father's latest favorite. Charity remained outside, crestfallen.

In five more minutes his voice bellowed, *"Robbie!* What the hell have you done with your room?"

— · —

Sundown paused as she passed Charity, hunched over the kitchen table and scribbling intently. "Homework?"

"A book. I'm writing a book."

"About what?"

"The plants and animals of Topanga. The flora and fauna."

Sundown looked out at their back yard. "Huh? Nothing much grows here."

Robbie had overheard. "Possums and poison oak? Who would want to read about that?"

Jackson had come in to wash his hands. "Well, I think it's a great idea," he said. "Charity's a fantastic writer. One day she'll be famous,

[47]

and you'll be saying, 'That's my sister.'"

Sundown snorted.

Robbie said, "Yeah, right."

Bret barged through the front door, clutching drooping marijuana plants wrenched out by the roots. "Goddamn male plants. *Male!* No damn use at all."

"Amen," agreed Sundown.

"Robbie..." he continued, "I want that shit off your wall by the weekend. Sundown—put the leftovers in the composter. And give it a stir. Here—" he said to Charity, dropping the plants and handing her a still-wrapped album. "Thought you might like this. She's new."

Charity took it and looked at the swirly painting on the cover. "Joni Mitchell?" She ran to her room and turned on her little portable record player. She was not thought worthy of a real turntable.

Reverently, she unwrapped it and slid out the disk. She knew to handle it by the edges, and she placed the pickup arm over the outer groove, lowered it gently and sat back, unsure what to expect.

The first track, "I Had A King," left her puzzled, but the second, "Michael From Mountains," captured her heart and she was hooked. For the first time in her life she heard songs, one after another, that resonated within and embodied what she felt love must be like, what being a woman today must be like. A whole new dimension of awareness opened up before her, sung in an achingly pure voice and coaxing unusual tones from her guitar. This was folk but not folk. Charity decided, right then and there, that the woman represented a whole new realm of music. She would always love The Monkees, but they now seemed old-fashioned, bubble-gum. If this was what the future sounded like, she was eager to grow up and into it.

2000

Sundown returned the draft notice to its drawer and slammed it closed, eager to get it out of sight.

Robbie, eager for a topic other than their brother, peered at the bookshelf. Its style was what they referred to as "early hippie"—a plank on two concrete blocks—which bore a well-thumbed library of books that used to be fashionable: In Watermelon Sugar; The Last Unicorn; A Book of Five Rings; The Electric Kool-Aid Acid Test; Steppenwolf; I'm OK, You're OK; The Teachings of Don Juan; Our Bodies, Ourselves; Walden. At the end was a paperback with a yellow cover. "Here's a copy of your book, Charity," he said, pulling out Flora and Fauna of Topanga Canyon, by Charity Sobieski. "First edition, too. Is it still in print?"

Charity nodded and gave a small laugh. "I sell about twelve in a good year."

"So, Charity," Sundown said, "what are you doing now?"

"What am I doing?"

"Y'know—what position do you hold in the church?"

"I'm a deacon."

"Cool. Can't be many women deacons."

Robbie couldn't resist interjecting, "Weren't you a Moonie once?"

"I joined the Unification Church, yes, to see what it was like. But I didn't like my religion mixed with politics." She looked at him with defiance. "How's your son?"

"Justin? Driving me crazy. He's out all night at raves, taking E."

Charity laughed. "Hah! Talk about karma!"

Robbie didn't appreciate the humor.

Charity regretted annoying him. "But I have another source of income."

"Oh?" Robbie's eyebrows rose. "Something new?"

"I supply white doves for weddings, other events."

"Really? What—breed 'em and everything?"

"No, no. Too messy. I subcontract that part. And they're pigeons—white ones. Doves are harder to find and breed. Besides, most of the pigeons return after being set loose, so it's a kind of recycling."

"How—?"

"A couple I was to marry requested doves be released at their ceremony, and it started a trend. It's very popular now." She pulled down a foxed copy of Be Here Now. "Wow!" she said, flipping through pages that had been laid out using a child's rubber stamp set. "I sat up all night reading this once."

Robbie picked up a colorful program for the San Francisco performance of Hair and showed it to Sundown. "Didn't you date a guy in this?" he asked.

She took it and flicked through the cast photos until she found one in particular. "Goddamn. I forgot how gorgeous he was."

Charity looked over her shoulder. "You were all beautiful in those days." She stared off wistfully. "I remember the party he came to. I was so impressed with all you grownups. You all seemed to have it together."

"Yeah, so together." Robbie's mouth twisted into a wry grin. "Jackson was there—in his uniform, if I remember right. Now I think of it, that took some courage, given mom and dad's crowd. I wish..." his voice caught in his throat, "I wish I had talked to him more. And listened."

"Yeah, Robbie," Sundown said, "You were pretty wasted that night."

Robbie turned on her and snapped, "I was high about as many times as you had a new boyfriend, Sundown."

Charity tried to make peace between them, as she often had. "Is it just my fantasy, or did Neil Young come to the party?"

Robbie laughed and shook his head. "Dad was always hoping."

5
SPRING, 1968
FOOLS ON THE HILL

Charity liked to hike up Zeidler Ranch Road—it was too steep to ride her bicycle—to a vacant lot where she could sit and look down on Topanga Center and watch the comings and goings of people as they shopped. It gave her a benevolent, subtly angelic feeling, to at once be a part of and yet separate from canyon residents. From this distance the tiny town had a dollhouse-like quality, and before the really hot days began it looked nestled in folds of green velvet. Soon, the green would turn gold.

She took her journal and pen from her backpack and began to write.

> *Please, God, take care of Jackson when he's gone. I know You must be hearing from a lot of people whose hearts are breaking at the thought of losing their loved ones to the war. But You are supposed to hear them all, so perhaps the quantity makes no difference.*

Then, because she didn't want to dwell on her brother's imminent departure, she changed topic.

> *In spring everything blooms, from the iceplant along the freeways to the jacaranda along suburban avenues. The jacaranda's entire dome of branches becomes a mass of blue-violet flowers that gradually fall to the ground over the next month. Homeowners tend to hate the blossoms, which make their cars sticky and smell, to some, like cat pee. Some suburban*

streets of Los Angeles have been planted solid with jacaranda by well-meaning civic engineers, and the trees lower the house prices.

Inland the desert heats up, drawing up a blanket of moist air from the Pacific and causing the June Glooms at the coast— gray days only brightened by sun midafternoon. The foot of Topanga canyon stays in the coastal climate, while the top joins the Valley's high desert zone.

— · —

"The tower" was the second-story room that Bret had had built in the center of the house. It was octagonal, with a view from all eight windows.

Maddy's workshop was about a third of the tower area. When the tower was first built, Bret tried to talk her into accepting a quarter, but when she kicked up a fuss he conceded a third, as if this were noblesse oblige. He argued that he needed more room than her, implying, without actually putting it into words, that his work was more important. Knowing how far she could push her husband, Maddy settled for this.

Bret's area was decorated with examples of his children's artwork, pinned or taped to the walls below the windows, along with some attempts of his own. Much to his frustration Bret had no discernible artistic abilities, his graphic skills limited to crude wiring diagrams. Only a few weeks earlier he had decided he could draw like Klaus Voorman's cover for the Beatles' *Revolver*. He bought himself some Rapidographs and doodled for hours, but all he achieved was something that resembled a spool of black thread that had been attacked by a kitten.

"That woman who runs the Canyon Kitchen..." Bret began.

Maddy glanced up from the sewing machine. "Susan."

"She's married to Neil Young, right?"

"You know she is."

"Why don't you invite them over for Jackson's leaving party?"

"Bret, I don't think they'll come. He's pretty private."

"Look, we're neighbors. He's probably heard about me just like I've heard about him. We Topangans have to stick together. We're a tribe, kinda; like the Laurel Canyon bunch but different. Ask her, at least. OK?"

"Hon, she told me that their party in March was busted by the police, supposedly for noise but they were looking for dope. Eric Clapton was visiting, wearing pink boots. The cops took them into Hollywood, told them to strip naked except for Clapton and his boots, and sprayed them with DDT."

"Did you say DDT? Why?"

"Why do you think? They wanted to humiliate them. They don't like longhairs. Susan wasn't specific, but I think Neil had one of his fits in the jail—he's been having more lately. Anyway, I don't get the feeling he's into parties."

— · —

Hophead Hills was strung with leftover July 4th bunting, Tibetan prayer flags, and peace signs. There was also a bizarre strand of Barbie lights. Just before Christmas, when Charity asked for another Barbie, Sundown had told her that Barbie was oppressive to women. Charity had gone to her room, pulled all the heads off her dolls—she had quite a collection—and jammed them onto a string of Christmas tree lights instead. They fit perfectly over the small bulbs, and the effect was surreal and slightly disturbing.

Bret barbecued hamburgers and chicken on the deck, as well as kielbasa—even though no one in California seemed to know what it was—while wearing an I'D RATHER HAVE A BOTTLE IN FRONT OF ME THAN A FRONTAL LOBOTOMY apron and holding court with anyone who would listen. He had the stereo hooked up within reach so he could control the music. He felt it his duty to turn people onto the latest albums, and last time he was in Hollywood he had bought several of the latest. Currently on the turntable was Steppenwolf's "Born To Be Wild."

Bret spent a lot of money on his music collection. He had his albums shelved and classified alphabetically by artist, and if an artist had more than one, then in strict chronological order. He took pride in owning the latest hi-fi gear—Garrard turntable, Sony receiver, JVC preamp, and Altec Lansing speakers.

Bret had also rigged up, with a bunch of Radio Shack parts and plastic elevator light diffuser panels, what he called a "color organ." When the music played, the treble notes triggered the green lights, the midrange the blue, and bass the red. The result was flashing squares of color that mesmerized his guests, especially, as the evening progressed, the most stoned.

Sundown regarded the array with scorn. If the lights had made interesting patterns that would be one thing, or if they gently shifted from one subtle color range to another, but to simply blink on and off was just some guy idea of cool, a kind of stoner's traffic signal.

Bret dominated the proceedings with his loud and penetrating voice, and was now arguing for the legalization of dope, one of his favorite topics, though he was preaching to the choir. "It's safer than booze," he was telling anyone who could hear him over the music. "It's just that there's a conspiracy by the alcohol lobby to outlaw everything else. Grass was being smoked in this country before the white man ever arrived. What d'you think was in the peace pipes? The State should stop busting people who smoke a bit of dope, and just tax packs of legal grass. The current laws have just made a whole bunch of peaceful people into so-called criminals. Kids are spending a year or more in jail for having a *roach,* for Christ's sake! Herb doesn't make anyone homicidal—they're more likely to trip out on the goldfish bowl. They're not gonna go out and kill anyone, not like someone tanked up on liquor."

Bret's work crowd was there, consisting of Doug, his best boy, and a couple of grips, and so was Maddy's pretty assistant Tess from Stitch Witches. Even the bikers from up the road, Cueball and his old lady Bonnie, had been invited, and their hog already stood in the driveway, all stretched forks, monkey bars and chrome, though its owners could have easily walked the few yards down the hill.

Rumors had spread of a major movie about to be released that featured motorcycle gangs, and this had given the local chapter down in the Valley, *Satan's Slaves,* a higher profile. Lately they had taken to strutting around town in faded jean jackets with the sleeves ripped off, their name in studs on the back.

Cueball's bald head was striking in such hirsute company, even covered as it was by a blue bandana. There were so many extravagant sideburns in the living room it looked to Maddy like an illustration from a Dickens novel.

Cueball preferred the countrier rock, disdaining the more pretentious art-school sound coming out of Britain and any album cover that featured men wearing chiffon scarves, and had brought his own albums. He especially disliked the Moody Blues, whom he considered a "bunch of Limey fruitcakes," and sneered at Bret's new copy of Tyrannosaurus Rex's *My People Were Fair And Had Sky In Their Hair.*

"O'course, Buffalo Springfield are almost no more," Bret said. "I'm doing the lighting for their last show in Long Beach in a coupla weeks."

"I never liked Neil Young's voice," said J.J., one of the neighbors, an older man with the previous generation's tastes and unintimidated by Bret. His was the only hair slicked shiny with cream, and he favored cigars. "Kinda whiny."

Bret's spatula froze in mid-flip. "How dare you! The man has soul. He means what he sings about, unlike bullshit singers like Pat Boone."

"Pat Boone's not so bad."

"'Not so bad'? He couldn't write a song if his life depended on it. He's just a performer."

"So?" J.J. responded, "What's wrong with that?"

"Today's bands are not just entertainers, they're trying to change the world with their music. They don't just deliver songs, they write what they feel."

J.J. laughed. "I don't need my world changed, thank you very much. And certainly not by a rock 'n' roll band."

"It's people like you that go to see Elvis in Vegas."

"So what if I do? You're a music snob, Sobieski. If it ain't longhaired, it ain't shit."

Bret considered kicking J.J. out of the party, but decided it would make him look bad. Instead, he just forced a laugh through gritted teeth and changed the subject.

— · —

Charity was clinically interested in gatherings of grownups. She listened to as much as she could, watched as much as she could. She felt it helped her grasp what adulthood entailed. She didn't understand everything she witnessed, like why two people sometimes went to the bathroom together, but it was intriguing.

She cornered Len, her sister's friend from school, to ask about the Civil Rights Act she had heard the President had just signed. She was puzzled because she had thought all Americans had the same rights under the Constitution, and Len spent some time explaining the disparities of race to her, especially—the focus of this particular act—when it came to housing.

"But that's racism, Len!"

He gave her a lopsided grin. "Yeah, that's racism."

"Well, we have to demonstrate!"

"Funny thing, Charity—I been on them demos and I always seem to end up getting hit on the head an' spendin' the night in jail. Next day, nothin' has changed."

"Well, we need to complain about that too! This is America, and—"

"Listen, kid, I know you mean well, and I 'preciate it, but your America is not my America. Two different places, two different rules."

"But..." she tried to assemble her thoughts in light of this new information, "we must fight to change things for the future."

Len shook his head. "They're on their own, kid. I ain't fightin' The Man no more. I like my head without cracks."

Charity subsided in frustration. She regarded Len's hairstyle. "Your hair..." she began, but wasn't sure how to continue.

"The afro?"

"The boys in my school don't wear their hair like that."

"They're probably still conking." At her blank expression, he added, "Straightening. That's gone outta fashion. That's what black folk did when they wanted to look less black. Now we wear it more natural."

"I wish I had hair like yours."

He chuckled. "No, you don't."

— · —

Owen showed up and looked with derision on a skinny joint that was being passed around. "That's a New York number," he said, and reached into his bag to roll a Jamaican-style spliff out of several joined papers. It ended up the size of one of J.J.'s larger cigars. "Now *this*," he said, holding up the end result and passing it around like a ceremonial pipe, "is a joint."

Robbie was pleased to see the guitarist again, and sat next to him on the floor. "It ought to be legal," he said, echoing his father's stand.

Owen passed him the joint, grandly. "Of course, all this is going to change."

Robbie looked around, puzzled. "It is?"

"Capitalism is dying. It doesn't work. The people won't stand for its inequities any more."

"They won't? Uh ... *we* won't?"

"The world that was divided between haves and have-nots is dead.

It was all a kind of slavery, and slavery is over and done with. Serfs and barons, peasants and lords, subjects and kings, employees and bosses—it's all on the rubbish tip of history."

Robbie's eyes became unfocused as he took a huge hit, held it in, and imagined the new world. It looked, in his rapidly fogging mind, a little like a Soviet poster, with smiling people striding forward in confidence, eyes filled with hope and undimmed idealism. "Y-yeah."

"All people have to do is organize. See, the government wants to keep us divided, and that's how we're kept powerless. As soon as we unite, we have power."

"Like in Russia and China, then?"

"Well, yeah."

"But didn't Stalin kill a lot of people?"

When the joint returned to them it was considerably reduced in size. Owen clipped the dwindling roach into the hemostat he carried for the purpose. "No global change can be made without some bloodshed. There'll always be resistance to it."

"So—there'll be fighting in the streets? Revolution?"

"Maybe. In some places. At first. But then things will even out, and people will see it's working."

"No government at all?"

"Only to manage the means of production—the factories and stuff. Not to hold people back, not to keep the rich rich and the poor poor. There's an old song where I come from, 'it's the rich what gets the money, and it's the poor what gets the blame.' Not any more."

Robbie's heart leapt in his chest. Yes, this was the world he craved. Each to his own. No money, no stifling office jobs. No credentials, no clock-punching, no "yes, sir/no, sir." Nothing to fight wars about. He was amazed he hadn't seen it before.

He stared at the skinny Englishman. Owen represented the man of the future. This was the kind of person who was going to bring down the old way. If the revolution were to start next week, he need never go back to school. Sign me up, he thought.

Robbie liked parties; they suited his fractured attention span, and he was able to bounce from one group and topic to another without being reprimanded. Soon he was drifting from room to room in a red-eyed haze, smiling vacantly and muttering short standard phrases like, "Far out, man." He overheard someone say, "Believe you me," and found it hilarious. "'Believe you me'?" he repeated, "What the hell does that mean? It's not even English! 'Believe you me'?"

Len, who was passing, patted his shoulder. "Don't be a dork, Robbie. Maintain."

Robbie's friends, meanwhile, were discussing the new film *2001: A Space Odyssey.*

"People are dropping acid and going to see it," one said. "They say it's really trippy, this whole bit where they go through space and time or something, into another universe."

"Yeah," another said, "but the ushers come around and shine their flashlights in your eyes to see the size o' your pupils. That way they can tell if you're loaded. An' if you are, they throw you out."

"They check your eyes at Disneyland now, too."

"Jeez. So much for being a free country."

— · —

The Allman Brothers' *Eat a Peach* had been on replay for some time when someone switched it, for a joke, to a 78 of Fats Waller singing "Your Feet's Too Big," which changed the atmosphere abruptly. *"Don't put that on again,"* Bret yelled, "You'll ruin my stylus." He replaced the heavy old record with The Grateful Dead.

Bret was now on his soapbox about alternate ways of getting high, a subject that always garnered avid participation. "The idea you can get stoned from banana peels is bullshit," he said. "And even if you could, it would take about fifteen pounds of bananas to get one good bowl."

"That explains why the Topanga store is always out of them," Maddy said.

"What about Jimson weed?" someone asked.

"Too dangerous. One seed'll get you high, ten are likely to kill ya."

"Mistletoe berries."

"Same. Too toxic."

"Morning glory seeds," someone else offered.

"I hear you can make a tea from them, but it's pretty weak. The best way is to grind 'em up and eat the whole lot." He turned the last of the hamburger patties. "Did you know Europeans in the middle ages used to trip? No, it's true. There was this fungus that grew on rye, and it looked like one of the grains so nobody noticed. *Ergot*, it was called."

Robbie was fascinated. "So what happened?"

"When they ate it in bread they hallucinated and stuff. For days on end. Must've thought they were going crazy. Can you imagine? Whole villages running around zonked. They probably thought they'd been possessed by the devil."

— · —

J.J. had cornered Jackson's girlfriend Shirley. "So I'm at the Sands in Vegas," he said, "and in the lobby I see Dean Martin waiting for an elevator. He's in his golf clothes and he's pretty toasted. Anyway, the elevator doors open, and Dean stands there rigid. Nothing anyone can do will make him get in. Turns out he's absolutely terrified of small spaces. Claustrophobic. 'Here,' I tell him, 'I'll take you up the stairs.' So I help Dean Martin up ten flights of stairs. We chat about this and that. He gives me two free tickets to his show that night. Front row."

— · —

Rain, the local self-styled shaman, appeared at some point during the evening and sat serenely on the patio. Bret offered her a hamburger but she declined, choosing salad.

Guests paid Rain their respects with a nod and a few words, but few engaged her in conversation—she was too daunting a presence, simultaneously there and above it all, as if she were the matriarch of some ancient tribe whose land they were camped on. She was so suntanned that it was hard to tell her race, but she spoke—when she spoke at all—with a refined Boston Brahmin accent that lent whatever she said a certain gravitas.

No one seemed to know much about her: where she came from or when, only that she occupied some obscure corner of someone's property somewhere up the hill. She could sometimes be seen hitchhiking down to the coast—never to the Valley—or buying mung beans or lentils from the health food store. Rain wore madras shirts and baggy pants, no shoes, and her long gray hair in a ponytail. Her one concession to personal ornamentation was a bone necklace.

Charity had always been fascinated by Rain. The woman popped in and out of her life like a wraith, and she was never quite sure if she was entirely real. The first time Charity had been introduced was when she was very small, and it happened to have been a wet day. Because of this, for several years afterward she assumed Rain was in charge of the weather.

— · —

Bret's topic now switched to conspiracy theories about Martin Luther King Jr's recent assassination. "A black man with that much power," he said, "They didn't like that."

"Who's 'they'?" J.J. taunted, "The Mafia? The KGB? Fidel Castro? Do you have a theory?"

Bret tried to ignore him. "The FBI's in charge of the search for the killer!" he said in wonder. "What kind of sense does that make—putting the fox in charge of the hen house?"

"Hoover's probably got a file on you, too," J.J. said, intending it as an insult.

This pleased Bret. "Yeah, well, I wouldn't be surprised. All the rabble-rousers go on his list."

Maddy let her husband have his moment. She privately believed the FBI had bigger fish to fry, though perhaps in the future there'd be a file on everyone, like in Russia and East Germany. "Robbie," she said, eyeing her younger son, "Don't get any ideas. Best to keep a low profile and not draw attention to yourself."

"Aw, ma," he said, "They're not interested in punks from Topanga."

"Good," she told him. "Keep it that way."

Maddy made a point of being a gracious hostess, though she too had taken a hit or two before anyone showed up. She swayed from deck to living room distributing hamburgers and picking up the discarded Solo cups on her return trips, since no one else was likely to.

During her travels through the house she joined conversations in progress. In the corner, a group was discussing song lyrics with the intensity of the stoned.

"How could anyone put 'et cetera' in a song, like in 'Elenore'? That's just lazy!"

"What the hell does 'someone left the cake out in the rain' mean? Is it some acid reference?"

"I heard it wasn't 'Mrs. Robinson' at first, it was 'Mrs. Roosevelt.' They changed it for the movie. What a sell-out, man."

"'Lucy in the Sky with Diamonds' spells 'LSD,' see?"

"But I don't understand that creepy line, 'The girl with colitis goes by.'"

"What's with the title 'In-A-Gadda-Da-Vida'? Sounds like a kid trying to say 'Garden of Eden.'"

"Maybe it was."

Charity listened to some of this too, since she had a child's affinity for learning lyrics, and joined in. "What *was* Billie Joe McAllister dropping off the Tallahatchie Bridge?" she asked.

"A ring!"

"Flowers!"

"A baby!"

"Gross!"

Robbie had overheard this last part, and remembered a song from his childhood. "Owen—that song, 'Puff the Magic Dragon'—what was it really about? Is it about smoking grass? Y'know—'puff' and 'paper,' and all that?"

Owen laughed. "No one says 'puff' a joint, man. The song's just about a kid who grows up and no longer plays with his favorite toy."

Robbie felt like a fool. "Oh."

— · —

Cueball was showing Bonnie how he could strike a match on the zipper of his fly when the head flew off the match and burned a hole in the carpet. Maddy, who was passing at the time, stamped it out.

Outside, Bret was onto overpopulation. "You should read 'The Population Bomb,'" he was telling his immediate audience. "The human population is doubling so fast we'll use up all the food in a few years. We have to limit family size before the race starves."

"How you gonna do that?" J.J. wanted to know. "You can't tell people they can only have one or two kids—that's fascism."

"Not *order* them, maybe, but give 'em a tax break if they don't. That's the way to do it."

J.J. laughed. "You've got four kids, Sobieski. No tax break for you."

— · —

Sundown arrived with her current boyfriend, a strikingly handsome man she met at a concert in San Francisco. "My dad thinks of Topanga as a kind of bigger Laurel Canyon," she explained. "Or Haight Ashbury South." She introduced him to everyone as Sebastian, part of the touring company of *Hair*. Sebastian tried to answer people's questions about what it was like to perform all week, and what "The Age of Aquarius" actually meant, though even he seemed uncertain. Someone asked which part was his, and he sang a few bars *a Capella* from "Let The Sunshine In," but found it too difficult with other music playing. For those who hadn't seen the musical, and this was most, he recited its famous line, "The draft is white people sending black people to make war on yellow people to defend the land they stole from the red people," and everyone except Jackson and the bikers broke into spontaneous applause.

Soon Sebastian and Sundown made their surreptitious exit and walked outside through the crickets' wall of sound to the tree house. They turned the stolen hotel room sign at the foot of the ladder to "Do Not Disturb," climbed inside, shucked their clothes and made love in every position they could think of for an hour and a half before they fell asleep in each other's arms.

— · —

By now the music had changed to Motown, and those who could still stand were dancing to The Supremes, and Sly and the Family Stone. Bonnie joined in as Maddy and Tess swayed and twirled in their gypsy-styled skirts, watched by the rest, who were sprawled about the furniture and floor and now largely incapable of movement.

It had been a good year for pot growing, and a shipment of Panama Red was in town, much stronger than the usual weed, and three times as potent as the stuff Bret tried to grow down by the creek. Stanley, from a commune in Northern California, spoke earnestly of experiments in crossing marijuana with hops, since they were related plants, to camouflage them from the authorities. Someone else brought up the new lights, under which plants could grow all day and night in a closet, avoiding the risk of being identified in the open by police helicopters which, it was said, could tell pot from other plants.

— · —

Robbie kept one bleary eye on his father throughout the evening. Bret couldn't complain about his younger son smoking dope, since he'd always smoked openly in front of his family, but he drew the line at Robbie

getting into pills. Grass was one thing, he believed—a mark of re-
bellion, a broadening of the mind—whereas pills represented something darker: a cheap dependency, a heedless reach for oblivion, the
attitude of a drunk. And grass was natural, unlike the pills that came
out of factories owned by greedy capitalists.

Robbie couldn't grasp the finer points of this difference in drugs.
Getting high was getting high, wasn't it? The songs talked about it,
musicians and movie stars he looked up to touted it. Getting high
was not some stupid felony; it was a statement, a way of life. It said,
"I don't like your world; I'll inhabit my own."

The previous generation, the war generation, the generation that
came of age after prohibition—their high was booze. Cocktails, beer,
wine. All the old-fashioned ways of getting a buzz. And their singers
sang about it too—Frank Sinatra, Dean Martin, Peggy Lee. Now, a
new generation had a new kind of high. A more natural high, too,
that didn't annihilate brain cells in payment.

What was the big deal about getting high, anyway? The police
probably smoked in private; took pills. They kept everything from
busts and took it home. Bunch of hypocrites.

So when Robbie decided to try to score something other than
weed, he made sure to do it on the sly. He cornered Owen and asked
if he ever took speed.

"Leapers? Sure. 'Specially when touring. Keep you going."

"Well ... got any?"

"I'm not sure I—"

"Just one. I could use a boost."

Owen looked around for Robbie's parents. "All right, mate," he
muttered, and slipped him a small blue tab. "Just this once."

Robbie took it out of sight of anyone. The speed revived his
flagging energies and made him a little over-bright. He engaged
people in conversation, and for a while they were captivated, but he
soon began to repeat himself and they drifted off.

— · —

Doug had Tess cornered in the kitchen. He was leaning close,
explaining something in low, urgent tones.

"I'm studying Tantra. Tantra teaches that sexual experiences are really spiritual acts. You see, by worshiping the divine in each other, we can raise this energy called *Kundalini*. This releases a slower, deeper intimacy. It can even lead to ... *multiple orgasms*."

"E-excuse me," Tess said, squirming away.

— · —

Bret was now holding forth about the war, and how, though he loved his elder son, everyone had been brainwashed by a bunch of warmongering armchair generals in league with the arms industry. "How many boys does it take, LBJ?" he slurred, to no one in particular. "We'll never win against an enemy like the Viet Cong. We've been bombing them every day for three years and it hasn't made a damn bit of difference. Two million bucks a day it costs us to fight this war—*two million!* Think what we could do back home with two million a day."

Maddy had heard all her husband's stories, and usually more than once. After enduring a few minutes of his latest pontifications she leaned over to Tess, her assistant at the shop, and whispered, "I sometimes wish he would just shut up."

Tess's big eyes glanced over at Bret. "He's a classic Leo with Aries rising. A natural leader. He has to run things. It's just the way he is. He's always going to be like that."

"Always?"

Tess nodded. "You knew what he was like when you married him, right? And you're an Aries with Cancer rising! Of course you would be attracted to him."

Maddy's mind slid back to Philadelphia, 1946, and her friend Michelle's party. Maddy had been seeing a boy who turned out to be far too much under the thumb of his mother. The woman had thought he could do a lot better than Maddy, and he didn't have the spine to stand up to her. Maddy's father had died the year before, and now, looking back on that time and her frame of mind, she must have been unconsciously seeking a strong male figure to replace him. Bret had seemed to fit the bill: likely to go places, likely to succeed. And he had. Movie business hours took getting used to, but it was a union gig and gaffers made good money.

"What are you again, Tess?"

"Aquarius! That guy Sundown brought—the actor. He's my type. Oh *boy*, is he my type."

"Hang around, then. She'll be finished with him by the weekend."

Tess leaned close and whispered, "Who's the guy with the blond hair and beard?"

"That's Doug. He's Bret's best boy on the movie shoots. Why?"

"He's a walking hard-on. Jeez, what an asshole."

"Yeah, he's always that way. Ignore him."

"I'm trying to. He keeps hitting on me."

— · —

Shirley had been invited by Jackson, but remained uncomfortable throughout. Her relationship with the young man was one-on-one, and had never expanded to allow for friends or parties. She was young and inexperienced, and without the privacy to do the things she knew how to do—play with his hair, light his cigarettes or hang on his every word— she was at a loss how to behave. So for most of the night Shirley simply sat next to him and sipped a beer, putting up with Duke and Cueball's crude jokes. Both Maddy and Tess tried to pry her away to dance, but she resisted, as if a girlfriend's duty was to be glued to the side of her boy- friend, her fun depending on his.

"She won't last long," Maddy said in an aside to Tess.

Tess nodded. "Typical soldier's wife—*enduring*."

Maddy winced. "Don't say that. I don't like the words 'soldier' and 'wife' together when it comes to Jackson."

Jackson managed to maintain an even keel throughout the party, and he and Duke sat in their green fatigues and spent the night drinking Cue- ball's Budweiser, smoking only Camels. They looked with bemusement on the antics of the guests around them, feeling on one side of a rift that for the last couple of years had split the country. Yet there was no animosity in the house. All were welcome at Hophead Hills. Jackson tried to capture the evening in his mind, to look back on when he was gone. This was the Sobieskis, like 'em or not. He could relate to them less and less these days, but they were still his family.

— · —

High, Robbie felt omnipotent, every word out of his mouth brilliant, every move the coolest.

One of his mother's friends, Cindy, caught his eye—a late twenties beauty with Caribbean skin and upturned eyes. The fact that she was more than ten years older struck him as insignificant.

"Hi," he said, "remember me?"

"Of course I remember you, Robbie," she said, "I've watched you grow up."

This was not exactly what he considered foreplay talk, and so he tried to change the subject. "You hear Jackson's off to 'Nam?"

Her mouth puckered in distaste at the thought. "Yeah. Bet your dad's hacked off about that."

"Hell, yes. But Jackson always was straight."

"Will you go, if it's still on when you're eighteen?"

"No way. You won't get me over there."

"No? Where would you go, then?"

"I have friends in England. I'll probably go over there and play guitar."

"You're a guitarist? Maddy didn't tell me."

"Oh yeah, big time. Hey, what say we go outside and smoke a J?"

She gave a small laugh. "I think I've had enough, thanks."

Unwilling to give up, and misinterpreting her smile as one of interest, he said, "I forget—are you married?"

"No."

"Seeing anyone in particular?"

"Yeah, I see a guy sometimes."

"But he's not here."

"No, not tonight."

"How about I show you the tree house?"

Her eyes twinkled, and she smiled a dismissive smile. "No, Robbie, I don't think so."

— · —

"I hear you do Tarot readings, Mrs. Sobieski," Jackson's friend Duke said to Maddy. It was late, and he was pretty plowed, but he had stuck to beers and was more coherent than most of the other guests. "How 'bout giving Jacks one? See how he's gonna do over there."

Maddy shook her head. This sounded like a terrible idea. She was about to leave, but Jackson had overheard.

He was drunk too. "Yeah, ma. Tell your son what the future holds."

"No, Jacks. I don't think—"

"Aw, c'mon, ma. It's OK. We don't take it that seriously. Hell, we don't take *anything* that seriously."

By now others had gathered around to witness the show, and she was cornered. She fetched the velvet bag from her bedroom and held the deck briefly over a stick of sandalwood incense as a token cleanse.

Maddy now regretted the hit of hash on top of a beer. *Just get through it quickly*, she told herself. But she had a nasty premonition. Nevertheless she put on her professional face and looked through the pack for the *Knight of Swords*, a young man in armor charging off to battle on a white horse.

"I'll use the pentangle reading," she told Jackson, showing everyone the card, "and this will be your significator." She placed this card face up in front of her, and then began to place other cards around it at the pentangle's five points, starting at top right.

She turned over *The Devil*, and groaned quietly. "Well, best to get this over with, I suppose. This is your earth card—it represents what's holding you back. The Devil often means addiction, but in your case I think it means you're too comfortable with bourgeois life, and eager to get out into the real world."

Everyone laughed. Jackson was enjoying himself, gazing at the cards with a naïve faith in her that threatened to break her heart.

Maddy started to place the next card in the bottom right position. "This is your air card—what others are saying about you, the external forces affecting you." It was the *Ten of Swords*, a man lying prostrate, ten swords buried in his back. Maddy began to sweat. Her smile became a strained rictus of jollity.

"What is that?" Duke asked. "A kebab?"

"This just means a surprise," Maddy told Jackson. "Perhaps … perhaps your friends are surprised at your choice to sign up." There—she took a deep breath—that should do it. Looking around, it seemed as if her audience had bought her downplaying of its significance.

Eager to leave the sinister image behind, she turned over the next card and placed it at bottom left. *Please let it be something uplifting.* It was *The Hanged Man*. "I know, I know," she said, and quickly tried to put another brave gloss on the interpretation. "This is your fire card, and represents internal conflicts at play. In this position, this just means sacrifice. For you, it's the sacrifice of the soldier giving up his safe home for the … the front."

Next she placed a card at top left, *The Fool*, reversed, a motley-dressed man with his nose in the air about to step unknowingly off a cliff. Several people laughed again. Maddy wanted to be anywhere else at this point. "This is your water card—what your intuition is trying to tell you, so you can learn from its advice. Upside down, it can mean recklessness, risk-taking. In other words," she looked at Jackson, "Don't take chances."

Duke laughed. "That's for sure, huh, Jacks? Good advice, man."

"And finally..." Maddy took the next card and placed it at center top. It was *The Tower*, showing what looked like a lighthouse being struck by lightning, people falling out of its windows. A feeling of horror crept up her spine and she had to repress a shudder. Was it possible to have a worse reading? "This ... this is your spirit card, representing the end result of ... your present path. I know it looks scary, but in this instance," she extemporized, "it's a catalyst of change—a change from peace and harmony. About what a soldier leaving home would expect."

Quickly, she scooped the cards together and returned them to their bag.

Several of the guests slapped Jackson on the back. None seemed to have picked up on his mother's extreme discomfort. As the group dispersed she hurried outside and threw up. Luckily, no one saw.

— · —

Big Brother and the Holding Company were playing now, with Janis Joplin's hoarse voice galvanizing her audience. Bret had turned on the blacklight, eerily illuminating the skull on a Grateful Dead poster and showing up J.J.'s dandruff along with all the debris on the fake-Persian rug. Those women wearing pale lipstick looked corpselike.

Bret, stoned but unslowed, was onto nuclear power. "Now they're heading toward World War Three. Russia and America have built enough nukes to wipe out all life on earth. Only cockroaches will be left. And the utilities want to switch to nuclear power stations. Why? Because it's cheaper for them. Do you trust 'em with plutonium? And all the radioactive waste it generates? Where are they going to put it all? Dump it in the ocean? Probably bury it all in one of the poorer states, like Nevada— they've already contaminated it with atom bomb tests."

J.J. wasn't about to let this comment slip by uncontested. "You wanna fall behind the Russkies? We have to keep ahead with A-bombs, or they'll end up ruling the goddamn world."

"But you can't trust the government," Bret insisted. "A hundred nuclear tests so far. All those people downwind—they're poisoned for life. The ground's contaminated for thousands o' years."

"I'd rather have radioactive sand than live under Joe Stalin," J.J. told him. "It's a necessary part of our defense."

"Remember that movie *The Conqueror* from the fifties? Some crap with John Wayne as Genghis Khan? That was shot in Nevada near a test site, and now all the actors are dying of cancer."

"Bullshit," J.J. said.

"It's true. Dick Powell is already gone, and others are sick."

"You can't prove that."

"Boys," Maddy said, "That's enough. You're never going to agree."

— · —

The moon, almost full, was rising over the ridge, and as word spread the guests indoors wandered outside to see. The moonlight silvered the meadow's drying grass, and an owl flapped in eerie silence from an oak. Someone began a kind of pseudo-Indian chant, and others joined in. Then someone else brought out a conga and started slapping it. Tambourines were found, and added a jangly percussive overlay.

Sundown and Sebastian descended from the tree house, smiling with an I-know-something-you-don't smugness and sat, heads together and holding hands. Owen plugged in Robbie's guitar and starting picking out a melody. Maddy, who had a fine voice but rarely used it, recognized Pete Seeger's "Turn! Turn! Turn!" and began to sing along.

This proved too sappy for Cueball and Bonnie, and their chopper started with a roar and drove, *potato-potato-potato*, back up the hill.

The moon was overhead by the time the party wound down, starkly illuminating the party's debris in blue and black. Most guests had left, a few had passed out, and the hangers-on were just looking for somewhere to crash. Maddy walked around finding the sleepers and covering them with blankets and gaudy Tijuana ponchos. Then she flopped onto the bed next to her snoring husband.

Parties were too much work.

6

"*I pledge allegiance to the Flag of the United States of America, and to the Republic for which it stands, one Nation under God, indivisible, with liberty and justice for all.*"

Forwitchit Stands, Robbie muttered to himself. Perhaps that would make a good band name. A damn sight better than Strawberry Alarm Clock, the local band that had just played at the school. When he approached them afterward backstage they wouldn't even talk to him, let alone consider him as a guitarist, and the memory still stung. When he got a band together, he certainly wouldn't name it after fruit.

"Sobieski," his teacher said, when they were done and seated, "The vice-principal would like to see you."

Robbie disliked vice-principal Hanke. With his tight-cropped hair, his muscular build, and his air of smug confidence, the man struck him as a grownup version of all the jocks that had ever given him a hard time.

"Sit down, Mr. Sobieski," Hanke said, and stared at him. "This isn't the first time I've had to talk to you, is it? You know, I keep receiving complaints about you: your attitude, your work. Or lack of it. Seems you're not often here, and when you are, you're not paying attention."

Robbie looked away from the man's well-fed face to the clock on the wall. Plastic. The whole country was becoming plastic.

Hanke tried the avuncular approach. "Now, I don't believe you're stupid, Robert; you're just lazy. Am I right?"

Robbie did his best to tune the man out. The vice-principal inhabited a bygone era, when teenagers were trained to become part of the machinery of the Establishment like good little cogs. He was still sold on some vague American Dream, believing in an Uncle Sam who, if you played his game, took care of you from cradle to grave. In his universe you paid a university to get credentials, then you landed a straight nine-to-five and moved up, bought a house, started a family, got a bigger house, and sent your kids off to be groomed in the same way. Then you retired, began drinking whiskey at breakfast, bought a La-Z-Boy and played golf until your heart attack. That was the old way, and Hanke's kind hadn't noticed the country—the whole world—was now on a different course.

"Your parents' taxes pay for us to educate you, Mr. Sobieski. They expect us not just to house you during the week, but also to infuse you with learning, with skills, with meaningful social interaction, all of which will benefit you once you leave. To stretch and mold you physically, mentally, and hopefully even morally. Hm?"

They were at the beginning of an age where people's real talents determined what they became, where love and not greed ruled, where a price tag wasn't attached to everything. Society was changing, and the old divisions, into which all these students were being slotted, would soon be meaningless.

Hanke's demeanor, now that he saw no response from Robbie, hardened. "You'd better shape up, Sobieski, or you'll find yourself without any marketable skills. Do you want to be a laborer, a ditch-digger? Your family expects us to make you a useful member of society, and we expect you to learn, and grow, and become someone they can be proud of. Do you think your parents would be happy with us if we allowed you to end up a janitor? I don't think so. Now," he smiled a humorless smile, "you have just one more year here at Pali High. Why not follow in your brother's footsteps and become a useful and respected member of society? If you buckle down and study, you'll be amazed at the difference it makes in your attitude, and in the way others treat you." He steepled his fingers. "There's still time. Tomorrow is the first day of the rest of your life."

"Yes, sir."

"Oh, and your hair is touching your collar again. See to that, will you?"

Robbie was in time for the second half of music class, where a nightmarish clamor met his ears. Everyone was attempting to play "Michael Row the Boat Ashore" on plastic Fitchhorn song flutes, *always in tune*. He felt like ramming one up the teacher's ass.

— · —

Robbie's CT90 slowed as the canyon steepened. Cars zoomed by. Once he was even outpaced by a man on a racing bicycle. This was where he needed the power, and the Honda didn't have it. He liked the little bike, but as he rode he fantasized about driving something bigger. One of the new Yamaha DT-1s, maybe; a Triumph Bonneville. Or forget the bikes. A Porsche Roadster, or a Ferrari like Owen's.

His speed dropped to a walking pace. Then, with a loud *clang*, his chain snapped. He wobbled to the side of the road and dismounted, cursing. He looked at his surroundings; though he was so familiar with the road he knew exactly where he was. Across to his left was rising hillside covered with chaparral, a small natural spring dribbling into the ditch. To his right was a steep drop-off to the creek a hundred and fifty feet below. No houses, no phone, no way to call for help.

He removed the snapped chain, covering himself with grease and dirt in the process, and wound it around the seat stem. Then he grabbed the handlebars and began to push.

— · —

In the tower, Charity wrote in her journal as her mother worked.

> *In early spring, entire meadows blossom with yellow mustard flowers, four or five feet high, which last a month or so. Like most wildflowers in Southern California the mustard is not native, and some say Gaspar de Portola brought the seeds from Spain in 1769 and planted them to mark his trail north from Mexico. It's probably untrue.*
>
> *Next the lupines appear, little blue-violet cones of dense-packed flowers only six or seven inches tall, cropping up in bright clumps on the hillsides. Later, as spring slides into summer, the wild radishes bloom, tiny Easter-pastel flowers on long stalks that if eaten taste of their namesake.*

"Mom? D'you think I should have a chapter on weeds?"

Maddy looked up from pinning patterns to fabric. "I don't think 'weed' is a botanical class, Charity. A weed is just a plant growing where you didn't plant one."

"Huh?"

"What's scorned as a weed in one place is admired as an ornamental in another. It's a judgment we put on plants. Good or bad."

"Oh."

"I guess humans put their judgments on everything. Bees good; wasps bad. Daffodils good; dandelions bad. It's just what we do."

This was a new concept to Charity. She considered how this moral duality applied to everything in life. Christians good; pagans bad. Men smart; women stupid. Right-handed good, left-handed bad. What a trap it is, she realized. Either this or that. Life was more complicated, surely. It was a childish way of looking at things—sorting them into just two buckets—this one or that one. She determined to try not to do it in future.

She picked up her pen again.

> *Jackson is going off to war. None of us want him to, but he thinks it's his duty. He loves granddad, and always wanted to be like him, I guess. Dad says this war is nothing like granddad's war, but Jackson says it's the same. They'll never agree, and he's old enough to go, so he's going. People are on one side or the other. If only they could get together and discuss it, they would see it isn't just black or white.*
>
> *I think war is silly, and it just shows how little we have changed since being apes, but I suppose sometimes it's necessary. I wish someone could tell me why this one is.*

— · —

The city of Long Beach had hoped to change its reputation as a dive for drunken sailors by allowing the recently retired *Queen Mary* liner to be moored in the harbor as a tourist attraction. The Long Beach Arena worked on luring high-profile acts to also help put the city on the cultural map. On May 5, it hosted the "Electric Carnival." Bret had been hired by Omega's Eye to design and manage the light show, though since the start time was four p.m., when the sun was still up, the audience wasn't likely to appreciate it much until the main act hit the stage around seven.

Not only was his idol Neil Young performing with Buffalo Springfield, but Canned Heat were booked, along with Country Joe & The Fish. The Hook, an L.A.-based band led by Bobby Arlin, and known for their one hit "Hey Joe," were also on the bill.

Bret quickly took charge. As far as he could tell, the skills of the people around him were at high school level, and in a curt voice he ordered the position of the key light and accents, managing to alienate most of the hands in a very short time.

Once he had finished directing his staff with the stage lights and their gels, and making sure the kaleidoscope and slide projector were hooked up and properly focused, Bret turned to the liquid projection part of the display, the wet show. He waved over his assistant, a young girl whose bangs kept flopping into her eyes. From his bag he took out a bundle wrapped in soft rags, and from this he placed a large glass clock face crystal on one of two bottom-lit overhead projectors and carefully poured a small amount of clear mineral oil into it. Then, from eyedropper bottles of artist watercolors he dripped small amounts of three different colors—blue, orange and red. Next he placed a smaller clock glass on top, which squashed the colors between the two bowls in blobby, amorphous patterns. When projected onto the stage, the effect veered between looking like chromosomal mitosis, squirming bacilli, and an animated Rorschach test.

"Trippy, man," the girl said, staring open-mouthed at the resulting display.

"Goddammit—*concentrate!*" Bret told her. "Now," he said, "Two things: First, don't spill it. Liquids and stage shows don't mix. Secondly, nudge the top glass around in time with the music, just a little. Don't overdo it. Also, three colors max on each, or they'll mix into a dirty purple."

"What's the other projector for?" she asked.

"We swap 'em out, so it doesn't get boring. Second song, second projector, third song back to number one. Your friend can be changing the oil and the colors while you're working."

As the five thousand-strong audience took its seats and the show began, Bret became lost in his work, almost oblivious to the music. The projectors threw their images—of lovers kissing, soldiers firing guns, flowers, police with riot shields, plus the blobby colored abstracts—across both performers and stage, and as the sun set the scene became vivid and alive.

It soon became clear that the audio board had a problem. Bret hoped it would be fixed by the time the main act took the stage, but he was disappointed.

[74]

Buffalo Springfield walked on, Richie Furay and Neil Young's hair and sideburns making their heads look as if replaced by shaggy coconuts. They managed to get through "Rock & Roll Woman," with its supremely sing-alongable chorus, the twangy country of "A Child's Claim To Fame," and "Nowadays Clancy Can't Even Sing," with its signature change in tempo from 4/4 to 3/4, before fans rushed the stage.

The electricity was cut, abruptly dousing the lights, silencing the instruments and stopping the show cold. To Bret's horror the venue's director, in incongruous sport jacket and tie, walked onstage to a chorus of boos and raised his hands for quiet.

"Buffalo Springfield will not play until your return to your seats! Buffalo Springfield will not play until your return to your seats!" he announced, to more whistles and catcalls, but the audience, realizing he meant business, relented.

During the pause Bret pushed his way back through the crowd to the men working the audio board. His lanyard pass let him into their booth, and they looked up at him with curiosity.

"The vocals are getting distorted whenever the singers are hot on the mics," he told them.

"We have it under control," one said.

"But—"

"Go on back to your snot slides."

— · —

Then came "Good Time Boy," and "Mr. Soul," with its jangly guitar, "Uno Mundo," its Latin beat bolstered by added trumpets, congas and maracas, and "For What It's Worth," its *Stop! Children what's that sound* like a gunshot, all interrupted by more stage rushing.

The performance was capped by a twenty-minute rendition of "Bluebird," with Young and Stills acting as usual—clashing fiercely with lead guitars like stags in rutting season.

— · —

As soon as the curtain had dropped after the last song, Bret barked instructions to his crew and quickly made his way back to the dressing rooms.

"Which is Neil Young's?" he asked one of the guards.

The man blocked Bret's way with a burly, tattooed arm. "You can't go back there."

"I'm the lighting director."

"I don't care if you're Lyndon fuckin' Johnson, you're not going back there."

Bret gave in, temporarily, vowing to return later. But before he could, a limo snaked off into the night, carrying Buffalo Springfield into history.

— · —

Sundown left her new yearbook on her desk for a moment, and someone stole it. When it reappeared half an hour later, scrawled under her photo was, in letters far too large to ignore, "Most likely to do all the members of the Doors." Her father wouldn't pay for another, unadulterated, book, and now she was stuck with this one.

Fuming, she went to her English room. Mr. Vandevere had requested she see him after class.

"Is it about my essay?" she asked him, once the rest of the class had left. She had written a long piece about broken Indian treaties entitled The Trail of Torn Paper, and she was proud of it.

"No, not really, Sundown. 'Sundown' … that's an interesting name."

"Yeah, well, my parents are kinda hippie."

"You know," he said, looking her up and down, "you're quite the most beautiful girl I've ever had in my class."

Sundown was surprised and flustered. This was the last thing she expected him to say. "Oh. Thanks."

"Are you sticking around over the summer?"

"What?"

"There's a pool at my house. Quite private."

"Uh … I'm not sure…"

"I just thought a girl like you might appreciate an … *experienced* man for a change."

"A 'girl like me'?"

"I meant an open-minded girl. A *modern* girl."

"Isn't that against the rules?" she asked him.

He smiled a lascivious smile. She had never noticed before that his teeth were yellow and his gums were receding. "Since when do girls like you play by the rules? Besides, in a few days you'll have officially left the school."

[76]

Sundown's eyes narrowed as she looked him up and down, too. "I used to think you were a good teacher. You're just a lech like everyone else."

— · —

Sundown fumed. At least she would soon leave all this behind. Screw college—that could wait. She flicked lazily through a copy of her mother's *Life* magazine and stopped at a photograph of Jackie Kennedy taken when she was First Lady, getting out of a limousine. "Where's Jacks?"

Maddy looked up. "He's in the garage."

Sundown found Jackson under his car. "Jacks?"

"Yeah?"

"Know anyone who works at a funeral home?"

He slid out and blinked at her. "Huh?"

"I need a hearse. Just for one day."

"Oh." Jackson nodded. This seemed like a perfectly normal request to him. "Duke has a friend that drives an old hearse. I can borrow it, for a full tank o' gas and a six-pack, maybe."

"Great. OK, just let me know what he wants."

— · —

A late fifties Desoto hearse, its length and fins making it look like some kind of grounded rocket ship, pulled up to the main entrance of Taft High. The mass of students and parents milling there for graduation stopped and stared.

After a dramatic pause Sundown slid out of the back, wearing a black Jackie Kennedy-style raffia and ribbon hat with veil instead of a mortarboard, and a black mini skirt under her robe.

The high school band played "Mighty Quinn." Then a school folk group called Pioneer Quilt sang "Both Sides Now."

After the ceremony, their ears still ringing from the poorly amplified *Pomp and Circumstance No. 1*, Spencer, who fancied himself the school poet, said, "I like your hat. Great statement."

"Thanks."

"Who was the guy with the short hair who dropped you off?"

"My brother. He's going to 'Nam."

"Really? What is he—the white sheep of the family?"

"Fuck you, Spencer."

"Sorry. Just a joke."

They sat and regarded the mass of students and their family members. Despite the crowd she felt isolated and alone. She had urged her parents not to come, and now she wished she hadn't.

"Where you going?" Spencer asked.

"College? I dunno. The thought of more classes makes me ill. I may take a year off, make some money."

"How do your folks feel about that?"

She laughed. "Haven't told 'em yet."

— · —

Len turned to her in the back of the hearse as they drove back. "You going to Grad Nite?"

Sundown made a face.

"C'mon—it'll be fun."

Sundown was torn. Disneyland represented her childhood, and she remembered getting happily lost in the brightly colored and simplified world Uncle Walt had created. Now, from her new adult perspective, it seemed middle-class and manipulative, but she was embarrassed to find she still looked forward to going. "I suppose."

— · —

Not many trees in Southern California are native. The jacarandas and mimosas are from South America, the magnolias and ficus from Asia, the crape myrtles from India, olives from Italy, even the tall fan palms are from Mexico, and the eucalyptus, so common across the southland, is Australian.

Early white settlers in California quickly set about cutting down its trees, as they had in other, more northern states. But California's forests were not as abundant. When the Tree Culture Act of 1868 offered a dollar for each tree planted and nurtured for four years, landowners complied wholeheartedly. A dollar was a lot of money then, and dozens of trees could fit into an acre. Early promoters promised that eucalyptus could be used for timber, fuel, medicine, wood pulp, honey, and provide medicinal oils that would combat malaria. Also attractive was its speed of growth: a Blue Gum may grow sixty feet in six years. But young eucalyptus wood turned out to be useless for construction and furniture building—it warped and cracked as it dried—and its other supposed uses turned out to be a bust, too. Only the growth rate was real, but at the cost of valuable ground water. But by the time people understood its limitations, Eucalyptus had been planted everywhere.

— · —

In the parking lot Sundown and Lenfound a place behind a van and out of sight of the chaperones to take a quick hit from a pipe, and by the time they got through the turnstiles they were giggling uncontrollably.

Everyone immediately made for the surreal shrinking atom ride—Monsanto's *Adventure Thru Inner Space* in Tomorrowland—and inside was a chaos of similarly loaded kids. Security guards tried to calm them down, with only limited success. The five security personnel were far outnumbered by a morass of manic graduates.

After they had completed the ride, Sundown and Len wandered over to watch the Sam the Sham Revue at the Fantasyland Theater in time to hear "Wooly Bully," which sounded pretty dated now, and then moved on to the Plaza Gardens to catch Bill Elliott and the Disneyland Date Niters. Bored with this show, which they considered watered-down and too middle-of-the-road to waste time on, they headed back to the Tomorrowland Terrace and caught the end of The Mustangs' performance.

At midnight were fireworks and the Joe Tex Orchestra & Revue, but they had paid an extra 75 cents each for an E-ticket to United Airlines' Tiki Room, and headed there next. The god out front spat water into a bamboo tube, which Sundown suspected was some erotic Tahitian god Disneyfied into something acceptable to families. In the lanai area they waited, serenaded by canned music, for the show to start.

Inside, the musical show was hosted by four animatronic macaws whose plumage matched their supposed countries of origin. José was red, white, and green and spoke with a Mexican accent; Michael was white, orange and green with an Irish brogue; Pierre was red, white, and blue and had a French accent; red, black, and white Fritz had a German accent. The birds had real feathers, and their little chests breathed in a lifelike manner.

Over two hundred talking, singing, and dancing birds, plus flowers, the magic fountain, tiki drummers and totem poles performed "In The Tiki Room," and "Let's All Sing Like The Birdies Sing," for whose chorus José crooned like Bing Crosby, Fritz scatted like Louis Armstrong, and

Pierre sang like Maurice Chevalier.

Blaine, one of the jocks, came up to Len. He smelled of liquor, so while they were toking outside he was probably chugging miniatures. Either that or he and his friends had done their injecting oranges with vodka trick and eaten them on the way. "What's this one sing in, huh? Gospel?"

Sundown couldn't understand why anyone would want trouble in a place like this, on a night like this. "Oh piss off, Blaine."

"Go on," Blaine persisted, prodding Len, who was almost a foot shorter, "do a calypso for us. Do the 'Banana Boat Song'."

Len hesitated. He was embarrassed, but rapidly losing his temper.

Sundown looked around in desperation for the rest of the jocks. "Call him off, will you? He's bumming us out."

Jordan, Blaine's best buddy, repeated in falsetto, "he's *bumming them out*, guys! Hey, Blaine, stop *bumming them out*, man!"

They erupted into snide laughter. Other guests started to edge away.

"Go on—" Blaine began again, before Len stamped on his foot, hard. As the boy doubled over in agony, Len gave a short, hard jab upward to his face. The jock fell backward and sat; now holding his nose, which streamed blood.

The "Hawaiian War Chant" started playing.

"OK, that's it!" said one of the guards, speaking urgently into his walkie-talkie. "You lot—out!"

As the students filed outside, they were met in the walkway by a bevy of security, who marched them to an electric golf cart and drove them to the exit, watched by curious Grad Niters.

By two a.m. Sundown and Len were tired and sober. They sat in the back of the bus, the jocks and the driver in the front, with an angry teacher assigned to sit between them. Sundown looked out of the windows at other students as they wandered and ran about, still doggedly enjoying themselves.

She yawned. "It was bourgeois anyway."

— · —

Sundown touched her big brother's muscled bicep. "Jacks, can we talk?"

"Sure." Jackson looked around the house. The usual chaos reigned. Robbie and Gilligan were having a tug-o-war with an old T-shirt and it would rip at any moment. Their father had the stereo cranked up with The Supremes' *Reflections* on the turntable. Their mother was grinding coffee beans. At home with the Sobieskis. "Let's go outside."

"Tree house?"

"Too hot. Let's sit under the eucalyptus trees."

One of a flurry of projects their father had tackled when the nascent Sobieski family had first arrived from Philadelphia ten years earlier was a circular bench around the largest tree. Eucalyptus didn't offer much shade, since they were tall and their leaves tended to clump high up in their branches, but it was still a peaceful spot, and the trees smelled good.

Brother and sister regarded each other in the dappled light.

Jackson saw Sundown's beauty as if for the first time—the freckles, the perfectly formed nose, the long blonde hair, the big bright eyes. She looked very little like either of her parents, but he figured his father's Polish genes had predominated, since his mother's looks were Italian, and darker. He would miss her. It was just like that lyric, *you don't know what you've got till it's gone.* "Lemme guess," he said. "The war."

Sundown glanced at his olive T-shirt and shorts. He was a boy in a man's body. It wasn't all that long ago he'd been playing out here with a BB gun, and soon he'd be handling real ones. "Yeah, well, all this violence is freaking me out."

Jackson shook his big head. "These are tough times. People keep talkin' about peace, but it ain't that easy. Peace comes at a price."

This sounded to Sundown like propaganda the military had put in his mouth. "What kind of price, Jacks? Dead American boys?"

He frowned. There wasn't much he could do about this kind of talk from strangers, and he tended to walk away from it, but from family... "We're highly trained by the time we get to 'Nam. I'll be OK."

"So the Viet Cong don't train their soldiers?"

"We outnumber 'em, and we have all the equipment."

"Aren't the Chinese supplying them now?"

Jackson made a dismissive sound with his lips. "They don't hold up to ours."

Sundown thought one bullet was much like another. "You hope."

A scrub jay squawked from one of the branches above. A gray lizard did pushups from the tree trunk.

"Jacks ... you sure you just don't want to get away from dad? I know

I do."

Jackson laughed. "He's a pain in the ass, but he's not why." He stood. "I just have to go. Maybe you'll never understand."

"I'm trying." As her brother turned away, Sundown called after him. "You be careful, OK?" She followed him back to the house. Well, that was Jackson talked to. Now it was time to deal with her parents.

Inside the house, quieter now, Bret and Maddy were making a shopping list in the kitchen. Only a fraction of their needs could be found in Topanga itself, and shopping entailed a long trip down to Woodland Hills and back. Because of this, and to minimize trips, the family spent serious consideration on what was needed.

Sundown decided the direct approach was best. "Mom, dad—I want to put off going to college."

Bret looked up, startled. "What? You were planning on Pierce, like Jacks."

"No, *you* were planning that. I need some time off. I've had enough of sitting in classes for a while. More than enough."

"But—you'll lose momentum," Bret said. "You'll drop out and never be able to get back in. You end up in a succession of lousy jobs—waitress or typist—"

"Thanks for your faith in me."

Her father's face took on a dangerous hue. "Sundown, really. We want you to—"

"I can't just go back to homework and exams and boring teachers right now."

"You have the summer—"

"Not enough. I'm going to be a model for a year, then look at it all again."

Maddy stepped in before Bret could reply. "Just a year, and then you'll go to college?"

"Maybe."

7

Los Angeles International Airport was crowded with travelers; most, by the looks of them, either going on or coming back from vacation.

Levi's had belatedly jumped on the fashion bandwagon and marketed bell-bottoms, and even the straights wore them now. The story was that a designer for Levi's had modified a pair of her own jeans with a triangle of denim inserted at the hem, and was in the process of being kicked out of the boardroom when she ran into the president, who approved the new line.

Charity looked around, fascinated. Everything about the airport—its eclectic mix of peoples, its air of urgency, its constantly changing lists of exotic locales—intrigued her, gave her a heightened sense of excitement, as if she were in the eye of a storm of important events. Any of these passengers lugging suitcases could be famous: an artist, writer, politician. Or they could be visiting from any country in the world: Madagascar, Switzerland, Mongolia. Even Great Britain, like Owen, like … the Beatles. She peered intently about in search of rock stars, but it was hard to tell. For all she knew, all the hippie types with messy hair and sunglasses could be in a band.

Still, the airport's energy was invigorating. It would be wonderful to work here and witness this parade every day. She became determined to become one of these stewardesses in their smart uniforms and perky hats, jetting around the world, free of the earth and belonging to nowhere.

Among the crowd were men obviously not embarking on a vacation. Men in drab green outfits and with short hair carrying shapeless kitbags like Jackson. Each had his own entourage, equally conservatively dressed. Only Jackson's group was mixed. Several officers walked by, and when Jackson stopped and saluted, they looked curiously at the colorful Sobieskis that surrounded him.

Robbie was uncomfortable here. A year ago he'd have been stoked to look for one of the new Boeing 737s, but that was when he was a kid. Now he was an adult, and wiser. This was the straight world, and not just any part of it—the gateway into the war and everything else he despised. He wanted to be back with his friends, smoking, laughing. The fact that his brother was leaving home only marginally impinged on his consciousness. All this concrete and glass had nothing to do with him. He had dropped out, with no intention of ever dropping back in.

Sundown was still having trouble with the whole idea of Jackson going to war. Some of her friends' brothers had returned from Vietnam disfigured, and she dreaded Jackson becoming one of the casualties. But there was no changing his mind. She felt the grip of fate, and a powerlessness to change it. The world was fucked up. The older generation had ruined it with their petty values, their greed, their colonies. Hers would do a better job.

The flight was delayed, and they found seats at the gate, where a group of hippies glared at Jackson. He held back. "I'll stand," he told his parents. "I'm not going to sit and have this bunch of longhairs tell me I'm a baby-killer."

His mother looked from them to him. "Surely not."

"Every day, ma, from someone or other. Only the bikers accept me, and I never wanted to be one of them."

Bret had to look up at his son; there was a good five inches' difference between them. "You know I don't agree with this, Jacks. The whole war is crazy. But..." he looked around, momentarily at a loss for words, "you look after yourself, OK? The others need their big brother. Your mother ... well, she'd go nuts if anything happened to you."

Jackson nodded. "I'll be fine."

The gate agent's announcement saved them from further discomfort by calling Jackson's flight. Each family member hugged Jackson in turn, and then stood, hands clasped awkwardly, waiting for the situation to be resolved by him leaving.

Jackson grinned. "'Bye. Dad—say hi to Neil Young for me." He turned at the boarding gate, waved once and was gone.

— · —

Charity looked in Jackson's room. Empty, it seemed strange. In the past, her older brother had either always been there, or was due back shortly. It still smelled of cigarettes, Aqua Velva, and ... *boy*, but it had a lifeless, stale quality now.

She walked to the bedroom she shared with Sundown, and took the opportunity of her older sister's absence to sit at her desk and write in peace.

> *The mockingbirds move in, strictly temporarily. They court new mates with their wide...*

She consulted the thesaurus for a couple of minutes

> *... repertoire of short phrases, while flying from tree to eave and back in display, their dark gray wings flashing white patches.*
>
> *Scufflings heard in the dry leaves are often signs a quail family is about, their silly headdresses bobbing. They're skittish and shy, and they'll whirr up and move somewhere else at the slightest noise.*
>
> *Hummingbirds come in two kinds here, the ruby-tuxedoed and the emerald. They live on flower nectar and the sugary contents of plastic porch feeders.*
>
> *Down at the foot of the canyon, where the road dead-ends at Pacific Coast Highway and the beach, the seagulls raid the dumpsters and sleep on the sand.*

— · —

Now Jackson had gone, Robbie felt one of the governors on his behavior lifted. His father was off filming again, too. He was free to do as he pleased. He ought to go on a vision quest, like the young men in Indian tribes were said to do, to find themselves and come back a man, with their true name.

He considered scoring some peyote, but he didn't think his surfer connections were into that, and besides, it sounded a little scary to do solo.

He remembered someone at the party mentioning getting high on morning glory seeds, and decided to explore the possibility. After school he steered his bike inland toward West Los Angeles, and turned down Sawtelle, a street full of Japanese nurseries.

When he entered the first and asked for morning glory seeds, the tiny old man that ran the place smiled briefly. "All sold. To young men like you," he said. "Very popular all of a sudden."

When Robbie tried the next he got the same result, though the owner this time was a little more articulate. "As soon as I get some in, the long-hairs buy them. I'm waiting for another batch."

"Well," Robbie replied, "what does it look like?"

The nurseryman smiled. "You don't know morning glory vine? Here—" he led Robbie out the back of the greenhouse to a corner of his overgrown lot, where a sprawling mass of heart-shaped leaves and bright blue trumpet-shaped flowers with white centers covered the wall. A hummingbird dipped its long beak in and out of the blossoms, and then zoomed away when they came too close.

"How long does it take to grow this big?"

"Too long for you. Ten, twelve years."

"Are they always blue?"

"No, purple, white—sometimes deep red or pink. But most blue, here."

Robbie thanked him, and feeling obligated to repay the man for his time bought a packet of carrot seeds to give to Charity.

All the way home he looked for morning glories. Most people here chose magenta bougainvillea as their vine—it grew and bloomed whether or not you took care of it. It wasn't until he was back on Pacific Coast Highway that he was lucky enough to see any. Up one of the smaller box canyons he passed on the way home, he glimpsed its blue flowers spilling over a stucco wall.

He parked a hundred yards away and scoped out the area as he walked toward the vine. It was a well-off enclave of Spanish-styled houses and, being Los Angeles, there was no one around on foot. He yanked off as many flowers as he could, cramming them into his bag. Then he continued home, parked his bike and walked down to the tree house. Once inside, he strew the flowers on every available surface. He knew it got hot enough in there to dry them quickly, and if anyone asked why they were there he'd say it was for some kind of hippie festival.

But nobody discovered the dead flowers, and in a week they were desiccated enough for him to extract the seeds. He was disappointed to find there weren't very many for all that work, but he hoped there would be enough for a true psychedelic experience. Borrowing his mother's mortar and pestle from the kitchen, he ground the seeds into a damp gray puddle. Now what? Without anyone to ask the proper procedure, he mixed them with marmalade and spread the mixture on toast. It left a disgusting aftertaste.

Then he went back to the tree house to await its effects.

In about twenty minutes he felt nauseous, but this didn't worry him. Everyone knew that peyote first caused nausea, so all good psychedelic drugs, he reasoned, must trigger this. You just had to get past it. He threw up out the window and sat back down to read a comic and wait. But when, after another hour or so nothing happened, he climbed back down, disappointed. The ladder felt odd, but he had probably gotten up too quickly and become a little dizzy.

The house seemed … *wrong* somehow. What was different? Nothing visual; it was more a vague *feeling* of wrongness. He walked in through the back door. His mother and sisters were in the kitchen, clattering about as they prepared dinner.

"Oh, hi, Robbie," Maddy said. "Ravioli tonight."

Robbie stood staring at them. The overhead light in the kitchen cast shadows into their eye sockets and made their faces look skull-like. Their movements were those of zombies. This was not his family. These were impostors.

Maddy looked back at him. "You OK?"

"Y-yeah," he said, and turned away to the living room. Their new Admiral 27-inch TV was showing *Mr. Magoo*, and its flickering colors seemed to leap out of the screen like flames from a small fireplace. The show's manic sounds yammered like chipmunks in his head. The shadows cast by the TV's brightness flitted about the room as if couch and chairs were trying desperately to leave.

Horrified, Robbie went to his room. When he flicked on the light all his furnishings were thrown into stark relief, each item looking as if it had just frozen to stillness.

What was going on? He sat on his bed, but the mattress tried to swallow him, so he jumped up again. He took his guitar from the chair and threw it onto the bed so he could sit there instead. This, too, felt as if it was trying to engulf him somehow, but at least it wasn't soft, and he thought he could deal with it.

His shelf of books leaned this way and that as if on a storm-tossed ship. His lava lamp looked amoebic and hungry. The light on his stereo receiver glowered with a dull and persistent malevolence. His Peter Max-inspired wallpaper pulsed and throbbed.

"Robbie!" his mother called. "Dinner!"

Could he deal with dinner? He decided not to try. He struggled out of the chair and tried to open the door, but the doorknob felt spongy. Finally he got it open and called out, "Not feeling well. Think I'll pass, thanks."

Hoping that would settle the matter, Robbie sat in the middle of the floor, clutching his knees to his chest. Should he turn off the light? No way. Was that an earthquake?

He tried closing his eyes, and though that limited the visual effects to a kind of primitive cartoon show projected on his inner eyelids, it made him paranoid about what might be happening around him that he couldn't see, so he had to open them again.

He decided the overhead light was too much and snapped it off, leaving just the lava lamp. This was not enough, and he turned on the reading lamp at his desk and his old Fred Flintstone nightlight in the wall socket. Now the illumination was more manageable, but it left far too many menacing shadows. He was about to try some music when there was a knock on the door and Charity opened it, staring at him. But was it *really* Charity?

"Mom said to see if you were OK."

"Y-yeah. Upset stomach. Must have been the school lunch."

Charity stood there without answering for what seemed like hours. Eventually she said, "Do you want me to get you some Pepto-Bismol?"

The thought of the gelatinous bright pink liquid made Robbie's gorge rise again. "No, I'll be fine. Thanks."

Charity turned away and closed the door. A vague outline of her shape remained behind for a moment, like smoke. Or a ghost. Were they ghosts? Was he dead? He should never have eaten the seeds—they'd poisoned him. Should he get his stomach pumped?

He tried to get a grip on himself. What would Jackson do? Jacks would laugh and light a Camel. Robbie could hear his brother's voice in his head, clear as a bell: "Well what d'you expect, Robs? Not all drugs are cool."

"Other people take 'em," Robbie muttered.

"But everyone's different. Ask a doctor—drugs affect everyone differently. Some people can't even take aspirin."

"Jacks ... where are you?"

Jackson gave his laugh, the laugh that made everything seem all right. "In your head, you little turdbag."

"Where are your cigarettes?" Robbie asked.

"My dresser. Top right."

Robbie went to the door and opened it. The sounds of dinner being eaten—knives and forks clinking on china, talking with food in the mouth—came from the breakfast nook. He scurried furtively along to Jackson's room, ran in, found the pack of cigarettes, and ran back to his room. Then he pulled one out and lit it. He coughed. It tasted intense, but normal. It calmed him.

"Jacks?" he said, but his brother had gone. Now a breeze was dragging the palm fronds across the screen of his window with a metallic scratching. He tried to ignore it, but the more he tried, the louder it sounded.

Out of the corner of his eye he noticed his hand holding the cigarette. It seemed too far away, as if his arm had lengthened. His fingers looked wrong too, as if they were the legs of a spider.

Would this never end? Sleep began to look extremely attractive—a dark amnesia in which to forget this new, twisted world. He'd look shitfaced at school if he didn't sleep. They'd know he was into something illegal if he arrived with bags under his eyes, and he'd get into even more trouble.

He climbed into bed without taking off his clothes or brushing his teeth, and eventually the personal cartoons faded and he slept.

— · —

First, Jackson had to complete his eight weeks of Basic Training.

At Fort Ord, he was greeted by a 105 howitzer with "Canned Heat" painted on its barrel, which brought a fleeting grin to his face.

The drill sergeant took them into their assigned barracks and pointed out where they were to sleep, how to clean the wooden building, and the importance of placing a fireguard at night. He explained that once he gave the order to form up, they had to do so in less than thirty seconds.

Then, just as they were beginning to relax and unpack, he gave the order. It was a minute and a half before they managed to get in satisfactory formation. As punishment he made them crawl under the barracks on their elbows, the length of the building, over and over again, until they were coated inside and out with dust.

They were told they would not be allowed to leave the company area that first weekend. Not until they were voted the best platoon during weekly inspection would they be allowed a day pass. It took a month before they won. In this time, the world narrowed to their barracks and the base. There was no television, and their links to their old life withered.

Only some of the men wanted to be there. At least half had been forced to by the draft, and resented the orders, resented the way their individual egos were being systematically stripped away before they could be rebuilt as soldiers. Jackson did not exactly enjoy the process, but he understood its necessity and thought he could rise above it. Fighting it was futile; it just had to be endured. Life was going to be hard from here on in; it would be harder still if you tried to swim upstream.

On the way to the training area they were usually ordered to march "double time"—jogging with full pack and rifle. If they were not judged to be doing it correctly, the drill sergeant would yell *"Charlie's gonna getcha!"*

Soon the memory of his family in Topanga began to recede until, after a few weeks, it was like an idealized Polaroid in his mind—pretty and bright but fading, disconnected from his new surroundings. Reality was now jungle green and olive drab. Reality was barked orders and kit and bed in order. Reality was a drill sergeant screaming abuse in your face.

This strict indoctrination was difficult to get used to, but easier for Jackson than most of the others. He realized now that he detested the lack of discipline at home, Hophead Hills' sloppy, mañana attitude. He needed the structure, and now he had it in spades.

He liked feeling a part of a bigger group, all working in unison toward a common goal. He liked having a purpose. The rest of America began to resemble a theme park in his mind, all mindless distractions and indulgent snacking. His reality was grounded in duty, and effort, and often pain. He had yearned to test himself against something bigger and stronger, and now he had his chance. First he would tackle the U.S. Army; next he would tackle its enemies.

8

"We have to do this outside," Maddy told Charity, "and you have to wear old clothes."

"OK."

"And rubber gloves."

Once they had changed, mother and younger daughter spread a tarpaulin on the grass, and Charity arranged two white T-shirts, latex kitchen gloves, two buckets and an assortment of little aluminum dye containers, all while humming *na na na nana na na* from "Hey Jude," which had been on every radio station for weeks.

"First, we have to rinse the T-shirts to get the starch off," Maddy explained, and dunked the shirts in the pail of plain water.

"Mommy? Do you believe in God?"

"I do, Charity, yes."

"Then why don't you go to church?"

"Squeeze these shirts out till they're just damp, then lay them out on the tarp. When I was a kid I had to go to Mass a lot. My parents were Catholic. But I didn't like it much, and I'd stopped going by the time I met your dad."

"So you're not ... spiritual?"

"I didn't say that. A person can still be spiritual without going to church. Now squinch up the part of the shirt you want to be the center of the design, like this, and put a rubber band around it."

Charity's small hands grasped and twisted a clutch of fabric and tied it off. "So how do you get spiritual without a church?"

"Spirituality is how you treat people, how you look at things, what you believe. No one can tell you what to believe; you ... kinda look inside yourself. Now choose a color."

"Pink. How do I know what to believe?"

"Good question. Everyone's view of the world is different. Put the dye in the bucket and add half a cup of salt. Then stir it with the stick."

"But if everyone has their own God, are there billions of gods?"

"No, maybe there's only one. But each person has his or her own kind of faith. Now put your shirt in and poke it under. Right."

"Now I take it out?"

"No! We leave it in there for hours. Here—I'll do mine. I'm going for—"

A throaty rumbling came from the driveway, and they looked up to see the bright red Ferrari pull in.

Owen climbed out and waved. Today he wore a blue cowboy shirt with black embroidered yoke. "Hey!" he called, cheerfully. "I was out for a spin. Am I interrupting anything?"

"Tie-dye," Charity told him.

"I'm afraid we were just about to leave," Maddy told him. "I have to take Charity to her best friend's house."

"Oh? Where's that?"

"Pacific Palisades. Ten miles or so."

"Up or down?"

"Down."

"Well then, I'll take you. I don't like the Valley side. Fancy a ride in a sports car, Charity?"

"Wow!" Charity jumped up and ripped off the gloves. "Oh boy!" She ran inside to change.

Maddy looked at Owen. "Are you sure? We—"

"'Course. I'm one of those doped-up dropouts everyone complains about. I have all the time in the world."

— · —

The car sped away with a roar, Charity happily jammed into its cramped back seat and playing with its power windows.

[92]

"Keep the speed down in town," Maddy warned. "The police here love to hand out tickets."

Owen complied until they passed the liquor store at Fernwood, and then the car surged forward with a gargly roar.

"And there are some t-tight turns."

They tore down the twisty canyon road toward the beach, Charity and the tires squealing at every bend.

Owen was clearly enjoying himself. "So where's Bret today?"

"Off on a shoot. New Mexico, I think he said—I lose track. He'll be back in a week or so." Maddy experienced an exhilaration she hadn't in years. She felt as young as her daughter in the back seat. And why not? She was riding in Italian sports car that made everyone turn and stare, driven by an oddly good-looking rock star.

Pacific Coast Highway was lined with surfers' woody wagons and VW buses, whose owners stood on the beach dispiritedly regarding an ocean calm as a paddling pool.

All too quickly they reached Pacific Palisades and turned inland.

"Governor Reagan lives here," Charity informed him, as they roared up Temescal Canyon and into the small, neat town.

"You have an actor for governor?" Owen asked, incredulous.

"Bret says he was head of the Screen Actor's Guild once."

"I suppose that'll help. Is Bret's job union?"

"Oh yes. Very strict." She waved him to a stop and turned to Charity. "Be good. See you tomorrow."

"OK, mom. 'Bye Owen. Thanks for the ride. Is your band on TV today?"

"No, luv, don't think so. No boys in your room, now."

— · —

"This is the life," Owen said, as they returned. "Not at all like dreary old London."

Maddy turned to him. His hair was blowing all over his face, and he looked a lot like Custer. She ought to warn him against visiting any Indian reservations while he was here, unless he put his hair in a ponytail. "What did you do in England before Sunday Joint?"

"Art School."

"What does your dad do?"

"Builder. After the air raids during the war it was the builders who made the best rescue units—they knew how a house was put together, see, and how it collapsed. I suppose he found so many dead people that my playing in a band seems frivolous by comparison."

"My dad was in the war too. He didn't get wounded, but I think it haunts him."

Owen nodded. "So now, we're making a different kind of world. No more fascists. No more royalty. No more super-rich. Nothing to fight for."

"You don't like the queen?"

"Nothing personal. Just don't like the whole bunch. We should do it the American way—have an elected president. Make Buckingham Palace into artists' studios. Turn all the castles into tourist hotels and nightclubs. I think everyone except thugs and murderers should be let out of prison. Everyone should get free grass. Perhaps the milkman could deliver it every morning." He laughed, imagining it. "Two pints and a lid, please. And some papers."

"You're an anarchist," Maddy said.

"Anarchist? Perhaps you're right. My parents used to take me to the London Zoo, and at four o'clock they had the Chimpanzee's Tea Party. All the kids loved it. The chimps would sit around a table, with tablecloth and china tea service and everything. It would start off fairly civilized, and then descend into absolute chaos. Cups flung and broken, tea, sugar and milk spilled everywhere. Screaming. I thought it was fantastic. I wanted to live like that, without all the manners and stifling conventions."

"But—"

"I know—what would life be like if we all flung our teacups? It just looked *freeing*, y'know?"

"What about your mom?"

"She's like you—a dressmaker. She loves to dance. She's a bit on the chunky side now, but light on her pins. She and dad still go down the Palais at the weekend—it means a lot to 'em. In their heyday, that was the way you got your jollies—dancing close."

They turned back up into Topanga Canyon. Owen still took the bends too fast, and Maddy had to hold on with a death grip. Around one corner a deer leaped out in front of them.

Owen yelled in surprise and swerved to avoid it. But then they were past and he cackled with glee.

Maddy wasn't sure he would live long. "So..." she said, looking nervously down the sheer drop to the creek, "are things much the same in England as here?"

"The same?"

"Regarding the war, and drugs, and rock 'n' roll—"

"And free love? Yeah, more or less, I suppose. Students are against the war, and nuclear bombs. Religion is a lot less popular than it used to be. So's marriage."

"But the Brits aren't fighting in Vietnam, so it's not quite the same for you."

"True. Still, most people support the protesters, the draft-dodgers. Sort of the what-if-they-gave-a-war-and-nobody-came idea."

"'Society is changing,' you said at the party. A revolution."

"There are whole communes that barter instead of using money. Where bringing up children is shared."

Maddy laughed. "Shared among the women, I bet. And I tried that barter system at the shop. Tess—my assistant—was exchanging the clothing for grass."

"How did it go?"

"She smoked it. And I still had to pay the rent on the place and buy more fabric."

He was silent for a moment. "I think a bell ought to ring around the world at a certain time each day, and you should stop work and make love to whoever is next to you."

"What, anyone? Old and fat and everything?"

"It would make the world a happier place."

"Maybe you should stick to music."

Owen laughed and wrenched the car around the final bend before the town. "Where's your shop?"

"Just down here," Maddy said, pointing. "Actually, let's look in on Tess. She's a bit of a dingbat, so I need to keep her alert by dropping in unannounced every once in a while."

Tess, sure enough, was having a toke out the back door of the shop. The whole place was filled with savory smoke. "Oh, hi!" she said, choking.

Owen shook her hand. "Owen. We met at the party."

He looked around at the Stitch Witches' wares. Strangely popular were military-style jackets. The older the better, apparently—confederate-styled, First World War—though current fatigue jackets or British combat blouses were there too, sometimes adorned with medal ribbons, actual medals, peace signs, and patches.

As if reading his mind, Tess said, "Can you send us some British uniforms?"

"Why all the military stuff if you're anti-war?"

"We're co-opting the symbols of violence, man," Tess said.

Also on racks were long-collared flowered shirts, Nehru jackets, blouses with flared sleeves, long pioneer dresses, a couple of John Wayne-style double-breasted cowboy shirts, hand-painted kipper ties, skirts made of unstitched jeans, fur vests à la Sonny & Cher and Brian Jones. On various stands hung jewelry—bracelets, rings, ankh and peace symbols, beaded headbands, granny glasses, feather boas dyed pink and orange.

"I love it," Owen said, winking at Tess. "Far out. Isn't that what you say here?" He grabbed a shirt and a bright tie.

When he opened his wallet to pay, Tess gasped at the amount of hundred-dollar bills. "So..." she began, "what are the shops like in—what's it called?—Carbony Street?"

"Carnaby Street. Oh, very groovy, though nobody I know shops there any more. It's all been taken over by the nellies. The hip place now is the King's Road. All kinds of crazy togs."

"I'd love to go one day."

"Well, let me know if you do. I'll show you the town."

Maddy was sick of the flirting. "Any customers?" she asked Tess, coldly.

"No, it's been quiet."

"Try to maintain. It puts people off buying if you're wasted."

Tess smiled a lopsided smile and brushed her bangs out of her eyes. "I'm fine."

— · —

Charity watched her friend Cindy sleep and wished she could too. But she was worried about her mother and Owen. She plugged her earphone into her transistor radio and turned on her favorite station, then pulled out her journal and uncapped her pen.

> I like Owen, but I think he may have an evil side. He seems nice at first, but he's fooled mommy and Robbie. He doesn't fool me.

Then she flipped the page and returned to her Flora and Fauna of Topanga Canyon.

> Mule deer, so named because of their large ears, travel around in clans, stepping delicately through the chaparral and freezing, heads turned, whenever they hear anything. The bucks have antlers—not a huge rack like their cousins farther north—and their skulls can sometimes be found in out-of-the-way areas. Trees they've passed are munched neatly up to five feet, as high as they can reach, so they provide a kind of natural tree-trimming service. They'll eat anything, though, so flower and vegetable gardens have to be sturdily fenced to survive.

— · —

After graduating from Basic Training the men found out where their Assigned Individual Training would take place. Jackson was sent to helicopter maintenance at Fort Eustis, Virginia, where there were two schools. One was for the OH-6 Cayuse "Loach," the teardrop-shaped light observation helicopter. The other was for the UH-1 Iroquois "Huey," originally designed for medical evacuation but so successful it was now used, in variations, as medevac, gunship, and troop carrier.

His ship was to be the Huey.

Their instructor gave the new trainees a brief introductory speech. "This is not a grunts-on-the-ground war," he told them, "though we have plenty, and we're the ones that drop 'em off. Nor is it a battleship war, though the Navy does great work in small boats in the Mekong Delta and sends in its fighter-bombers from the carriers when we need 'em. No, this is a helicopter war. The helicopter gets men in and gets them out, in much greater numbers than the old paratroops, and carrying more equipment. The helicopter can carry guns, rockets, stretchers—"

The *whump-whump-whump* of returning Hueys underscored his comments.

— · —

Completion of the five-week basic maintenance course conferred on Jackson the Military Occupational Specialty code of 67A10. Those who excelled had the option of further training to become MOS 67N20, and Jackson was about to sign up for this when one of the other trainees warned him off. When Jackson asked why, the man explained that 67N20 would give him crew chief status.

"So?" Jackson asked, "What's wrong with that?"

"You go on *every mission*, man. Crew chiefs don' last long. You do what you want, but I'm stayin' where I am."

Jackson decided to wait and see.

9

The morning sun revealed the overgrown lot at the end of the street, vacant for the last three years, was now occupied by a large and colorful former school bus. Its chrome yellow had been covered by a riotous mishmash of rainbows and stars, a moon on one side, a sun on the other, and peace symbols scattered seemingly at random. On the rear was a green pyramid with an eye at its top, like on the dollar bill. Around the bus were folding chairs, a cable drum table and a cheap barbecue.

Maddy assumed these were temporary squatters, and as long as they kept themselves to themselves she doubted anyone would complain. The authorities equaled The Establishment, and nobody in Topanga wanted any more laws enforced than were strictly necessary. Most had moved here to be away from close scrutiny, and the canyon had a history of representing a refuge where people could get on with their lives without interference. It may have been one of the smallest of small towns, but unlike most insular communities its neighbors did not pry.

Shopping at the health food store later in the day, Maddy ran into an older couple that introduced themselves as Summer and Heath, the owners of the bus. The three chatted amiably for a while, and Maddy, on an impulse, invited them over that night for dinner. Heath asked if their being vegetarians would be a problem, and Maddy promptly bought a slab of tofu, steeling herself for the reaction from the children.

— · —

That night a small procession approached the house in the dusk—two older adults, a young woman, and a dog of indeterminate breed. Gilligan trotted up to inspect the newcomer, and after the preliminary sniffings decided to be friendly. As everyone walked out to the deck for drinks the two dogs romped together on the grass.

Heath looked about forty-five or fifty, with a graying beard that had never seen scissors. Summer was about the same age, and her hair and skin, Maddy thought a little unkindly, hadn't visited a beautician in under a decade.

"So, Heath," Bret asked, "where are you from?"

"Oregon. We usually stay in the forests. Felt like a change."

Summer added, "Went a bit stir crazy after five months of rain."

"And your daughter's name?" Bret asked.

"Freedom. But she's not our daughter. She kinda ... adopted us."

Freedom smiled. "They've been very good to me."

Robbie was fascinated with the young woman, unable to tear his eyes away. His mother had to nudge him to introduce himself, and he did so, shyly.

Sundown warily shook hands with the new girl. She was used to being the most beautiful creature in the room, and while Freedom was not as conventionally pretty, with her knowing gaze and her fringed chamois dress she radiated a casual but powerful magnetism. It seemed that nothing could faze her, and so it gave her an aura, a mystique.

Charity was pleased to have visitors, and asked a lot of questions about living in a school bus, and Oregon, and how long it took to drive down.

"They're vegetarians, Charity," Maddy told her. "They don't eat meat at all."

Charity was fascinated. "Why are you vegetarian?" she asked.

Heath explained. "We think that killing animals for food is unnecessary and elitist. Unnecessary because humans evolved as omnivores, and so we can get our nutrition from plants. Elitist because animals were here first on the planet, and so we can't tell ourselves they were put here for our menu. It's the worst kind of slavery, to be bred as food and slaughtered."

"Wow," Bret said, forcing a smile. "Heavy."

"So what *can* you eat?" Charity persisted.

"Oh, there's plenty of things. We get protein from nuts and beans. The Indians made a complete protein from combining corn, beans, and squash."

It was Robbie who first noticed the gray cubes in his Bolognese sauce. He poked one suspiciously with his fork. "What the heck's *this?*"

Maddy put on a bright smile. "It's tofu. Bean curd. Full of protein, without having to eat meat."

Robbie pouted. "But I like meat."

"But our guests don't. Don't make a fuss, Robbie. Half the world eats it."

Robbie doubted this, but didn't want to cause a scene in front of Freedom. Bret and Charity put on brave faces and pretended, for their guests' sake, that they were enjoying it. Sundown simply piled her tofu in a wall around the edge of her plate.

"So, Bret," Summer said, "What is it you do to be able to live here?"

Bret visibly inflated. This was his favorite topic: himself. "I'm in the movies. Gaffer. I'm the one who handles all the lighting. The proper name is really Chief Lighting Technician. Anything to do with lights, I'm in charge of it. I have to know all the techniques, but also know the set and the script." He leaned forward. "People don't realize how much light film needs. That's why the early film industry settled in California. Weather, sure, but more important—*light*. And there are all kinds of different lighting. Film noir, for instance, uses a look borrowed from German expressionist cinema. Stark, shadowed—what Italian painters call *chiaroscuro*.

"And light can be flattering and unflattering. It all depends what the director's going for. I'm known for flattering actresses, so I'm popular with the female leads. My crew and I work twelve, eighteen-hour days for weeks on end. It's tough. It's a question of maintaining teamwork and dealing with tempers and egos. There's a shitload of stress, and if you're not careful, a lot of accidents, too."

"What was the last film you worked on?"

"*The Sundance Kid and Butch Cassidy.* Robert Redford and Paul Newman, and a new girl—Katharine Ross. They originally wanted Steve McQueen or Marlon Brando for Redford's role. The director—Hill—hurt his back, so he spent most of the film lying down. Newman was spooked by the horses, which was a problem with a western—the goddamn creatures were everywhere. There's a great part where the two leads jump off a cliff into a river, and I heard the screenwriter ripped off the idea from *Gunga Din.* Stuntmen, of course, not the leads themselves. Insurance wouldn't allow that."

"Whereabouts was all this filmed?"

"All over the place. Zion and Grafton in Utah, Durango and Silverton in Colorado, Taos and a place called Chama in New Mexico, Monument Valley in Arizona, even a few scenes in Cuernavaca in Mexico, to stand in for Bolivia."

"So that must mean you're gone a lot."

"Yeah, but once the shoot is over there's often a lot of down time till the next. So it kinda evens out. Huh, Maddy?"

Over the years, Maddy had developed a stock answer to this question. "It's good to get rid of him for a while," she told them with a wry smile, "But it's good to get him back at the end."

"And you, Maddy?" Summer said. "You don't look like the type to just stay home and wait."

"I'm a fashion designer. I have a shop in town, but lately I've been making outfits for bands from home."

"How exciting! You must be very talented. And you get to meet famous people, too. Your lives make ours seem very drab."

"Not at all," Bret assured her, in a slightly patronizing tone. "Your life must be very ... serene."

Summer laughed. "Oh, it's serene all right. Serene and mildewed. But I have my writing, and Heath has his work."

"What work is that? Logging?"

"No, no," Heath said, "I don't believe in logging. I do a bit of well-digging, backhoe stuff."

"Is there a lot of logging up there?"

Now it was Heath's turn to laugh. "All the Northwest. Biggest employer, so you can't talk anyone out of it—I've tried. They're leaving the trees alongside the roads while they clear-cut and sell everything that's out of sight."

Charity put her hands to her cheeks in shock. "That's awful!"

Maddy hurried to head off one of her husband's tirades, this time on the indiscriminate logging of natural resources and the policies of the Bureau of Land Management, which she knew could keep him going for half an hour. "And your writing, Summer?"

"Poetry. And I teach a little. Doesn't pay much, but we don't need much."

Heath helped himself to more carrot cake. He looked as if he hadn't had a good meal in years. "When's your next movie, Bret?"

"Next week. I'm in San Francisco and Mt. Tamalpais."

The youngsters grew bored and drifted outside, leaving the adults to talk over a pipe. When they had gone, Bret asked how they had met Freedom.

"She was hitchhiking in Bend," Heath said, "and looked a little messed-up. She'd 'been in a heavy scene in the city,' she told us, and was looking for a place to chill. So—"

"'Heavy scene'?"

"I dunno, man. We didn't press her. Gave her her space, know what I mean?"

"Sure."

"Anyway, she's been hangin' with us over the winter. Healing, maybe. Expect she'll be gone soon."

Maddy watched the others fooling around with a Frisbee in the dark. The dogs were joining in. "And you two? What are your plans?"

Summer smiled. "Stay here until we're kicked off, I guess, then head north again. Don't want to go to Mexico in case they don't let us back across the border. I hear it happens."

"You can camp on the beach just across the county line into Ventura," Bret told them, "at La Jolla Canyon. They allow campfires, too."

"Might just do that."

Summer and Heath toured the house. More bowls were smoked, more music played, more stories told. Heath helped Bret repair a leaky faucet. Summer toured Maddy's workshop and accepted some clothing samples and ends of fabric.

Finally, Heath stood and belched. "Well, guess we should head back."

Summer called for Freedom and, when the girl returned with the others, explained they were leaving.

Freedom looked at Maddy. "I wonder—could I have a shower? It's been so long."

"Of course! Go ahead."

"I'll get my towel and come back."

"No, use ours—I'll get you a fresh one. Just let yourself out when you're done."

"Thanks."

— · —

Once Summer and Heath had left, the household members dispersed to their various areas—Robbie to his room, Charity and Sundown to their shared bedroom, Maddy to the master bedroom, Bret to the tower and his storyboards. He had another shoot coming up soon, and needed to plan.

Robbie tried to sleep, but the hiss of the shower and the mental image of Freedom naked in it kept him awake. After a while the shower stopped and he drifted.

When his door opened to reveal the silhouette of a towel-wrapped Freedom, he thought he must have been dreaming. A wishful-thinking kind of dream; the kind he was having a lot lately.

She walked in and sat on his bed, not caring if her towel sagged. "Hey, Robbie," she whispered. "D'you have a girlfriend?"

"Uh, no. Not right now."

"How old are you?"

"Sixteen. A-almost seventeen, really."

"Really." She smiled. "Ever had a girl?"

Robbie swallowed. "Well, yeah. Of course."

"Of course," she teased, sliding her hand under the sheets and finding him. "I think this guy could use some exercise, huh?"

Robbie found he couldn't reply.

Freedom dropped the towel and climbed in with him.

— · —

Bret shuffled down the spiral staircase to the kitchen and poured himself a glass of milk. As he turned away from the refrigerator, he came face to face with Freedom, her hair still wet. "Oh, hi. You still here?"

She smiled. "Got carried away. Sorry."

"Oh, that's OK. Glad you liked it."

Freedom walked to the dark window. "Did I see a tree house out there?"

Bret laughed. "Yeah. Funky little thing."

She clasped her hands together. "Oh, I always wanted a tree house! Could I see it?"

"What, now?"

"Were you going to bed?"

"Nah, I'm a bit of an insomniac. Maddy's used to it."

"Then let's go."

They walked out into the cool air night air and across the grass to the foot of the two trees.

"Gimme a second," he told her, "and I'll go up and light a few candles." He climbed the ladder and in a moment a buttery light filled the windows. "Come on up," he called down softly.

— · —

He was a man now.

Robbie looked in the mirror, grinned, and tugged on his hair. He couldn't wait to get out of school so he could grow it long. Outrageously long.

Maybe he should grow a mustache, though his earlier attempts at doing so had resulted in just a few wispy strands on upper lip and chin. Now he was a man it would all work better.

What was with the pink patches on his cheeks? It looked as if he'd been slapped. A dead giveaway that he was young. Maybe if he got a tan they'd disappear. He would lie out in the sun at the weekend and get bronzed.

He practiced stern gazes, turning left and right, clenching his jaw and narrowing his eyes. Robbie S, lead guitarist of … the Scorpions, the Rat-catchers, the—

"Robbie?" His mother's voice came from outside the bathroom door. "You in there? Hurry up."

As he walked out, he looked so cheerful Maddy commented on it. "You OK?"

"Yeah, sure. I'd better get to school."

This was unusual enough to be suspicious. Maddy frowned. "You sick?"

"No, no. Just got stuff to do."

Robbie even forgot to get stoned on the way.

— · —

Bret was late for breakfast, and when he did show up, Maddy sensed something different in him too. Something different from Robbie's elation.

"Busy today?" she asked.

"Huh? Oh, yeah."

"Want eggs? Toast?"

"Sure."

When Maddy slid his breakfast in front of him, she said, "Summer and Heath were nice people, huh?"

"Oh. Yeah."

"And Freedom. So pretty."

"Was she? I didn't notice."

"No, of course not."

— · —

After listening to the news on her transistor radio, and some clips of statements from presidential hopefuls, Charity took out her pen and best writing paper.

> Dear Mr. Nixon,
>
> My name is Charity Sobieski, and I am 13. I hope you will become our new president, because you said you would find a way to peace with honor. I hope you will stop the war soon because my brother is going.
>
> Yours respectfully,
>
> Charity Sobieski

And then, in case he might think her name was that of a foreigner, she added,

> American citizen.

— · —

Robbie's euphoria lasted four days. Then he became worried, and worry soon turned into desperation. He drove his motorcycle down Pacific Coast Highway, past the foot of the Santa Monica cliffs and up the ramp into Venice. He swung inland through block after block of bungalows to the ugliest commercial street in the area, Lincoln, all repair shops, used car lots and fast food joints. Then he pulled behind a lime green stucco building, looked around furtively and locked his bike.

"Well, Mr. ... *Smith*," the clinic's doctor said, after a cursory examination, "it looks like a case of plain old gonorrhea. It'll clear up with antibiotics, but we should really notify your other partners, or they'll spread it around to more people. We don't want that, do we?"

Robbie said nothing.

"Don't you want to tell your current partner? I know it's awkward, but otherwise—"

"She's gone. I don't know where."

"Ah. I see." The doctor, a young man himself, sighed. He handed Robbie a small bottle of white pills. "OK, then. Take one of these two times a day until they're gone. Take them all."

He had some other advice, about how to avoid this kind of thing in the future, but Robbie wasn't listening.

He had just seen his father in the corridor.

— · —

Maddy looked up as Bret came into the kitchen. "The bus has gone."

Bret nodded and reached into the cookie jar.

"I liked Heath and Summer," she continued. "They were sweet."

"Yeah."

"Sundown said she thought she saw Freedom hitchhiking on Sunset the other day."

"Oh yeah?"

"Bret ... are you feeling all right? You getting a cold?"

"What? N-no, I'm fine. Just ... too busy."

10

"Canned Heat's at the Corral again Saturday!" Bret announced. "Who's going?"

"I'm in," Maddy said.

"Me too," Robbie added.

Bret shook his head. "You're underage."

Robbie looked smug. "I'll get in."

"Can you get me in too?" Charity wanted to know.

"No, sorry, honey. One day, when you're older."

"Well, damn, I'll be there," Sundown said. There was nothing she liked better than a concert, and though Topanga's were small and cramped, the Corral was their own, local venue featuring local bands. As far as she was concerned, the Corral was the only good reason to live in Topanga. Funky, but still a focus of energy and raw talent.

— · —

Charity watched the others leave with mixed emotions. It was good to get rid of her siblings, but it was frustrating to be denied the performance. She played outside in the twilight until she noticed a tick in the grass and ran inside to grab her notebook.

> California is blessed to be relatively free of insects, at least compared to Canada and its blackflies, the flying cockroaches of Florida, the chiggers of Alabama, and the mosquitoes of

Maine. Its lack of humidity and standing water for breeding
has kept it free of many of the plagues of other states. But it has
the tick and the flea, two tiny vampires. The tick climbs trees
or grass to wait—some say for years, if necessary—for a warm
mammal to pass below. Then it drops, burrows in, a tiny and
hard-to-find passenger at first, but if left alone bloating to the
size of a grape. The flea prefers small mammals, but will settle
for humans if evicted from a better host. If it can't find fur to
lay its eggs in, it settles for carpets.

— · —

The Sobieskis, minus Charity and Jackson, walked the ten-minute stroll through the warm evening.

Cars were lined up all along the verges of Topanga Canyon Boulevard and down its narrow sidestreets. The Corral was packed, even an hour before the posted performance time, with far more people than a fire marshal would have allowed, were one there to see it.

The dance floor had a poorly painted naked couple hung over it, named *Pisces Dancing*, but tonight it was far too crowded for anyone to actually dance. Those inclined to move would have to merely sway in place.

It was hot too, despite the ceiling fans.

Of all the bands that played here—Spirit, Little Feat, Taj Mahal—Canned Heat were considered the locals' favorite. This was a year after their first, eponymous, album, and in January they had released *Boogie with Canned Heat,* which everyone Bret and Maddy knew had bought to show support for their own.

When its members finally walked onstage the crowd went berserk. Bob Hite, known as "The Bear" because he weighed over 300 lbs, grabbed the microphone and adjusted its stand's height. You could hear the stage creak. Alan "Blind Owl" Wilson stumbled over to his Les Paul guitar, arranging his harmonicas in his different pockets, one for each key. Larry Taylor strapped on his bass and stooped to set the controls on his amp, and their newish drummer "Fito" de la Parra settled himself behind his kit and adjusted the angle of his cymbals. Henry Vestine hooked up his Stratocaster and parked his Les Paul on a stand, on the side of the stage away from Taylor—it was said they didn't get along.

After a brief "Hello again, Topanga!" from Hite, they pitched into their signature "Going Up The Country," with its catchy falsetto, perky flute, and vaguely back-to-the-land lyrics. The crowd roared its approval.

Robbie had managed to get in. Though short and baby-faced, and as yet unable to grow sideburns, he pulled tufts of hair in front of his ears to approximate them. This fooled no one, but the bouncer knew him, if only because of his beautiful sister, and turned a blind eye.

Sundown had gone alone, wanting to stay unencumbered in case she met anyone interesting. She wore a peach halter top, faded cutoffs with a braided leather belt, and about a dozen Indian bracelets that jangled. Her blonde hair was almost waist length and an embroidered ribbon headband kept it out of eyes made up like a Mary Quant ad she'd seen. Her lipstick was so pale it looked as if her lips had disappeared.

The band played Elmore James and Robert Johnson's "Dust My Broom," a standard for all blues bands because of its locomotive rhythm and soaring slide solo that, here, bounced off the Corral's wooden walls.

Maddy wore a caftan, Bret a Grateful Dead T-shirt and Levi's he had painstakingly shrunk to his body in the bath. They found a spot near the back, since their older ears were more sensitive to the volume. The short distance from the stage did little to diminish the decibels, but the mass of people between them and the speakers absorbed at least some of the sound. Bret, claimed a pitcher of beer early. He knew the bar would immediately be surrounded by patrons ten deep and stay that way.

"I've been a big Canned Heat fan long before they became popular," Bret told the bartender. "Their first drummer, Frank Cook, was great, but he left after their Denver bust."

The bartender looked at him blankly, and then turned to the next customer.

The band played B.B. King's "Sweet Sixteen," a slow, standard 12-bar with plenty of room for arabesques high up the neck of the lead guitar.

Joints were handed around to friend and stranger alike, and a smoky camaraderie soon pervaded the place. Bikers mixed with hippies, squares with freaks, and even off-duty soldiers like Jackson would probably have been accepted, though if any were there they were wisely out of uniform.

"They got their name," Bret told another stranger, "from an old blues song by Tommy Johnson, about an alcoholic who drank Sterno." The man drifted away.

The band launched into a syncopated "Wish You Would," with plenty of cowbell and a hypnotic repetition of the main motif.

— · —

Robbie caught the eye of a girl he thought was around his age, and edged closer through the crowd. "Hey," he said, when he had made it to her side. "Like Canned Heat?"

She smiled. "Love 'em. You?"

"Yeah. I live just round the corner, so they're my local band."

"That must be so groovy, living in Topanga. I'm down in L.A."

"It's so cool here—no one cares if you smoke."

"Yeah—I thought I smelled pot."

"You ever get high?"

"Sure."

"I have some if you want a toke at the break."

She nodded. "I'm Polly."

"Robbie."

The band played "Bullfrog Blues," with its driving drumbeat and whining guitar, for about eight minutes.

— · —

Sundown caught the eye of a tall, handsome man who looked in his early twenties. At first glance he seemed to be what her father disparagingly referred to as a "weekend hippie"—straight-dressed but with longish hair and sideburns. When he sidled over, she gave him the cool treatment, but he persisted.

"I'm Jimmy," he said. "You from the Valley?"

"Sundown. No, just round the corner."

"A canyon girl, huh? Must be nice."

She shrugged.

"Didn't I see you on American Bandstand?"

Sundown smiled. "No."

"But you are a dancer, right?"

"No. But I'm thinking about being a model."

"I know an agent. He has an office on Sunset. I can give you his name if you like. He handles top models."

Sundown's mask of indifference faltered. "Sure."

"Hey—want to get high?"

She feigned indifference. "Maybe."

After getting their hands stamped with green peace symbols at the door, Robbie and Polly walked out to the parking lot. The eastern sky glowed a dull orange with the lights from Los Angeles, over the hills, and the smell of burning pot floated on the night air.

Robbie lit up and handed the joint to Polly, cupping it in his hands in case a police cruiser passed. "You here with someone?" he asked.

"My big brother," she said, giving a delicate cough. "Good grass."

"Yeah. Good band too, huh?"

"Yeah." Robbie noticed Sundown talking to a man nearby.

"You know her?" Polly asked.

"My big sister."

"Wow. She's gorgeous. Hey—wouldn't it be funny if my big brother and your big sister got together?"

"Yeah, pretty weird."

"So what school d'you go to?" she asked.

"Pali High."

"Really? That's a long way to go."

"No high school in Topanga. Not big enough. What about you?"

"Fairfax High."

"The one off Melrose?"

"Yeah."

"That's a hip place. Phil Spector went there."

She shrugged. "It's OK. It's school, y'know?"

"Yeah."

The lights blinked and they went back in.

— · —

The second set began with "Evil Woman," with its sneering guitar tone, followed by "I'd Rather Be The Devil," a shuffle heavy on brushes and harmonica.

Like the Rolling Stones, Canned Heat had started with Chicago blues and bent it into their own version of rock 'n' roll. But unlike the Stones' carefully cultivated aura of inner-city menace, Canned Heat's output had a jaunty irreverence, one that, in Southern California at least, seemed to encapsulate the attitude of the times.

Tonight was one of those rare performances of any band where both audience and musicians were fused with a kind of mutual magic. Everyone felt it, except for those too wasted on downers or booze to feel anything at all. The atmosphere made you feel as if the evening would never end; that you had reached a state outside of normal, boring life where everyone was related in a kind of glorious, high, family. The Corral was a rough venue, unsophisticated and seedy, but that night it was transformed for a while into a kind of rock shrine.

The band played "When Things Go Wrong," another 12-bar slowed to the point of lethargy, a second and a half per beat, leaving room for intentionally sloppy drumming. Couples shuffled together close and slow.

— · —

But it had to end. Canned Heat had saved "On The Road Again" for their finale. Wilson played a long-necked tamburato, giving the song a spacy drone, joined after a few bars by eerie harmonics picked from the guitar. This song featured Wilson, not Hite, as the singer, with a haunting falsetto vocal. It turned it into a long drawn-out boogie of a jam, but after half an hour, Wilson could blow no more blues harp, Parra threw down his sticks and Wilson and Vestine unplugged and unstrapped their guitars and gratefully accepted a beer.

Once it was clear there would be no encore, people drifted out into the sudden ear-ringing vacuum of the night. Robbie thought he was going home with the girl he had been talking to—or shouting at—all night, but she climbed into her brother's Jeep and waved a sad goodbye. Maddy and Bret walked down the boulevard to the fork and around to their street, with a surly Robbie following at a discreet distance.

A passing raccoon hissed at them. An owl hooted somewhere. The hills smelled of hot sage.

"That was righteous," Maddy said, as their house came into view.

— · —

Sundown and her new friend Jimmy walked away from the Corral with their arms around each other.

"You like clubs?" Jimmy asked.

"I prefer the Hollywood kind," she said, partly because she thought it made her sound more in-crowd. She had only ever been to one.

"Let's go, then."

They drove his Dodge Dart up Topanga Canyon Boulevard to Mulholland and turned right into town. To their left, below, twinkled the grid of the San Fernando Valley. To their right stretched the dark expanse of the Santa Monica Mountains.

At this time of night it took no time at all to get to Hollywood and Sunset Boulevard, which was still very much awake. Huge billboards had begun to hawk the latest albums, *In-A-Gadda-Da-Vida* by Iron Butterfly, *Feliciano!*, and Simon and Garfunkel's *Bookends*, along with nights in Vegas for $13.95. Cars—some of them elaborately tricked out—jammed the Strip, cruising slowly up and down, and every tenth one was a police black-and-white. Crowds lined up outside It's Boss, Coconut Teaszer, the Hullabaloo Club, the Red Velvet, Ooh Poo Pah Doo's, Gazzarri's, The Trip, Filthy McNasty's, the Whisky A Go-Go, and London Fog.

"They all seem full," Sundown said, disappointed.

"I know someone at the Whisky," he said, "Let's give it a try."

He found parking on a side street and they walked, laughing, down to the Strip and along to the club. The bouncer, once he recognized Jimmy, waved them through and into a wall of sound and light and seething dancers.

"I saw the Doors here last year," he told her, raising his voice. "It was wild. Scary, actually."

Strobing lights and colored oil slides projected over the stage. Illinois Speed Press was playing, one of the "druggy" bands, as opposed to the love and peace kind out of San Francisco. The floor was filled with gyrating couples doing all kinds of bizarre dance moves. Some were dressed fairly straight, with some men even wearing short-sleeved white shirts and ties. Some were dressed in the current hippie look—men in striped bell bottoms with wide belts, flowered shirts with long collars, women in mini skirts or colored flares, muslin tops, layered necklaces. Others, she presumed the freaks she'd heard about, dressed outrageously in all kinds of fantastic garb. One woman had a stovepipe hat with feather—God knew how she kept it on—and one man wore a white tuxedo jacket with painted stars.

In a raised cage next to the stage were the go-go dancers, writhing girls in fringed skirts so short as to be almost nonexistent, bustiers to match, and low white high-heeled boots.

The atmosphere was thrilling, electric, bruising, and just a little gauche. Sundown was fascinated. She wanted a drink to mellow her out, and after yelling this at Jimmy he disappeared for a while and returned with two rum and cokes.

The band played long songs to work in solos for each player. The drummer's devolved into a lot of crashing about, losing the rhythm entirely, and so the audience stopped dancing and just gathered in front of the stage staring at his flailing arms until the song resumed.

The pulse of the place began to take over. Someone handed Sundown a joint, and she took a hit and passed it on. She became entranced by the lights reflected in the chrome stands of the drum kit, the way the lead singer's face was half-orange, half-blue from the side spots, the trails the drumsticks left in the air behind them. The bass notes moved through her feet and up her spine, while the high notes of the lead guitar tried to pry the top off her head. She forgot about Jimmy for minutes at a time; once in a while he would appear briefly in her vision and say something. At some point he placed a beer in her hand, and the cold glass felt good.

She had no idea what time it must be now—two? Three?

Jimmy opened his hand to show a small white tablet. "Pill?"

Sundown grinned. "Already took one."

Jimmy was puzzled for a moment, and then, understanding, he grinned too.

They kissed, and Sundown felt a surge of passion for him. Perhaps they should leave and go somewhere.

A commotion began in one corner of the dance floor, and dancers staggered in her direction. One woman fell over and had to be helped to her feet. Behind them glinted the cap badges of the Los Angeles Police Department.

— · —

"Dad?"

"Where the hell have you been?" Bret exploded into the phone. "We've been worried sick!"

Sundown tried to keep the tears in check. "I was at a club on Sunset. It got busted. The stupid pigs threw us all in jail for the night. This is the first chance I've had to call."

"Jesus. Did they charge you with anything?"

"No, but they only just let us out."

"Who were you with? Is he bringing you home?"

"I don't know what happened to Jimmy. They split up the men and women. Maybe he's still there. Can you come and get me?"

"Where are you?"

"Googie's."

Bret snorted. "Be there in forty-five."

— · —

The Camaro sped through the empty Sunday morning streets of Hollywood. At first, neither Sundown nor her father spoke.

Bret gripped the steering wheel tightly. After several miles, he said, "Look, you're eighteen—"

"Dad, I wasn't doing anything—"

"You oughtta know better than—"

"It was just the Whisky. Everyone goes there."

"The pigs love to bust places like that."

"How was I supposed to know?"

Bret took the onramp onto the freeway and floored the gas pedal. "Sundown, you have to be careful who you hang out with, where you go."

"I am, dad. I—"

"You're a good-looking chick, Sundown. You need to—"

"I'm not a kid any more."

Bret said nothing, seething. It was on the tip of his tongue to say you are to me, but he bit back the words. "So this guy you went with..." he finally said.

"Jimmy."

"Where did you meet him?"

"At the Corral concert last night." It seemed like a century ago.

"What does he do?"

"He goes to USC. Majors in business."

It could be worse, Bret told himself. She could be dating a drummer.

"Dad?" Sundown asked, "Can you get me into the movies? I want to be an actress. Can you get me ... what d'you call 'em ... tryouts? Auditions?"

Bret shook his head. "You don't want to get into movies. It's a lousy business for girls. I don't know anyone in casting, anyway. That's a whole other area. Takes place long before I'm involved."

"Well ... how do I get a modeling agent, then?"

Her father stiffened. "Sundown, you're not getting an agent. They're scumbags, all of 'em. Give it up."

Sundown wasn't about to. "Dad—I'm eighteen."

He turned to her, red-faced. "If you want to get into modeling, I can't stop you. But don't say I didn't warn you."

— · —

Although he had not managed to go home with the girl he had met at the Corral concert, Robbie had her number.

He waited until no one was around, picked up the kitchen phone, hesitated. There was always that chance, on the first call, that Polly would say "who?," but to his relief when she answered she remembered him. When he suggested getting together, she told him she was heading downtown to an antiwar demonstration in Pershing Square and asked if he wanted to meet her there. She lived in the Fairfax district, a lot closer than he, and her brother was taking her, as he had to the Corral concert.

For Polly, it would be a fifteen-minute jaunt. For Robbie, on the Honda, it was an expedition. He couldn't take that small a bike on the freeway, and so had to travel the whole way on surface streets, over an hour's ride.

As he headed downtown Robbie wondered if every American city looked like this: pro- and anti-war graffiti, flags flying from porches, dull green National Guard trucks seemingly everywhere, floridly illegible concert posters on fences and telephone poles. It seemed almost half the cars he followed sported AMERICA—LOVE IT OR LEAVE IT bumper stickers.

Here was another STOP sign with WAR added in spray paint. Here was another VW bug decorated with stick-on flowers. Here was another monstrous Detroit gas-guzzler driven inexpertly by a bluehair.

To those he passed he occupied a position between the rival factions—too young to be a threat to anyone, hair neither long nor short enough to be a statement one way or another. Soon he would be out of school and regarded as one of the freaks the straights detested, but until then he slipped between the cracks.

He ought to move up to Haight-Ashbury. Or Greenwich Village. Coconut Grove was supposed to be far out—residents applauded the sunset from the beach each night. Or Hawaii. Hawaii represented a hippie's idea of paradise—no need for clothes or money. Yes, Hawaii.

Eventually he made it to the square, filled with a vocal mob of long-haired men and women. A large banner read NO MORE WAR, and others proclaimed LOVE & PEACE, and WE ARE ALL ONE FAMILY. A squad car waited warily at one corner.

One young man in particular was holding forth about U.S. imperialist forces and the military-industrial complex. *"Don't let them sell you on this war!"* he yelled into a bullhorn, and the sound bounced off the older, tall buildings. *"These aren't Nazis we're fighting this time! They're farmers!"*

Robbie stood as close to Polly as he could, while keeping one eye on the squad car. So far the police were choosing not to interfere.

"We've been in Vietnam for four years. How much longer? More boys get drafted every week. Who's next—you? Your neighbor? Your brother? Before long it'll be every man gone. And what for?"

Robbie and Polly smiled at each other, indignant at the war but exhilarated by the energy of the participants and the heart-pounding feeling that violence could break out at any moment.

"Does anyone know what we're doing in Vietnam? Where it is, even? Can anyone tell me why the United States thinks it can decide how other countries are run?"

A wild-haired young man pushed his way forward, waving something in his hand. *"I've just been drafted!"* he announced, *"and here's what I think of my draft card!"* He lit the corner of the document and threw it into the air.

This triggered several others to do the same. A small bonfire of draft cards began.

Polly looked at Robbie expectantly. She didn't know he was too young to have been selected for service. He fumbled in his wallet, pulled out his school bus pass, and set it alight from the corner of another burning card. Her eyes sparkled with admiration.

He grinned. But then he saw the heat moving in, and recalled that burning a draft card was a felony, or misdemeanor, or something illegal. "Come on," he said, "time to go."

They ran off down Olive and into a store. Inside, they pretended to shop, giggling, for fifteen minutes, until they judged it safe to leave. Then he bought her an Orange Julius and they strolled back, feigning nonchalance.

"Need a ride home?" Robbie asked, and then added a little inaccurately, "I pass through Fairfax on the way back to Topanga."

"Sure."

He leaned close to her ear. "Anyone home?"

She smiled conspiratorially. "Not right now."

"Let's get the bike."

They reached the side street where he'd parked the Honda. The square was being cleared by police, with some of the card-burners being handcuffed and manhandled into a black bus. But his motorcycle was still there.

They rode off. It was just like a Honda ad, with the girl laughing on the back seat. Of course it was slower now, but he didn't care. He could feel her warm thighs next to him, her arms around his waist. Now he knew what the phrase "a stirring in his loins" meant.

"Tell me how to get there," he said, his voice husky.

— · —

In twenty minutes they passed the huge art deco Pan Pacific Auditorium, and Polly directed him onto her street. In half a block they pulled into the driveway of her parents' two-story house.

"My folks won't be home till this evening," she told him. "But we have to be careful."

Robbie was so excited he could hardly see straight. They went up to her all-pink bedroom and fell on each other.

"That was so brave of you," she murmured, and gave him a clumsy French kiss.

Robbie was so aroused he felt stoned, even though for once he was straight. He and Polly fumbled with each other's clothing and flung it onto the floor, writhing around naked on the pink coverlet. Robbie felt like a compass needle pointing to magnetic north, and was about to climb on top of Polly when a honk came from the driveway outside.

Polly jumped out from under him and immediately began dressing in her just-castoff clothes.

"What?" Robbie asked, confused, "What's going on?"

"My brother! He's back!"

[119]

"Well ... he'll understand."

"Like hell he will! Get dressed! Quick!"

Robbie crammed himself painfully back into his jeans, straightened his shirt, and picked up one of her album covers, pretending to read its liner notes. The type swam, meaningless, before his eyes.

Polly straightened the bed and then sat on it, grabbing a hairbrush from the nightstand and running it through her hair.

The door burst open and her huge brother stood in the doorway, looking from one to the other suspiciously. "What's going on?" he demanded.

Polly waved the brush vaguely. "Oh, Robbie ran me home and we were discussing Bob Dylan."

Her brother looked at the album Robbie was holding. "But that's Leonard Cohen."

"They have similarities," Robbie said. "Riffs," he added, sounding lame even to his own ears.

Polly's brother frowned menacingly. "Riffs, huh? Well, you two, I think riffing time is over. Your friend can go home now, Polly." He looked back at Robbie. "Thanks for giving her a ride."

"N-no problem."

All the way back Robbie cursed big brothers and their lousy timing. Was it true you could die from blue balls? He guessed he would find out.

Halfway up the canyon one of the local bikers pulled alongside on his Harley, throttled back and looked over at Robbie with a grin. "Wanna race?"

— · —

Charity was on a mission to gather wildflowers, and the best, in her opinion, were Matilija poppies. But they were only found in a few places in the canyon, and all were private property. Her father had warned her never to trespass on private land, since many of the landowners in Topanga were trigger-happy cowboys intent on protecting their privacy, and she was likely to have the dogs set on her or get herself shot.

But along Entrada was Trippet Ranch, and its hundreds of acres were in the process of being deeded over to California to become Topanga State Park—she had read about it in the *Times*. And in certain places on Trippet Ranch at this time of year there were Matilija poppies by the hundred. Who would stop a little girl taking her dog for a walk?

Gilligan followed her trustingly—though a little grumpily, since he wasn't used to walking this far—through the fence and across the meadow, sniffing the undergrowth's unfamiliar smells.

She kept an eye out for rangers, but midweek there seemed to be no one around. Through a grove of stumpy oaks they strolled, and out the other side. There, in a narrow gully in the hillside ahead, she saw them—crepey white petals surrounding a bright yellow pompom, on stalks five to seven feet tall, looking like an illustration from a Dr. Seuss book. She picked an armful. What a pity they wouldn't last long in a vase. Wild-flowers never did.

— · —

Tonight was one of the rare evenings when the entire family sat around the TV, like some ideal family in a magazine ad. Not since *Mission Impossible* four years earlier had they all been glued to the screen like this, though *Laugh-In* usually attracted whoever happened to be home on Monday nights.

Charity walked in expecting to be thanked for providing such spectacular wildflowers, and in such quantity. But her reception was a hushed and red-eyed silence.

"What?" she asked. "What happened?"

"Kennedy," her father said. "He's been shot."

Charity was confused. "I remember … kinda. Why is everyone still so upset?"

"His brother," Maddy explained. "Robert."

"He was our only good choice for president," Bret muttered.

"I was going to go down there!" Sundown said.

Charity turned to her sister. "Where?"

"The Ambassador Hotel. Jimmy had tickets, but he had to study."

Bret stood in frustration, unable to sit still. "They're killing off all the Kennedys. It's some crazy right-wing conspiracy. Who's next?"

Robbie pointed at the TV. "They say he's still alive."

"Not for long—you'll see."

— · —

The images from the TV flashed in front of Charity, chasing away all hopes of sleep. These killings didn't fit with the picture of her country she was being taught at school. She turned on her bedside lamp and slid her locked journal out of the nightstand.

> If America is so civilized, how come Americans shoot their leaders? This is the kind of thing that happens in Africa or South America, surely, but not here.

She walked out for a glass of water. The poppies had already wilted.

11

Lance Bowman, theatrical agent, nodded eagerly. "Sure, I can add you to our modeling books. Blonde chicks are always popular. You a cheerleader?"

"No."

"If you dress as one I can get you Dodgers and Lakers gigs at conventions and stuff. I just need your details. Name?"

"Sundown Sobieski."

"Wow. What's that—Russian?"

"Polish."

"Huh. Want to change it? Sundown Seven, Sundown Skybeach..."

"No."

He slid her an index card. "Here—fill out your height, weight, sizes." When she was done, he placed it into a file. "All right. You'll need head shots." He handed her a business card. "This guy's good, and reasonable. Five minutes east on Sunset. Can you dance?"

"Yeah."

"Y'know, I can get you work as a dancer in Tokyo. They love blonde chicks over there..." he leaned around his desk and looked her up and down, "'specially with long legs like yours."

"Uh ... no, thanks."

He shrugged. "Please yourself. Willing to do topless stuff?"

"No."

"Pays well. Nothing smutty, you understand. OK—I'll get back to you."

— · —

Sundown thought she might as well get the photographs taken right away, since she was in town. It belatedly occurred to her that she should really have brought a change of clothing, but they were just headshots, after all.

The photographer's place turned out to be small, the interior just a large room with a Hasselblad on a tripod in front of a roll of blotchy gray velvet, and reeking of developer. Peter, the photographer, was a middle-aged man with longish hair and wearing a caftan, looking as if he were trying a little too hard to be hip.

"Lance sent you, huh? Yeah, he sends a coupla chicks up here a week. Must be busy. So—how many d'you want?"

Sundown wasn't sure. "Hundred, I guess, for now."

"Sure." He looked her up and down. "That all you got? Hmm. We'll take a few wearing that, then," he waved to a fitting room in the back. "See what you can find and we'll try something different."

He fiddled with the lights and aperture, and then ran off a dozen similar poses.

While Sundown was trying on the slightly sour-smelling tops in the fitting room, Peter poked his head around the door. Sundown clutched a blouse to her chest. "Find anything?" He leered. "Why don't we try a few topless? Never know what kind—"

"No thanks."

— · —

Lance's first gig for Sundown was at an address in downtown L.A., so she consulted her Thomas Bros. map book, jumped in her car and drove down Highway One until it angled inland as the 10 freeway. In the distance, downtown's handful of tall buildings rose out of a brown puddle of smog. The Corvair had a damaged frame from a previous accident, which is why she had gotten it cheap, and it shimmied at any speed over fifty, and so to the annoyance of the drivers behind her she kept her speed down.

Once downtown, she turned on West Pico to a brick building marked

1112, and parked. The street was dotted with homeless and a woman with a trash-piled baby carriage who was yelling something unintelligible, but inside the place seemed well kept-up, and she took the elevator to the fourth floor.

The doors opened onto a wide expanse of studio, with various coves built for simultaneous shoots. Tripods and lights filled the place, and assistants scurried back and forth with clothing, food, and equipment.

"You Sundown?" a woman asked, and gestured her over to a far corner, where two women and a man were posing under lights wearing colorful sweaters. A box fan was attempting to cool them off.

"This is for J.C. Penney's winter line. Here—" she picked a stack of clothing from a portable rack. "Get into these. Dressing room's over there."

Sundown posed over fake snow holding skis, wearing knitted caps, boldly striped sweaters, high boots. She soon got the knack of posing the way the photographer wanted. It was a little like dance choreography, but with no follow-through, just freezes. And so much smiling her face muscles began to ache.

This was it. She was a model. No more school, and soon, no more Topanga.

All too quickly it was over. She had to sign a release, put her street clothes back on, and that was it. Relieved to get out of the hot clothing, Sundown was about to leave when an assistant called her to the phone. It was her agent, Lance.

"Can you do another gig?"

"When?"

"Right now. South Pasadena."

This is it, she thought. My fame is already spreading. "Uh, yeah. Sure. What's the address?"

— · —

The location this time was a scruffy industrial park populated by cabinetry and car body shops. A metal shutter door had been rolled up to reveal several chopped and tricked out motorcycles surrounded by cheap lights. Other young women stood around in skimpy outfits, smoking, while men arranged Rolleis on tripods. This was not nearly as sophisticated an operation as the previous studio.

A young man with a wispy goatee leered at her and handed her a bikini on a hanger. "You're Sundown? You can dress in the restroom over there."

In the toilet, which was about as clean as she would have expected in a motorcycle chop shop run by men, she squeezed herself into the bikini. Then she opened the door and leaned out. "Didn't the agency give you my sizes? This top is a size too small—maybe two."

Wispy beard grinned. "That's the idea. Now we need you to bend over the Triumph."

Sundown regarded him, and the motorcycle he indicated, with distaste.

"Hey," he added, "put on these big sunglasses."

"But no one will be able to see my eyes."

"It ain't your eyes they'll be looking at, babe."

"What's this for?"

"*Biker* mag. We do the covers. Now hurry up, we've got more to do before we lose the light."

Sundown considered leaving, but she was here and might as well get on with it like a pro. She leaned over the machine in as many positions as she could think of while the shutters clicked away, until bearded guy waved her off.

"Great. Thanks," he said. "I'll tell the agency you were fantastic."

— · —

On the way home Sundown berated herself. But by halfway, she had rationalized that these kinds of gigs were what modeling consisted of. Not every assignment was for *Vogue* or *Elle*. And it was for a magazine cover. Perhaps someone would see her and book her for a better magazine. Even Veruschka and Twiggy and Jean Shrimpton had to start somewhere, though somehow she doubted it had been *Biker*.

— · —

The Tongva tribe named the canyon that formed the western border of their territory "Topanga," which is thought to mean, "place above." In some spots you can still see their mortars carved into outcroppings. The rock hereabouts is mostly sandstone, and skulls found in the area have teeth ground down to stubs, which seems to indicate everyone was getting a little grit with their meals.

The first Europeans moved in in 1839. In the early 1900s, Lower Topanga was a Japanese fishing village. Perhaps the Arundo reeds reminded them of the bamboo of home. William Randolph Hearst then owned the area for a time, and turned it into a weekend getaway spot with beach shacks for his guests. Famous residents of Lower Topanga have included Humphrey Bogart, Bertolt Brecht, Carole Lombard, Peter Lorre, Ida Lupino, Shirley Temple, and original screen Tarzan Johnny Weissmuller.

By the 1920s, the upper canyon had become a weekend getaway for the new Hollywood stars, who built cottages there to get away from fans and photographers. In the 1950s, black-listed actor Will Geer sold his Santa Monica home and moved his family to a small plot in the canyon. Geer's friend Woody Guthrie had a small shack on the property.

— · —

Maddy handed the phone to Sundown. "It's for you."

Sundown took the receiver. "Hello?"

"Lance. Hey, babe—your first two clients were really happy with you. I have your paycheck. I could mail it, but why don't we have a drink to celebrate, talk about upcoming assignments?"

Sundown hesitated. But she was a model; she had to play the model game. "OK. When?"

"You free tomorrow night? Meet me at the office at six."

— · —

Sundown looked around in fascination at the Brown Derby's signed headshots. She was part of Hollywood now, like all those other famous people, complete with—she glanced across the table at Lance—oily agent. Her face could be up there one day, with a scrawled "Love, Sundown," across the bottom. She ought to practice her signature.

"So here's your check," Lance said, sliding over an envelope. "Good job."

Trying to be blasé, Sundown placed it into her purse without opening it and staring at the amount, though she was tempted. "Anything else going on?"

"Yeah, yeah. I'm working on lots of stuff. Any day now."

She took a sip of her martini and leaned forward. "What kinds of stuff?"

"Oh, y'know. Commercials, training films, magazines. It's a busy time, and there's a lot going on in the City of Angels." He gestured the waitress for more drinks, and lit a cigarette. "You have a classic look, y'know? In the past, stars would get discovered at Schwab's, but that was the old days. Now, it's through people like me—people with connections." He waved the cigarette in airy emphasis. "It's all connections. And I have other irons in the fire…"

"Like what?"

Lance leaned forward and lowered his voice. "Don't tell anyone, but I'm *trademarking* the *smiley face*. That way, everyone has to pay me every time they use it."

Sundown blinked. She hadn't realized such a thing was possible. "Oh."

He leaned back, smiling smugly. "Yeah."

"Lance Bowman, telephone please. Lance Bowman."

"See what I mean?" He smiled apologetically and stood to take the call.

While he was gone, Sundown looked around the restaurant to see if anyone famous was there. Was that Jack Benny? And surely that was Sandra Dee over in the corner, entertaining a gaggle of admirers.

Lance returned, lit another cigarette and attempted smoke rings.

"Anything important?" she asked.

He grinned. "Nah. I have the restaurant page me every now and then. Sounds good, and gets my name around. It's all part of the game."

Sundown looked at him through a filmy haze of intoxication. She'd had two drinks before her surf and turf arrived, and was feeling pleasantly blurred. She wasn't really into booze, but it had its moments. Like tonight.

— · —

After dessert, Lance paid the bill and smiled at Sundown. "Hey, babe," he said, "I know you live in Topanga, but I bet you haven't seen the Hollywood Hills properly. The view from my place is far out."

What the hell, she thought. Tonight was a night for new experiences.

"You can leave your car at the office," Lance said.

A warning bell went off at the back of her fuzzy mind. "No, I'll follow you up."

As Sundown drove behind Lance's little Sunbeam Tiger around the narrow streets above Sunset, she tried to memorize the route, but it was all but impossible in the dark.

Eventually he pulled into a driveway and waved her to park next to him. The single-story house was unprepossessing from the street, but when they walked inside she was confronted by a glass wall with a vertiginous view of Los Angeles, spread below like an electric ocean.

"Wow," she said.

"I'll make drinks." He turned on the stereo, and a Frank Sinatra album started to play.

This was his generation's make-out music, she understood. She half began to decline, but her willpower seemed to be waning. He made the drinks strong, too.

"Yeah," he continued, slurring his words slightly, "This is the age of the model. Some of them—*supermodels*—can make big bucks. You've seen the magazines—they all want a pretty face on the cover. Why? Because it sells. Same with billboards, calendars. No end o' work out there. If you have contacts."

He slid beside her on the wide couch, unnecessarily close. "Of all my girls," he said, slopping his martini over the edge of its glass, "you're by far the prettiest." He leaned over to kiss her, but she leaned away and he lost his balance for a moment.

"No, Lance, I have a boyfriend..."

He was undeterred. "So? It's the business. We all just have fun."

Yeah, she thought, the men have fun. The women... "I should be going."

"What? You just got here, babe. You hafta see the view from the bedroom."

Sundown stood. "No, I don't think so, Lance. I've got some stuff to do in the morning."

Lance seemed to realize he was being turned down, and tried to save face. "Well, it is a weeknight, and I've got a busy day tomorrow. Some other night, huh?"

— · —

Driving back down soon took on the quality of a nightmare. The Corvair's steering wasn't great to begin with, all the roads looked the same, there were no streetlights, and she was seriously tipsy. But she figured if she kept heading downhill she should eventually get to a street she recognized.

After what seemed like ages she appeared at an unfamiliar section of Sunset. Unwilling to tackle the Hollywood freeway, she just continued west, through the residential areas and down toward the ocean. She wound down all the windows and called into the night, "Sundown on Sunset!"

— · —

Sundown was never sure, but her next modeling assignment might have been by way of revenge on Lance's part. She was sent over to a scruffy address in Chinatown, which apparently specialized in the cheesier of cheesecake photos. She was given a baby doll nightie and told to take off her bra, and was supposed to pose on a bed clutching a stuffed teddy bear and looking sultry.

"I was hoping your nipples would stand out more," the photographer complained. "Can I bring over an ice cube?"

Sundown glared at him. "Don't you have retouchers?"

"Retouchers expensive. Ice cube cheap."

"Go to hell."

12

Sundown looked at Jimmy as they sprawled across his Venice apartment's bed. Then her eyes refocused beyond him on one of his posters, which showed a peace sign woven out of flowers and ribbons, and she jumped up, and pointed to it. "We should make a big peace sign and put it up somewhere for everyone to see!"

"Well, I—"

"It would be an antiwar statement, see! It would get in the papers!"

Jimmy looked doubtful. "Where would we put it?"

Sundown scrambled to put on her clothes, thinking. "I know—there are two big water tanks above Topanga. You can see 'em for miles. We could just climb up."

"'Just climb up,' huh? If it's big enough to see from a long way away, it won't be that easy." He held his hands out sideways. "This is six feet. It would need to be at least double that."

"Sure. Twelve feet or so." Sundown stared out of the window at the palm trees. "It would be round, so if we built it light enough, we could roll it up the last part of the hill. Then one of us would hoist it up the side."

Jimmy could see she was selling herself on this whole idea. He could also see she would get someone else to do it if he declined. "If we did this ... *if* ... it couldn't be wood. Metal, but not steel—too heavy. Aluminum— it would have to be aluminum. I know an aluminum welder who works on the oil rigs off Long Beach. I bet he'd do it if we bought the materials."

Sundown nodded. "We'll tell the papers so they can take photos and run stories. Hey—the Strawberry Festival is coming up. Tons of people'll be there. They'll all look up and see it! Then maybe the war will be over by the time my brother Jackson is sent over there."

"Is this about Jackson, then?"

"It's about all the killing! The assassinations, the war! It's about ending violence!"

Jimmy held up his hands. "All right, all right."

— · —

Snakes slither through the grass on the hotter days. The striped racer, dark gray with white line along each side; the gopher snake, like tan basket weave; the coast mountain king snake with its striking coral, black and white rings; and the western diamondback rattlesnake.

Local lore has it that a rattler's years can be counted by its rattles, but it's a myth—rattlesnakes grow a new rattle each time they shed their skin, and they shed more often when young than when older. Juvenile rattlers are thought to be the most dangerous because they deliver all their venom at once, whereas adults dole it out in smaller quantities.

The venom dissolves muscle, which is how the snakes digest rodents, and so an untreated bite will often leave a crater in an arm or leg. A rattler can sometimes be found lying across a path, looking like one of those beaded Indian belts, dropped on a hike.

— · —

The finished peace sign was fourteen feet in diameter. Jimmy's friend had built a stand, too, to keep it upright. Though large and unwieldy, it weighed surprisingly little.

Sundown was excited. "Put it on the top of my car—I brought a blanket—and we'll go up first thing in the morning, before it gets light."

Jimmy shook his head. "We can't possibly strap it to your car roof—it'll stick out too far and the pigs'll pull us over. We need a pickup. Does your dad or your big brother have one?"

"No."

Jimmy was starting to regret having agreed to this. "All right, I think I know where I can borrow one."

At two on Saturday morning they left Venice and drove the borrowed pickup, with the construction tied down, up the coast and into the canyon. Once they reached Topanga Center they wound up a steep side road into the silent hills until they reached the peak, its two massive cylinders black against the purple-gray sky. Jimmy pulled the truck back down the hill slightly, away from the fence, and yanked on the handbrake.

"We'll have to climb the fence somehow," Jimmy said.

Sundown nodded, a determined look on her face. "Push the sign over first."

Once this was done, they clambered up the chainlink and rolled the sign toward one of the shapes. Each had a metal ladder up the side for servicing, and Jimmy climbed one with a rope attached to the sign. From the top he hoisted the construction up the side of the water tank, then helped Sundown up beside him. They stood on top, viewing the sleeping town below. Only a few lights showed, along with the blinking red beacons of the radio masts on the nearby hills.

Their intent was to have had it done by dawn, but the eastern sky was already lightening.

"Damn," Jimmy grunted, "this is taking longer than I thought."

They wrestled the sign upright on its frame, and then Jimmy insisted on wiring it upright so the wind couldn't blow it over.

All this took even more time, and the sun had crested the horizon. To their horror, the unmistakable sound of motorcycles starting up came from the town. Dozens of them.

"It's the bikers!" Sundown said. "Off on their weekend ride."

"Shit. Perhaps they won't notice. Let's go."

But the roar of the motorcycles grew louder. Instead of north to Mulholland, they were coming west. Their direction.

Sundown and Jimmy scrambled down the metal ladder and over the fence.

"No!" Jimmy said, steering her away from the pickup. "They'll catch us. Here—" and he pulled her off into the trees. They hurried through the undergrowth for a while until they reached the edge of the hill and had to stop. The ocean glinted in the distance. A mockingbird awoke and began to sing.

By the crashing that followed, it was clear the bikers had ridden over the fence. Then came the sound of bootsteps up the side of the water tank followed by the sound of the sign being smashed to pieces in a frenzy.

"Go back to Russia, fucking Communists!"

"Traitors!"

"Asshole hippies!

— · —

Maddy sliced a trayful of still-warm brownies into squares. Bret had requested some "adult cookies" as he referred to them in front of Charity—though she knew better—to take with him on the shoot for those times he couldn't light up. She had crumbled a sizable amount of brown hashish into the mix. Last time she hadn't added enough and it failed to have the intended effect, for some chemical reason she was never able to determine. This time, despite the cost of the ingredients, she was determined he'd have no complaint.

This weekend was Topanga's Strawberry Festival, and she had rented a space for a Stitch Witches booth. It was almost time to set up. She put six brownies in a baggie and placed it on her husband's suitcase, grabbed a floppy hat and made her way out to the VW.

— · —

When the motorcycles finally roared back down, Sundown and Jimmy crept back out. The van was untouched, but the sign and the fence were a mass of tangled debris.

Sundown looked down the hill to where the Festival was setting up, and the reporters that she had imagined would have been aiming their cameras up at their glorious statement of a sign. "No story now," she said.

Jimmy started the pickup with a sigh of relief. "Well, least we're alive." He looked at her. "Coming back into town?"

She would rather have attended the festival, but she nodded. "I have to. My car's at your place."

— · —

Maddy and Tess laid out the Stitch Witches' booth with their wares while the other Strawberry Festival sellers set up around them—the dulcimer tent, the macramé booth, food stands with Coke and beer, corndogs, tacos, and churros, and Lance Sterling's gypsy wagon full of women making leather sandals, belts and bags. There were two painters—a watercolorist and a specialist in oils, and a woman who made candles. A local potter sported his clunky unglazed earthenware, debossed with seagulls and sunsets. Lucas, one of the local artists, was there with his metal sculptures—it looked as if he had made some small and affordable ones especially. Similarly, Maddy had narrowed their stock to low cost items geared for quick sale—shirts and vests, scarves and headbands, and a few bracelets, necklaces and rings.

— · —

A flatbed truck rolled into the middle of the space ringed by the booths. Roadies ran to hook up the equipment on the back—amps, speakers, guitars and mics—and soon fat wires snaked across the dirt.

Canned Heat played first, a rambling jam, their big sound echoing off the hillside. Maddy, though she loved the band, soon began to look forward to them stopping, since as long as they were playing everyone stood around to watch and forgot to buy. During the break everyone, including band members, headed for the food booths. Only once they had been fed did people return to browsing and occasionally purchasing.

Next, Taj Mahal climbed aboard with drummer Earl Palmer, his Native American guitarist Jesse Ed Davis and his Telecaster, Gary Gilmore and his bass. They started with "Corinna," one of the band's most well-known songs, and people again stopped their shopping to crowd around. This time, though, as soon as they broke into "She Caught the Katy, and Left Me the Mule to Ride" with its infectious rhythm, people began to dance.

Charity turned to her mother. "Is he saying 'she complicated'?"

A browser at the booth overheard. "No, honey. 'She caught the Katy.' The 'Katy' is the train that serves the Mississippi Delta."

By now Tess was seriously loaded, swaying with the music and, much to Maddy's annoyance, only with difficulty focusing on customers. After Tess had served a couple while Maddy was tied up with another buyer, Maddy asked what Susan Acevedo and Neil Young had bought.

"Oh, shit!" Tess said, horrified. "I didn't notice it was them! She bought a shirt for him! How much did I charge them?"

Maddy looked after the couple as they walked away. "That was sweet of Susan to buy something. She's a brilliant seamstress herself."

Taj Mahal launched into "Leavin' Trunk."

Charity ran to the truck and started jumping for joy. *"Mailbox!"* she shouted, though it was doubtful anyone could hear her. To her delight the band played "Going Up To The Country, Paint My Mailbox Blue."

— · —

After the bands had left and the music truck had driven away, Charity ate a corndog and a churro, and then became bored. The interesting part of the Festival was apparently over, and the crowd was thinning. Besides, her pocket money was long gone. She waved goodbye to her mother and walked the four minutes to the house, intending to play with the dog. *"Gilligan!"* she called, *"Gillie!"*

Robbie opened the door. "Haven't seen him."

She ran past him into the house, flustered, her face red. "Dad? Where's dad?"

Robbie pointed vaguely out toward the road. "Off on a shoot. Left when you did."

"Something's happened to Gilligan! I can tell." Her small, slender body dashed back outside and across the grass away from the house.

The creek seemed the natural place to start, but Gilligan was nowhere to be seen. Charity tried to think of the places the dog liked to hang out, and remembered his love for squirrel chasing.

She ran back up the hill toward the street. A clump of three eucalyptuses grew here by the road, the kind with bark that peels off in strips. Squirrels could sometimes be seen cavorting in them, though the trees bore nothing edible.

At their foot, half covered with leaves, was a dark shape, moving slightly.

"Gilligan!" Charity yelled, crouching over him.

Gilligan was on his side, panting shallowly. He looked grotesque. Half of his muzzle was swollen to twice its normal size. One eye was closed; the other looked at her in pain.

With her father gone, she was in charge now. She scooped the dog into her arms and stood with difficulty. Gilligan was far heavier than she had imagined.

Robbie saw her staggering toward the house, and ran out to meet her, taking the dog from her. He knew immediately what had happened.

"Snakebite," he told her.

Charity's eyes filled with tears. "Will he be OK?"

"We'll have to take him to that damn vet in town." But his father and mother were gone. "Where's Sundown?"

"She's at her boyfriend's in Venice."

"He needs a vet. I'll have to drive him." He looked up to the empty driveway. His father's and mother's cars were gone, and Sundown was down in Venice with hers. Only Jackson's was waiting in the garage for his return, its fender still damaged. Jackson had been planning on draining the oil, but that was when he had finished basic.

Robbie staggered into the garage, and when Charity had opened the GTO's door for him, gently placed the dog on the back seat. Then he sat behind the wheel and stared at the fake wood dash with its four large dials, the tachometer his brother had installed on top, the big three-spoked steering wheel. His feet couldn't reach the pedals, so he scooted the seat closer.

Charity climbed in and looked at him nervously. "Do you know how to drive?"

He had never driven before, apart from little experiments in a big parking lot once, when his father had felt like imparting some tips, and certainly never his big brother's car, always off limits. "'Course I do. Piece o' cake." Robbie jammed the key in the ignition and with false confidence turned it on. The powerful motor sprang to life, filling the garage with sound and fumes.

Robbie looked at the gearshift and the three pedals. Terrified but trying not to show it, he released the brake, shoved down the clutch and pushed the shift knob into first. The car leapt out of the garage. Charity squealed.

With a crunch, Robbie shifted quickly into second and turned onto the street. Luckily there was no one else around. Now third. This wasn't so bad. Fourth. Easy.

But the car was huge. From Robbie's low viewpoint it seemed to fill the street. He wished he'd taken the time to find a cushion to sit on so he could see better. Too late now.

They drove, slower than normal, narrowly avoiding scraping the side of a parked van, past the emptying festival to Fernwood, where there was an overpriced veterinarian named Leuchauer.

Robbie slewed across two parking spaces and slammed on the brakes.

Inside, the receptionist told them to wait while she told the doctor of their arrival. Gilligan lay on the carpet, his body motionless, only his bloodshot eyes moving.

"It's a snakebite!" Charity told the doctor, when he finally appeared.

He ignored her and poked around in Gilligan's muzzle. The dog whimpered softly.

"It's snakebite," he declared.

"We *know* that!" Robbie snapped. "Give him something for it!"

Leuchauer looked from one to the other with a bland expression. "I'd have to order the antivenin sent up from L.A. It'd take too long. Your dog will have either died or not in the meantime. I suspect he'll be OK. He lived this long, after all."

Charity scowled. Why didn't he keep the antidote handy? "Isn't there something you can do to ease his pain?"

The doctor shrugged. "I'll give him a shot."

Afterward, the receptionist said, "That'll be fifty dollars."

Robbie hadn't thought about money. He had five dollars on him; Charity had nothing at all. "You'll have to bill us," he told the woman, and wrote down their address.

As they stood outside again, Gilligan woozy on his legs and drooling, a primer gray Mini Cooper with black-tinted windows zoomed by.

"Hey!" Charity said, "That was Neil Young's car! Dad'll be so angry he wasn't here to see."

By this time it was late, and the festival was done. Attendees had drifted off, the music truck and the gypsy wagon were gone, and volunteers were picking up trash.

"Let's help mom and Tess," Charity said.

Robbie parked, badly, and helped his mother dismantle their booth while Charity fetched the dog some water, and then he drove everyone home. He glanced sideways at his mother. "It was an emergency," he explained.

Maddy continued to watch the road. "Robbie, I see why you had to take Jackson's car. But you could've been arrested for driving without a license. You'd better make sure your dad and Jacks don't find out." She looked at Charity. "We won't say anything about this, all right?"

Charity began to protest. "But—"

"It's a white lie. They're OK."

[138]

As they all walked to the house from the cars, Gilligan still staggering, they came face to face with a man in a suit and tie.

Maddy assessed him warily. In Topanga, men in suits meant either authorities or religion, and neither was welcome. "Can I help you?"

The man singled out Maddy to address, since she was the adult of the group. "I'm from the Los Angeles City Planning Department. Are you Mrs. Sobieski?"

"I am. Come in. We were just at the vet's."

"Oh. The dog is sick?"

"Snakebite." Maddy ushered him into the kitchen and indicated a seat at the table. "He'll be all right."

The man sat, looking alarmed. "A-anyway, it's about your extension."

"Extension?"

"The … ah … structure in the middle of your house. It seems your husband neglected to apply for planning permission."

Maddy was careful in her response. "My husband's away at the moment. I'm sure he took care of all the necessary forms."

"Apparently not. The rules in Topanga are a little looser than in the city suburbs, of course, but there are still rules. And they must be followed."

Maddy had an idea. "Would you like a brownie? I put some in before we left—they should be cool now." She walked to the tray on the counter. "Perfect! Fresh brownies."

Charity and Robbie looked at each other but said nothing.

Maddy put a piece each on two plates. "Here."

"Thank you. Isn't anyone else having any?"

"Oh, no. It'll spoil their dinner. They'll have some later."

The man took a tentative bite. "Very good. You must be quite a cook."

Maddy nibbled hers. "Why, thank you. Anyway, you were saying…?"

"If planning permission has not been applied for and approved, then any structure must be removed."

"Removed? Taken down?"

"Yes."

"Dismantled?"

"Yes."

"But that would leave a huge hole in the middle of the house."

The man hoisted his briefcase onto his lap and clicked it open. He withdrew a sheaf of pale yellow papers and sorted through them, waving one in triumph. "Here—'the inspector'—that's me—'has the power to order any unauthorized structures removed within thirty days.'"

Maddy's eyes filled with desperation. "Let's go up and look—I'm sure you'll find everything is in order."

He swallowed the remains of his brownie and followed her up the spiral staircase.

"See?" Maddy said, as they regarded the octagonal room. "It's very well made. Wired properly and everything."

"Mrs. Sobieski, we have specialized inspectors—structural, plumbing, electrical—that must sign off on each stage of construction. There are no such approvals on file." He walked around the walls, stooping to examine details and prod things with his ballpoint pen. "Oh." He touched his forehead, leaving a smudge of chocolate. "I must have climbed the stairs too quickly."

"Oh, that often happens," Maddy assured him, and led him to the swivel chair. "Sit. Charity! Bring the gentleman a glass of water. And another brownie."

The inspector sipped his water and looked around with a bemused expression. "Quite a view," he said eventually, loosening his tie.

"Yes," Maddy agreed. "That's why we had to build it, you see?" When he didn't respond, she prompted, "So, the paperwork..."

The inspector looked away from the bright view beyond the glass. "What? Oh—paperwork. Yes." He looked down at the briefcase on his lap as if he had never seen it before. "Yes, most important."

"So what's the next step?"

"Oh, I'll have to ... ah ... have to file a report..."

"Really?" Maddy smiled at him. "Is that really necessary? After all..." she gestured to include the tower, "It's all solidly built, and it's not harming anyone."

The inspector shook his head and marshaled what remained of his officiousness. "That's not the point."

"No? What is, then?"

He blinked. "I think I ought to be going. I feel ... I feel..."

"It's hot today. And the heat collects up here. I'll walk you to your car." She helped him out of the chair and down the spiral staircase, which now seemed to fascinate him. "Thank you for coming out. I'm glad everything was OK."

"OK? Yes, I suppose." He wandered toward his car and sat in it for several minutes before starting up and driving hesitantly away.

"So..." Charity said, as they all watched his car disappear over the hill, "is he going to cite dad or something?"

Maddy wrapped the remaining brownies in foil and put them away. "We'll see. Somehow I doubt it."

2000

On the shelf among the books was a James Taylor album. Robbie took it down and extracted a buckled LP.

Sundown glanced at it. "You ever listen to that kind of music now?"

Robbie shook his head and returned the record to the shelf. "The country's whole mood has changed. Those emotions I felt back then—I don't feel them any more."

Charity smiled, vaguely. "I still listen to Joni."

"This must be yours, Charity," Sundown said, handing over a Christian comic book by Jim Phillips entitled *Eternal Truth, No.2*.

Her sister took it without embarrassment. "Yes, I remember that. The Hitchhiker. Probably worth something now."

Robbie chuckled. "You went off the deep end there for a while."

Charity finally lost her cool. "You're one to talk," she snapped back. "Who was so wasted all the time that he got no education at all? Did you really want to be a car salesman all your life?"

Now it was Robbie's turn to be annoyed. "There's nothing wrong with car sales. I make a good living. Besides, I'm general manager of a dealership in Santa Monica. I make more than you."

"That's true. But I think mom and dad had bigger things in mind for you."

Robbie struggled to control his feelings. He was good at it. Every day he was friendly to people he despised. Every day he cheerfully burned people who clearly could not afford to be. "Charity, doesn't your belief teach you not to be self-righteous?"

Charity reddened. "You're right. I guess I'm not perfect."

"But forgiven, huh?"

"That's enough," Sundown said, putting down the copy of Steppenwolf she'd been thumbing through. "We all dealt with growing up in different ways. God knows I paid the price for my decisions. I always tried to follow my heart," she said, "And you know what I found? My heart was fucking stupid. Perhaps a bit more faith would've helped me, but I was like dad—godless."

"We could talk about that, if you like," offered Charity.

"No thanks, sis—a bit late now."

"It's never—"

"No."

13
SUMMER, 1968
MAGIC CARPET RIDE

Summer. Temperatures rise. Days start hot and just get hotter, building to a peak in midafternoon. A cloud hasn't crossed the pale blue sky for months. It's at times like this that convertible drivers wonder if having an open car was such a great idea, as their faces become parchment and their hair turns to straw. The steering wheel is too hot to hold, the seats could bake potatoes, and the radiator might boil over at any minute and strand them somewhere nasty. And rain? No rain, unless some freak storm wanders briefly up from Baja. It is now that the Los Angeles basin drains the rivers of its neighboring states to water its lawns and golf courses.

Topanga is a glimpse into what the rest of Southern California looked like before the large-scale import of water from upstate and out-of-state—dry, without glamorous and glossy vegetation.

— · —

Charity loved Camp Wildwood. Not that it was all that different from her own back yard—it was a mere half-mile away and its appearance was much the same. But she loved the big swimming pool, the carved Kilmer poem "I think that I shall never see / A poem lovely as a tree," and the run-down cottages with the cutesy names left over from its prewar resort days: Seldom Inn, Come On Inn, Tip Toe Inn, and Snuggle Inn.

The only drawback was some of the other children. Almost all were from down in the basin—the Valley or the Inner City—and some had clearly been shunted off to the hills by exasperated parents who couldn't deal with them at home all summer. Problem children who reverted to savagery as soon as they were freed of the constraints of parents and school.

She found one boy, Phil, about to pick red-leaved plants by the creek.

"Don't touch that," she told him, "it's poison oak."

Phil looked at her suspiciously. "How do you know?"

"I live here. Everybody in Topanga knows poison oak."

"Hey, Caroline," he said to a girl wandering nearby, "She says it's poison ivy."

"Poison *oak*."

"We should call her Poison Ivy! She lives up here!"

Caroline wore dusty patent T-strap shoes and an impractical mini-skirt. "You live here at the camp?"

"No," Charity explained, pointing. "Down the road."

"Then why do you come here?"

"'Cause it has a pool. And new people."

Caroline assessed Charity. "What's your name?"

"Charity."

"What kind of weird name is that?"

"A hippie name," the boy said. "She's a hippie-dippie. Do you smoke pot? I bet she smokes pot. Do you have any?"

"No."

"Can you get us some? I have money."

"No."

"I bet she can—she just doesn't want to."

"I don't smoke."

"Bet you do. All hippies do. My dad says."

"*My* dad," Caroline added, "says hippies don't do any work. Does your dad work, *Charitee?*"

"He works in the movies. He does the lighting."

This, finally, impressed them.

"Wow," said Phil. "Can your dad get me a *Planet of the Apes* outfit? I'll give him a hundred bucks."

Caroline tossed her head in disdain. "I bet he just plugs things in." She sashayed away, her city shoes glinting in the sunlight.

"That Caroline—she's snooty," Phil told Charity. "I hate her."

"Why? What's she done to you?"

The boy looked uncomfortable. "I showed her mine but she wouldn't show me hers."

Charity was horrified. "Perhaps she didn't want to see yours."

"Why not? It's just a game. It's fun."

"No it isn't—it's disgusting."

"Everyone does it at camp."

"No they don't."

He apprised her. "You're snooty too, then."

"No, I'm not. I just don't want to see your private parts."

This struck him as funny. "Private parts!"

"Although I guess with you they're not private now."

He folded over with mirth. "Shit, that's funny! You're OK, Poison Ivy."

Charity left him laughing to himself, not wanting to give him any time to undo his clothing.

— · —

Poison oak is common—not poison ivy, which is an East Coast thing—though it usually only grows beside the creeks. Its serrated leaves grow in groups of three, which led to the rhyme "leaves of three, let me be," that hardly anybody seems to know. In spring, the oak-like leaves are dark green and shiny, but by fall they begin to turn shades of red and orange. So the autumn is the easiest time to identify them, since the real oak trees around them don't turn colors like oaks of the East and Midwest.

Topanga residents know it as one of nature's most vicious plants, though its corrosive oil doesn't protect it, like thorns. It's only some hours after touching it that human skin starts to blister and itch, Once the oil has been touched by brushing a leaf, or from stroking a dog that has brushed against it, an inflammation will result that lasts, it's said, an average of three weeks, and that's once you stop scratching. Calamine lotion doesn't work, and a shower will just spread it.

Some of the older residents hire a goat to wander about the areas of their property infested with poison oak, since the animal, with its notoriously cast iron stomach, can eat it with no ill effects.

— · —

That night, at about two, there was a commotion in one of the girls' cabins.

"*My face!*" Caroline wailed. "Something's wrong with my *face! I can't see!*"

Charity jumped up and turned on the light. To her horror, she saw that the girl's face had turned a lurid pink, ballooned alarmingly to twice its normal size, and her eyes had swollen shut. Charity dressed quickly and ran for the counselor's cabin.

"Poison oak," the counselor said, as soon as he saw the girl's condition. "How did you get it all over your face?"

"I don't know! I didn't go near it!"

"I'm calling an ambulance—we need to get you to the hospital."

By the time the ambulance arrived, its lights flashing around the oak trees, the whole camp was awake and standing around in their pajamas. The counselors, in an excess of belated zeal, were burning Caroline's bedclothes in the fire pit.

Phil wandered over to Charity's side. "Hey, Poison Ivy," he said. "Did you poison ivy Caroline?"

"No! Of course not!"

He smiled. In the light from the flames and the ambulance his face looked satanic. "I did. Rolled her pillow in it. That'll teach her to be snooty."

— · —

Sundown came out of the apartment's tiny bathroom and sat on the end of the bed.

Jimmy looked at her with concern. "Why so bummed, babe?"

"I was ... kinda hoping my period would've arrived by now." She looked at him to gauge his reaction.

Despite the warm day, the atmosphere had suddenly turned frosty.

He got up and dressed self-consciously. "You mean ... you might be pregnant?"

"Yeah, that's usually what it means."

"Well, shit, Sundown, I thought you had that taken care of." He looked down at her, and then away to the view from the window. A neighbor was playing "Chain of Fools."

"So did I."

"Well ... you'd better find out."

She nodded. "I'll let you know."

"Yeah. OK."

— · —

After the night's drama, camp resumed with its normal schedule: Monday was water balloon fights and a scavenger hunt, Tuesday was crafts, during which they wove multicolored lanyards—all except for Phil, who declared the exercise "too sissy," and climbed trees instead. Wednesday was supposed to be swimming and diving lessons, but on the way to breakfast one of the other girls found a dead bat in the deep end.

"*Cryptosporidium!*" declared one of the counselors in panic, and after scooping out the small corpse dumped several jugs of chlorine into the water. After that, the pool reeked eye-wateringly of chemicals.

Instead, they played Civil War. "The idea's simple," a counselor explained. "Get more points than the other team. You get points by capturing the other team's soldiers, and by stealing their flag. We'll start with the sound of the bugle and the flourhawks are launched. The Union begins up the hill, which is 'Cemetery Ridge,' and the Confederates start at the bottom, which is 'Seminary Ridge.'"

Charity wasn't at all sure this would go well, especially since Phil seemed overeager to get a flag at any cost. She was just glad she was on his side, or she felt sure she would at least end up with a bloody nose by afternoon's end. She would have preferred the counselor to have added a few rules, but he was a bit on the loosey-goosey side.

The bugle sounded. Socksful of flour burst spectacularly in the trees.

Charity stormed a stronghold, but she had no one else with her. The moment she grabbed the flag, the Union soldiers launched themselves at her. She was buried beneath bodies, her face in the dust and prickly oak leaves.

At the end of a frantic couple of hours, bruised and bloodied, uniforms torn, the kids shuffled back down to the camp for pizza.

— · —

Phil waited until the adults had retired to their cabins and then ran around to each of the kids' windows hissing, "Let's do the Weegee!"

Charity was puzzled until he produced a battered Ouija board. The campers gathered hesitantly in his hut as he lit the candles meant for emergencies and flicked off the overheads.

There was a momentary silence, since no one could decide what to ask the board first. Then Phil asked the spirits if anyone had died at the camp. The planchette laboriously spelled out J-A-N-I-C-E. "Who's Janice?" they asked each other. Phil wanted to wake up the counselors and ask, but the others talked him out of it. Charity hoped this marked the end of the game, but Phil impulsively demanded to talk to someone recently passed.

After a pregnant pause, the planchette lurched around to spell K-E-N-N-E-D-Y.

"Which one?" Phil asked rudely, "JFK?"

The pointer headed to NO.

"Wow!" Phil said to the others. "We got Robert!"

Charity looked at the group. In the dim light their faces were scared, with that hesitant half-smile that tried to camouflage the fear.

"So did that Sirhan guy really blow your brains out?"

"Damn," a boy named Peter reprimanded him; "You need to talk to it with some respect, man."

The planchette zigzagged back and forth across the board, eventually skidding off into the dark. The children looked at each other in horror.

"That's it," Charity told them, getting to her feet and flicking on the electric light. "I'm leaving." She hurried back to her cabin long enough to throw her things in her backpack and collect some dimes, and then fumbled her way to the phone box.

The house phone rang for a long time, and she was about to hang up and reluctantly walk home in the dark when her sister picked up.

"Hello?"

"Sundown! It's Charity! You have to come and get me!"

"Huh? Why? What's happened?"

"All kinds of things! They're crazy! Poison oak! Talking to the dead! Bats in the pool! I've had enough!"

"OK, OK. Gimme a coupla minutes. Meet me at the street."

Charity made her way up the steep, dark driveway toward the glow of a streetlight. Phil—at least she hoped it was Phil and not some conjured spirit—was still making noises down in the dell.

In a few minutes Sundown's Corvair pulled up at the camp's entrance, its engine loud in the night. Charity ran to meet her and threw her backpack and sleeping bag onto the back seat.

"What?" Sundown asked, as she drove away. "Got tired of it?"

"The city kids. They spoiled it."

Sundown seemed distracted. "Yeah."

Charity chatted on about her experiences until she sensed her sister's lack of attention. The car abruptly swung off to the side of the road, and Sundown opened her door and threw up.

"Sundown! What's the matter?"

Sundown wiped her mouth with the back of her hand. "Just an upset stomach."

14

Charity helped prepare her mother's traditional Sunday lunch: spaghetti and meatballs. She had always helped with this in the past, but now she not only refused to eat meat but also expressed her revulsion at the thought of handling it raw. Maddy's compromise was to make an occasional vegetarian version, which the rest of the family reluctantly accepted. Today was no-meat meatballs, and Charity was standing on a stool and mashing together chickpeas, mushrooms, oatmeal and onions in a bowl, and then rolling balls of the mix in flour while her mother watched.

Sundown came up behind them and looked at the mixture with distaste. "Mom? Can we talk? Not here."

"We're in the middle of cooking."

"It's OK," Charity assured them, "I can do it."

"The pan's already hot," Maddy told her. "When you're done, put them in on low. Keep turning them."

Maddy and Sundown walked outside.

"Tree house?" Sundown asked.

Maddy hesitated.

"Don't want to climb?"

"No, no. I'll be fine."

They mounted the ladder and lit candles. Sundown looked around the little cabin without meeting her mother's eyes.

"So?" Maddy prompted.

"I think I'm pregnant."

"*What?* I set you up with the pill! I had to get them prescribed for *me!*"

"Yeah, well…"

"How? You forgot?"

"Maybe."

"Who's the father?"

"Jimmy, I guess."

Maddy stared at her daughter. "You *guess?*"

— · —

Charity found she didn't have enough room in the pan for all the meatballs she'd made. Should she start another pan or cook them in two batches? She ran outside and down the hill to ask her mother. When she reached the pepper trees she quietly climbed the ladder. She could hear her mother and sister talking within.

— · —

Maddy bit her lip. "Sundown, this is serious."

"You're telling me! I'm a high school senior. I don't want a baby!"

"Well," Maddy continued, "a woman in your position has three choices: keep, put up for adoption, or … terminate."

"Abortion."

"That's right. It's only just become legal here."

"No—abortion. I want one."

Maddy scowled. "Sundown, abortion is not the same as birth control. You're ending a life. It's supposed to—"

"Ma, that's just your Catholic upbringing—"

"How dare you say that!" Maddy put her face in her hands and began to weep.

Sundown was bewildered by the extent of her mother's reaction. "What? *What?*"

"I … I had an abortion once. It was before I met your dad. I made a horrible mistake, and I didn't want it to affect my whole life. In those days it was illegal. Still is, most states."

Sundown looked away, flustered. "Look, I'm sorry you went through

[152]

that, but can we get it done soon? I'm going away with Jimmy at the weekend."

"I don't like your attitude, young lady. If we do this … *if* we do … this must never happen again."

"Of course."

"No 'of course'!" Maddy looked fiercely at her daughter. "I mean it."

Sundown nodded and looked away. "I'll find out for sure."

— · —

Charity ran back to the house and threw meatballs into the pan with the flame turned up much too high. They sizzled and filled the kitchen with smoke.

— · —

After her mother had returned to the house, Sundown stayed in the tree house, trying to harness the turmoil in her mind. How could life turn from good to bad in such a brief instant? Why couldn't she have been more careful? Why couldn't Jimmy have been more careful, goddamn him? It just wasn't worth it—a few minutes of pleasure, resulting in … a new person. He wasn't even that great of a lover. It was insane. The two things were totally separate. Sex was one thing; starting a family another. What kind of sick God had linked the two? It made no sense at all.

It was all wrong. Having a child should be an agreed-on thing. *Not* having a child should be the biological norm. Motherhood should need to be unlocked, and unlocked by mutual agreement, not triggered by accident after a joint and half a bottle of Mateus Rosé.

To think that if she didn't have an abortion she would soon have a helpless, needy baby was appalling. She wasn't ready to be a mother. And she was pretty damn sure Jimmy wasn't ready to be a father. They were young, good-looking, about to embark on talented, exciting lives, exploring their potential, exploring the world. They weren't meant to be frumpy stay-at-homes with epaulettes of puke, changing shit-filled diapers all day and night.

She would probably want a kid someday, but not now, not when she was just starting her life. When she'd done the things she wanted to do, been to the places she'd always wanted to visit—then was the time to stop and settle and start a family.

She pictured her new future in her mind. Suburbs. Station wagons. PTA meetings. A spare tire of fat from the pregnancy she would never be able to shed. Tupperware parties. Getting the mail in her robe and slippers. No concerts, no money, no freedom, no fun.

She gagged.

Besides, what kind of world was this to bring a child into? There was always a war going on somewhere. If you had a boy, he would grow up playing with guns and then, as soon as he was old enough, get scooped up by the army and sent off to fight. Chances are he wouldn't live to middle age. Is that what mothers were for these days, to produce more cannon fodder? And if you had a girl, she would always be in danger of being knocked up.

She pictured Jackson, and the tears started again. She had never known how much she loved him till this instant. OK, she told God, a deal: I'll have a kid if you keep Jacks safe.

— · —

Once her mother had relieved her at the stove, and opened all the windows and doors to let out the smoke, Charity clattered up the spiral staircase. Her father was in his swivel office chair, flipping through a typewritten script, adding marginalia about lighting cues with a red ballpoint. "Dad?"

"What's up, honey?"

"Dad, are you religious?"

Bret looked at his daughter. "Religion's bullshit, Charity. You're old enough to understand that now. Some people set themselves up as the mouthpiece of God. And other people believe them."

She blinked. "So ministers, rabbis—they don't really talk to God?"

He laughed, briefly. "There's no God, Charity. It's all a scam."

Charity looked horrified. She threw out an arm to include everything around them. "So who made … all this?"

"Nobody. It's just hard for humans to believe. It all just … happened. It evolved."

"And … when we die?"

"We just die. That's it. Finito."

"So who have I been praying to?"

Bret shrugged. "Beats me. There's nobody there, honey. Sorry."

"But Mommy taught me to pray!"

"When?"

"Ages ago. When I was small."

"Well, there you go—praying's for kids."

Charity stamped a foot. "You *lied* to me! *All* of you! Grownups *all* lie!"

"No, no, Charity. Look, hon—people like to believe in something. It makes them feel as if there's some purpose to life, and—"

"But there isn't?"

"No, but that doesn't mean—"

"So there's no one who made all this, and no one watching over us?"

"No, but—"

"If God is crap, then our *lives* are crap!"

"Look, I didn't say that. I just—"

"Yes, you did! You're all pigs!"

"Charity! Charity..."

But Charity had gone.

Bret sighed and meditatively rolled a joint. He lit it and looked out at the hills.

The door opened and Maddy stormed in, a fierce look in her eyes. "What did you tell Charity?"

Bret dropped the joint. "We were just discussing—"

"You told her there was no God."

"I tried to explain to her how organized religion worked."

"Well, you did a lousy job of it."

"Why? What's she doing?"

"She's gone, that's what. She's really upset. And all because of your clumsy efforts at *en-fucking-lightenment*."

"Maddy, I—"

"You should know better than to burst a kid's bubble like that."

Bret stood, a sick feeling in the pit of his stomach. "Where'd she go?"

"God knows, Bret. Ask Him."

— · —

Charity climbed into the tree house and sat inside, shivering uncontrollably. She was far from cold; it was what her father had said that sent a chill through her. All the things she had thought interconnected and made for a purpose—a special purpose that she wasn't yet old enough to understand—were just ... *random*. She felt as if her heart had been torn out of her.

Martin Luther King, Jr. and Robert Kennedy had been shot, her sister was going to abort a baby, and there wasn't even a heaven for people to go to after they died. They were just snuffed out, like the flame from a candle.

Gilligan sat at the foot of the ladder, whimpering. Since Jackson had gone the dog had latched onto her. He could tell she was upset. She leaned out and looked down at him. The dog looked back up at her, hopefully. He didn't want to go up; he wanted her to come down. She would have laughed in the past; he looked so comical with the bandana around his neck and his goofy expression. Now she knew he was just a bag of atoms driven by chance. "Go away, Gillie," she said. The dog hesitated for a moment, and then got to his feet and padded back in the direction of the house.

Charity drew her knees up to her chin, thinking bleak thoughts. She had always believed there was meaning to her life, that she was alive on earth for a reason. She had always thought she and the people she loved were special. Now they all seemed flat, like cinema lobby standees, with no dimension and no purpose but to take up space, along with all the billions of other cutouts. They were as significant as ants. It couldn't even be God's little joke if there wasn't any God. She had never understood the word "spiritual" before, but she did now, now that it was meaningless. What was she supposed to do with the part of her that yearned to be part of something bigger?

"Charity?" Maddy's voice called. "You up there?"

She didn't answer. Her mother must be in on the secret too; must know nothing meant anything. She had been hiding it from her, like the others.

She felt the tree house tremble as Maddy climbed up.

Charity would have liked to throw herself at her mother, to be cuddled in her arms, but she did nothing except stand awkwardly.

"Did dad say something? You mustn't take everything he says too seriously, y'know." When Charity still said nothing, she prompted, "What did he tell you?"

"He ... he said that God was bullshit. He said nobody made the world."

Maddy shook her head. "Yeah, well, your dad's what's called an atheist. He doesn't believe in a God. But that doesn't mean he's right. There's plenty of people who do."

"Do you?"

"I do. Not in a churchy way, maybe, but I do. I can't believe that all this—" she waved his arm in a broad, all-encompassing gesture much like Charity's earlier, "is just a big accident. And you," she tapped her daughter gently in her narrow chest, "are very special to all of us."

"*Charity!*" Robbie called from the deck. "You up there? Dad said to come find you."

Maddy looked at her with concern. "You come talk to me if you need to, OK?" She climbed down and walked back to the house. "She's up there," she told Robbie. "Be nice to her."

Robbie walked to the foot of the ladder and looked up. "We're going to the movies in Woodland Hills. Wanna come?"

Charity regarded him with a wounded expression. She suspected he had been told to invite her, since he and his friends had never before included her in their outings. But she loved movies. "Maybe."

"Well hurry up an' decide. We're leaving soon."

— · —

Bret's round face was a deep and dangerous red, and his eyes, always a little bulbous, seemed about to pop out of his head. "I told you to look after her! And you took her to see *that*? Why do you think it's rated X?"

Robbie looked at his feet. "But she likes movies. We thought it was gonna be just, y'know, a scary movie we could laugh at."

"But *Rosemary's Baby*? You took Charity to see *Rosemary's Baby* when she was already rattled? Robbie, I swear you can be a real dumb little fuck sometimes."

"Oh yeah? Who was telling her there was no God?"

"How did you get in, anyway?"

"A friend let us in the back."

Bret ran his fingers through his hair. "I'd better talk to her."

"She's gone."

"Where?"

"Dunno."

— · —

Bret consulted the family address book and jabbed the wall phone's buttons.

"Jackie? Bret Sobieski. Is Charity there? No? OK, thanks ... what? No, everything's fine."

"Bill? Bret. Is Charity over there, by any chance? OK, catch you later."

"Sandra—Bret. Is Charity over there with Kitty? No? OK ... no, no problem. See you."

He looked in alarm at Maddy. "Who else?"

"I guess she could be at the Robinsons."

Bret punched numbers again, a little more forcefully this time. "Peter? Bret Sobieski. Is Charity over there with the kids? She was? She what? Where? Really? OK. No, that's OK. Thanks, man."

Maddy looked at him, concerned. "What?"

"She bummed a ride with them into L.A. Told 'em she was meeting a friend. Some Jesus freak place. God*damn*." He shook his head in wonder. "God*damn*."

As he replaced the receiver, the phone rang.

"Mr. Sobieski?"

Bret frowned at the phone receiver. "Yes?"

"I'm Reverend Williams, the pastor at Haven Home in Los Angeles. I thought you'd like to know your daughter's here."

"Charity? Charity's there?"

"Yessir. She's fine."

"We've been looking everywhere for her."

"That's why I'm calling. To let you know she's OK."

"Well, thanks, but ... what's going on?"

"Nothing's going on, Mr. Sobieski. We're a halfway house for troubled youth, and—"

"Troubled youth? Charity's not troubled!"

"Perhaps not. But she's pretty upset about something, otherwise she wouldn't have run away."

"Run away?"

"She's fine here for a while, if you want to leave her with us. Of course, since she's underage you can come get her whenever you like. But she seems to be looking for something maybe we, and Jesus, can provide."

Bret said nothing for a moment. Maddy saw his congested face and mouthed "What?"

He waved her angrily away. "What do you do there?" he asked.

"Discuss the bible. Pray together. Break bread together. Witness."

"Witness?"

"Go out and share His love with others."

"I see. Tell you what—it's late. Tell her I'll pick her up tomorrow morning. Give me your address."

— · —

The room in the old, rundown house was too strange for Charity to sleep. Besides, the noises from the street outside were too foreign for her. The two teenaged runaways that occupied the other beds were, on the other hand, deeply asleep, one muttering in her dreams.

She reached into her bag and fumbled among the belongings she had impulsively grabbed before she left home: One of her Troll dolls, a red and white PEZ space gun dispenser, a crocheted beret, her transistor radio, her signed photo of Davy Jones. She pulled out her pen and her journal, and then began to write in the light of the streetlamp outside.

> *Sundown is pregnant and she's going to have an abortion! It's the worst thing I could think of. And mommy said she had one too, once. I can't believe it. I don't think God would like it, but dad says there's no God, so I guess no one cares except me. Sundown is too young to be a mother anyway, but I'm sure she would get used to it. In India girls of my age have children and they manage somehow.*

She blinked, and almost jumped out of bed. That was the answer. *She* could be a mother! Why not?

— · —

Once Bret had driven off, Maddy and Sundown exchanged brief glances heavy with a coded significance. Maddy crooked a finger and they walked outside into the late morning heat.

"I found someone," Maddy began. "He—"

Sundown stopped her. "False alarm. My period was just late. Stress, I guess."

Her mother sagged with relief. "Thank God. I was dreading this."

Sundown began to cry.

Maddy put an arm around her. "Jimmy must be happy."

"I haven't told him yet. I'm going over there now."

Charity stood, dwarfed by the streamline moderne exterior of the May Company at the corner of Wilshire and Fairfax, a rounded corner of gold tile looming four stories above her diminutive form. As Bret approached she was handing leaflets to indifferent shoppers, half of whom immediately dropped them on the sidewalk.

He walked up to her, and at first, not recognizing him, she tried to hand him one too.

"Charity—it's me, dad. Look, honey, I'm sorry about what I said. I didn't mean to upset you. I'm so used to being an unbeliever myself that I forgot the whole thing means a lot to some people. You mustn't take any notice of me. Truth is, I don't know if there's a God or not. But I'm sure glad you're here, and you're my daughter. So there must be something good in the universe, huh?"

She looked at him with hurt eyes.

He winced. "1 Corinthians," he quoted softly, *"And now abideth faith, hope, charity, these three; but the greatest of these is charity.* See? I believe in that. Let's go home, hon."

They drove for a while in silence, Charity uncharacteristically quiet, still clutching her handful of tracts: *GOD'S NOT DEAD—And Neither Will You Be If You Truly Believe.*

Bret said, "So ... why did you leave?"

At first Charity said nothing. She looked out the window at the passing streets. "Sundown is going to have an abortion."

Bret was shocked. Maddy had told him, but he hadn't realized Charity knew what was going on. He almost denied it, but at the last minute decided this was not the time for a lie, not even a well-intentioned one. "Well, honey, if she does, it'll be a very difficult decision for her. Nobody does that kind of thing lightly. Your sister's getting pregnant was an accident, you see."

"Still, it's a baby."

"I know, but—"

"*I'll* adopt it if she doesn't want it."

Bret swallowed. "That's a great thought, hon, but you're too young."

"Then you and mom can."

Bret nodded. "It's a possibility, I suppose. We'll all talk about it."

Charity glanced at him with a look he recognized. It was a you're-just-stringing-me-along look.

"I promise, Charity. I'll talk to mom about adoption."

— · —

Sundown felt giddy with relief. She stopped at a store and bought Jimmy a gag gift—a Gerber baby bottle and a small bottle of whiskey, with a card on which she scrawled "Just kidding!" Then she drove on to Venice to give him the good news.

But when she reached Jimmy's apartment, there was no answer to his bell.

"Mr. Jimmy—he no here," said a voice behind her.

She turned to see the landlord. "Do you know where I can find him, Mr. Lee?"

"No—he no here."

Served her right for not calling first, Sundown told herself. She considered leaving a note in Jimmy's mailbox—*Hey, I'm not pregnant after all. Let's celebrate*—and then decided against something so impersonal.

Instead, she drove back home to Topanga and immediately called him.

"I'm sorry," said a recorded voice, *"You have reached a number that is disconnected or no longer in service. Please check the directory and dial again."*

— · —

When the family members finally sat down for dinner, each had their reasons to want to be elsewhere. Robbie was in the doghouse for taking a vulnerable Charity to see a horror film, Sundown was hurt by her boyfriend's disappearance and furious with men in general, Maddy had been uncomfortably reminded of an incident in her personal history she had thought successfully buried, and Bret felt like an insensitive brute in his dealings with Charity.

Charity was in a kind of shellshocked bubble, confused and disillusioned. In her mind, scenes from *Rosemary's Baby* overlaid images of the Haven Home house and Sunday school pictures of heaven that she now knew were a fantasy. If Jackson were here she would have gone for a walk with him and poured out her heart. He would've understood. Without him, the Sobieskis seemed off-balance. Even Gilligan was morose.

15

Sundown and her friends liked to hang out at Topanga Plaza, where Topanga Boulevard crossed Ventura Boulevard in the Valley. It was only four years old and said to be the first covered mall in America.

If they had money, they'd cruise the May Company, Montgomery Ward, The Broadway, Joseph Magnin, Kay Jewelers, and end up trying on shoes at Florsheim's. Once in a while they'd skate the Ice Arena at the southeast corner.

If they had no money, they'd just people-watch, and it was a great venue for this. Once in a while there would be a much-touted grand opening, attended by Hollywood personalities like the always sequin-clad Zsa Zsa Gabor, sad-eyed Buster Keaton, the inseparable Steve Allen and Jayne Meadows, the woman who played Kate on *Petticoat Junction*, Bea Benaderet, and Lorne Green from *Bonanza*—though she would have been more interested in the smoldering Pernell Roberts, who played his son Adam.

Today Sundown had planned to meet her friend Jeannie to shop, or at least pretend to. Sundown waited by the Rain Fountain in the South Court, in front of Treasure Isle and Silverwood's. This sculpture consisted of several circular arrays of almost invisible lines stretching from floor to ceiling, with droplets slowly descending along each. This was where you always met people at the Plaza, but when half an hour had passed it was clear that Jeannie had either forgotten or received a better offer—with teenage girls, you never knew.

Reluctant to go home, Sundown walked instead to the Topanga Theatre to watch an early showing of *The Thomas Crown Affair*.

She left the cinema two and a half hours later in haze of wonder. She understood it was just a movie, but it encapsulated the things her life lacked: Excitement, exotic locations, and sophisticated men. As she walked back into the mall, she felt the glamour drain from her. Why couldn't she meet a man like that, who could take her to spectacular places? Why couldn't she live in a beach house, sip cocktails on private jets, make love in huge silk-sheeted beds in a white house on a Greek island with the blue Mediterranean outside the window?

Yes, she lived in a house larger than most on a parcel of land larger than most, but with a tyrant of a father and a shared bedroom.

The world was changing. A woman could do things she never used to be able to. But she still needed a man. Why date these deadbeats from Topanga and Woodland Hills when she could be going out with powerful men, moneyed men?

Annoyed, Sundown strolled though The Broadway, absently checking out the women's purses. Muzak played a syrupy version of "California Dreamin'." An older man was there, examining each bag with a baffled concentration she found amusing.

He looked at her. "My niece is fourteen," he said. "D'you think she'd like this one?"

Sundown wondered if this was a pickup line. If so, it was rather an elaborate one. She pointed to a stewardess-style bag with bold op-art pattern. "That one."

"Yeah? OK." He smiled at her.

She gave him the once-over. He was smartly dressed, well fed, like an executive of some kind.

"Are you a model?" he asked her, as he paid for the purse.

Now this was definitely a line. "As a matter of fact, I am."

"Wow. Don't know if I've ever met a model before." He held out his hand. "Frank Westerby. Architect." One of his eyebrows rose, as if waiting for recognition of his name.

It meant nothing to her. "Sundown Sobieski." She turned to leave.

"Wait. All this shopping has made me hungry. Where's a good place to eat here?"

She nodded toward the May Company. "There's a restaurant called the Terrace on the top floor."

"Ah, good. Let me buy you lunch for helping me."

"No, I—"

"Please. I hate eating alone. I always feel as if everyone's looking at me."

She laughed and acquiesced.

— · —

Sundown ordered a club sandwich, and when it arrived regretted the extra slice of bread and had to dismantle the sandwich to extract it.

Frank watched her with amusement. "Counting calories?"

"Models have to."

He patted his stomach, which was not huge, but not exactly flat either. "I should start that." He looked out the windows. "Interesting place."

"A scene in *Divorce American Style* was shot here last year. Debbie Reynolds was shopping where we were. You don't live around here?"

"No. San Marino."

Sundown blinked in surprise. San Marino was across town at the foothills of the San Gabriels, old money and one of the richest cities per capita in the U.S. "Then why on earth are you shopping here and not over there, in Pasadena or something?"

"Business meeting. I'm working on a new building just to the east of the plaza. You like it here in ... what is this? Woodland Hills?"

Sundown pointed toward the smog-tinted hills. "I live up in Topanga."

"Topanga. What an exotic name. What's it like?"

"It's like a chunk of goddamn West Texas in L.A."

He blinked. "I see. Where—?"

"There's a city down the road called *Tarzana*, for God's sake, after Tarzan of the Apes."

"That is a bit odd. Where would you rather be?"

She smiled. "Monte Carlo."

Frank laughed. "Wouldn't we all."

She liked his laugh, and liked the way his face looked when it was laughing. He reminded her of Robert Vaughn from *The Man from UNCLE*. She looked down at his left hand. "So you're married."

He grimaced. "For a little while longer. We're separated."

"I see."

— · —

Robbie retrieved the mail and handed Charity a tan envelope.

When she ripped it excitedly open, she found a hand-written response from Monkees management, on Brendan Cahill—David Pearl letterhead, showing high-contrast images of Davy, Michael and Micky. Peter was missing.

> *Dear Charity,*
>
> *Thanks a bunch for your letter. I was in Topanga once—it's a cool place, and you're lucky to live there.*
>
> *The boys in the band appreciate your wishes to bring back the show, but there comes a time when everyone has to move on, and we came to that point. But there's a movie out soon, and maybe a TV special or two. Keep in touch, and who knows what might happen in the future?*
>
> *Love & Peace,*
>
> *David Jones*

Hand-written! Davy had written this himself! She held the paper to her nose and inhaled, trying to extract some part of his essence. All she smelled was printing ink.

Excited and inspired, Charity clutched the letter, grabbed her journal and pen, and walked outside. She ran to the tree house, climbed inside, and after thinking for a moment began to write.

> *Raccoons come out at dusk and operate during the night to investigate trashcans with their little paws. Their prints, when seen in mud, look like miniature human hands. Most animals here are nocturnal, in fact, no doubt finding it easier to hunt without people everywhere to chase them, shoot them, or run them over.*
>
> *Skunks patrol with an arrogance that comes from having one of the mightiest defenses of any small animal—an ability to deliver an almost otherworldly stink. A stench that can easily blanket four square miles, and at its center completely overload the human sense of smell.*

— · —

Jackson got out of his friend's car, shouldered his kitbag and walked to the house.

Compared with Basic Training, with its orderly cots, neat uniforms, and rigorous discipline, the inside of Hophead Hills looked to Jackson like some kind of freak show. Messy, disordered, with rock and folk music playing from morning till night.

Maddy noticed him first. "Jacks! You're back! I didn't know!" She hugged him and looked up at his face, scanning it for change and possible injury. "Are you OK?"

"I'm fine, mom. What's new?"

Maddy turned back, briefly, to her family. "New?" She laughed. "Same as ever."

Bret clasped his son's shoulder. "Great to have you back, Jacks. How long are you here for?"

"Just a few days, dad."

"And what's it like?"

"Pretty brutal. But OK, I guess."

— · —

For the family members, Jackson's return from Basic was anticlimactic. He was surly, antisocial and jingoistic, and seemed to just work on his car and smoke too much. To Maddy's surprise, he rearranged his room until it was unrecognizably neat. Too neat, she felt.

But he was rarely home. He and Duke hung out together, comparing notes and speaking in the new jargon they had been learning. They were already soldiers in their minds, merely on leave from the front, though they had yet to be sent there.

For his part, Jackson was uncomfortable at home. He had been successfully indoctrinated into the all-male barracks environment, polarized into its hypermasculinity, and now experienced difficulty remembering how to deal with females. Besides, he was in a brief limbo before being assigned overseas, and he knew he would shortly be wrenched out of Hophead Hills' chaotic milieu. Relaxing now would not only unravel his training, but also make him more vulnerable when in country. His soldier's psychic armor was too new to be breached.

— · —

Outside, a flatbed truck bearing a green and yellow John Deere riding mower backed awkwardly into the house driveway. The winter's rains and the first hot days of spring had triggered a growth spurt in the chamise, deerweed, sugar sumac, and buckwheat. The county had ordered the property's brush cleared by midsummer to avoid potential fire risk, and Bret, about to leave, had instructed Jackson to take care of it.

Robbie watched his older brother sign off on the tractor and briefly discuss its operation with the driver. He was eager for a chance to ride it, and once the truck had left he approached shyly. "Hey, Jacks."

"Hey, Robbie."

The two rarely talked these days, with little in common to discuss. They had shared the usual sibling rivalries, fights, trespassings, and short but memorable periods of hilarity and injury. But not recently. The split in America was now represented in miniature in their relationship, though neither saw it that way. Jackson thought that Robbie was squandering his life and intellect on weed and rock 'n' roll trivia, while Robbie thought Jackson was irredeemably straight and wasting his time in service of a lost cause.

But Jackson was leaving soon, and Robbie felt he should say something about it. Something that showed how important he was as an older brother, how his younger brother looked up to him. The trouble was, his vocabulary was not up to the task.

"Uh ... spare a Camel?"

"Mom and dad don't like you smoking, but OK." Jackson handed him the pack and his Zippo.

Robbie winced as he drew on the cigarette. He preferred filters, especially first thing in the morning. But he thought it made him look cool, and older than he was. "So ... can I have a ride on that thing?"

"In a minute. Let me get the hang of it first." Jackson turned on the ignition and the tractor chugged to life. He sat astride it and began to experiment with the simple controls.

Bret hurried out from the house, buttoning the bib of his Farmer Johns. "Here," he said, waving Jackson off, "I'll show you how to work it."

Jackson relinquished the seat with a glance at Robbie that said *what can you do?* The brothers watched as their father churned up and down on the tractor, tried reverse, performed tight circles. Finally, he dismounted with a superior smile. "There you go. Keep your hands away from the blades underneath, whatever you do. Watch out for rocks and stumps— we don't want to break the damn thing and lose our deposit. Try not to gouge any grass down to the dirt or star thistle'll take hold, and we'll never get rid of the stuff. And watch out for rattlers—they'll be pissed."

Then he swaggered back up to the house to pack.

"So..." Robbie began, walking alongside the tractor. "You really going over there?"

Jackson nodded. "'Nam? Looks like it."

"When?"

"Soon."

Robbie's words ran out. "Well, shit. It looks ... rough."

"Yeah, well, I'm a soldier."

Robbie's face puckered with anguish. He looked ten years old again, not sixteen. "But why? Why be a soldier?"

"It's just something I have to do, Robbie. You'll understand one day."

They took it in turns to mow the acre of meadow, chugging in long rows back and forth as the day became hotter. Every half hour they would switch, and during one changeover Charity brought them each a Coke from the house.

Jackson pulled out another Camel. "You smoking much weed?"

Robbie shrugged. "Everybody does these days."

"But you're getting your school work done, right?"

"Yeah. 'Course."

Jackson looked at him askance. "Robbie, I always thought you were a smart kid. The time for partying is when you're older, when you've got your high marks out of the way. In college ... well ... there'll be time for a bit of fun. Later."

Robbie looked away. "I do the stupid lessons."

Jackson nodded. "Good. Y'know ... all this hippie stuff ... it's just a fashion. I like rock too, but I love my country more. America's fighting for its way of life. One you take for granted. Russia, and now China—they want to ram their system down our throats. They're trying to take over our world."

"So what business is it of ours?"

"We're the only country strong enough to stand up to 'em."

Robbie fidgeted and looked longingly at the house. This was like the interview with the vice principal, for God's sake. "Yeah, well, it's all a crock."

Jackson stubbed out his cigarette underfoot. "No, Robbie, it's serious.

I don't want it to come between us. And I don't want you to throw your life away on hippie bullshit. All these demonstrations—they just prolong the war."

"Jacks—"

"The country's coming apart. Right when it needs to stand together." Jackson handed Robbie a rake. "Now we have to bag all this crap."

"Can't we have a bonfire?"

"Not allowed. Too dangerous."

The brothers raked the brush into piles and then helped each other stuff them into huge plastic lawn bags. It was dusty and prickly work.

Finally, after another hour, they stood beside a pyramid of bags.

Robbie had imagined, if he had thought about it at all, that he would have some profound parting with his older brother before he went off to war, some memorable bonding scene. Instead, Jackson leaned on his rake and fixed him with a piercing gaze.

"I heard you talking to that Limey at the party. You know communism's a crock, don't you?"

Robbie was taken aback. "I ... I thought it was an interesting concept."

Jackson laughed. "'Concept' is all it is. There isn't one place in the world it's working. If you gave communists a choice, which they certainly don't have, they'd all come here. Why is that? Because there's no freedom under communism. You have to do what the state says. He's just repeating Leftist bullshit he's heard somewhere. Stalin's as big a murderer as Hitler, and Mao's not much better. Don't you go falling for it, Robs."

Robbie reddened. The trouble with being a younger brother was that you were always reminded of it. He tried to salvage some self-respect out of the exchange, and said in a sarcastic tone, "So America's the only way, then?"

"Not the only way, maybe, but the best way we've found so far."

"Jacks," Robbie said, "You'll be OK, right?"

Jackson grinned. "I'm comin' back to kick your scrawny butt."

— · —

To celebrate Jackson's temporary homecoming after Basic, Maddy had spent all day making paella. Now it sat in the center of the dining table, colorful and fragrant, in a huge hand-painted dish. Chicken, chorizo, mussels and shrimp dotted with peas, onion and red pepper, surrounded by a sea of saffron-tinted rice and seasoned with some of their own bay. She knew in Spain they usually added rabbit to their paella too, but she couldn't face it. Hundreds of rabbits made their homes around Hophead Hills, and though they were pests they were a little too familiar to make into a meal.

Everyone eagerly dug in, and for once the family was too busy eating to talk. When they did, it was all about the food.

"You've outdone yourself this time, hon," Bret said. "This is even better than your lasagna, and that was great."

Maddy blushed, pleased. "Oh, it's just a little something I threw together."

Jackson piled his plate high. "I'm making the most of it. I'll be eating rations in future."

"Hey," Robbie reprimanded him, only half-joking, "save some for us."

Charity approached her meal tentatively, though Maddy had tried to persuade her that seafood wasn't really meat, but soon forgot her reservations.

Every now and then, each family member would sneak a glance at Jackson. He seemed like a stranger now, or at least partially so. He exuded a martial aura, a kind of bottled-up energy that seemed likely to burst out at any moment. His face had changed slightly over his weeks away: more defined, the muscles under the skin taut with endurance, the eyes jaded and guarded. His hair, of course, was painfully short, making him look like some other kind of creature than the rest of the Sobieskis.

"Gilligan seems excited you're back," Sundown said, waving her fork at the dog, who was leaping about in a manic fashion outside.

Maddy looked out the window. "He's going to miss you when you're … over there, Jacks."

"I'll take care of him for you," Charity said.

Gilligan scratched at the back door and barked.

"He smells the food," Charity said. "If I let him in, remember not to feed him at the table."

Sundown opened the door and the dog rushed by. Her face contorted in horror. "Oh Jesus!"

"Oh my God!" Charity said.

"*Get him out of here!*" Jackson yelled.

"I'm not touching him!" Maddy said, wiping her eyes.

Charity burst into tears.

"Christ alive!" Bret said, in horror. "He's been skunked!"

The smell was so overpowering that everyone, in desperation, rallied to eject Gilligan back out into the night, but by then the damage was done. The reek flooded the kitchen and spread throughout the entire house. Gilligan ran up and down outside, agitated. If a dog's sense of smell was so much better than theirs, he must have been in agony.

"Light some incense, someone!"

"What about the bathroom spray?"

"That too! Anything!"

"Open the windows!"

"No! That'll let the stink in!"

"What we gonna do?"

"Where's an all-night market?"

"Nearest is Woodland Hills."

"OK, Jacks," Bret said, "drive down and get a whole carton of tomato juice. At least a dozen big cans."

"Huh? Tomato juice?"

"We have to bathe the dog in it. Maddy—give him some money. *Go!*"

After Jackson had driven off into the dark, Maddy and Bret stood outside and looked at each other with pained expressions.

"Fuck!" Bret said. "You'd better get a motel room for the night. I'll bathe the bastard."

Maddy took one last, sad, look at her meal. "But my paella..."

— · —

When Sundown and Charity and Maddy returned next morning, Gilligan, now a startling deep red, was rolling about in the grass, still trying to deskunk himself. Opened cans of tomato sauce overflowed two trashcans. The house still smelled, but not nearly as much. Bret was in the bath, exhausted and asleep, surrounded by scented bubbles.

16

Bret was oblivious to Jackson's discomfort at the idea of a going-away party on his behalf. He loved parties—they provided him the platform he enjoyed, whereas Jackson, now that he knew where he was going and when, just wanted to get on with it without any more fuss.

Even Maddy was uncharacteristically insensitive. "We have to have a party, Jacks. Who knows … uh … when you'll be back?"

"We should get a band!" Bret decided. He looked expectantly at Maddy. "What about Sunday Joint?"

"No, I don't think—"

"Why not?"

"Because they're famous. They don't do parties. Would Canned Heat come?"

Bret reluctantly conceded defeat. "OK, OK. Maybe Neil Young'll show up this time."

"His wife closed down the café. Said it was too much work. I think her husband's on tour."

"Well … we could still get a local band, couldn't we?"

Maddy nodded. "I'll ask around."

"But we're going to do it differently this time." Bret turned to glare at his youngest son. "Not so wasted this time, Robs, all right? *Pace* yourself."

"Yeah, dad."

"And Sundown—don't just disappear with your latest boyfriend. Help your mom serve."

Sundown sighed. She was good at sighing, and it was usually her father that triggered one.

"Charity—you can help with the food. I thought we'd cook a whole pig this time."

Charity had been thinking about Jackson leaving for the war. It gave her a queasy feeling in the pit of her stomach. Up until now, Vietnam was just a word on the TV and radio, with no association that made it personally relevant. Now, her big brother was actually headed there. When her father's words filtered through her consciousness, she looked up in alarm, her eyes large and her face chalky. "What?"

"A whole pig. I may hire those Hawaiian guys down the road—they know how to do it much better than me."

"A ... pig? On a spit? Going round and round all night?"

Bret nodded with enthusiasm. "Yeah—you can help carve. It'll be spectacular."

Charity ran out, whimpering.

"What? What did I say?"

Maddy glared at him. "Bret—Charity's a *vegetarian*."

He shrugged with indifference. "Oh, that's just a phase. She'll come around. We all do."

"Honey, even if it is a phase—and I'm not sure it is, knowing Charity—we still have to respect her choice."

Ultimatums never worked with Bret. "We're having a pig."

— · —

This time Bret's apron read LIQUOR IN THE FRONT, POKER IN THE REAR, which Maddy had unsuccessfully tried to talk him out of wearing.

"It's funny," he had told her.

"It's crude," she had countered.

"Crude is funny."

The Limey, Owen, arrived with a 12-pack of imported English beer. "None o' your American cat piss," he announced cheerfully, angering Cueball and his biker friends, who maintained their allegiance to Budweiser.

"So if you're in a band," one of the guests said to him, "play us a song."

Owen exhaled a long and fragrant stream of smoke from a joint someone had passed him. "I don't have my guitar with me."

"You can use mine," Robbie told him.

"OK," Owen said, and while Robbie hurried to his bedroom he told his audience, "I'll play you a song I wrote recently. The recording company said they wanted more of a psychedelic feel to our stuff, since that's what's selling these days, and I wrote this one—'Did You Know I've Been To The End Of The Rainbow'—as a parody, to make fun of trippy songs. But they liked it, and it'll be on our next album."

Robbie returned, and handed him his cheap electric guitar. Owen quickly tuned it by ear, and jumped straight in. Its sound, without amplification, was trebly and insipid.

"Did you know, I've been to the end of the rainbow
And I'll explain what I found lying there—
Among the silver chestnut trees
And golden-plated bumblebees
Fanned by a lukewarm autumn breeze
I found the other half of me..."

"See?" he said when he had finished. "Dumb but catchy." He handed the guitar back to Robbie and rubbed his raw fingertips. "Bloody hell, that action's shit."

"So..." Robbie said, his eyes glowing with intensity, "should I get a Stratocaster or a Les Paul?"

Owen looked surprised. "They're pretty expensive, y'know. Are you sure—?"

"Yeah, yeah, no problem," Robbie assured him, envisioning future pot sales. "I have some money coming in. Which d'you think?"

"Well, they're very different guitars. Hendrix plays a Strat. It has a thicker, more rounded neck, and the neck's a little longer than the Les Paul. It's lighter to play, and it has single coil pickups, which give it a sharper, more pointed sound that cuts through the noise of the rest of the band."

Robbie's eyes unfocused as he imagined himself on stage, ripping though a solo, blowing everyone away. "And the Les Paul?"

"The Les Paul's pickups are humbuckers, which give it a rounder, warmer, bell-like tone, and more sustain. And it's the heavier of the two, so if you play a lot it can get tiring."

Robbie considered this, nodding solemnly. "I think I'm a Les Paul man."

— · —

The grass behind the house was scruffy. What little had escaped being undermined by gophers and seared by the summer sun had been killed off by Gilligan's urine. The band Maddy had hired, The Canyon Critters, showed up at seven and set up there—a pile of scuffed Marshall amps, a mismatched Premier drum kit, two microphones on stands, and a Vox Continental organ with cheerful red lid and its keys reversed—whites black, and blacks white.

Their sound echoed off the hills, and soon after they began the local kids wandered over and accumulated along the fence to listen. Several of the guests—mostly women—started dancing in front of the band, until this mass of movement overexcited Gilligan and Bret had to order Robbie to lock him in the garage.

— · —

A posse of the youngest children, ranging from five to ten, ran to and fro between the inside rooms and the yard, pausing to watch the band and then hurtling off again. Food disappeared in huge quantities as guests with the munchies descended on everything like locusts.

Charity had stayed away from the Hawaiian men who set up the roasting spit and fire, trying to ignore the sight of an entire pig, head and all, rotating and slowly browning, its fat dropping onto the coals and sizzling. She considered it barbaric and disgusting, all the more so because the smell made her mouth water in betrayal. But it was hard to avoid. Knowing how long it would take, the cooks had started in the early afternoon, and now they were slicing great slabs of steaming meat off its flanks and handing them out on paper plates.

Instead she stayed inside, where the party was well underway, the air blue with smoke from various sources. Cueball was discussing something intently with Rain, and Charity sidled closer to listen.

Rain was saying, "Karma is like a kind of cosmic scorecard, where you rack up points."

The biker frowned. "How's that?"

"You do bad stuff; then bad stuff happens to you. You do good; good stuff happens."

"Well, that's the same as Judeo-Christian belief, then, right?" he said.

"Do as you would be done by. Golden rule."

"Well, yes, except..."

"'Cept what?"

"With Christianity, the payoff is in heaven or hell. With Buddhism, the payoff is here and now. And there's something else..."

"What?'

"With karma, you could be paying for something you did in a previous life. It stretches across generations, you see."

"Jeez, that's rough. How far back does it go?"

"I don't think there's a statute of limitations."

"So if I come off my hog it could be because I stole a fuckin'—oh, s'cuse me—tomato in the Middle Ages? That sucks, man."

"But you can balance it out by doing good."

"What—bein' nice to old ladies? Well shit, man, I'd better get started."

— · —

The Critters were a cover band. Their singer introduced every song, even though they were familiar to just about everyone in earshot. Nobody cared what he had to say, but it quickly became clear that he thought he was witty, but wasn't. The drummer—two bass drums were *de rigueur* these days, like Ginger Baker—was too loud, and the organ had a tone like a bee in a bottle. The rhythm guitarist was solid, but the lead guitarist's solos tended to wander off into foreign keys and have trouble finding their way back.

Bret, uncomfortable at being eclipsed at his own party, tried to laugh off the band's eccentricities. At the musicians' first break he asked the drummer if he could take a turn at his kit. To his great irritation, since he was the one paying the piper and thought it gave him rights, the drummer refused.

The band members headed for the refreshments, and Bret cranked up "Sunshine Of Your Love" on the turntable.

When the band reassembled after the break, the bassist was missing. The singer switched on his mic. *"Jeff? Anyone seen Jeff?"*

Charity thought she had seen him heading down toward the creek, and so to be helpful she ran down to tell him he was needed. When she got there she heard a rustling behind the trees, and when she investigated she saw the bassist and one of the female guests half naked, making love in the grass, his hairy buttocks jerking up and down. Shocked, she hurried back and considered telling the band, or her father, or both. In the end she told no one, and tried hard to purge the image from her mind.

During the break the drummer, who apparently subscribed to the Keith Moon style of partying, had imbibed three tequilas and a beer, then took a long hit at a bong. By the time they started again he was incapable of performing his role. His timing was off, and during one song he took a swipe at the sizzle cymbal, missed and fell off his stool. Bret, still stung from the earlier rebuff, stormed over and berated him for some time before, chastened, the man climbed back up and resumed.

— · —

Sundown attended without male accompaniment, for once. She was sick of men, and fended off several advances during the evening, including persistent attempts by her father's best boy Doug, who was running around, she decided, like a dog with two pricks. Life was better without a boyfriend, she tried to tell herself. To depend on men was a sign of weakness. Her mother was right—they were only interested in one thing.

Lucas, the artist friend of her father's who lived up-canyon, showed up in his usual Beat era garb of goatee and a black turtleneck. He came up beside Sundown on the deck. "Hey," he said, raising his voice to get over the racket of the band, "remember me?"

"Sure," she told him. "The sculptor. How did you do at the Festival?"

He shrugged. "Money. It just gets in the way, y'know?"

"Not so well, huh?"

"Kinda. So—your brother's going over there?"

"Yeah. I wish he wouldn't."

"So what happened? He get drafted?"

"No. Worse. He *wants* to go."

Lucas shook his head. "Crazy."

They watched and listened as the Canyon Critters massacred "Hello, I Love You," though the singer did a fair impersonation of Jim Morrison about to keel over.

"So," Sundown said, "what are you working on?"

"I'm doing some portraits. I heard you're a model now. How 'bout posin' for me one day?"

"Portraits."

"Yeah."

"Faces."

"Yeah."

"Maybe."

— · —

J.J. was talking to Cueball and Bonnie. "I'm at the Sands in Vegas," he said, "and in the lobby I see Dean Martin waiting for an elevator..."

— · —

"Here—" Tess said, eyeing Owen from beneath her bangs, "I'll give you a reading."

"What—tarot?"

"No, Maddy does that. I do astrology. What's your sign?"

"Gemini."

"Thought so." Tess took a blank birth chart and small ephemera out of her big tooled-leather purse, and uncapped a pen. "When were you born?"

"December 12, forty-seven."

"And where?"

"London, England."

Tess consulted the ephemera. "Ooh! You were born on the zero-degree longitude line! I've never seen that before."

"Well, yeah—the Greenwich Meridian and all that."

She started to fill in the spaces of the form while toking on a joint someone had handed her. "Time?"

"Four in the morning. Just to be difficult."

Tess scribbled some more, until the circle on the chart was crisscrossed with lines. Then she sat back, regarding the results. "So, you're a Gemini of course, with Sagittarius rising. That means you're artistic, mercurial, with a tendency toward inconstancy."

"Incontinence?"

She giggled. "Inconstancy. Flighty in love."

"Flighty, eh? Feel like a flight?"

Tess giggled some more. She was about to reply in the affirmative when, to her dismay, Robbie inserted himself into their group.

"So," the boy asked, "what's it like being in a band?"

[178]

Owen pulled a wry expression. "A bit like being married to four or five people. We've been on tour for seven months, living in each other's laps. Gets old really fast. Every little thing that pisses you off about someone, something that wouldn't normally bother you because you wouldn't see 'em that often, gets blown up out of all proportion. In the end you explode; have a punch-up about it. Then it's all over for a while."

Robbie considered this, slack-jawed, imagining fistfights on a tour bus, backstage, at rehearsals.

"So..." Tess persisted, trying to ignore Robbie, "are you the leader of the group?"

"Nah, not really. Just 'cos I'm the singer and lead guitarist people assume I am, and the journalists like to have a central figure to write about, but it's not my band. We started it together, in school."

This, too, excited Robbie. The thought that you could become famous from starting in a high school band. "So—"

"But you write the songs," Tess persisted.

"Most of 'em, yes. Royalty checks twice a year."

Oblivious of Tess's interest, Robbie continued, "It must be great, being on tour, playing different places..."

Tess got up and wandered off in a huff.

"We've only had ten days off in the last year. My girlfriend's buggered off with some other bloke, my friends have forgotten who I am, and when I get home they're jealous anyway. It's not that glamorous. Performing's a kick, at least some of the time," Owen continued, warming to the subject. "Venues are a bit scuzzy, and promoters disappear with your money half the fuckin' time, but it's a blast getting that feedback from the audience. Best high of all, apart from sex. Oh—" he looked around guiltily, "don't tell your parents I said that."

Robbie thought Owen was downplaying band life in order to talk him out of it. If these were the problems of a rock star, he would happily settle for them.

"Well, what about recording? What's that like?"

"I dig recording. It's more creative than performing, because you can mess with it; doesn't matter if you make a mistake. You can overdub, get a denser sound. And if you can't think of a good ending, you just fade it out. Besides, the gear here is much better than the pokey stuff in England— eight-track, not four. Very sophisticated."

I'll be doing that soon, Robbie thought. Eight tracks. I could harmonize with myself. "So ... what do people get high on in England?"

"Well, grass, of course, but you can't grow it there. Hash comes in from the Middle East and North Africa—green and powdery, or dark brown like chocolate. We—the band—like a combo of grass and mandies."

"Mandies?"

"Mandrax pills. I think they're called something different here. Downers, kinda, but not too much of a blitz; mellow. It's a high you can sustain without conkin' out." Owen looked at his watch and stood. "Well, gotta go. Zappa's havin' a party. He doesn't like drugs, so I'll roll one for the drive. Which way's Laurel Canyon?"

Robbie drew him a map on the back of Tess' chart. He wanted to ask if he could go too, but didn't want to risk the inevitable rejection. One day *he* would be the one throwing the party in Laurel Canyon.

— · —

Shirley was there, uncomfortable at the thought of her boyfriend going to war. Being with a soldier awarded her a certain cachet, but she was unused to her role and unsure how to act. She hung around Jackson, smiling at anyone that talked to him, but contributing little to the conversations.

She and Jackson had never talked about their future together, and his leaving without any firm plans was starting to make her feel abandoned. But she assumed that when he got back, his tour of duty completed, they would marry and start a family.

Jackson had been enjoying the party and the band until they played the Country Joe and the Fish song, "I Feel Like I'm Fixin' To Die Rag," and people started to look at him to gauge his reaction. He sought out his father.

"Dad—didn't you tell the band what this party's about?"

Bret, fairly drunk now, was even more garrulous than usual. He had the politician's trick of placing his pauses mid-sentence, and then running his sentences together without pause between, leaving no room for anyone to interject. He had been regaling his immediate audience with a story about how Robert Redford had screen-tested for the part of Benjamin in last year's *The Graduate*. "So the director—Nichols—can't see Redford as playing an underdog, but Redford disagrees. Nichols asks him, 'Have you ever struck out with a girl?' Redford says, 'What do you mean?' Nichols nods and says, 'That's precisely my point.'"

"Dad," Jackson interrupted, "they're playing an anti-war song."

Bret made a dismissive gesture. "Oh, it's just part of every band's song list these days. They don't mean anything by it."

"Well, I don't appreciate it. Tell 'em to shut the hell up."

Bret stared at Jackson. "I'm not gonna stop 'em in the middle of a song, Jacks. It's almost over. Cool it."

— · —

The Critters took a second break at around nine-thirty. Robbie, who was so high by now he occasionally lost track of whose party he was attending, took the opportunity to ask one of the guitarists to let him stand in.

"No, kid. Sorry. We don't do that."

Robbie had been harboring fantasies of astounding the crowd with his unsuspected talents. To be called a "kid" began to filter through his foggy awareness as a put-down. "Why?"

"We just don't. Bands don't like that."

— · —

Rain came up to Charity when she was outside listening to one of the band's long and rambling solos. The lead guitarist was lying on his back, playing with his eyes closed. She sat and looked up at the sky. "Trippy, huh?"

Charity eyed Rain nervously, unsure what she meant. "Uh, yeah."

"You know what's strange about reality? It doesn't really exist. All this..." Rain waved an arm above her head, "is just what we all agree it is. See?"

"No."

Rain nodded, unperturbed. "No, of course not. It's a weird concept. What I mean is, we all here, tonight, decide it's a party. And so it's a party. But if we decided it was a bare mountaintop in the snow—if all of us agreed to imagine it—then it would be a snowy mountaintop."

Charity thought about this. It had never occurred to her that reality was so flimsy that it could be changed by group consensus.

"I see you don't buy it, and I don't blame you. But it's true. Nothing exists without us believing it does. And that," she looked at Charity intently, "is why changing people's consciousness is so important. If we can imagine world peace, we can have it. But we have to imagine it first, we *all* have to imagine it, and then it can happen. Trouble is, all we see on TV is murders and war, and so that reinforces the opposite. Our shared reality is negative, see?"

"But we need it to be positive."

Rain's eyes, even in the dark, lit up. "Right on! You get it. See, kids are in tune with it. Adults lose the ability to understand what it's all about." She looked back up at the dim stars. "All those billions of stars. Some of them must have planets like ours. And some of those planets must have life, like here on Earth. I think they're looking down on us, waiting for us to grow up."

When Rain drifted away Charity remained, still gazing up at the sky.

— · —

Maddy saw Doug and one of Bret's grips giggling to themselves in the corner. "What are you two up to?" she asked them suspiciously.

They looked at each other, and Doug shrugged and said, "We put acid in Lucas' beer."

"Oh, no. You didn't."

"He'll be OK. He was goin' on and on about religion. Now he'll get to see God for himself."

Maddy lost her temper, but there was nothing she could do about the situation now, apart from keep an eye on Lucas. "How long ago?" she asked.

Doug grinned. "Oh, 'bout fifteen minutes."

So in about half an hour Lucas could be expected to start acting strangely.

Sure enough, next time she looked, Lucas seemed inordinately interested in the pattern of the rug at his feet. Everyone ignored him. Soon he was lying back on a beanbag with his mouth open, staring at the ceiling fan.

— · —

By ten The Canyon Critters' performance had disintegrated into rambling songs that didn't so much end as peter out in unintended syncopation. Sundown found them an embarrassment, far worse than the bands she'd been seeing on Sunset during the year. But most of the guests were out of it by now, and no one else seemed to care.

She was bored. She had no boyfriend, no one here that she found interesting. Her thoughts kept returning to Frank, the architect. But he was married. Even so, if he called she thought she would probably see him one more time, just to see what happened. Just for closure's sake.

— · —

Charity found Jackson looking through the album covers, Shirley hanging onto his elbow. "You know Rain?" she asked him.

"The song or the shaman woman?"

"The woman. Who exactly *is* she?"

"I heard she was a doctor in Boston and someone died under her care. So she retired and came out here."

Bret, passing, overheard. "I heard she was a Blackfoot who went back east and got a PhD."

Tess said, "Some say she murdered her husband and is hiding out here."

Maddy said, "Why doesn't someone just ask—?"

Blue lights flashed around the deck as three black and whites swerved melodramatically into the driveway, as if in an episode of *Hawaii Five-O*. The effect on the guests was immediate. The band's song dribbled out, leaving the drummer hammering on for a few bars until he belatedly became aware what was going on. Several people stumbled off into the dark, and both toilets busily flushed away illegal substances.

Officers with flashlights the size of billy clubs walked warily toward the house.

"Who's the owner here?" one asked.

Bret stood in the door and hooked his thumbs in his belt. "I am."

"We're responding to complaints of noise. You need to shut this down."

Most people, confronted by eight armed policemen, would have backed off, but Bret immediately became belligerent. "We're not bothering anyone."

The cop's eyes narrowed. "Well, *sir,* apparently you are, judging by the calls we've been getting from your neighbors."

"I'm a taxpayer like everyone else. This is harassment."

"No, sir, after ten this is disturbing the peace. You need to stop the music now."

"Or what?"

"Or we'll have to take you in." The policeman hooked his thumbs in his belt too, and waited for Bret's decision.

Maddy had appeared at Bret's side by this time, and grasped her husband's arm with a painfully tight grip. This penetrated Bret's fuzzy brain, and he nodded. "I'll tell 'em."

— · —

Despite the band unplugging and loading their gear, and their insensate drummer, into a van, the party showed no sign of stopping.

Charity had grown bored with the adults' antics, and made her way to the bedroom she shared with her sister to try to sleep. The beds were piled high with guests' jackets and purses, and one bed—hers—was moving. Underneath the heaving mound were two people, by the look of them naked. The woman was gasping, "You ... filthy ... little ... *bastard!*"

Charity turned around and returned to the party, where she ran into Lucas, now looking very strange.

"I had this vision, man," he told her, gripping her small shoulder and staring into and past her with alarmingly soulless eyes, "It's like all the stale doughnuts of the world are collected an' fired ... like, by a Roman catapult or something ... an' the animals have all 'scaped from the zoo an' chargin' through Griffith Park in a long conga line, man. Till the ground under their feet turns into Cream o' Wheat. There's, like, rays comin' outta the sun that pull everyone around like puppet strings, but we can't see 'em. But they're there anyway, an' if you start talkin' about them you get, like, *disappeared* somewhere, to some big warehouse in the desert full of people who know the *truth*, man..."

Maddy steered her away. "Just because someone's talking to you, hon, doesn't mean you have to stand there and listen. Especially not Lucas when he's wiggy."

"But—"

"He'll be OK tomorrow."

When Maddy looked around, Lucas had gone. She found him in the kitchen, building a Stonehenge out of her Rice Krispy treats. "Come on, Lucas," she said. "I have a couch for you."

— · —

Robbie gazed enviously at Doug, who was seated on the rug, looking down and shaking his head, while a good-looking woman gave him a neck rub. He always seemed to get the girls.

"It feels like I've lost brothers," he was mumbling. "First Martin Luther King, and now Robert Kennedy. I can't deal with it all."

"There, there," she stooped to kiss him. "We're all upset. It'll be OK."

He turned and grasped her hand. "Why don't we—?"

A shape swooped by Robbie and stopped in front of Doug. It was his mother.

"Brothers, huh?" Maddy asked him, hands on hips. "I distinctly remember you saying MLK was a pompous hypocrite. And last time you were here you called the Kennedys 'Papists and rapists'."

With a look of betrayal at Doug, the girl extricated herself and backed away. Doug glared up at Maddy but had no response. She glanced back at Robbie with a "don't-fall-for-that-shit" expression, and flounced outside.

— · —

Once the police, the band, and most of the guests had left, Maddy was left with the cleanup. Someone had apparently thrown up in Gilligan's bowl, and Gilligan was still locked in the garage. Bret was mumbling to himself in the papasan chair on the deck. Three people were wedged onto one beanbag, asleep. Someone was singing off-key in the driveway. Lucas was on a couch, playing with his shirt buttons.

Maddy sighed. Parties were too much work.

— · —

Jackson, the only one who hadn't mixed grass with booze, was the first up next morning. The house looked like a war zone as he stumbled to the refrigerator for orange juice—empty bottles and cans everywhere, overflowing and reeking ashtrays, bits of food and ham bones on paper plates being attended to by tiny freeways of ants, and a few guests passed out on sofas, armchairs, and floor. The sun, well up in the sky, was illuminating it all with a callous and sordid clarity.

He sat and regarded the house interior for a minute, grateful that the unappealing vista made it easier for him to leave. Then he got up to find an aspirin. By the time he returned to the living room, he was surprised to see his father sitting in his robe. He looked comical, his eyes bleary and jowls patchy with stubble. His hair stood up all over his head, showing receding patches at his temples and a thinning spot at the crown.

"Hey, dad."

"Hey, Jacks. Quite a scene, huh?"

Jackson nodded, immediately regretting it. "Ouch. Yeah."

The house was silent for a moment.

"Jacks, how 'bout we take you to the airport again?"

"No, dad. Once was enough. I just want to go by myself."

"But the family wants to see you off."

"They did. Last night."

Bret considered this. "OK. When you going?"

"Soon. Duke's driving me down."

— · —

When Duke arrived, Sundown and Robbie had contrived to be elsewhere. Maddy and Bret hugged Jackson and wished him luck, and he hugged them stiffly back. Charity watched from the tower window, crying. She didn't care if there were no God; she sat and prayed to Him anyway.

17

Robbie clutched his cheap Teisco guitar and practiced his Pete Townshend windmilling arm swing in front of the mirror, throwing his head back but still keeping on eye on his reflection. If only his hair were longer. If only his sideburns would grow. Could you get sideburn wigs? He'd have to ask his father—he must know the makeup people.

Down Beat magazine had an ad for Les Paul Standards. They only came in gold, apparently, and they sold for $395. That was a hell of a lot of money. He'd have to sell a lot of dope to save that. Maybe he'd better get a part-time job.

Perhaps his band should be called something with "psychedelic" in the name. Psychedelic Psychos. Psychedelic Saints. Psychedelic... No—what was that phrase Owen had used? *Blue Language.* Yes.

He put down his guitar and ran out to the kitchen.

"Mom!" he said, excited. "I need outfits for my band, Blue Language. I was thinking black and bright blue. Blue looks really good on color TV."

Maddy stopped mixing dough and looked up. "Robs ... you don't have a band."

"I will soon! I've got it all figured out."

"Maybe you should practice—"

"I practice all the time, ma. Now I'm gonna get the rest of the guys together. Maybe a chick singer too."

"Please don't call women 'chicks.' It's degrading."

"It's just slang, ma. Anyway, the guys'll alternate black pants/blue shirt, or blue pants/black shirt. Only *I'll* be in all blue."

"Robbie, I'll be happy to help once you've got the band together and I can get all their sizes."

"You don't believe in me!"

"Of course I do. You're a talented kid—"

"Kid?"

"Guy. Bring the others here—and the girl—and I'll take their measurements."

Robbie stormed off.

— · —

Jackson had assumed he had arrived in Saigon during a rainstorm, but when it was not only still raining when he reached the central highlands but worse, it became clear it was monsoon season. Growing up as he had in the dry southwestern U.S., Jackson had never seen this much rain. It was hard for him to conceive that mere vapor could produce this much liquid. It bucketed down from endless banks of low cloud, limiting visibility to at most a quarter mile.

The C-130 Hercules landed in Pleiku, and as Jackson stepped off he looked around admiringly at the air-conditioned buildings, neat lawns and huge Base Exchange. But instead of being allowed to dry off, get a meal and stock up on necessities, he was pointed to a bus with windows covered by wire grille. When he took a seat, the man next to him stuck out his hand.

"Willie Wyckoff, Henderson, Nevada."

"Jackson Sobieski, L.A."

"Well," Willie said philosophically, as they drove off into the rain, "They're bound to call me Whack-off, and you ... you'll be Sobi, or Ski, I guess. 'Less you do something weird and get yourself another nickname."

As the bus splashed away from the town, Jackson gazed out at the tiny huts with tin roofs and cardboard walls, the sour-smelling rice paddies, the plodding water buffalo. These people were the poorest he had ever seen, small and concave-chested, often shoeless and hatless, some with teeth blackened by betel nut. Many stood beside the road in the rain, begging. Their army driver threw trash at them.

Camp Holloway was six miles east of Pleiku, a huge treeless base consisting of rundown buildings on what looked like Georgia clay, now a dull red pond as far as the eye could see. Its parking area was on a slope, and as they juddered to a halt Jackson watched a jeep pull up alongside. One of its passengers jumped out and threw a sandbag under a front wheel to halt the vehicle's slide down the hill.

"God—what's that smell?"

Willie laughed. "Shit burning. They use jet fuel."

"Why?"

Willie shrugged. "No sewers. A lot o' men. What you gonna do?"

No one seemed to have been assigned to introduce him to anyone or explain anything, so he was forced to ask often-inane questions of old-timers who wanted little to do with one of what they labeled as the Fucking New Guys. He eventually managed to find out that during what he thought of as winter it was dry and hot, a bowl of dust that the helicopter rotors fanned into choking pink clouds that rose to a height of thirty feet. But at this time of year—a swamp. And he and the other mechanics were the Swamp Rats.

Holloway's runways were pierced steel plank, and between them sandbag revetments helped protect the helicopters—the largest collection in Vietnam, he had heard—from attack.

Several helicopter companies were based here, most using the Hueys he would be working on—some for troop transport, the Slicks, and some modified with rockets and machine guns, referred to here as Hogs. These were marked on the noses with "Gator" and "Croc" badges. Little Loach observation helicopters were lined up too, ready to find and mark the bad guys. The term "bad guys" seemed to be used un-ironically to refer to the North Vietnamese Army regulars and the Viet Cong.

In one area were the new and strikingly aggressive-looking Cobra gunships, the Snakes, which were essentially flying rocket and gun platforms, carrying nothing apart from as much ammunition as they could hold, since they burned through it all quickly. In a far corner were the large and relatively slow helicopters that hauled the big loads, the tandem rotor Chinooks and the skeletal Skycranes, which looked to him as if most of them was missing.

There were also three types of small, fixed-wing aircraft: Broncos, with their twin tail booms joined with horizontal stabilizer, and Mohawks, with their triple tail, both used to scout and mark bad guys' positions with their smoke rockets. Fragile-looking Cessna Bird Dogs were ready to observe, direct artillery and zero in the Snakes.

Jackson's hooch was a Quonset hut with about twenty other mechanics, filled with standard bunk beds like one big foul-smelling and leaky dorm. When Jackson asked about air conditioning, everyone laughed uproariously.

His bunkmate turned out to be Willie. Wyckoff was a mystery man, at once equally new to Holloway but experienced in Vietnam in general, so Jackson surmised he had been transferred from elsewhere, possibly demoted for bad behavior. Their beds had mosquito nets, and Willie warned him to learn to sleep without elbows or knees touching the netting, or the opportunistic bloodsuckers would immediately find them.

Hooches had Vietnamese maids who were paid to make the beds, do the laundry, polish boots and keep the place clean. They spoke only a limited set of interchangeable English phrases, and were made fun of by most of the men. Jackson and Willie's hoochmaid was Mai Dinh.

Electricity was provided by massive diesel generators, which to save fuel ran only in the morning and evening. Jackson was warned that if he returned late the latrines would not function, and so between midnight and dawn the toilets could get ugly.

The rain drove the rats inside.

One of the older mechanics explained that in '65 there had been an attack serious enough to be written up in *Life* magazine, and he showed them a tattered copy. Their protection had been improved since, he told them, but despite this Holloway was usually still hit three or four times a week. These were always at night, and the mechanics were supposed to run out to the bunker beside the hooch. The bunker's walls and ceiling were piled with sandbags, which protected against mortar shrapnel. Nothing, he explained blithely, protected against the rockets.

— · —

The bell of Community Church rang faintly from Old Topanga Road.

Jackson was gone and the family awaited word from him. Sundown was sleeping off a late night. Charity was at a sleepover at Cindy's in Pacific Palisades. Robbie was visiting his surfer friends. The bikers, judging by the distant rumbling, were beginning their weekend ride to the Rock Shop on Mulholland.

Maddy and Bret sat drinking espresso and smoking his Marlboros as they shared sections of the fat *Sunday Times.*

Maddy pointed to an article. "This says LSD use is on the rise."

"Not surprised," Bret grunted. "People are sick of this reality."

"Did you ever drop acid?"

"No."

"Want to try?"

Bret put down his Sports section and frowned. "You have some?"

"Yes. Owsley."

"Wha—where did you get it?"

"The Limey. Owen. At the party."

He considered this. "Do you trust him?"

"He took it. Said it was smooth, not harsh." When her husband didn't answer, she added, "We talked about doing it one day."

"I know, but..."

"Nothing going on today. No commitments. Kids are gone. Your shoot doesn't start for a week, right? "

Bret shuffled the newspaper together carefully. "I guess. Shouldn't we take it with someone with experience? Just in case?"

"Just in case what?" Maddy asked him. "We're in our own house. Sundown's here if we get off the wall."

Bret nodded. "What the hell." He slapped the paper. "I've had enough of this reality too."

Maddy stood, went to her purse and retrieved a tin of mints containing two microdots. She handed him one. "Put it under your tongue."

He hesitated a moment and then did as she said. Then he looked at her. His eyes showed a flicker of fear. "Now what?"

"We wait. He says it takes a while to come on—forty minutes, maybe."

He looked around. "Let's get the breakfast stuff put away. I'm sure we won't feel like it later."

They pottered around the kitchen, wiping up the morning's mess—bags of granola from the local health food store, a few dried apricots, a mason jar half full of almonds, a carton of Cap'n Crunch cereal, a *TV Guide*, and a half-empty baggie of weed with Rizla rolling papers.

Once everything was put away, they sat and stared out the window.

Maddy asked, "Feel anything, hon?"

"I don't think so. Things look brighter, maybe."

She joined him at the window. "What are all those birds doing on the ground?"

"Looking for seeds, I suppose. Too dry for worms."

"They're so ... beautiful."

Bret frowned. "They're just crows."

"Still, like in those Castaneda books—they're supposed to be magical, right?"

"Look at the way the sun hits those hills. It's all golden. Like El Dorado."

Maddy gazed into the distance. "Wow. There's no air in here—let's go outside." She grabbed Bret's hand and they jumped at the electricity when they touched. At an experimental kiss their eyes widened. "I feel funny."

"Me too." Bret struggled to slide open the doors. They seemed heavier than normal. But soon they were standing on the back deck. He looked down and became fascinated with his feet in their sandals. They seemed to belong to someone else, yet at the same time familiar.

Maddy shaded her eyes and began to walk toward the tree house. Its blue paint shone with such an astonishing *blueness*. And all the trees—they were so alive to every nuance of breeze. She was just a transient being compared to their calm longevity. She must look like a flicker to them, with their elongated sense of time. She turned to explain this observation to Bret but he was miles away, staring at something on the ground. No words came to her lips.

Bret felt intimidated by the enormous complexity of the world around him. Why, every step he took crushed hundreds of blades of grass, dozens of insects. There was an entire universe at his feet, going about its business, indifferent to the big clumsy beast that was stomping over it. What details humans missed every waking minute. He felt like a baby again, overwhelmed by his surroundings, his senses as yet unfiltered, every input staggeringly strong.

Maddy felt drawn to the tree house, though walking was not as straightforward as it once was. She was momentarily concerned that she might lose her husband on the way, but the breeze was so inviting, and it carried some enticing scent. A bee approached, a single bee, and she turned to watch it as its sound grew louder and it passed, on some important apian errand no doubt, and dwindled into the distance. She felt part of its world and yet an intruder.

The ramshackle blue box atop the two trees had a clumsy affability about it, as if it were alive in its own right, a nexus of the family's energies. It had the unnatural square corners of something made by humans, and the contrast between it and the free-form nature of the trees was striking.

At the foot of the ladder she considered climbing up to the tree house and shuddered. She much preferred solid ground, and besides, she was unsure of her new sense of balance. The two pepper trees and their lacy leaves fluttered in the slight breeze like enormous ferns, their bunches of pink berries rustling drily. Their trunks were knarled and lumpy, like some kind of Disney cartoon, and she half-expected a face to appear in the bark.

Bret walked up behind her. "I ... guess I'm coming onto it," he said.

She turned to look at him, his Beach Boy hair, his longhorn-shaped eyebrows, the splayed rib cage that reminded her of the Neanderthal diorama at the Natural Science Museum. This was the man she married. What a *heavy* thing to have done. How strange human beings were, and what choices their hearts made. She felt an overwhelming fondness for him wash over her, but it wasn't exactly love. It was a recognition, an acknowledgment of another being in this strange material world. Had she always known him in some greater universe than this? Is that what was love was—the re-familiarization of a soulmate throughout time? Would she know him again in the future? Would their paths continue to cross throughout eternity, just encased in different bodies for each lifetime?

"Were you going up there?" he asked her, squinting up at the tree house.

"No, I don't think so. Not right now."

"Yeah. It's a long way up. And it's so blue."

Maddy laughed. For some reason this seemed unutterably funny. "It's paisley, too!"

Bret frowned. "So it is. When did that happen?" Eyes already drawn upward, he watched turkey vultures wheel overhead in circles, their wide black and white wings tilting almost imperceptibly as they rode the thermals. Then Maddy took his hand again. Her warm touch bridged the wide cosmic gulf between them, and he followed her down the hill to the edge of their land and the series of red metal property markers that marched authoritatively across the grass.

Maddy thought it strange that white people had to own pieces of the earth's surface, and mark what was theirs. What a primitive idea, and yet so-called primitive tribes didn't subscribe to it. They respected their mother earth too much. Was this what triggered wars, this need to possess the land and steal it from others? Is this what Vietnam was about?

A wave of sadness punched her in the gut, and she stopped and sagged.

"What?" Bret asked, alarmed, his eyes comically large.

"Jackson. I'm worried about him."

He patted her shoulder, clumsily, as if reassuring a child about her homework. "I know. But he's OK. I'm sure he is. Don't put yourself on a bummer."

"I shouldn't have let him go."

"I offered to send him to Canada. And he'd been accepted into engineering school. He could've gotten a deferment, but he wanted to go."

Maddy looked over to the shining hillside. The yuccas were in bloom, each improbably tall stalk crowded with creamy flowers. Why had he gone? What was it in men that made them need to prove themselves in war? She shrugged. Some questions just didn't have answers, or if they did, she didn't have the wit or the patience to wait for them to occur to her. And anyway, the mind's answers didn't change anything—they just made things easier to think about. "Let's take a walk," she said.

"Where?"

This was unlike Bret. He was normally the one in charge, deciding where to go and when. He was a big man in all kinds of ways—big-bodied, big-voiced, with big appetites. He lived large, as people often said; loved hard, partied hard. But this drug, this acid, had shown another side of him, revealing him to be just a big boy.

"Outside. On the road. We could climb the hill and look at the ocean."

Once this was out of her mouth it seemed to both of them an obvious goal. They strode off east, toward the fence along the road, and when they reached it they climbed over, laughing.

The asphalted road struck them as a mild affront to the senses, an oafish plastering-over of the earth that radiated the sun's heat in a most unnatural way, but it led them easily up toward a bend below a hill. Here was another marker of ownership, a ranch-style three-barred fence, but they climbed over that too.

The hills pulsed like the flanks of some sleeping creature. Late California poppies blazed from the hillside like orange-hot magma spilling from the slopes of a volcano.

Bret's heart pounded in his chest. Amazing how it knew how to beat without being told. He felt his lungs laboring as he clambered up the slope. What a complicated thing a body was. And it always knew what to do. For a while he wondered if he ought to be controlling his own breathing, but luckily his lungs knew how to function without orders, otherwise he'd go mad.

Finally they reached the crest and sat together, hearts thudding around inside their chests. There, a couple of miles away at the foot of the canyon, the Pacific began. It shone like hammered nickel, sunlight glinting on the waves in scintillas so bright they looked like holes in reality.

The view, the very air itself, was tiled into patterns. Layers of hillside paled into the distance like a Chinese watercolor. The sun was like a hot breath on the skin, its rays visible, golden. Beetles bustled about at their feet, busy breaking things back down into their component elements in the great wheel of life.

They sat, silent, for a measureless moment.

Maddy squinted briefly up at the sun. "How long have we been out?"

Bret had been thinking about the interconnectedness of everything; how glorious it would be if everyone could take a trip and feel this way: nonjudgmental, full of wonder. The astronauts on the moon must have felt like this. From their vast objective distance the world was a precious little ball of struggling creatures in the middle of a cold and airless void— miraculous and vulnerable. A lattice of interdependent life. He wanted to hug it, protect it.

So much was lost in growing up. Children knew so much already, and by the time they became adults we had trained it out of them. "What did you say?"

"The time. What time is it?"

Time. It seemed as if he and Maddy had lived a year in a day. The minutes had become stretchy, like taffy. Time was a human construct, obviously, imposed on the world to break it down into manageable chunks, but it wasn't real. His father fought the Battle of Saipan every night while he slept, because his subconscious had no sense of time, and now Bret understood. Everything was *now,* but humans couldn't deal with the ... *chaos of simultaneity.* He was proud of the phrase; wanted to hold onto it, but it was already gone. "I don't know. I've lost track."

They stumbled back down the hillside, now in the shade. Monarch butterflies shamed their clumsiness with their own effortless, gravity-defying grace.

At the foot of the hill by the road, Maddy smiled at him nervously. "Bret—where are we?"

"We're ... ah ... we're near the house, right? We didn't walk that far."

"I know, but I'm lost."

"Well..." he looked around, blankly. Nothing looked familiar. Every landmark he had taken for granted had somehow lost its label. "It has to be down this way."

They began to walk along the road. The air hummed with distant traffic noise from the town. Cueball's hog started up. Someone was using a chain saw across the valley, a raw and brutal ripping of the air. Insects chirred in the grass. High above, a plane scratched across the sky on its way to LAX. Were its passengers looking down on them? Maddy waved to it, just in case.

As they rounded a bend a black and white police squad car abruptly slid to a halt in front of them. Its engine switched off, and a burly cop got out and appraised them both. His vehicle sighed and ticked behind him, smelling of gasoline and hot rubber, looking aggressive. His pants, the deepest blue-black, radiated of a kind of fascist authority, as did his creaking leather belt and holster, his shiny back boots, his tight tan shirt.

Bret bristled.

"Afternoon," the policeman said.

"Afternoon, officer," Maddy replied.

"Out for a walk?"

"Yeah. Nice day."

"Sure is." He turned and looked down the road. "Live around here?"

"Yeah," Bret told him. "Off Old Topanga Road."

"Ah. Hippies."

Maddy smiled. "That's right."

The officer took a step closer and looked into her eyes, and then into Bret's. He smelled of aftershave and tobacco and pastrami. "You feeling OK?"

"Fine, thanks."

"You two know your way back?"

"Of course."

Nobody moved. Maddy began to panic. Were they about to be sent to jail? If so, she didn't think she could bear it.

At a sound, they all turned to see Rain strolling toward them, fanning herself with her hat.

The policeman addressed her. "Hey, ma'am—do you know these two?"

Rain glanced up at Bret and Maddy and smiled. "Of course. They live down the road."

"Can you take 'em home?"

Rain looked momentarily puzzled, but then smiled again. "Sure." She walked forward and replaced her hat on her head, took one of their hands in each of hers, and drew them down the road on either side of her. After a few minutes, the police car drove past them and back into town.

They fumbled their way back to the house. It sat waiting for them, glowing complacently, radiating the heat of the day. The scent of the star jasmine that grew around the front porch was heady, honeylike.

Rain let go of their hands and looked into their eyes. It was as if she understood what they were feeling. "There—he's gone. You'll be all right now."

Maddy smiled at Bret in relief, and when she turned back to reply Rain had gone; the street was empty. Had she ever been there?

Sundown looked up briefly from painting her toenails as they walked in. The reek of the polish was like an assault on the nasal passages. "Oh hi," she said. "I wondered where you were." Then she looked back at them and frowned. "You two trippin'?"

"Yeah," Maddy said. She waited for more words to reach her tongue but none did. She was at another stage now, apparently, and was starting to feel like a typewriter whose keys had all been mashed down together.

"How long ago did you two drop?"

Bret tried to remember. "No idea."

"You were still asleep when we left," Maddy told her, as she reevaluated her kitchen utensils.

"Jeez, ma, that was hours ago. You OK?"

"Fine," she said, vaguely. "Fine. What's new with you?"

Sundown was still concerned about their welfare. "You should drink some water. Don't want to get dehydrated." She poured them each a glass and made sure they drank.

"Wow," Bret said, looking at his glass in fascination. "That's amazing."

Sundown was enjoying the shift in power. "Yeah. New idea. Just comes out the faucet, as much as you want." She stood and slipped on her sandals. "Will you two be all right? I'm going up the road to talk to Lucas. He wants me to pose for a portrait."

Bret nodded in a distracted way. "Sure, honey. That sounds like fun." He looked at Maddy with unusual shyness. "We'll ... be here."

— · —

Sundown left the house and walked down to the main road and turned left, toward Lucas's studio on Rugged Trail. Everybody knew Lucas, and knew his studio, a jumbled mass of rusting metal objects around a small galvanized steel Quonset hut. Anywhere else it would have been considered a junkyard, but in Topanga it was an atélier.

Even though Sundown had passed it many times, she had never been inside. She stopped at its gate, welded out of bicycle frames. "Hey, Lucas," she called.

A face peered around the doorway. "Oh—hi, Sundown. I forgot you was comin'. Come on in."

She picked her way carefully between the chunks of dead machinery and walked into the gloom of the building, looking around. The inevitable odor of marijuana smoke, mixed with machine oil, hung in the stuffy air. "So ... you still want to do a portrait?"

"Yeah, babe. I'm diggin' portraits these days." He pointed to a corner of the room. "Stand over there—that's the best light. I'll need you take your top off. You can put your clothes—"

"W-wait a minute. Where's your stuff—easel, canvas, paints...?"

He waved a hand to brush away her comment. "Oh, I don't do that kind of bourgeois painting. I'm a constructivist. I'm more like Picasso."

Picasso my ass, she thought. "So what ... medium do you use?"

"Metal, o' course. I'm a metal man, can't you tell?"

"You plan to do a portrait of me in bits of metal?"

"Yeah, it'll be outrageous. Make us famous."

"Lucas, that's such bullshit. Why do you want me to take my clothes off if you're welding me out of metal?"

Lucas looked sheepish. "Worth a try," he said.

Sundown stormed out, shaking her head.

— · —

The best thing about LSD, Maddy decided, was the way it took everything else away. While on it, she could pretend there was no Vietnam War, no problems with Robbie's school, no worries about Sundown's moral development. On acid everything was beautiful, and fine, and unrolling exactly as it should.

How good it felt to just wallow around in bed, feeling. How much of our senses we ignored. Life was happening every moment, and it was priceless. Jewels weren't valuable, money wasn't important, property had no meaning. *Life* was the most valuable gift of all, and one we all took for granted.

Then there was love. Love, if we were lucky, was the second most valuable. And here she was—the day was warm, a breeze blowing in the window—with her man. Alive and loved. They were healthy, and they had healthy and beautiful kids.

She lay on the bed with Bret, both of them naked, touching. Certainly they had far from perfect bodies, but they *had bodies,* and that was what they were here in this material world for—to experience it with them. To touch it, feel it, taste it, hear it. How exquisite to be alive, breathing the dry California air, feeling the 300-count sheets, smelling the jasmine. These were life's real riches, and she was a billionaire.

Touch. Such an undervalued thing. Here, now, they could touch and be touched, just for pleasure. No worry about who had an orgasm and when, no required rules of foreplay, no taboos. Most touch was cursory, selfishly motivated, a brief means to an end. Touch ought to be indulged in like a fine meal—savored, prolonged, with no time limits, no preconceived plan, a languid sensory exploration.

"Bret," Maddy murmured, "away on all those shoots—have you always been faithful?"

The ensuing silence allowed a knife to twist in her guts.

Bret looked everywhere but at his wife. Finally, he responded. "Well ... you and I ... we always had an understanding, right?"

Maddy sat up in bed, pulling a sheet to cover herself. There would be no languid touching now. "What understanding is that?"

"That our marriage was ... open."

"'Open' honest, or 'open' free to fool around?"

"Not 'fool around.' More ... uh ... *non-exclusive.*"

"But we're married, Bret. When did we come to this understanding?"

"Relationships these days ... they're different from in our parents' time. The old way of doing things is breaking down, right?"

"For you it is, apparently. Have you had affairs, then?"

"Well, y'know..."

She felt sick. "No, I don't. Tell me."

"On those location shoots, far from home, everyone gets kinda loose. It doesn't mean anything."

"So you have."

"Uh ... only once in a while. Like I said," he added quickly, "it didn't mean anything."

"It means something to me."

"I thought we had—"

"An understanding. Yeah, that's pretty clear. You get to screw around."

"Aw, Maddy, you're the one I love. The others—"

"Don't mean anything."

"Right."

"Fuck you."

18

Soldiers in Vietnam thought of their current environment as belonging to some alternate reality unworthy of being labeled real, and from this remove the U.S was referred to as "the World." Likewise, the Vietnamese, whichever part of the country they came from, were all called "gooks," and generally considered at best backward and primitive, at worst subhuman. "How do you tell the good Vietnamese from the bad guys?" Jackson asked one man. The soldier looked him coldly and said, "If they're alive, they're VC."

At the end of their first week Jackson and Willie were given the traditional orientation ride. Since it was a just a maintenance check flight and not a mission the aircraft had no seats, no safety harness, and no crew chief at the open doors with gun. The two men had to sit on the floor holding on for dear life. While in the traffic pattern they peered down through the mist at the rice paddies, separated by rows of nipa palms. It appeared peaceful, but everywhere was said to hide an invisible threat.

Pilots treated mechanics with respect. After all, their lives depended on them.

The Army policy with helicopters, unlike with fixed-wing aircraft, was to assign the ships to the enlisted men who maintained them—and only loan them to the pilots for assigned missions. In essence the crew chiefs and flight engineers owned the aircraft, and because of this they treated them like their babies.

Each helicopter had to be serviced at double the rate of peacetime requirements, and Jackson's workday began two hours before dawn. He accompanied the crew chief to "his" Huey, helped check its head and stabilizing bar, oil gauges, hydraulic system, electrical systems, and fuel intake. Then he had to supervise loading to ensure a safe center of gravity. After a couple of hours the pilot showed up for preflight. Soon the air was filled with the whine of Huey turbines spooling up.

At day's end, once the mission was complete and the helicopter shut down, Jackson began his daily inspection. He cleaned and greased the head, rinsed the air filters with running water, checked the engine for worn fuel and oil lines, and lubricated the tail rotor. He examined the entire engine for loose parts and made sure all components were functional for the following day. Then the aircraft was cleaned, washed, and reinspected.

He and Willie had soon learned enough to be selected as senior helicopter mechanics. Jackson was given his "Swamp Rats" patch—a rat holding a wrench—and sewed it proudly on his coveralls.

— · —

Sundown answered the phone. "Oh, OK. Just a minute." She held out the receiver to her mother. "It's for you. Sounds like the English guy."

Maddy took it. "Hello?"

"Hey, Maddy," Owen said. "I was on my way up and got overheated. I'm in a bar in Topanga called 'The Nomad'—know it?"

Maddy stifled a laugh. The Nomad was the biker's hangout. "Sure."

"How about if we meet here instead? It's nice and cool. For some reason there are no windows."

"OK, sure. I'll be over in a few minutes."

"What's your poison?"

"What?"

"What do you like to drink? I'll have it waiting."

"Oh. Gin and tonic, I guess."

"OK. Cheers, then."

Maddy hurried up to her workshop and grabbed the latest pieces she had sewn for the band, along with the original sketches, and stuffed them in her big bag. When she walked outside to the car, she realized Owen was right—it was damn hot. Her VW bug was like an oven, and it had no air conditioning. She couldn't face baking in it, even for the four or five minutes it would take to reach the bar. Instead, she grabbed a hat and walked.

She felt a little self-conscious going to a bar during the day—it seemed something an alcoholic would do—but she reminded herself it was a business meeting. Besides, it was a break from routine, and she had to admit it was exhilarating to be asked out for a drink by a famous—or *relatively* famous—rock musician.

At the bar some kind of initiation appeared to be taking place. Two younger bikers were drinking beer from VW hubcaps—rusty ones, by the looks of them—and when they finished there were cheers.

Once her eyes had adjusted to the gloom inside, she picked out Owen in a corner booth with two drinks in front of him. As she sat, she noticed his face was unnaturally red and his nose was peeling.

He noticed her gaze. "Yes, nasty sunburn. Long night in the studio, see. Thought it would be fun to sunbathe on the beach in Venice, but I fell asleep. Woke up somewhat fried. That's why it's so nice in here." He looked at her bag. "Oh, good. You brought the stuff."

Maddy withdrew a blue vest with leather panels. Its beaded border twinkled in the lights. Chuckles came from the bikers at the bar as they watched this. To her discomfort, he stood and slipped it on.

Whistles and jeers came from the bar now, and she distinctly heard the word "faggot."

"Uh, Owen … you might want to try those on with the rest of the guys. *Later.*"

He understood her meaning. He looked at the drinkers across the bar and twirled. "What d'you think, boys?"

"Looks beautiful, darling," one of them said, and the others laughed.

"Owen, perhaps you should—"

He sat back down again, much to her relief. She didn't relish a confrontation.

"So the others are essentially the same but each with a different main color?"

Maddy nodded, taking the swatches out of her bag.

"Good."

"When are you wearing them?"

"A week from today. Enough time? We're on some kind of CBS show."

"Yes, that's enough time. I'll drop them off the day before."

"A thousand thanks, m'dear. More drinks. Same again?"

Maddy hesitated. Why not? "All right."

When he returned from the bar, Owen sized her up as he slid her drink across the table. "The Sobieskis are a good-looking bunch," he commented.

"Why thank you, sir."

"No, really."

Satan's Slaves were now requiring their inductees to do something in the men's room. She didn't want to know what.

"Well," she said, "I ought to get back to the house."

"Need a ride back?"

"Sure. Thanks."

They walked out of the door into a wall of heat.

"Damn," Owen said, struggling to put on his Ray-Bans, "I forgot it was still daylight. I always expect to come out of a bar at night."

Some of the bikers had followed them out, still clutching their beer glasses and hoping for a fight.

Maddy and Owen climbed into his Ferrari, left the bikers in a cloud of dust and gravel, and narrowly missed Louie Kelly's plumbing van—*If it's smelly, call Kelly*—that happened to be passing.

— · —

Maddy was glad she had left the air conditioning on. The house was refreshingly cool, like some kind of oasis.

Owen looked around. "Where are the kids?"

"At school—back around four. Bret's in Santa Barbara, shooting at the mission. Jackson is … God knows. Somewhere in Southeast Asia now, I suppose."

Owen put his arm around her and squeezed reassuringly. "I'm sure he'll be OK."

On an impulse, Maddy held his arm and squeezed back. He turned her to face him and they looked at each other. Before she knew what was happening, he kissed her.

Maddy's first reaction was to be offended, but there was an undeniable chemistry between them, a chemistry she either didn't feel with Bret or hadn't for a long time. Perhaps it was just the novelty of a new person and his taste and touch, perhaps it was answering some kind of longing she hadn't been aware of until now. At the back of her mind was Bret's attitude toward their relationship: open. She kissed Owen back.

Owen backed her against the kitchen counter and they kissed more. He ran his hands through her hair, holding her head to his. He pushed against her and an overwhelming arousal swept over her. She led him toward the bedroom, and then at the last minute swerved away from hers and Bret's and into Sundown and Charity's instead.

— · —

As soon as Sundown came into their bedroom, Charity fixed her with an accusatory glare. "Sundown?"

Sundown was in no mood to be confronted. "What?"

"Did you jump on my bed or something?"

"Are you crazy? No, of course not. Why?"

"It's ... *dented.*"

"Maybe dad was changing the light bulb and stood on it."

"Oh. Yes." Charity touched the items on her nightstand thoughtfully. "And does it ... smell funny in here to you?"

Sundown sniffed. "Smells the same as usual to me."

"Oh."

"Charity," Sundown fixed her with her own gaze, "You're not going wacko on me, are you?"

"No, I—"

"'Cos it's hard enough sharing a room with you without you losin' it."

— · —

Guilt weighed down Maddy like a suit of armor, making it difficult for her to move. Should she tell Bret? He hadn't admitted his affairs—she'd had to pry them out of him. *Them.* More than one. She had just had one little fling. Perhaps he was right; this was what relationships were like these days—relaxed, flexible, and that loaded word, open. It was touted as the natural union of humans: temporary. But if this were the natural state, why did it feel so bad afterward?

On the other hand, if she were to tell him, how would she do it? "Oh, by the way, Bret—you know the English guitarist guy? We got it on the other day. So I guess we're even. More coffee?"

She felt as if her unfaithfulness must be obvious to everyone, but at breakfast the children were indifferent, involved in their own worlds. Bret was late getting up, and for an agonizing half hour Maddy thought it was because he was waiting for the others to leave before he confronted her. But he had returned home late the night before, and eventually woke grumpy and disheveled.

"Morning, hon," Maddy said, tentatively. "Can I get you anything?"

Bret looked up, puzzled. He usually served himself in the mornings. "Uh ... sure. Eggs an' toast?"

"OK," she said, with false cheeriness, "Coming right up."

— · —

Charity sat in the playground, alternately consulting a book and writing in her journal.

> The basis of the early Topangan diet was the humble acorn. Because of the many varieties of oak, Native Americans in Southern California had no need to develop agriculture, and managed to avoid famine. But raw acorns are bitter and inedible, and several steps are needed before they can be eaten.
>
> The acorns were gathered in September and October and dried in their shells, and then they were cracked to remove the nutmeat, and pounded with mortar and pestle into coarse flour. Water was continuously poured over the flour, or if a stream were handy a basketful was left in the current, until the tannins were washed away. Dried again, the flour was used to make soup and bread.

— · —

After school, instead of heading home, Charity headed up a steepening path. It took a while, but she finally found the yurt that Rain was said to live in. The circular, canvas-sided structure sat tucked in an out-of-the-way corner of a clearing halfway up a hill. Colorful dreamcatchers dangled from the trees. The woman herself was sitting nearby in an old deckchair, weaving on a small handloom.

"H-hello?" Charity said.

Rain looked up and shaded her eyes with a hand. "Charity? Welcome."

Charity tentatively advanced, and decided to sit at her feet like a supplicant. Her mind went blank.

"You worked hard to find me," Rain said, after a moment of silence. "There must be an important reason."

"I'm ... I'm trying to understand about God."

"Ah," Rain nodded. "We all are."

Charity looked up, surprised. "Are we?"

Rain looked up as a bluejay flitted by. "Well, he's not. He's just being. Out of all the creatures, it's only humans who wonder why they're here."

"Well, why *are* we here?"

"I don't think I can tell you. I'm not trying to be difficult, it's just that why I'm here might not be why you're here."

"We're all here for different reasons?"

"If we want a reason, each of us has to find his or her own. It's not always easy."

Silences were comfortable with Rain, and the two sat without speaking for a long moment, the only sound a background summer drone.

"My dad's an atheist."

"Ah, well, a lot of people feel that way. But it doesn't mean you have to."

"How come you know so much about this kind of thing? Are you a minister, or a medicine woman or something?"

Rain laughed. "I was a court stenographer. I didn't like what it was doing to me. I got sick of typing out all the gross things people were capable of, year after year. I needed to get away, find myself, restore my faith in humanity. So I came out here."

"And you found more positive things?"

"Oh yes. No money, of course, but a lot of peace. Haven't quite solved getting both at the same time. If you find a way, please let me know."

Charity was flattered that Rain would ask her for help—it made her feel like an equal. The world didn't seem quite as cold a place as when she had set out that morning.

She tried another question that had been bothering her. "What is war all about?"

Rain gave a sigh. "You have all the hard questions. Some people think we'll always have wars, because humans are violent."

"Do you think that?"

"Humans are capable of violence, yes. Humans are capable of great love, too. It's as if we're not devils or angels, but both."

"So ... how do we ... uh...?"

Rain spread her hands palms upward. "We find our own path, I suppose. Mine is not yours. Yours is not your father's. Your brother, Jackson—he'll have to find his own, too. But I think the human race is learning. Learning not to keep making the same mistakes."

After this came a lull so long that Charity turned to see if Rain was still awake.

"You're always welcome here, Charity."

— · —

Hollywood's Musso & Frank Grill was a dark and musty place, old-fashioned, and with waiters that looked like lifers. The atmosphere was more like Sundown imagined in restaurants in New York or Boston, and not here in the sunbelt. She sank into the red leather booth and gazed at the menu.

"You must try the *Fettuccine Alfredo*," Frank said. "Douglas Fairbanks and Mary Pickford brought the original recipe back from Alfredo's in Rome in the twenties." When the waiter arrived, Frank ordered them Manhattans.

"So," he asked, "have you been on any shoots lately?"

"Oh God, you wouldn't believe it. It was incredibly stupid." She declined to go into detail. "I need to get away."

"I have a place up in Big Bear I like to get away to, whenever I can."

How civilized, she thought dreamily, to have more than one home. Tire of one, move to the other. The ideal situation.

Frank, as she appraised him, struck her as a representative of the establishment, of the straight, Republican business world. Not a world she had ever felt attracted to or aligned with. And yet its appeal was rapidly becoming evident. Having the money for a second home, or for that matter a first in San Marino, showed money's power. Perhaps it was a world she shouldn't be dismissing so lightly. Though she often wished it weren't so, her looks were an entrée into this world if she chose to use them in that way.

And why shouldn't she? We all made a living from our gifts, we all sold what we'd been handed. That was life, wasn't it?

Frank was a very different kind of man than her father—he seemed confident, without the need to hide behind bluster. By comparison, her dad came off as insecure.

Frank ordered wine. Sundown, finding it on the list, saw it was phenomenally expensive. "So … what are you working on right now?" she asked him.

"Some new developments in the Fairfax area, not far from the museum and the Tar Pits. They're a real problem because of gas leakage. Everything's tar under there, you see, and on top of it sits gas. Not gasoline, but gas. Masses of it. And it's flammable. So we have to cap each leak before we can continue."

"Wow. Fascinating."

Frank talked more about his architectural feats, his training in New York, his designs for a project in Hong Kong. She was content to let him talk, since by comparison she felt she had accomplished nothing. Yet.

After crème brûlée, a dessert Sundown had never even heard of, let alone tasted, Frank ordered them cognacs. By the end of the evening, Sundown's view of the restaurant was blurred and canting slightly. Life was a fine thing. She had arrived.

"Are you OK to drive?" he asked her when they stood to leave, a concerned look on his face. "I can call you a cab."

"A cab? To Topanga? It would cost a fortune. No, I'm fine."

"Tell you what—my company keeps an apartment on the Miracle Mile. We put visiting clients up there. It's not far. Follow my car."

Sundown took a deep breath of the night air. Then she turned to Frank. "Maybe next time."

— · —

I must stop drinking and driving, Sundown thought blurrily, as she found her car and eased out into traffic. This is the second time recently. One of these days...

Where the hell was she anyway? Hollywood Boulevard, with all its stars in the sidewalk. Maybe she would have one there one day. And her handprints in front of Grauman's Chinese.

Down here she had to turn up Highland to the freeway, right? In the dark it all looked a little creepy. Did all cities change at night? L.A. certainly did—from bright and colorful to lit only by neon, giving it the boozy and sleazy ambiance it hadn't managed to shake since the thirties. She wished she were home, without having to deal with the miles of street in between. From this perspective, Topanga wasn't so bad, especially at night.

Was this Highland?

The dash of the Corvair flickered with light. At first she thought it was more neon, but a glance in the mirror showed a police cruiser behind. Shit.

She turned the corner and pulled over, wound down the window and waited.

"Well, little lady," the cop began, "Having trouble driving straight, are we?"

"E-evening officer. No, I just don't know this part of town very well."

"Oh yeah?" He held out a meaty hand. "License." When he shone his flashlight on it, he looked back up. "Topanga, huh? You're not one o' them gals who comes down here to make money on the weekend, are you?"

"No, no. I was meeting a friend."

"Uh-huh. Had a few drinks, did you?"

"No."

The officer leaned uncomfortably close. "That's not what it smells like, little lady. I think I'm gonna have to take you in."

Oh no, Sundown thought, this is all I need. They'll find the other arrest on Sunset. I'll never get out. She forced a smile on her face. "Look officer—"

"Can you give me one reason I shouldn't?"

"Sir, I—"

"Of course, we might be able to come to some kind of understanding..."

"Understanding?"

"You do something for me, and I forget the whole thing."

Sundown looked around in panic. There were plenty of dark doorways and very few people on the street. Did he mean—?

A carful of kids screamed by, and one of them threw a beer bottle at him. It smashed in a thousand shards on the curb, glittering pieces everywhere.

The policeman ran back to his car, cursing, and tore off after them with the siren wailing.

Never again, Sundown promised. And thank God for carsful of hoods.

19

Sundown shoved her way into Robbie's room without knocking. He was listening to a Ravi Shankar album, and it was toward the end. The dense rhythms had taken on a frantic quality.

"Robbie—what the fuck is that racket?"

"It's a raga."

"What the hell is a raga?"

"Indian music. The Beatles are into it—'specially George."

"It's weird. Turn it down." She stormed back out.

Robbie took off the record. Truth be told, he thought it was weird too. But sitars were in everything these days. Perhaps he should learn sitar instead and sit in on recordings, make a fortune.

Nah. He was a guitar man.

Instead, he shoved the jack of his guitar into his little Sears Silvertone amplifier. The amp gave a satisfying roughness to the tone if cranked up fully—not exactly fuzzbox quality, but a tasty distortion from the overload.

He tuned the guitar poorly by ear, and strummed the couple of chords he knew well. He would write his own songs. Then he closed his eyes and sang in a nasal tone reminiscent of Bob Dylan,

"I'm arresting you for stealing my heart
And your sentence is to love me forever...

His face squinched up as he tried to come up with more lyrics.

There is nothing that can keep us apart
And you can never leave me, never..."

Some harmonica would go well here, he decided. He would get his dad
to stop by Wallich's and pick up a blues harmonica and one of those racks
that held it on your guitar, so you could blow into it hands-free.

"The Love Police gonna pull you over
Gonna have to put you away
So you won't be a menace to society
And keep your beauty from the light of day..."

And now for a chorus:

"I'm gonna stake out your heart
Till you set me free
We can never be apart
Till you surrender to me"

And here would be a mind-blowing solo.

Robbie remembered Owen warning him away from trying solos before
he knew the guitar better, but decided that was bullshit. He wanted to cut
to the good stuff straightaway.

He put on Jimi Hendrix's "All Along The Watchtower," listening
intently. Three times he attempted to pick out the guitar solo part, then
turned the record off to try it on his own. He tried to play the entire riff,
but it soon disintegrated into a cacophony of notes. He had a good ear but
no formal training in music theory, and so finding which string and fret
position was a haphazard hunt. But if he kept at it he hoped his memory
would take over, and his blisters become calluses.

Watching other guitarists on TV didn't help—they always made it
look so easy. He had seen a long clip of Hendrix once, and it was as if the
man had been born with a Strat's neck in his hand.

But, Robbie told himself, everyone had to start somewhere. He experimented with playing a note high up the neck and placing his guitar near
the amp to produce a screeching whine of feedback, like Clapton.

"Robbie!" his mother yelled, *"Stop that!"*

Reluctantly, he turned down the volume and sat on the bed, returning
to the D, G and A chords Owen had recommended. Then he worked on
reaching F chords. How did anyone do that? They must have hands that
worked differently from his. Jesus, that hurt.

If he just kept up this practicing, at least an hour a day, in a year he could be smokin' hot. He could go to London and be Owen's American buddy, sit in on all kinds of jam sessions. He would be an exotic addition to the scene. "Let's get the Yank in," they'd say. It was easier to get famous over there, because they were a smaller country, and because they were hipper. Then, in a year or so, he'd come back to California a legend.

Eventually he would hook up with some other guys and they'd start a new band. He had tired of Blue Language. He would call it … Five Finger Discount. Or Doobie Decimal System. Or Believe You Me.

He should change his name, too. He could be Robbie S. Or Sobie. Or Robbie S.O.B.

He played the "Satisfaction" riff Owen had shown him and then ran through the songs he knew—"Louie, Louie," "Memphis, Tennessee," and "Suzie Q."

He lay back on the bed and continued to play. He could call the band Poor Air Quality, or Parking Citation, or The Dry Heaves, or Nocturnal Emissions—no, maybe not. Urban Sprawl? What about local names—Wildwood, Fernwood? Red Rock, like that canyon off Old Topanga Road with the caves, where he and his buddies sometimes got high? But Red Rock wouldn't work with blue shirts, and he didn't feel like wearing red. Too Vegas.

"Robbie!" his father called. "Come help me with mom's car!"

— · —

The aptly named Swamp Rats worked a twelve-hour shift, eating, sleeping, then getting up and starting all over again. When the 119th Assault Helicopter Company's Hueys returned after a mission, Jackson and his fellow mechanics pulled all the maintenance according to the manual, and worked off any write-ups entered in the logbook.

After eight or ten hours of flying, many of the choppers were damaged, and Jackson had to check their A2408 forms. A red X meant unsafe for flight. A circled red X meant a deficiency, but may be flown under limits. A red dash meant inspection was required. A red diagonal slash meant the ship was unsatisfactory but not dangerous enough to be grounded.

Even without mission damage, a ship received an inspection after 25 flying hours, a major inspection after 100, and after 300 flying hours its entire turbine had to be replaced. At 2000 hours—if a bird lasted that long, and few did—it was sent away for a complete overhaul.

The Huey had only two rotor blades. They were supposed to last 1000 hours' flying time, but in the tropics they were lucky to last 300. If a bird developed a main or tail rotor vibration, the Swamp Rats tracked the blades at night using the landing light. If the rotors were shot up by bullets or shells and needed replacing, it took five or six men to change them. Jackson seemed to spend most of his shifts fixing main and tail rotors and steering leakages, and only once that was done could he switch to replacing the big Plexiglas windows. Then it was time to check the fluids with a metal detector to catch any metal shavings. Minor repairs, like patching bullet holes on the thin aluminum skin, were often made in a hurry with duct tape, which the Army provided in a conveniently matching green.

At first, if he wanted a snack when the canteen was closed, Jackson would tear open a C-ration. Until he noticed, when passing under a floodlight, that the date stamped on it was when he was two.

Rounds regularly penetrated the lower front windows, the chin bubbles, and these often had to be replaced. Since helicopters were flown using both hands and both feet, and an injured foot would effectively incapacitate a pilot, any spare flak vests were placed over them to stop bullets entering the cockpit.

By morning the birds would be ready to take flight again, the mechanics often still there to greet the crew when they showed up to begin their preflight checks at 0630.

— · —

Maddy sat in the foyer of the Reprise offices, waiting for someone to come out and collect the outfits she had made for Sunday Joint. She looked nervously around at the framed gold records of Frank and Nancy Sinatra, Sammy Davis, Jr., Dean Martin, Bing Crosby, Jo Stafford, and Rosemary Clooney. Nothing better reflected the label's extreme transition from "easy listening" than the poster of Jimi Hendrix looking wild and radical, the orange backlighting making his hair appear to be on fire. She glanced down at the parcel in her lap, on which she had written SUNDAY JOINT. Charity had used colored pencils to ornament the letters with flowers.

A tall, hawk-nosed man with wild hair in ringlets strode in and bantered with the receptionist in a singsong voice. It was not until he had disappeared through a door that she realized it was Tiny Tim, he of the recent falsetto hit of "Tiptoe Through The Tulips."

Who would pick up her parcel? *Please don't let it be Owen,* she prayed, not wanting to be confronted by her adultery—at least not yet, and not here. But after a few minutes Owen appeared, cheerful and just as he always had been, except she now knew what he looked like without his clothes.

"Hey, Maddy. How are ya? That the stuff?"

"Hi, Owen. Yes, all done."

He winked. "Thanks loads. Wish I could stay and talk, but they've got me in a business meeting." He rolled his eyes. "So f-ing tedious. But still—has to be done. Ring you later?"

"O-OK."

"All right, then. Cheers for now." He disappeared down a corridor.

— · —

Jackson was so busy, and so exhausted when he wasn't that he had no time to be homesick, nor even think of home. But at night his dreams returned to a simplified and sniper-free Topanga, idyllic and peaceful. He drove his GTO through flower-lined lanes and listened to soul music, his girlfriend at his side, and it wasn't raining.

One night his dreams were interrupted by sirens, intermittent at first, but then a constant wail. The generators shut down and everyone made their way to the reinforced bunker. Jackson crouched with Willie in the dark, waiting to see what would happen. Something hit their hooch, its shrapnel thudding into the sandbags before it could reach them. Sand blew into their eyes and mouths, reminding Jackson of family beach outings when he was small, when sand seemed to get into everything.

"Mortar," Willie said. "Let's hope they ain't got no rockets. Rockets make a five-foot hole in whatever they hit." He looked up at Jackson's scalp. "You need a haircut, Sobieski. Or the captain's gonna get on your case."

"Where's the barber's?"

Willie shook his head. "We use Mai Dinh. Or one of the other locals, but Mai's the best. If I see her I'll send her over."

Next day a tiny, middle-aged Vietnamese woman came a few steps into the hangar and stood waiting in the bright doorway. She wore a rust-colored *ao dai* and her hair was cut in a pageboy.

Jackson looked up from his work. "Can I help you?"

The woman withdrew from her clothing scissors and a comb. "You wan' haircut, Jimmy?"

He wondered if, to her, "Jimmy" was the same as "gook" was to them—a generalized name for all of them. "Yeah, sure. Uh..." Jackson grabbed a swivel office chair and rolled it over to the doorway, thinking it best not to let a civilian into the hangar's interior. He sat, and she efficiently began to comb and trim, comb and trim.

When she was done, Jackson ran his hand over his head and felt a consistent stubble. "Great," he told her, and handed her one of the funny money Vietnamese bills.

The woman bowed briefly and exited.

In the bar later, Willie was suitably impressed. "Ah—I see you had a visit from Mai. Good, ain't she?"

— · —

The phone rang, and Maddy was nearest. "Hello?"

"Maddy—it's Owen. Can you talk?"

Maddy looked over into the dining area. Bret was helping Charity with her homework. "No, not right now. I'll call you back."

"OK. Cheers."

Maddy hung up and turned back to Bret. "I have to go down to the shop."

"OK."

The VW, newly converted to a 12-volt system and its larger battery, started immediately, and Maddy drove off down the hill to the boutique. Inside, Tess was chatting in low tones with a customer, by the looks of him a townie, not a local.

She left them to their flirting and picked up the phone, dialing Owen's number, half-hoping he wouldn't be home. "Owen?"

"Maddy! I'm glad you called back. How are you?"

The sound of his voice made her blush. She stretched the cord as far as it would go, retreating into the curtained-off corner used for fittings. "I feel ... I feel terrible. I don't know what to do."

"Oh, Maddy, it's not that big of a deal. This monogamy thing—it doesn't work. People have too much love to limit it to just one person all their lives. It's unnatural."

"I don't know. It doesn't feel right to ... be involved with someone else."

"Look, I tell you what—come on down and see me. We're recording tomorrow. Say you're delivering more outfits or something. I'll tell 'em you're coming."

"I don't know, Owen, I—"

"It'll be fine. Come on down. A&M studios, on La Brea." Being a non-Angeleno, he pronounced it *Bray*. "We're there all day."

— · —

Maddy felt grateful to live in Topanga, which sat above most of the smog. The Hollywood air, by contrast, tinted the buildings and sky sepia.

As she entered the studio, there seemed to be some kind of altercation inside. Several excited girl fans had pushed their way into the lobby, and the receptionist and a guard were attempting to wrangle them back out to the street.

"*Sunday Joint!*" they were screaming.

"*Jeff!*"

"*Owen!*"

For a shared split second the staff glanced at Maddy in case she turned out to be another invader, but quickly dismissed her as being too old. She noticed, and felt offended.

A third employee appeared and helped shove the fans back through the doors, locking them once the girls were beyond the glass.

Owen came out and gave her a kiss. He seemed a little wired—his eyes were bright, the pupils larger than she remembered, and his words were rapid-fire. "This is the old Charlie Chaplin studios, they tell me. First recording here was that album by Sergio Mendes, *The Fool On the Hill*."

He led her inside to the freshly painted interior, all muted lighting and muffled sounds, hip-looking people sauntering to and fro. She felt frumpy by comparison.

"What are you recording?"

"*Trying* to record. 'Goodbye Cowardly Lion.' It's about Bert Lahr, who died last year. Always loved him in *Wizard of Oz*. It's not going so well. Anyway, we'll be taking a lunch break soon, so we can talk. Hang out here for a little while..." He led her into the control booth, one side of which was filled with a confusing board of sliders and dials marked

HAECO and manned by two men, with a female assistant hovering behind. They looked up and regarded her with disinterested eyes.

"This is Maddy," Owen told them. "She sews the gear."

The technicians nodded and returned to their console. The assistant looked pouty.

"Have a seat," he told her, pointing to a stool in the dark corner. Then he returned to the studio with the other band members. Through the glass she could see them arguing, then getting together over a mirror and snorting lines of white powder through a rolled-up dollar bill. After that, they adjusted their headphones and got ready to play.

The engineer said, "Roll tape. Take fourteen."

Apparently the vocals had already been recorded—she could hear them running quietly in the background—and the band was listening to them over playback as they laid down the instrumental parts.

"Goodbye cowardly lion
No more need to be afraid
Your courage has been proven by
All the friends you've made."

It sounded good to her, but Owen would continually get angry about something, stop them partway through and make them start again, suggesting different approaches. Recording, she belatedly realized, had very little in common with performing. No audience apart from the hypercritical engineers and producer, no atmosphere to respond to, no real energy anywhere except that produced by isolated musicians surrounded by equipment. It wasn't nearly as exciting as she'd imagined.

"You may not look like a hero
But your fearlessness has won
And you'll never need the wizard's help
In protecting anyone."

Maddy said to the men at the console, "I thought the instrumentals were recorded first, and the lyrics after."

The producer looked at her briefly, and then back to the view through the window. "Usually. But this bunch don't do anything the sensible way."

"They gave you a medal for courage
But I know you'll always be
The King of Beasts, the King of Clowns
And the King of the Forest to me."

At the end of a run-through, the drummer bounced his sticks off the snare and said, "What the fuck is this song about, Owen?"

Owen glared at him. "I already told you. Now stop complaining and fuckin' get on with it."

"I think we should let the groupies in and take a break in the back room," he said, with a leer.

"Even a groupie wouldn't want you, you fuckin' little spaz."

The producer clicked on his mic so they could hear him. "Boys, boys—play nice. You can punch each other's lights out on your own time. Right now this is costing us." He switched off and looked at Maddy apologetically. "Bands. Bunch of kids."

"Are Sunday Joint worse than most?"

He put his head in his hands. "God help me, they're all the same."

— · —

After one more take, Owen reluctantly declared they had it in the can. The recording engineer, sighing with relief, tweaked his sliders until he was satisfied with the mix.

The bandmembers crowded in to listen, nodded enthusiastically at the result, then left to pack up their gear, animosities now forgotten. This was the final track of their next album, and their obligations to their recording contract were fulfilled.

The drummer came back in, looking sheepish. "I think the drums need to be up in the mix a bit more. Y'now, drivin' beat an' all that. Otherwise it's just a soppy song."

The engineer glanced briefly at Maddy. "OK, I'll fix it."

"Thanks, mate."

The bass guitarist squeezed past the drummer on his way out. "The bass is getting lost," he announced. "And that piece of shit needs all the help it can get."

"OK," the engineer told him, "I'll work on it."

As soon as the bassist had left, Owen came in. "Sounds good, man. Can you beef up the lyrics a bit? It's a words-driven track, and people have gotta hear 'em all."

"Yeah, sure," the engineer assured him. "I'll take care of it."

Owen beckoned Maddy into an unoccupied room.

"It's good to see you," he said, stooping to kiss her. He had a ring of white around one nostril.

Maddy felt awkward. "You too. Uh…"

"Yeah?"

"I don't think I can do this, Owen. Have an affair, I mean. It's just too … weird."

Owen smiled unconcernedly. "You'll get used to it."

"But that's just it—I don't want to. I think I made a mistake."

"Hey! Owen!" a voice bellowed. *"Where are ya?"*

Owen seemed unsure what to say to her. "Why don't we talk—?"

"No, I'm sorry. I've made up my mind."

"Owen! Where the fuck are ya, man?"

He nodded. "Well, gotta go. Want to stay and watch more?"

"No, thanks."

Just as the guard was about to unlock the doors to let her out to the street, where the groupies still hung around hoping to meet the band, Maddy turned and returned to the studio. She had been too blunt. It wasn't his fault that she had compromised her marriage vows; it had been a mutual decision. There was no point in ending the relationship on a sour note. They could still be friends.

She pushed open the studio door and caught the band making fun of her outfits. The drummer was wearing one of her vests as a kind of diaper; the bassist wore one on his head like a bright turban.

The organist threw his across the room. "I don't give a toss what the label tells us, I ain't dressin' up like a trained monkey."

20

Between tasks the men sat around and read, played cards, drank beer. If it wasn't raining, they would lounge outside and work on their tans. Sometimes they hitched a ride into Pleiku, referred to as the "Ville." Jackson was reluctant to go to the Ville—he had heard GIs could get killed there. But Willie eventually cajoled him into going, and because Jackson was bored stiff from being confined to the base and desperate for a change of scenery and food, he agreed.

Willie had other reasons. "I need to get laid, man. How about you?"

Jackson shook his head. The thought of making love with a Vietnamese woman turned his stomach, not because he found them unattractive or racially unacceptable, and not because he felt any ties of fidelity to Shirley back home, but because he would always know they were doing it for the money to feed their family. He was also deathly afraid of catching something. He had plans for life back in the world, and they didn't include carrying a disease for the rest of his life.

"Please yourself," Willie said. "Better tail in Saigon anyway. You waitin' for leave, huh?"

Pleiku had the ramshackle quality of a Wild West town, all slapped-together with wood and corrugated iron. The streets were full of cyclos, mopeds, and three-wheeled Lambro cabs, along with American jeeps, deuce-and-a-halfs and occasionally a Walker Bulldog tank, plus pigs, goats, dogs, and pedestrians wearing their conical *non la* hats.

Jackson felt suffocated by the humidity, and wondered if he would ever get used to it. It was like inhaling a warm, wet facecloth. Topanga began to rise in his estimation as some kind of paradise on earth, with its dry air and short, civilized rainstorms, and best of all, no mud.

Here, mud was everywhere, piling up on the soles of his boots until he was almost two inches taller, staining every piece of clothing, and leaving slippery pink trails across the floor of the hooch. Jackson fell regularly, but so did everyone; there was no escaping it.

The moment the two men walked among civilians they were overrun with children selling everything imaginable. Jackson had only been there ten minutes when he felt a strange sensation on his right buttock. A child had slashed his back pocket with a razor and run off with his wallet, luckily slicing only denim. But his whole month's pay—$78—was gone, along with a photo of his family taken the previous Thanksgiving.

Jackson turned to Willie. "You'll have to pay and I'll give it to you next payday."

"Shit, man," Willie grumbled, "you're cuttin' into my screwin' money."

Willie took them to a bar and ordered beers. What they got was *Ba Muoi Ba*, Beer 33. Despite the label proudly proclaiming "Grand Prestige," it tasted lousy, with a chemical aftertaste. God only knew what they were making it out of, but it certainly wasn't barley and hops. On his way to visit the toilet to rid himself of some of it, Jackson was surprised to glimpse in a back room a stack of what looked remarkably like Viet Cong flags. An old man was punching holes in them and sprinkling them with blood from a dead chicken. When Jackson described this scene, Willie told him they were to sell to the GIs to take home and boast about.

— · —

Robbie watched as his mother selected pint cans of paint and stacked them in the shopping cart. Royal blue, ocean blue, cornflower blue, Indian turquoise, sunset peach... "But why paint the tree house ... what's it called again...?"

"Paisley."

Maddy considered divorcing Bret, or at least moving out. But where would she go? Down in the Valley? Hollywood? After spending so long in a semi-rural environment she couldn't imagine living somewhere urban. And what would she do for companionship? The majority of the people they considered friends were Bret's. Most of hers had been left behind when they came out to California all those years ago, and she supposed she had just relied a little too much on her husband's circle of acquaintances and his ability to connect.

No, she had no intention of starting again. She would never move out. The home was just too important to her as a family hub. Hophead Hills, she realized fondly, wouldn't work out of an apartment in the city. Like it or not, and at the moment she didn't, they were stuck with each other. Perhaps one day, when the kids were gone…

"Why are you painting it paisley?"

Maddy stopped, a can in each hand. "Robbie—it's a project. A crazy idea. I'm feeling creative."

"But mom—you don't like heights."

Maddy nodded. "I know. But it's not that high, and anyway, we have to confront our fears in life."

"Yeah? OK."

"You don't understand me, do you?"

"Uh, sure."

"No you don't. Look—we all have something that frightens us—snakes, the dark, cockroaches…"

"Heights…"

"That's right. We need to confront it, and not let it beat us, see?"

"I guess."

She looked at him intently. "Don't you have fears, inside?"

Robbie had no intention of talking about things that frightened him. That would make him a kid, and he wasn't a frightened kid any more. He shook his head. "Nah."

"If we've conquered our inner demons, we can't be pushed around by the ones outside."

"If you say so." He looked at the cans. "But paisley?"

"It's something your dad and I saw that time we … got high together. Everything had a pattern, and I could've sworn the tree house was paisley. So…"

"Oh." This made sense. Stoner sense. "OK. Far out."

"And you're going to help."

"Aw, ma…"

"Unless you'd rather pick the ticks out of Gilligan's ears?" This was

Robbie's least favorite chore, and she knew it.

"OK, OK. How about brushes?"

— · —

They needed extra ladders, not just the one used to gain entrance, and dragged two over from the garage.

Maddy teetered at the top of hers. "Ooh," she said, gripping the rungs and turning pale.

"Mom? You OK?"

"I'm fine. Just getting used to it." She peered in the window. "Oh—hi, Charity. We didn't know you were up here."

"Hi, mom."

"What are you up to?"

"Reading the Bible."

"Oh. Sorry. We were going to paint."

"That's OK. I was done." Charity climbed down and ran back to the house.

As she left, Robbie muttered, "She's weird."

"Don't be rude, Robbie. She's just ... trying to find herself."

"Why? Was she lost?"

"Very funny. Help me out here. Take the chalk and draw me some of these shapes." She showed him a piece of paisley fabric.

Robbie looked doubtfully at the cloth. "They're ... *blobby.*"

"I think they're leaves, stylized. Or figs, maybe."

"They look like amoebas to me."

"Whatever they are, draw them about three feet high. Then you can help me paint."

Maddy stepped down while he worked, stirring the paints. When he'd completed the sketches on one side, she said, "OK. Before you do them all, let's give one a try." But when she attempted to climb up holding paint can and brush, she froze halfway. "I ... don't feel well. You'll have to do it."

"Aw, mom..."

"It'll be fun. Look, just copy the fabric's design. I'll bring you a Coke. I'll make some guacamole later and bring it out."

"Jeez. OK."

— · —

It wasn't simple. The shapes were complicated, embodying a lot of detail. The tree house that Robbie had always thought of as small now seemed, when he had to paint all four sides of it with dumb Indian shapes, huge.

Gilligan watched, puzzled, as he worked, and was soon spattered with small blue spots.

In an hour, his mother returned with the promised snacks, and with relief Robbie stepped down. They sat on the grass and ate.

"So..." Maddy began, "How's things at school?"

Robbie fidgeted. "Fine."

"No, really, Robs. Anything you want to talk about?"

"Nah. It's just ... y'know, high school."

"If there's anything that's bothering you, you know you can talk to me, right?"

"Nothing's bothering me, ma."

— · —

At the end of the afternoon Maddy called up, "That's enough."

Robbie threw down his brush and sighed. His arms ached. "Good. I'm all paisleyed-out."

As his mother walked back to the house, Robbie climbed inside, now redolent of drying oil paint. He opened his father's stash box, took out a film canister of dope and rolled himself a joint, which he lit and inhaled deeply. Then he grabbed some paper out of the filing cabinet and worked on the lyrics of his song some more.

Where was he?

> I'm arresting you for stealin' my heart
>
> It's a crime the way you treat me...

No, this wasn't working. Better to try a new approach.

> The Love Police are gonna give you no peace
>
> The Love Police are gonna getcha
>
> Breakin' my heart is breakin' the law
>
> Breakin' my heart is...

Shit. What rhymed with law? Nothing. OK, something different.

> The Love Police will catch you and lock you away
>
> The Love Police will find you—

"Robbie?" his mother called back, "Don't forget your homework."

21

Sundown sat at the bar of Filthy McNasty's with her friends Sarah and Jodie. Sarah's brother had returned from Vietnam with an arm that ended at the elbow, and these days she liked to get drunk fast. They were there in search of guys; she was there to get out of the house. She still felt burned by Jimmy, and swore she would have nothing to do with men ever again.

A band named Moonburn was onstage, and after the third song Sundown felt herself drawn to the lead guitarist, a thin young man with a sensitive face, a mass of wavy dark hair and a way of playing that seemed to pluck at her very heartstrings. Rather than just fill the air with notes, like most rock 'n' roll musicians trying to show off, he knew to leave space between them; breathing room. He was her type—dark and moody, passionate.

Halfway through the evening two things happened: Sarah and Jodie disappeared with a group of guys, and the lead guitarist sensed her interest. He would glance in her direction, and when he had an opportunity to solo he turned her way as if he played just for her.

Around eleven Moonburn had to relinquish the stage for Annabelle's Tears, a far less talented group. Sundown was considering leaving when the guitarist she had watched appeared at her side.

"Like it?" he asked, waving to the bartender for his comped beer.

"Your band? Yeah. Far out."

"A pretty good night. I'm Alex."

"Sundown."

They shook hands, and she laughed at the formality of the gesture. "Been playing long? Sounds like it."

"Yeah. Got my first guitar when I was twelve. You local?"

"Topanga."

"Really?" He became animated. "I love Topanga. Have you ever heard of The Island?"

"No. What is it? A club?"

"A commune. Kinda. Based on Aldous Huxley's book. It's in Topanga, up in the hills. I go there all the time."

"To play?"

"No, no. To … kinda … tune in. Meditate. It's run by a guru guy, but not from India; an American. He's on some other plane."

"Oh yeah."

He laughed. "I know. Sounds weird. But it's a special place. Spiritual, y'know. You'd like it."

"How do you know?"

He looked at her with his soulful eyes. "I just know. You learn that kind of stuff there—to trust your intuition. Your inner eye."

She looked around the bar. Her friends were gone. Annabelle's Tears had emptied the place with their indifferent playing. It was late. She was tired. It was time to head home. "OK. When?"

"I'm going up there this Saturday for a festival. Meet me there." He scribbled the address on the back of a Moonburn flyer.

She looked at it, recognizing roughly where it was. "What time?"

"Oh, five, I guess."

"Do I bring anything?"

Alex laughed. "An open mind."

"Wait—it's not one of those swingers' places, right? No Wesson oil orgies and stuff?"

"No, no, it's not like that at all. It's spiritual."

— · —

"The Island" turned out to be a loose agglomeration of a small canyon house, a half-constructed geodesic dome, two nylon tents, a tipi, and an Airstream trailer with an incongruous orange extension cord umbilical to the house.

A tall, handsome man in his forties, with long gray hair in a ponytail, wearing white cotton *kurta* tunic, *churidar* pants and a serene smile, stepped from the trailer.

"Sundown, this is Baba Ji," Alex said, placing his palms together and bowing. "Baba Ji, this is my friend Sundown."

Baba Ji took her hand and held it overlong, gazing into her eyes. "I can see," he said, in a resonant tone, "that you were meant to be here. Thank you, Alex, for bringing your friend. She is obviously an evolved creature."

Sundown extricated her hand and gazed around the compound. Various young people strolled purposefully about, intent on their duties—gardening, babysitting, cleaning, carrying; men, women and children dressed in sundry pseudo-Indian garb. Except for a couple of toddlers who were left to wander about without diapers, with predictable results.

"Come," Baba Ji said, "The wives have begun cooking the feast."

"Wives?" Sundown repeated, looking at Alex. He shrugged.

Two of the men stirred the coals of a big fire pit to glow evenly under a hinged metal grille. Various foods were being prepared on long tables— saffron rice, some kind of chapati or tortilla, falafel, vegetables of all kinds seared on the coals, hummus, two kinds of beans, and urns of tea.

"No meat, of course," Alex explained.

Before the meal was a kind of prayer. Baba Ji sat, legs crossed, eyes closed, palms up, and chanted some tribute to the earth and sky. Incense was lit, which Sundown thought tacky, since her mother had taught her that incense during a meal interfered with the enjoyment of the food. Nevertheless, the Islanders dug in with gusto—some with forks, a couple with chopsticks, and some with fingers.

Sundown leaned over to Alex, who had a kind of beatific smile on his face. "Baba Ji's not eating?"

He smiled patronizingly. "He no longer has any need to eat. He's attained another level of existence."

Sundown wondered if Baba Ji had been at the hot dogs inside his trailer beforehand, and was about to share this jest with Alex, but one look at his face indicated to her that he had probably lost his sense of humor.

After the meal another prayer was offered up to the now darkening sky, and music started, a harmonium and finger cymbals. People began to chant the mantra "the river of light, the valley of love," over and over again until it filled the mind.

Some kind of joint was passed around. Baba Ji declined to participate in this too. Sundown took a hit when it was passed to her and was unpleasantly surprised. This was not grass, or it was grass treated with something else. Maybe the STP or Angel Dust she had heard about. The back part of her brain flared into some kind of activity, and her eyesight became enhanced—the lowering twilight took on a fluorescent luminosity. The trees against the night sky, which formerly she would have had trouble separating at this time of the evening, now stood out in accentuated depth. And the sky itself, a typical Los Angeles sky with a scattering of dim stars, took on the brilliant splendor of a mountain starscape. But she felt somehow soiled, and passed it quickly on.

She looked at Alex, and she could see in the firelight that his eyes were closed. Perhaps he had taken more hits than she had; at any rate he looked inaccessible.

"The river of light, the valley of love..."

When the joint returned once more, she passed it without even pretending to take another hit. Everyone looked zonked. Far from the feeling of wellbeing that good grass provided, this—whatever it was—left her uneasy and paranoid.

A woman was washing Baba Ji's feet. He was smiling, a smiling patriarch in radiant white. Strange that no one else was wearing white. Was that one of their rules?

"Brothers and sisters," Baba Ji intoned, waving away the foot-washer, "the fact that we are here tonight is no accident. The universe has willed it. You may think you chose to be here, but you were sent. Or rather drawn here, like bees to a flower, by instinct." His resonant voice, probably theater-trained, rang like a bell across the darkening compound. All were silent, listening. Only the coals popped and spat occasionally.

"Look around you. We have people of all races here, with skins of all colors. But it doesn't matter. We are all of the same tribe. Perhaps over the centuries our peoples were dispersed around the earth; now, at last, we are reunited."

It all sounded plausible, Sundown thought. At the very least it was a nice idea.

"Mankind has been given an opportunity to re-form, to remake itself. That opportunity is Island. Here, we're trying to move onto the next level. We're in the process of evolving into *Homo superior,* a better race."

Sundown was not exactly sure how vegetarian food and toddlers without diapers were achieving this. She suspected there might be some other plans at work.

"But no transition happens uncontested," Baba Ji continued. "Outsiders will not understand—they belong to the old race. Even we will not understand sometimes—after all, we are hindered by old race thinking from humanity's Dark Ages. Our minds, trained from birth into the old ways, will struggle, sometimes, with the new."

Sundown gazed at the crowd. Everyone was enthralled, still muttering the chant. She experienced a vague discomfort. Wasn't this all a bit Hitlerish?

"But we Islanders will prevail. We will show the outside world that what we have is not just desirable, but inevitable. Ours is the way of the future. A new and better humanity will, in time, make a new and better world."

He smiled and closed his eyes. Applause rippled around the fire. Sundown wanted to move, to get up and go home, but getting to her feet felt like a monumental task. Besides, where was the way out? Since the sun had set the place had become more and more odd and ... alien. It was a world within a world. She had fallen down Alice's rabbit hole and was stuck with the Mad Hatter. And the people ... they chanted about love but they radiated hostility.

A light glowed from within the tipi, making it look like an illuminated traffic cone. The trailer shone like a grounded blimp.

"Alex!" she managed to hiss. "Alex!"

"The river of light, the valley of love..."

A cool wind ran through the compound. Her mind felt violated somehow, stained. What was this Baba Ji guy up to here? The "wives"—were they all his? Were all the babies his too? What kind of religion was this anyway? He would probably deny it was a religion, but it felt like one. Or ... what was the word? ... a cult. She looked for the man, but he was gone from his spot. At the same time she sensed someone sitting next to her. Thank God—Alex had come back to his senses and they could get out of here. But no, it was Baba Ji.

"I thought I heard you calling me," he said, in his mellifluous, compelling voice.

"Oh ... hi." She summoned her energies and tried to focus. "I was ... about to leave."

"Leave? Why? You fit in here—don't you feel it?"

He gazed into her eyes and, try as she might, she couldn't pull her attention away from him. She felt skewered, his mind burrowing about inside hers.

Before she could speak again, he continued. "We are the Chosen of the Lord, Sundown," he explained, as if it were the most natural thing in the world. "It doesn't matter which Lord—they're all the same. That's what all the ancient religions have been trying to tell us. All gods are one, and we are parts of God. It's all very simple. And since we're all parts of God, it's only natural that we should get together. That's what we've been put here on earth to find out—how to find our way back together. You and I belong together, Sundown—the universe wills it."

Sundown tried desperately to reassemble her faculties. "No, I..."

"The Island is the way of the future. The Island is the world; or how the world will soon be. We are the Chosen of the Lord," he reiterated, "which means that everyone else is the chosen of Satan. There comes a time when we must all choose which side to be on. Which side are you on, Sundown?"

"I..."

"Armageddon is upon us, Sundown, and after the flood there will be wars between the saved and the damned. Of course Topanga won't survive, but we have land high up in the Sierras that will, and there we will reestablish the world. A newer, better world. You can be a queen of that world, Sundown, and rule with me."

Sundown's skin crawled. Her fuzzy mind fished around for a response. This was the pickup line to beat all pickup lines. "That's... that's a big decision to expect me to make, right here, right now. Give me some time to think about it and I'll let you know."

Something flickered behind Baba Ji's eyes. It wasn't friendly. He frowned, briefly, but then his smile reasserted itself. "That's only fair," he conceded, "and no one can say I'm not fair. Take a little walk; clear your head. Then come back and talk to me—I'll be here." He walked away, his white form shining like a specter.

Sundown took another quick glance at Alex. He was swaying from side to side with the chant, his hair almost covering his face, lost to her. She stood, shakily, and tottered off toward where she believed the entrance gate lay. On the way she passed faces of the Islanders—guarded, afraid, resentful of her contact with their spiritual leader. What the hell was going on here? And where the hell was the entrance?

The image of Rain came into her mind. She wished the woman were here now. Rain would set her straight; she'd have something pithy to say about the Islanders and Baba Ji. She'd say anyone who needs drugs for enlightenment doesn't get it. She'd say Baba Ji was a wolf in guru's clothing. This made Sundown feel a little better.

One of the commune people, a young man built like a wrester, was standing by the gate like a guard. Sundown didn't know if he'd been instructed not to let anyone leave, but she plastered a smile on her face and said "I just have to get something from my car."

He let her through, and she staggered up the dark road. This was where she parked, wasn't it? She could no longer tell direction. For a panicked moment she thought someone had taken her car, but at last she found the Corvair and clambered in, sighing with relief. But she was afraid someone would come after her, and so she fumbled for her keys and switched the car into life. She turned on the lights, shoved it into first, and swung the car around toward home.

— · —

Jackson had worked all night replacing blades on a ship, and was so tired he thought he could even sleep through the sticky day. As the sun came up he was steeling himself to go back into the oven of a hooch when some kind of commotion ran through the camp. An attack? No, there was no gunfire, no rush for the shelters, and men were looking up, not out toward the camp boundary.

He squinted to see a Huey smoking and swinging erratically back and forth across the brightening sky. As it came closer, he saw the white square with red cross on its nose—a dustoff flight that couldn't make it the couple of extra miles to the 71st Evac hospital in Pleiku. Its pilot was fighting bravely to keep it under control, but its turbine had quit and he was attempting to land on autorotation, a tricky maneuver at the best of times. Pilots were trained to deal with it, but hoped never to need it.

Instead of the Huey's usual steep, almost-vertical angle of descent, this one was coming in shallow and fast. Just a few feet above the ground the pilot pulled the nose up and flared, allowing some of the cushion of air from under the still-spinning rotors to lower his speed. All lift gone, the

Huey dropped the remaining distance with an ungainly thump, mashing its skids and spilling red-spattered bodies onto the metal runway.

Jackson ran toward the helicopter, and with the other men helped wrestle body after body onto stretchers. When they ran out of stretchers, they pulled down tents and folded them into impromptu pallets, dragging them and their burdens to Holloway's small medic area.

Soon the injured had been loaded onto another ship to be flown into Pleiku, so there was nothing more Jackson could do. Sleep was a distant memory, impossible now. Though he tried to rest, even with eyes closed all he could see were mangled limbs and blood pooling in the circular cutouts of the metal runway. This was what war was all about, he understood. This is what happened to the grunts. It hadn't hit him until now, until he saw blood pumping out of arteries and men with newly missing limbs, what was going on.

— · —

Charity took out her journal and pen.

> *Castor bean plants, large-leafed weeds that were once thought ornamental, grow wild in all untended parts of the canyon, especially near water. Their poisonous seeds have delicate tortoiseshell markings and look like little bugs. Mussolini's Blackshirts force-fed castor oil to dissidents, knowing full well its laxative properties.*

2000

Sundown looked around the tree house. "There's nothing of mom's here. Everyone else, but not her."

"She never liked climbing up here," Robbie said. "But she made the pillows."

"You know, I never knew what mom saw in dad," Sundown said. "I wish she was still around so I could ask her."

"I talked to her about it once," Charity said. "She grew up in a big family, and pretty poor. Dad seemed confident, she said. I think he represented a way out. She used to make a joke, too—she said that being a Lanzavecchia, she was attracted to his shorter name."

"So she exchanged a wop name for a Polack."

"One less syllable."

"And then, after Jackson ... I guess they felt as if they had to stay together."

Sundown picked up a roach clip made from small tongs welded to an Indian-head nickel pounded concave. "This looks like one of yours, Robbie. Didn't you hand these out with weed, like the gift in Crackerjacks?"

"Savvy marketing," he said. He stooped to push aside the beanbag and pick up a well-thumbed repair manual for the Pontiac GTO. He brushed off the silverfish and glanced at Charity. "Did Jacks come up here much ... after?"

Charity looked away. She was struck by Jackson's presence more than his absence, even though he had been gone three decades. "When he wasn't working on the car. Dad ... dad didn't know what to do with him. Nor did I, really, but I used to try. I ... should have tried harder."

Robbie turned to Sundown and changed the subject. "What about you? How's the beauty biz?"

"I don't model any more. I run a model agency that guarantees women fair treatment on gigs. It's the only one in L.A."

"When did you start that?"

"A few years ago, when I went on an assignment and some shithead looked me up and down and handed me a diuretic."

"So," Charity summarized, "We've all done OK. I think mom and dad would be proud."

Robbie looked uncomfortable at the mention of their parents. "How do you think they got along ... after ... Jackson?"

Sundown stared out of the window. "It changed everything. They were never as close after that, I think. Though dad tried to get back to what we all had ... before."

Robbie shook his head. "Mom kinda lost her ... drive, or spirit, somehow. She stopped making things. And then we drifted away."

Charity nodded sadly. "They still loved each other though, right?"

"They went through counseling. Dad tried living down in the Valley for a while."

A glint from one of the drawers caught Charity's eye. She pulled out a small coil of wire, spotted with rust. "What's this?"

Robbie took it and rasped his fingernail along the side of one strand. "It's a guitar string. Bottom E, looks like." He laughed. "From my illustrious career as a guitarist."

Sundown gave him a wry smile. "Things didn't work out the way any of us wanted."

Charity regarded them both with a smile. "But they worked out."

22
Fall, 1968
Those were the days

Fall, in Southern California shoved to the end of the year, takes place between Thanksgiving and Christmas. Topanga's oaks are live oaks, and their leaves stay on all year, so it doesn't announce itself, and even the sycamores by the creeks keep most of their big, dusty leaves. The tumbleweed bushes dry from green to pale tan, and the October winds uproot them and roll them across the roads to pile up in ditches. Warm days alternate with cooler, until before you know it the year is over.

— · —

After the school inspector had left, Bret's eyes filled with fury. He grabbed Robbie's shoulder and slammed the boy against the doorjamb. "Don't you *ever* lie to us like this again! You *have* to go to school—it's the law. All this time your mom and I—"

"I don't need school. You don't believe in it. It's all bullshit."

"That's *it!*" Bret snarled. "You're going to Ridgewood!"

Robbie paled. Ridgewood was a military academy in the Valley, used as a threat to get wayward boys in line. It worked. "OK, OK," he said, "I'll try harder."

Maddy said, "All the time you told us you were going to Pali High you were ditching! What the hell were you doing all day?"

"I was … hanging out."

"Hanging out?" Bret repeated. "What kind of job is that going to get you?" His voice took on a high-pitched, sarcastic tone. "'Yes sir, I was real good at hanging out. How much are you going to pay me for doing nothing all day?'"

"High school's no use to anyone. 'Sides, I'm going back to England with Owen. He's gonna get me work as a guitarist."

Maddy said quietly, "He already left."

Robbie turned to her with a stricken look. For a moment he couldn't speak. "He went back? To England?"

She nodded. "He was never going to be out here for good."

"But we had a deal."

His mother shook her head. "No, I don't think so, Robbie. He wouldn't want a sixteen-year-old in tow. You must've misunderstood." She looked away.

Bret glared at his son. "You'd better shape up, boy, or things are going to go really badly for you. You think you don't have to play by the rules, but it doesn't work that way."

Robbie fought back tears. He looked at his mother. "Why? Why did he go back? He said he liked it here."

"Foreign visitors are eligible for the draft after three months. He got his notice to appear for an army medical. He didn't like the idea of ending up in Vietnam."

Robbie, to avoid showing his feelings, hurried to his bedroom and slammed the door. He put his foot through the speaker of his amplifier. Then he took his guitar out of its case and wielded it like an ax, smashing it against the floor.

— · —

The mood in Hophead Hills was so tense that both sisters actually chose to be in their bedroom at the same time that evening, Charity scribbling intently in her journal, and Sundown flicking absently through a copy of *Seventeen*.

When their father yelled *"Sundown! Phone!"* they both looked up in alarm. The phone was starting to portend trouble, and Sundown in particular dreaded it being that guitarist Alex, or even worse, his guru Baba Ji.

She walked into the kitchen and reluctantly took the phone from her father as if it might bite. "Hello?"

"Sundown? It's Frank. How are you?"

The unease in her chest dissipated. "Oh, fine."

"Good, good. Uh … I was wondering if you wanted to do dinner again. I enjoyed Musso & Frank. There's another place I think you might like. Are you free on Saturday?"

Sundown thought quickly. She was, but she hesitated to admit it. On the other hand, if she stalled she'd have to call back, and she didn't believe in playing games. Besides, she couldn't deny it was good to hear from him again. Frank was mature. Frank was an intellectual. Frank was a possible way out. "OK."

— · —

Next morning, Maddy and Bret attempted to work in the tower.

Bret taped together three sheets of quadrille paper to make a wiring diagram. Despite the Robbie debacle, he was feeling good. His last paycheck had just arrived, so his bank account was flush, and he didn't have to go back to work for two weeks. His favorite situation: money without having to work for a while.

Maddy was using her sewing machine, one of the newer Swedish models, surrounded by bolts of bright satin, reels of binding and ribbon, colorful spools of cotton, and flimsy pattern sheets that flapped in the breeze from the ceiling fan.

'Maddy?" Bret said.

The sewing machine's chatter stopped.

"I don't know what's going on lately, I swear. Jackson's gone overseas, Robbie's a pothead, and Sundown's … kinda loose."

"Charity's OK."

"Charity's struggling to understand it all. Kids these days—they never had their own culture before."

"What d'you mean, culture?"

"Their own music, their own books, their own fashions. It makes 'em think they're adults, but they're not."

"I think it's cute, in a way. They want to change the world for the better."

"What—with beads and dope? Ain't gonna happen."

"Maybe. But you can't blame them for trying. Look what a mess we've made of things."

Bret's face reddened. "I hate idealists."

"It's the younger generation's duty to at least try, Bret. And it's the parents' duty to get frustrated with them."

"They need more discipline."

"You can't expect Robbie to stop smoking pot if you do it. And..." Maddy looked away, out of the windows, to the hazy distance.

"And?"

"And you can't call Sundown 'loose' if you sleep around. Kids hate hypocrisy."

"Honey, I explained all that—"

"No, you didn't; you just came clean. It doesn't make the facts go away."

"Maddy, I'm sorry. I was stupid. Can we ... move on?"

She was not about to let him off that easy. "Lay off the kids. They need love, not lectures."

"You sound like a flower child."

"Oh? Is that such a bad thing?"

They were silent for a moment. Neither resumed work.

Bret looked askance at his wife. "Hon? You OK?"

Maddy paused and glanced at him briefly. "Sure."

"You seem ... different lately. You getting sick?"

"No, I'm fine."

Bret gave up, puzzled. He decided it was probably her period. Or was she past the period stage now? He didn't know how to ask. Better not.

Maddy looked out of the window. It was going to be a hot day—she could tell by the metallic sheen of the sky. Any outside work would have to be done before eleven or after four. "Bret?"

"Yeah."

"Y'know what we were ... talking about?"

Bret's earlier good mood disappeared, replaced by a sinking feeling in his gut. "What was that?"

"About ... open relationships."

"Oh. Yeah."

Maddy swallowed. "I had one."

Bret frowned. "Had one what?"

[239]

"A-an affair."

All blood drained from his face. Finally, he managed to form words. "Who?"

Isn't that a typical man, Maddy thought. Not "why?" but "who?" "I'm not saying. But it won't happen again."

Bret's mind ceased working properly. "Who?" he said again.

"I'm not saying. It just happened." She looked at him with a blank expression in her dark eyes. "Like it did with you, I guess."

His eyes narrowed. Color returned to his face. He stood and clenched his fists. "It was the Limey, wasn't it?"

"Bret, I—"

"It *was!* Goddamn! Behind my back!"

"Bret, you did the same."

"But I said I was sorry! Now you go and..."

"We had an 'open relationship,' you said," Maddy reminded him, a hint of cruelty in her tone.

Bret looked on the verge of tears. "H-how long?"

"Just once. It was just a spur of the moment thing. I didn't plan it."

"'Spur of the moment,'" Bret repeated dully.

"Yes. It's not important."

"Not important." Bret looked around. "Not important."

"No. You said it didn't mean anything, right? Well, I understand completely—it was the same for me."

"Don't keep throwing my own words back in my face!"

"Why not?"

Bret threw his diagram across the desk and left. In a minute Maddy heard the sound of the Camaro roaring away.

— · —

Robbie was sitting in the corner of the quad, seething about the ruins of his rock star plans, when the new kid came up to him. The boy's hair was in the process of growing out messily from a shorter cut, like many teenage boys lately, and he was paler than most. He looked like a senior.

"Hi," the new kid said, leaning against the wall beside him. "I'm Henry."

"Robbie."

"Hey, Robbie."

Despite feeling homicidal, Robbie made an effort to be friendly. "Where you from, Henry?"

"Indiana. Just moved here. Dad's in construction."

"Mine's in the movies. Gaffer."

"Wow. Now I *know* I'm in L.A."

They were silent for a while, watching girls file by, clutching their books to their chests like shields.

Henry finally turned to Robbie. "I don't have any connections here yet."

"Connections?"

"Y'know. To score. Weed."

"Oh."

The bell rang.

Robbie looked at Henry, assessing him quickly. "Later."

— · —

Jackson and Willie worked even later than usual. A mission had gone spectacularly wrong, and almost all the Hueys involved, slicks and guns, needed repairs. The two men toiled into the night, and when they were done they slouched back to the hooch past the parked ships silhouetted against the horizon's predawn glow.

"You miss home?" Willie asked.

It was unusual for the man to express anything that smacked of emotions. Jackson put it down to his tiredness. "It's so far away, it all feels like a dream."

Willie grunted. "Wish *this* was the dream."

A moving shape separated from one of the gunships and, surprised that anyone was still working, Jackson flicked on his flashlight to see who it was.

Its beam illuminated a small face with pageboy haircut.

"Mai, isn't it?" he said in surprise. "What you doing here, Mai?"

The diminutive figure turned and ran away, and Jackson, after a shocked hesitation, ran after her, while Willie ran to examine the Huey she had been beside. As he reached the fence an explosion blew him onto his face in the mud. One of the Hueys was now a cat's cradle of aluminum and magnesium.

Willie was dead, shards of metal embedded in him from face to crotch.

Jackson spun and fired his pistol in Mai's direction, but it was futile. She was gone.

— · —

Robbie sat through classes, hopelessly behind in the work from all his absences. He felt humiliated and angry, an outsider misunderstood by everyone, family and school alike. His gaze would return over and over again to the view outside the window—tree ferns, palms, open blue sky. Outside was freedom; people doing important things. Outside bands were recording, performing, touring. Outside people were demonstrating about the war. Inside ... inside was Social Studies.

Following that, a showing of *Red Asphalt*, a cheesy public service film intended as a warning about the hazards of driving distracted, drunk, or too fast.

After school Robbie looked for Henry, finally finding him in the parking lot about to get into a battered dune buggy. Dune buggies were hot since *The Thomas Crown Affair*, which featured a long, exhilarating sequence of a dune buggy actually on sand dunes, whereas most here were just street vehicles. The nearest beach you could drive on was Pismo, over two hours north.

"Hey," he said, "Nice wheels."

"My brother's."

"I've got some smoke if you're still interested."

"Great. How much?"

"Twelve. It's not primo, but it's OK."

Henry smiled. "All *riiiight*."

They crouched down inside the fiberglass shell of the car and completed the transaction.

"OK, cool, man," Henry said. "Thanks."

"Later."

Robbie walked to his motorcycle, started it, and drove down Temescal Canyon to Pacific Coast Highway. He was elated with the deal, and of escaping the school environs, at least until tomorrow. It was crappy weed, and the money would allow him to get some better stuff.

There were still a few hours of daylight left, and he would have time to stop and watch the surfers at Will Rogers Beach. Perhaps he could take orders there for some more deliveries tomorrow. Perhaps—

A police car siren whooped behind him. Damn. Had he been going too fast? Impossible. The CT90 was notoriously underpowered. He pulled onto the hard shoulder by the cliff and switched off the engine.

Two policemen walked up and stood on either side of him.

"You Robert Sobieski?" asked one.

"Y-yeah."

"I'm arresting you for possession of narcotics, and for unlawful sale of narcotics to a minor, on state property." He took a card from his pocket and read from it in a stilted monotone. "You have the right to remain silent. Anything you say may be used against you in a court of law. You have the right to the presence of an attorney to assist you prior to questioning and to be with you during questioning, if you so desire. If you cannot afford an attorney, you have the right to have one appointed for you prior to questioning. Do you understand these rights?"

"I guess."

"Do you understand these rights?"

"Yeah."

The other policeman clicked handcuffs on him and led him to the back seat of the police car.

"What about my bike?"

The policemen laughed. "No one would want to steal that piece of crap. But we'll send someone out."

— · —

Robbie's absence went without comment at the house—he was often out late. Charity took advantage of him being gone by writing at the kitchen table, instead of hiding out in her room.

> *Although there are many butterflies in Southern California, the orange and black Monarch is the most eye-catching, and probably the best known. There are two populations of Monarchs in the US. The group east of the Rockies migrates south to spend the winter in Mexico, while the western group migrates to the coast of central and southern California. Some fly over 1,000 miles, and many don't make it. By November, the survivors shelter from San Francisco to San Diego. Topanga doesn't host a significant number, but a few miles north is Sycamore Canyon, and thousands make their winter home here. After—*

The phone rang. Charity was closest, and so she picked it up. "Hello?"

"Charity?" Robbie's frightened voice came over the line, "I've been busted. Tell dad I need a lawyer."

"What's 'busted'?"

"*Arrested,* dammit. Get dad."

Charity waved her father over. "Robbie's been busted."

Bret grabbed the phone. "What for?"

"Possession."

"How much?"

"Not much, but I sold it."

"Oh, well—"

"At school. To a narc."

"Jesus, you little fuckwit. Where are you?"

"West L.A. I gotta go. I need an attorney pronto."

Bret hung up the phone and walked outside to Maddy. "Uh ... hon...?"

— · —

The judge's chambers were all shiny wood and leather. The Sobieski family members sat in the bulky chairs, dressed as conservatively as they could manage. Robbie looked very young and very frightened. One of his legs twitched uncontrollably.

The judge looked sternly at the boy. "Robert, the evidence against you is conclusive. Not only did you, a young man who should know better, carry narcotics onto state property, you sold them, and to an underage person. If this were just possession, given that you have no prior offenses, I would probably have let you off with a fine and community service. As it is, the state guidelines are clear: selling drugs in a school is one of the most serious offenses. It's also morally reprehensible. The State is alarmed at the increase in drug use, and citizens are adamant it *will not take place in schools.*" He steepled his fingers and scowled. "I have no choice but to sentence you to a year in juvenile hall. I hope that by the end of it you'll have seen the error of your ways. That's all."

Bret looked about to burst. He stood, quivering with indignation. "But he's a high school junior!"

The judge glared at him over his glasses. "I presume you are his father, sir. If so, you should know better. Of course I know he's a minor. That's why he didn't get prison. Bailiff, escort these people out."

23

Crammed into the Camaro, the Sobieskis leaned this way and that as Bret wound the car through Malibu Canyon. In the past the kids would exclaim at the twisty road, make risqué comments about the naked "pink lady" painted on the rock above the tunnel entrance and demand the horn be honked halfway through, but this morning the atmosphere in the car was tense, and everyone was unusually quiet. Today Robbie was going to jail.

Camp David Gonzales announced itself by just a small wooden sign, and was easily overlooked in a passing driver's peripheral vision as a utility company's storage yard. Bret missed it at first, and had to hang a U-turn. Then he drove the Camaro down the short, tree-lined lane as the family peered from its windows.

What stretched before them was not the minimum-security "honor farm" they had imagined, but a large full-security facility. What the trees had hidden was a twenty-foot brick wall around the main prison, and a dusty oval yard, as large as a football field, surrounded by a tall cyclone fence topped with vicious-looking razor wire. Huge metal poles held clusters of floodlights.

In the sickly green front office the guard consulted the ledger, which was chained to the countertop. He checked Bret's driver's license, examined his face as if he might also be an inmate, and entered Robbie's name. Then he ordered Robbie to empty his pockets.

On the man's desk appeared a motley collection of keys, a Marlboro soft pack, and the piece of paper with Owen's phone number. Robbie looked at it and recognized, as everything was swept into a bag and labeled, that a whole part of his life was over.

"Well," Maddy said to Robbie with a strained smile, "It's new."

"I looked it up," Charity added. "You're only six miles from us, as the crow flies."

Robbie gave his sister a weak grin. Six miles could be a thousand when you weren't free to leave. No dope, no wheels, no good music, and no freedom. No girls, either.

"And it looks just like Topanga," his father said.

Robbie looked around, trying to stifle the panic rising in his chest. Malibu Canyon was the next canyon up the coast from Topanga. It was relatively unpopulated and much wider, and consequently a little hotter, but it looked a lot like home.

It was just that it wasn't. It was prison. Prison for punks.

"Did they find my bike?" Robbie asked his father.

"No, sorry. By the time they got back there it had been stolen. I filed a report."

Sundown squinted around the compound. "What does everyone do here?"

The guard, overhearing, said, "It's like school, mixed with boot camp."

Robbie grimaced. "Jackson would love it." He steered Sundown out of earshot of the others and whispered, "Hey—we won't be able to smoke dope here, but can you get me some reds?"

"Reds?"

"Y'know—Seconal. No one'll know if I've taken those, and I can hide 'em easily."

"Robbie, I can't possibly smuggle in pills for you. What the fuck is the matter with you?"

He looked at her in desperation.

His mother came over and patted his shoulder. "We'll try and get you out on a Christmas pass. And the attorney said if you behave yourself they're likely to cut it to nine months."

Robbie winced at the thought. Nine months? Nine months might as well be a year. Nine *days* would be hard enough to endure.

And then what? He'd been expelled from Pali High. He'd have to start somewhere new. He felt like crying, but if he did and was seen, he'd be beaten up for sure the moment his family left. He wrenched his face into a mask of bravado. "OK, ma, cool. I'll be fine."

— · —

Sundown waited to pack until Charity was out. This will be the first batch, she told herself, and I'll just grab another load each time I come back.

Into a large suitcase she stuffed the clothes she wore most, makeup and hairbrushes, shoes and boots, and a few books and magazines.

Her mother caught her on her way out. Maddy looked at the suitcase and back at her daughter. "When were you going to tell us?"

"When I saw if it was working out."

"Who is this guy?"

"Frank. He's an architect."

Her mother's eyes narrowed. "He's married, isn't he?"

"Divorced."

Maddy was about to say more when Bret came in and looked at the suitcase.

"What's going on?"

"Sundown's leaving."

"Leaving? Leaving?" He glared at her and balled his fists. "You can't just leave!"

"I can. I'm eighteen."

"You can leave when you're twenty-one."

"Don't be ridiculous. I can do whatever I like, and you don't have a say in it."

"You—"

"I would have left to go to college, right? Well, I'm leaving to live somewhere else, just not a dorm. I'll do the college thing later."

Bret's face had by now deepened dangerously in color. Maddy had to restrain him.

"Sundown, this is a big deal," she said quietly, trying to defuse the situation. "You're an adult now, and you get to make your own decisions. But be careful out there. You'll be on your own; no one's looking out for you except yourself."

Sundown, on the verge of tears, nodded and made her way downstairs. Bret made as if to follow her, but Maddy slid quickly in front of him to block his way.

"She wants to make you the reason she leaves," she told him quietly. "Don't make it easier for her."

Bret stopped, puzzling out what his wife had said. Then he sagged and turned away. "I didn't think it would happen like this."

They watched from a window as Sundown shoved her case into her car and drove off.

"It's OK. It's just … life."

— · —

Sundown stepped inside and looked around. The place looked stylish, as she would expect with an architect's taste, but sterile—a movie set of an apartment, with no lived-in touches. It smelled of wood polish and air freshener, but no food, no cigarettes. "Won't somebody complain?"

He smiled. "It's my company. I can do whatever I like."

Sundown poked her head into the bathroom and saw a second porcelain convenience. "Oh…"

"Yes," he said, "we get some Europeans in town, so I put in a bidet."

"Of course. Good idea." She looked through the window and down onto Wilshire Boulevard's bustling Miracle Mile. The traffic hummed incessantly—she would have to get used to that. But this was what she wanted, wasn't it? Urban, in the center of things. Certainly about as far from a dusty canyon as she could get while still staying in Los Angeles.

She turned back to him. "For how long?"

Frank wandered around, straightening cushions. "Long as you like. I can always put up clients at hotels."

Sundown paused for a length of time she thought would not make her seem easy. "OK."

Frank kissed her. This would normally be the prelude to their lovemaking, but this time he reluctantly pulled away.

"I have to get back to work. See you this evening?"

On an impulse, Sundown said, "I'll make you dinner."

Used to their dates at restaurants, Frank hesitated. "That's OK, we—"

"I want to."

Frank's uncertain expression bent into a smile. "Great. Thanks. I'll bring the wine."

— · —

Bret and Maddy sat in front of the TV, a gulf between them. Charity sat on the floor, stroking the dog.

Bret's anger made him unapproachable, and his resultant isolation made him angrier still. He felt as if he had lost his family, or at least alienated each of its members. Nothing was going right.

Sundown had replaced him with another man, as old as him, maybe. Robbie had turned into a petty criminal. Charity was apparently getting religion, and he had messed up his opportunity of talking her out of it. Jackson was in a foreign country crawling with people who wanted to kill him, and how long could that last? And Maddy, now that he had admitted his affairs—his face burned as he recalled the day—had had one of her own.

The family had been, in the past, like an engine, all its parts working together. Certainly there had been times when it misfired and stalled, or needed repairs, but it ran. Now, it was coming apart. And he didn't know how to rebuild it.

Now there were just three of them at the house. Hophead Hills had abruptly emptied, far earlier than he had anticipated. It was weirdly quiet, with no one to interrupt him, rev a car engine, play music too loudly, yell at a sibling or the dog. Even the television seemed to be talking to itself, with stiff interviews with presidential hopefuls and their self-appointed shills.

This would pass, wouldn't it? Things would improve. The war would be over soon and Jackson back tinkering with his car instead of helicopters. Soon he would be telling stories of near misses and drunken stupidity on base. Bret swore silently that he would cheerfully listen to them over and over, as Jackson got older and began to tell them to his children.

Sundown would find a nice boy her own age and leave her wild years behind. Robbie would straighten himself out and get a job. Charity would ... well, she was young. Anything could happen in the next few years.

As for Maddy ... he would have to show her he had made a mistake and knew it.

He stared at the television. "Nixon'll wind things down in Vietnam, you'll see, now LBJ's out."

Maddy was not so sure. "He looks shifty to me. Devious."

"I wrote to him," Charity announced. "I told him we all want the war to be over so Jacks can come home."

O to see the world through the simple eyes of a child. "That's nice, honey," Bret said, getting up from the sofa and patting her shoulder. In the kitchen he poured himself a large glass of wine. After a hefty swig, he turned back to the living room and assessed what was left of his family. Everything was turning sour; at least that's how it seemed. He pulled down the one postcard they had received from Jackson and stared at its tantalizingly terse scrawl.

> Hey all. Wet here and never seem to get the mud off my clothes. Send a washing machine. The biggest enemies are the mosquitoes. Never see the VC. Could use some magazines—maybe MAD and Car & Driver. And some of mom's cookies. Love to all, Jacks.

— · —

For a while Sundown bustled about the apartment, trying to make it home. She hung her clothes in the closets, put her few books on the shelf in the living room, draped a scarf over one of the bedside lamps to tint its light rose. She opened the windows to enjoy the refreshing newness of the city sounds, but soon tired of it and closed them again.

She sat on the bed and stared for a while, appreciating her new state of aloneness, noting the lack of the static and angst of family life. Then, not wishing to deal with these kinds of feelings, she locked up and took the elevator down to the street. Just a couple of blocks west was Orbach's department store, and she bought some cheerful, Indian-inspired cushions with tiny mirrors sewn into them, and a lava lamp. Outside again, she was tempted to walk along to the La Brea Tar Pits behind the Museum, but there really wasn't time if she was to prepare dinner. She chuckled, remembering her Spanish lessons. "The La Brea Tar Pits" literally translated to "The The Tar Tar Pits," but no one seemed to notice the tautology.

From a convenience store on a side street she assembled the ingredients for a spaghetti meal. The prices were inflated, compared to the suburbs, but she supposed city dwellers were used to it. Real Italian pasta and the subtle fixings her mother would have used were not on the shelves, so she had to do her best with what was. Then, burdened with bags, she made her way back to her new home.

— · —

Suddenly energized by her sister's departure, Charity took down Sundown's posters and replaced them with her own. She put away the Jim Morrison photo and the ads from European *Vogue,* and arranged her tissue paper flowers in their place. Then she sat complacently, surveyed her new domain, and opened her journal.

> *The cats of Topanga come in differing sizes and states of wildness. The domestic cat, if let outside, is often flea-riddled with fur matted with foxtails. Then there are the feral cats, once domestic but gone back to the wild, training their young to kill—mostly mice and baby rats—because there'll be no more food out of cans. There are true wildcats, like a chunky house cat with bigger ears with a lynx-like tuft of fur on top, but they are not often seen. Lastly there is the mountain lion, the cougar, which rarely attacks humans but nevertheless leaves a trail of persistent stories of when it did.*
>
> *Coyotes can appear anywhere and at any time, and look a little like mangy gray German Shepherds. They seem fond of domestic cats, and sometimes corner them when hunting in a pack, leaving the head and spine uneaten.*

— · —

Sundown and Frank lay in bed, the sweat drying on their bodies.

"I like what you've done with the place," he said with a grin.

"Sorry about the meal. It was—"

"It was fine." He stifled a belch. "Great. I appreciate it."

"I like it here."

"Good. Listen ... I have to take a shower and get outta here. See you tomorrow?"

She sat up. "Can't you stay?"

"No, not tonight, hon. Some other time."

— · —

Thoughts of Jackson in Vietnam keep running around Bret's head, resulting in an insomnia-inducing tangle of worry, guilt, and regret. He tried to distract himself by imagining how he would demand his ten bucks back from the shitty John Lennon and Yoko Ono album he had just bought that turned out to be just a bunch of wailing, but it didn't work. He thrashed around in bed for an hour before giving up on sleep and walking outside into the cool night air.

There in the distance, its dark bulk dimly visible against the night sky, sat the tree house. Bret recalled the summer, ten years ago now, when he and Jackson had built it. Jackson was only eight then, and so he hadn't been much help, but it had been good for the kid. It gave him a sense of accomplishment, and he was able to show off to his sister Sundown. Robbie had been too young, then, to appreciate what was going on.

They had chosen the trees—not difficult, since there weren't many suitable—and then driven to the lumberyard to buy two-by-fours and planks. Then it was off to the scrapyard at the foot of the hill for old tires, one to hang below as a swing and two more to slice into protective collars for the trees.

Jackson's serious, deliberate manner became evident that summer, his interest in planning and executing ideas. It had been no surprise to Bret that as soon as the boy had become old enough to drive he had transferred his energies to fixing and modifying a car. There was no public bus service in Topanga, and so any teenager that wanted to go places without having to wait on rides from friends had to have a car, or at least a motorcycle.

Wheels were a prerequisite in Los Angeles—the city was so spread out that it was almost impossible to get around without them, unless you were willing to waste great chunks of the day transferring between sporadic buses. Consequently, cars could be bought cheaply, and down in the Valley stretched mile upon mile of dealerships and used car lots. To teens now, especially to boys, owning wheels was crucial, a symbolic entrée into manhood. No boy could be taken seriously by a potential date without one. No matter if it were jalopy, pickup, hot rod, dragster, convertible or coupe, a guy had to drive *something*.

Now Jackson had entered another phase of his life. Unfortunately. In retrospect, Bret viewed the boy's car tinkering as a golden age, never be revisited. Even without the war, Jackson would have been growing away from the family and out on his own, but Vietnam added its polarizing weight to every decision these days, and would interfere with Jackson's destiny in ways yet to be seen.

Sleep was impossible. Bret pulled on shorts and sweatshirt, slipped on sandals, and paused in the kitchen to roll a doobie. Then, lighting it, he slipped outside. The grass underfoot was dry and scratchy, and the foxtails would just irritate his feet if he walked on the property, and so he chose the silent road.

He strolled uphill, and soon reached more open ground that allowed views between and over the oaks. Birds were beginning to stir in their dark branches. The eastern sky was lightening, fading the meager smattering of stars.

What kind of sky was Jackson viewing? His stomach clenched at the thought of his son, subject to the murderous intent of a guerilla army just across the barbed wire. There were no rules in this kind of war. Jackson may not be a soldier per se, but to the North Vietnamese he was an invader just the same.

A *tick-tick-tick* made him turn. A low black shape was trotting toward him, wearing a bandana just revealing itself to be red.

"Hey, Gilligan. Come to keep your old man company?"

— · —

Although Camp David Gonzales was new, its systems seemed to Robbie medieval. The inmates were divided into dorms whose doors were locked at 10:00 and unlocked again at 6:00 by a jailer with jangling keys.

In his short time as an inmate, Robbie had already adopted the custom of walking outside as soon as he could in the morning, both to get out of the stale secondhand air from a dozen adolescents and to avoid confrontations with boys with too much contained resentment. At the same time he tried not to appear unsociable, which would have brought its own revenge; just taciturn. A delicate balance.

In the cold morning air, as Robbie and a hawk atop an oak regarded one another, a boy from another dorm sidled up to him.

"So—what kinda name is Sobieski anyway? Russian?"

Robbie turned to see a kid with the pugnacious air of a gang leader. "Polish. So what's yours?"

"Fratelli."

"Is that Italian?"

The eyes flashed. "It's American. What—you think I'm mafia?"

"N-no. My mother's Italian."

"Oh yeah?" Fratelli acted indifferent to the information, but his aggressive demeanor softened. "Hear you was busted for dope. How much you sell?"

"A lid."

"A *lid?* You got busted for a *lid?* Shit, man, I got busted for five keys. You shoulda made it worth your while. Least you coulda had some bread when you got out, like me. What you got? Ten fuckin' bucks? Some expensive vacation you got yourself."

Reaching for something to respond, Robbie came up empty.

Two Air Force fighters flew low over the camp, to practice among the hills of the canyon. Jackson had told him once that the eroded sandstone hills there looked a lot like parts of Vietnam.

As Fratelli wandered away, Robbie reflected how much had changed in just a couple of months. Both he and his brother were now behind barbed wire, just for different reasons. As for the rest of his family ... he didn't really know. "Family" meant more than just being related. Proximity was a crucial part, being around one another enough to keep up with their lives and the changes they were inevitably going through.

It was only now he recognized the true meaning of home, now he'd been excluded from his.

— · —

Back at the house, Bret shaved. He reflected that a man got to know his own face better than almost anything else, he spent so much of his life shaving it. He had long ago learned how to look up to stretch his chin in order to reach all of the folds of flesh. He knew to be careful of the little bump under his left ear, or he would nick it and it would bleed like a bastard. Sideburns had to be handled carefully, or they would end up uneven and take weeks to grow back properly.

He had not envisioned his elder daughter leaving like this. If he had thought about it at all, he pictured a dinner with a suitor one evening in the distant future, then, if all went well, the young man would ask for her hand in marriage, like in the old days.

But for her to just walk out and live with someone, someone older, in some downtown apartment ... this wasn't right. Sure, things were changing, morals were changing, relationships were changing, but not like this. It hurt. His little Sundown, so cute, so pretty, so interested in everything around her, now a woman, making love with a man he might never even meet. It was too painful to consider. He wished he could talk to his wife about it, but he had forfeited his standing as wise patriarch, especially on the subject of sex, and any attempt at discussion of it would probably return to his infidelities.

Luckily it was time to leave. This time it was to Stockbridge, Massachusetts, for some scenes for *Alice's Restaurant* with Arlo Guthrie and Pete Seeger. Much too far to drive, he had booked a flight out of LAX.

He felt like a deserter, bailing on his wife and kids who all seemed lately to need his help. But he couldn't deny he was looking forward to getting away. Nothing was going right. He yearned to be in an environment where he was in charge.

He scrawled a note to Maddy and left it on the refrigerator door.

Back soon hon. Miss you already.

24

A crew chief explained the situation.

Earlier in the day, gunships had flown in ahead to a hot area and hosed the tree line where VC soldiers were hiding. Then, as usual, the slicks flew in the men, who quickly deployed. But the ARVN forces that were supposed to help the Americans refused, leaving their numbers low and their strength weakened. The enemy held firm and returned fire. It had been, he told the mechanics, a total cluster fuck.

By sunset twenty or more men were trapped in the clearing, wounded, and five Huey crewmembers lay dead. The enemy withdrew, and fresh Hueys flew in to rescue the remaining men in the dark. But two helicopters were shot up enough to be left behind. It was too dangerous to send in the big, slow Chinooks to lift them out.

They needed a maintenance recovery team, he told them, to get the ships fixed and flown back to base, or they might fall into the hands of the enemy and be used against them.

Willie had always reminded Jackson that no one in his right mind volunteered. But Jackson vowed revenge for his friend's death. "I'll go," he said.

— · —

Their lovemaking was different now. Not as passionate. Instead of getting lost in it, Sundown felt as if a part of her were hovering above, uninvolved, objective. She told herself this was mature sex; that she and Frank had gone onto another level, that was all. She had just never before had a long enough relationship to have reached this point.

Sometimes, though, she felt like a kept woman. "Frank?" she asked.

He had been falling asleep, and jerked awake. "Mmm?"

"We don't always have to make love when we get together, you know."

He grunted, then seemed to realize more was expected of him. "No, of course not. I enjoy your company in all kinds of ways."

"So—what should we do at the weekend?"

"Ah—I'm a bit tied up Saturday and Sunday, I'm afraid."

She was disappointed, but that would just give her more time to decorate.

Sundown decided she liked older men as lovers. They were more considerate, more experienced, more careful, and grateful. They didn't run out of things to say the minute they'd gotten their rocks off, like teens.

So what if Frank was married? Marriage was an old-fashioned and outdated institution anyway. Besides, anything called an "institution" couldn't be good. And anything sanctioned by the church and the state had to be oppressive, by its very nature. People weren't meant to be chained to each other for their entire lives—it was unnatural.

But where were they going from here? The thing was, with short affairs you never had time to think about the future. Now they had made the commitment to live together—sort of—the future demanded to be dealt with.

"Frank?" she asked, "Where are we going?"

He had fallen asleep. "Going?" he asked, groggily.

"I mean ... are you going ahead with the divorce?"

Frank's eyes twitched around the room. "Well, it's complicated."

"Complicated how?"

"Well, Dianne ... owns the house."

"The San Marino house? She owns it?"

He nodded glumly. "And under California law, half the company."

"So if you leave..."

"I'd have nothing."

Sundown sat up, pulling up the sheets to cover herself because she suddenly felt exposed. "So ... you're not divorcing."

Frank sat up too. "Well, now, I didn't say that. It's just..."

"Complicated."

He winced. "I just have to sort things out before I make any sudden moves."

Sundown stooped to collect her clothes from the floor. "I see."

"No, honey, you don't. It's a matter of timing."

"No, I get it. You're just hoping she'll conveniently die. Until then, nothing'll change."

"No, Sundown—"

"I'm just your piece on the side!"

"No—"

— · —

The guard pulled the gooseneck microphone toward him. When he spoke into it, his amplified voice boomed from the outside loudspeakers. *"Sobieski, R! Sobieski, R! Front office immediately!"*

Robbie put down his mop and headed to the office. He assumed it was his family back for a visit, but when he entered the main building he saw Polly and her big brother, looking uncomfortable.

"Oh, hi," he said. "Uh ... thanks for coming."

"Hey," Polly said. "So ... I called the house. I heard you got busted."

Robbie glanced at her brother, whose face wore a grim, you-dumb-little-asshole expression. "Yeah. A little bit of grass."

"On school property," added the superintendent, behind him.

Robbie shrugged. He had no idea what to say.

Nor had Polly. Her eyes darted around the pale green walls and the small barred windows. Eventually she said, "Well, at least it's not a real jail."

To Robbie, who was indifferent to the view of the chaparral through the fencing, it was all the same. His freedom was a thing of the past, and he was in an even worse school than high school used to be.

"You look ... fit," she said.

"Shit, yeah. They make us work out. We have to jog around the damn perimeter twice a day. There's a..." he swallowed, "gym."

"How long you in for?" her brother asked.

"A year, supposedly. We'll see if I get some time reduced."

"No guarantee," the superintendent said.

"Uh ... anything you need?" Polly asked.

Robbie understood she had really nothing much else to say. They hardly knew each other, after all, and two hostile adults were listening to their conversation. They had nothing in common, and they were unlikely to ever see each other again. Any chance they might have had as boyfriend and girlfriend had been tarnished, along with his record. And the only things he needed—freedom, a fat joint, and a time machine to go back and kick his own ass before trying to sell to a narc—she couldn't provide. "No. Thanks."

"Well," her brother said, "We have some other stuff to take care of. Just wanted to make sure you were OK."

"Yeah. Thanks. See ya."

Polly and her brother drove off in his Jeep. Robbie went back to mopping, plagued for more than an hour by the memory of her body under his, willing, ready. Life was cruel.

— · —

The hottest weather is reserved for September. While vast chunks of the country are getting out the snow tires and dusting off storm windows, California is baking. The Santa Ana winds spring up off the desert to heat things up even more.

The vegetation turns to tinder. One careless match, a sloppy campfire, or the hot exhaust pipe of a car that pulls off the road so its passengers can admire the view, can start a wildfire that rips across the meadows and any houses in its way.

The aftermath of a fire is almost as fascinating as the fire itself. The gray moonscape left behind shows the myriad trails of all the wildlife not normally seen because of the undergrowth, a kind of road map of animal wanderings. Then the wildflowers germinate, held back by the bigger and faster-growing plants until a fire gives them their opportunity.

— · —

Bret and Doug watched the rain run down the windows. The New England weather had called a halt to outdoor shooting, and all the interiors were complete, and so everyone was temporarily at a loose end. Actors huddled in their trailers, the caterers shivered in their tent, hair and makeup were talking shop at the local beauty parlor. The director and cameraman were ensconced in the hotel lobby desperately reworking the shooting script, and the gaffers and grips were lounging in the diner's vinyl booths, drinking too much coffee and smoking too many cigarettes.

Doug was reading the *Boston Globe*. "Looks like the rain'll last for a coupla more days at least. Hot as hell back in California, though." He waved the waitress over and gazed at her cleavage as she refilled his coffee.

Bret pointed at the paper. "What else is going on?"

"Apollo 7's launching tomorrow. They're gonna broadcast live from orbit." He shuffled through the newspaper. "Oh, and there's wildfires in Southern California."

Bret sat up. "Lemme see that." He grabbed the paper and studied its map. "Glendora."

"Is that anywhere near your place?"

"Not really. But the conditions are right for it to happen anywhere—Santa Ana winds after a long, dry summer, jerks with cigarette butts..." He handed back the paper and stared again through the window, this time seeing Topanga, California, and not Lee, Massachusetts. Then he stood and reached for his parka. "Back in a while."

— · —

The Production Coordinator was not happy. "Three days? Three days only?"

Bret nodded. "Yeah—I just have to be sure they're prepared. Then I'll come straight back."

"On your own dime?"

"Yeah, yeah. I'll take care of it."

Back at the diner, Doug was half asleep, an ashtray full of butts in front of him.

"Doug—drive me to the airport."

"Huh?"

— · —

Maddy looked sadly at the lasagna and the mound of garlic bread she had made. She would have to learn to scale down her cooking in future, now the family's size had shrunk.

"There are fires over in Canyon Inn," she told Charity. "Perhaps you heard. You haven't seen the damage a fire can do, or how fast it can do it. So—"

"But Glendora's miles away," Charity said.

"It's a lot like Topanga, and they've both been dry for months, and now the Santa Anas have blown in. That means the same thing can happen here."

"We're always careful with matches," Charity assured her, "like you and dad tell us. There's sand buckets all over the place out back, and one in the tree house."

"Yeah, well, a bucket of sand won't do much if fire rolls over that hill out there. Tell your friends not to start any campfires."

Maddy decided to freeze half the lasagna. The garlic bread wouldn't keep. Perhaps she could drop some off at Robbie's camp.

— · —

As the sun set and the sky over Malibu Canyon deepened to a dull purple, an unnatural glow became visible in the east like an early, angry dawn. Robbie and several of his fellow inmates gravitated toward the camp's fence to gaze in that direction.

"Fires," one said, unnecessarily.

"Hey, Sobieski," said another, "Your folks are in Topanga, right?"

Robbie had quickly learned not to respond to potential taunts, and said nothing.

"That's them, man. They crispy bacon now."

"*You boys!*" the supervisor called from the office. "Get the hoses hooked up. You need to soak the perimeter."

"They're gonna send us to help the fire department," the boy continued. "Free labor."

Robbie thought about this. If he were put on fire duty he could hightail it off into the smoke. But where would he go? Hophead Hills would be the first place the police would look.

Being a fugitive sounded romantic, but was probably just a way to end up cold and dirty. He abandoned the idea. He'd made enough stupid mistakes, and he mistrusted his own judgment. It was time to go straight.

Robbie shuffled along the outer fence of the camp under the wary eyes of the guards, waving his hose without enthusiasm. The odor of the distant fires reminded him of a lit joint. He wished he could smoke one now, and retreat from this offensive reality.

Moistening the dust was useless anyway. The fires were miles distant and would take hours to travel this far, whereas this topsoil would stay wet for ten minutes at most. It was just one of the many make-work campaigns that the institution devised to keep inmates out of mischief.

Robbie's face flushed with humiliation, mercifully unnoticeable in the dark. He should be home, acting as the man of the house with his father and Jackson gone, reassuring the women and hosing down *their* property, not the boundary of an outdoor jail. How could his life have taken such a dive so fast? Jackson had been right—he should've shaped up. How hard would it have been to just knuckle down and pretend to study for a few months longer? Then he would have been free.

— · —

Bret ran through the terminal and out to the parking structure. Throwing his bag onto the back seat, he started the Camaro and roared off into the Los Angeles night. His worry about the house had made him unable to sleep on the flight out west, and he was feeling jumpy and wired.

Once he had negotiated the car onto the freeway, Bret fumbled in the glove box for a tape, slid The Byrds' *Sweetheart Of The Rodeo* into the under-dash player, and was pleased to hear the first track was "You Don't Miss Your Water," one of the only country rock songs he really loved. But the music faded down in the middle of the song, and there was a loud *kachunk* as the tape changed tracks before the song faded up again, effectively killing whatever mood the song had generated.

Bret gritted his teeth. He was starting to hate 8-tracks. The format chopped an album into four programs and split some songs in two. This was a monstrous system, devised by tin-eared morons.

The night sky in the northeast, over the San Gabriel Mountains, glowed a sullen orange. With the windows down he could soon smell the burning vegetation on the air.

— · —

Charity had gone to bed. Maddy sat alone in the kitchen, contemplating her empty nest. Though Robbie would be back, as would Jackson eventually, this was a glimpse of the family's eventual diaspora. It happens to all families, she tried to tell herself, as she pulled a cigarette from the pack and smoked it morosely.

She climbed the spiral staircase to the tower, leaving the lights off in order to see outside better. The smell of smoke was stronger here, seeping in through the open windows. In the distance hung a malevolent sky above the mountains, much as she imagined the sky above a volcano must look.

A moving flash of light caught her attention, and she glanced down to the road in front of the house. A car pulled into their driveway, and when the glare of its headlights turned off she saw to her surprise it was Bret's. Back already? Surely he was only halfway through his shoot.

She hurried back downstairs to meet him at the front door. "What's wrong?"

His hair had blown all over the place. He pushed it out of eyes that were wild and red. "The fires. I was worried about you. I had a bad feeling."

She decided he had been smoking too much dope. It made him paranoid sometimes. "Oh," she said, dismissively, "it's miles away."

"No, it's not. I passed some spots closer."

"Bret—I was just up in the tower. I didn't see anything close."

"That doesn't mean anything. Wildfires move quickly. They get outta control."

She personally thought it was he who was out of control, but she humored him. "OK, we'll keep an eye out. How about I make some coffee and we'll stay up, on guard?"

He hesitated, not wanting to appear frightened. "You go to bed. I'm cranked anyway. I'll be up for a while."

They both walked back up to the tower and regarded the dark landscape outside. Soon, Maddy's eyelids started to droop and she had to stop herself falling off the swivel chair.

"You go to bed, hon," Bret said again. "I'm fine."

— · —

Afterward, no one could remember who saw it first. Bret was half asleep on the loveseat in the tower when Charity and Maddy burst in. The knowledge that the fire was at the property somehow spread through them as it would through animals in the veldt, and they all panicked at once.

"*Get in the car!*" Bret yelled, "and head down toward the coast, not up into the hills."

Maddy looked at him, her large eyes even wider than usual. "What about you?"

"You take my Camaro. I'm gonna try to save the house."

"But the fire department—"

"They'll save the town first! They won't get here in time!"

"What about Jackson's car? And mine?"

"Leave 'em."

Charity pointed out the window at the pepper trees. "What about the tree house?"

"Nothing we can do. It'll have to take its chances."

"No!"

Maddy grasped her hand and tugged. "Come on, hon."

The family members scrambled around, rummaging through their rooms for things too important to leave behind. Charity rescued her journal, her Monkees letter and a few favorite books. Maddy went from drawer to drawer, wrenching out documents, letters, a manila folder of stock certificates from her father, a framed photo of Jackson, and the family album. She ran back upstairs. "Where's your important stuff?" she asked Bret.

"In the rolltop desk. A blue envelope. I've got my wallet with me."

"Anything in the tree house?"

"Nothing worth risking your neck for. Go on, get outta here."

She kissed him and ran out to the car.

Bret grabbed a recently rolled joint and matches, and hurried downstairs after them. In the kitchen he found a pint of Jose Cuervo and stuffed it into his back pocket. On the deck he picked up the nozzle of the hose and turned the water on full. Then, dragging the hose with him, he climbed up to the shed roof, and from there onto the roof of the house.

From here he could see Maddy and Charity in the driveway, trying to shove Gilligan into the Camaro. Cueball and Bonnie roared past, intent on their own survival. A clan of mule deer ran diagonally across the meadow and disappeared into the hills.

He turned back to the view down the hill. A gray wall of smoke was approaching, lit from below by flickers of orange. The smell of burning sage and grass was rapidly becoming overwhelming. The sky was tinted gray-violet, and the moon was a strange tan. Ashes began to fall like snow; once in a while a glowing ember. Surely, he thought, if the wind gets any stronger the whole canyon will go up.

He walked up and down on the warm tiles, hosing down the roof thoroughly, and then focused the stream below to form a wet ring around the house. As he did so he heard Maddy and Charity drive away. The wail of sirens echoed from the hillsides.

One of the sirens came closer, and out of the corner of his eye Bret could see one of the red Topanga fire trucks easing its way along the narrow street toward the house. There was a loud click as one of the firemen turned on its loudspeaker.

"Sir? Please vacate the premises, sir." When Bret did nothing, the amplified voice came again, *"Sir! Please turn off your hose—you're draining the resources the fire department needs to fight the fire. And vacate your premises NOW, sir—it's not safe to stay."*

Bret had no intention of following either of these orders. His initial response to authority was always defiance. Besides, he intended to protect his house. He took the tequila bottle out of his back pocket, fumbled off the cap one-handedly and took a mouthful. He belched and waved.

The truck drove away. A helicopter passed overhead, the downdraft of its rotors pushing the smoke down and away in a huge, ever-expanding ring.

He sat, watching a rising sun the color of a blood orange.

— · —

"Dad?" Charity called.

Maddy looked nervously at the unscorched walls of Hophead Hills.

Charity ran around the outside of the house and returned to the front door. "House is OK. Hose is still running."

Maddy peered up to the roof tiles. "Last time I saw him he was climbing up."

"I'll go look," Charity said, clambering up the shed roof to the house eaves. "Oh God! He's here!"

Maddy climbed up too, straining her eyes to see against the glare.

Charity stared down at her father. He was curled in a fetal position and covered with a thin coating of gray ash, making him look like one of the victims of Pompeii. Smoke inhalation? "Is he dead?"

Maddy bent down to take the pulse at his neck. She smelled the liquor and laughed. "Dead drunk."

— · —

Opuntia cacti grow on exposed patches of hillside. Their flat oval pads produce bright red flowers, which after dying leave a fat fruit that must have been enjoyed by the original settlers of the canyon. They're still eaten in Mexico and the Southwest, where they are called tunas. *Even the pads, though their sharp spines make them look scary, are edible. The skin is sliced off and they're cooked along with a new penny to separate the slime, and called* nopales.

Also on the sunnier slopes of the upper canyon grow agave succulents, huge and majestic rosettes of dusty green, sometimes with stripes of white or yellow along their fat, gel-filled leaves. This filling is distilled into mescal and tequila. Each leaf has small barbs along its edge, and one vicious thorn at the end. Hikers know to be wary of these—blundering into one can be extremely painful.

— · —

The clearing at night looked like a scene from a cheap horror movie. Rice fog drifted off the paddies, seemingly dissolving the silhouetted jungle. Armed men surrounded the damaged Hueys in a ring facing outward, as Jackson climbed up the recessed footholds of one to its roof.

On top, he removed the damaged rotor and told the other mechanics to hand up its replacement. Huey blades were wide and long. The length and flexibility of the carbon and steel mesh blade made it awkward to manage, and four other men stationed themselves at the tail boom, the turbine cowl, and on the top greenhouse window.

It was too dangerous for lights to be used, but Jackson was experienced enough by now to do the work by feel. He tried to avoid looking out at the dark palms and bushes that could be hiding Viet Cong, as a climber tries not to look down.

The work went quickly, and he sensed the men around him beginning to relax. He climbed back down to the ground and stood watching as one switched on the battery, turned on the main fuel, yelled *"Clear!"* and pulled the start trigger, his face lit red by the gauges and dials. Blades begin to slowly turn. He gave the thumbs up.

Jackson waved in the pilot, and was about to climb in behind him when a *pop* came from the forest. Everyone froze.

"Incoming!"

Flashes erupted across the clearing, coming closer.

25

Charity sat on her bedroom floor surrounded by the items she had collected for Jackson's care package: Kool-Aid, Tang, and a jar of instant coffee; bottles of Tabasco and French's mustard; bags of pretzels, candy and chewing gum; a can each of Spam, Vienna sausage, fruit cocktail, and corned beef. A Tupperware container of her mother's peanut butter cookies, his favorite. In a stack were *Life*, *MAD* and *Car & Driver* magazines, the most recent Sunday comics from the *Los Angeles Times*, and letters she had hounded each member of the family to write. Now it was time for hers.

Dear Jacks,

Expect you heard Robbie got busted. He's in this new camp in Malibu Canyon for a whole year and he's very unhappy about it. Sundown moved out to live with a boyfriend in the Miracle Mile. We haven't met him yet.

We got a new president, Richard Nixon, and he's going to stop the war so you can come home soon. Gilligan misses you and so do I.

My book is coming along well and I plan to send it to a publisher next year. Do you think they will need pictures? I'm not so good at drawing plants. I'm better at horses. Mom and dad seem sad these days they don't talk and laugh like they used to. I suppose it's the war.

Topanga is the same. I heard they're going to change

the name of the Strawberry Festival to Topanga Days.
I think you and I should have a booth there. Mom showed me
how to tie-dye, and we could sell tie-dyed T-shirts. We could
make a million...

The door opened. She looked up to see Sundown, and for once she was happy to have her big sister in the same room again. "You're back! Why—?"

"It was time to come home. I missed you, you weirdo." She regarded the items strewn about the floor. "Need some help?"

— · —

When he saw Sundown walk downstairs, Bret smiled with relief. "Hey—we're off to the Corral to see Taj Mahal. Coming?"

"Sure."

Maddy said, "Let's not mention this to Robbie. He loves Taj."

"I hope he plays 'Giant Step,'" Sundown said, with a forced cheerfulness. *"Take a giant step outside your miiiind..."*

Charity, as usual, could not go. But she had one trump card to play. "I saw Mr. Mahal in town. He was wearing a sheriff's badge on his bell bottoms."

Sundown said, "Robbie used to like 'Statesboro Blues,' with that boss bottleneck guitar. He—"

A dull green car with military plates drove up and stopped. Both front doors opened simultaneously and two tall men got out, all crisply creased uniforms and boots that glinted in the sunlight. Their taut expressions said they'd rather be anywhere else than this particular place and time.

Gilligan growled.

"Mr. and Mrs. Sobieski?" one said. "May we talk ... inside?"

Maddy sagged and had to be held up by Bret and Sundown.

"Sundown," Bret said, "take Charity and try to get her in—we'll meet you down there."

"No! I want to hear!"

Maddy, her face white, ushered the men inside and bade them sit on the sofa. They did so, perched stiffly. "C-can I get you some iced tea?" she asked them.

"No, thank you, ma'am," one said. "Uh ... you might want to sit down, ma'am."

The other swallowed and continued, "Tech Sergeant Jackson Sobieski ... I'm sorry to say he was ... was injured in action on Tuesday of last week, in Kontum Province, in a place the pilots call the 'Plei Trap Valley,' over by the Cambodian border and almost all the way to Dak To." He apparently felt more comfortable reciting the details than dealing with the emotions involved. "He was part of a military operation there. I'm afraid I can't give you any more specific information than that."

A strange relief filled the room. The family members finally took the collective breath they had been holding in the belief that the soldiers' appearance heralded a death announcement. "Injured" wasn't so bad.

It was Bret who managed to speak first. "*How* injured?"

"The bombardment was severe. An explosive device went off next to him—probably a mortar—and he was hit by shrapnel. Some to his head."

Maddy prompted, "And...?"

"He will need ... full-time care, ma'am."

"But he'll get better?"

"I'm not a doctor, ma'am."

"Tell me! How bad is it?"

The soldier consulted a form. "They're the kinds of wounds we call grade three, ma'am. But he has P.I. ... uh, psychological injuries ... too. He can't speak, he can't move properly. He has all his limbs, but he..."

"He's a basket case!" Sundown said. "You're telling us he's a basket case!"

The soldiers looked uncomfortable at the phrase used. One said, "He was awarded this purple heart, sir, ma'am," and held out a small box.

Bret took it, not sure what to do with it.

"We get a medal?" Sundown said, in a choked voice. "A medal? His health in return for a big coin?"

Now the shock set in as they began to comprehend. They looked at each other and quickly away, as if this were some trite part of a movie, a clumsy read-through of a play. It couldn't be happening. Jackson couldn't possibly be less than he was when he left—full of youth, and energy, and life.

Maddy and Charity clutched each other. Tears streamed down their faces as they looked at the box, trying to parse what it meant.

Sundown's face was dark with anger, her eyes flashing. "Fucking war," she spat, springing to her feet and pacing. "Fucking, fucking, fucking—"

"Sundown!" Bret said, putting the box on the table and touching her shoulder. "That won't help."

"No? It feels good to me."

One of the soldiers handed Bret a small leaflet that listed numbers for further information and support, and saluted again. They were obviously eager to leave, having nothing else to add, and he led them to the front door.

"Did … did you know Jackson?" he asked one, hopefully.

"I'm afraid not, sir."

"No, no, of course not." He turned back to his family. Meeting their eyes was the hardest thing he had ever done.

— · —

The day they picked up Jackson at the Westwood V.A. hospital was incongruously beautiful. But no one could imagine sunbathing at the beach, going to a restaurant, or watching a movie. No one could imagine doing anything fun, frivolous and carefree ever again. It felt as if their lives had been not just changed but irreparably tainted.

Bret had rented a wheelchair-accessible van, and first they picked up Robbie, who had been granted a pass from the camp once the supervisor had been informed of the situation. No one spoke. Bret turned on the car radio and tuned to his favorite AM station, KHJ. Robert W. Morgan introduced "Killing Floor" by The Electric Flag. Maddy flicked it off. Bret turned it on again and changed the station. This time it was Country Joe and the Fish playing "Feel Like I'm Fixin' to Die Rag." Maddy flicked it off again.

"Why the fuck did you let him go?" Robbie burst out.

"Robbie!" His mother swung around to face him. "Don't talk to your father like that!"

"But—"

"I know you're upset. We all are. But that won't help."

Sundown stared out the window, not seeing anything. "He coulda been at school, with a deferment."

Maddy turned to Bret. "You're going a bit fast, honey."

Bret said nothing. The muscles in his jaw were bunched as if refusing to let any words pass his lips, in case he burst into tears when he tried to speak. All those differences he'd had with Jackson that had seemed so insurmountable at the time all seemed so trivial now. And in a corner of his heart he suspected that he, the father, had caused them. Perhaps Jackson had turned out the way he was because of the way *he* was. Perhaps—

"Shit, dad!"

Blue and red lights flickered around the interior of the van.

"Fuck it." Bret pulled over to the hard shoulder and wound down his window.

The highway patrolman took his time. He radioed in their license plate, and then he got out of his cruiser and sauntered toward the van. When he was level with the driver's window he peered in at Bret. "Out of the vehicle, longhair."

Maddy leaned over to look up at him. "Officer, we were—"

"I didn't ask you to speak, ma'am."

Robbie leaned forward from the back. "Hey! You can't talk to my mother like that!"

"You can shut your mouth too, you little punk, or I'll throw you all in jail." He turned back to Bret. "You. All of you. Get out."

The whole family exited the van and stood uncomfortably on the hard shoulder. Curious drivers peered at them as they sped by. The policeman peered in the back of the van. Bret reached into his fringed jacket for his wallet.

"Put your damn hands down!"

"I was getting my—"

"You do what I tell you. You were driving dangerously."

Maddy tried once more. "We were going to—"

"I won't tell you again, lady. You hippies are a menace. Look at the state of you. Anyone would think the goddamn circus was in town." Sneering, he wrote them a ticket and left them standing, shaken, by the side of the freeway.

— · —

Jackson was in a large ward. The family members, pointed toward his bed by an orderly, approached it warily. As they drew close they saw a man with half his face bandaged.

Maddy thought she'd better speak before her throat closed completely. "Hey, Jacks," she said softly.

The man lying on the bed looked at her with no light of recognition in his eyes.

"Everyone's here," she continued, waving the others forward.

He looked at them without acknowledgment of any kind, as if it were only the movement that drew his attention.

Bret looked around in desperation. "Isn't there a doctor here?" He ran over to an orderly and grasped his arm. "We need a doctor."

"Doctors all busy," the man said. He indicated the rest of the injured—there must have been forty beds, each filled with a man either wrapped in bandages, hooked up to tubes, or both. "There'll be one along soon."

As they waited, awkwardly, the Sobieskis attempted to connect with Jackson, one at a time.

"Hey, Jacks," Robbie said, "I got busted—did you hear? I'm in juvie! No surprise there, huh?"

Jackson looked at him as long as he was speaking, but as soon as the boy stopped his eyes slid away.

Sundown tried. "Hey, Jacks." She waved a hand. "This is all a real bummer, but we'll get you well again." She waited, but received a similar non-response. "I'm gonna be a cheerleader for the Lakers—can you believe it?"

Charity walked up and kissed him. "We've come to take you home. Gilligan misses you."

Jackson's expression showed no recognition of his little sister, or at the mention of his dog.

Then Bret took his place at the side of the bed. He fumbled for his son's hand under the sheet and grasped it. "Hey, Jacks. I'm … I'm sorry all this happened to you, son. We're taking you home as soon as I've talked to the doc." He whirled around again. "Goddammit, Sundown, go find a doctor, will you?" He turned back to the figure on the bed. "We're going to bring you back, Jacks," he said, though his voice lacked conviction even to his own ears. "Back to Hophead Hills, back to health."

Sundown returned with a woman in a white coat.

"Dammit, nurse," Bret exploded, "I need to see a doctor!"

"I am Dr. Conover, sir." She glanced at Jackson's chart. "You're Mr. and Mrs. Sobieski?"

"Oh, sorry, doctor. I just wanted to know what's going on with my boy. What—?"

The doctor led them away from the bed and lowered her voice. "I had wanted to discuss this with you in my office, but we've had a mass of emergencies this afternoon. Your son has severe brain injury. Specifically, shrapnel lesions to the lower back part of the skull, affecting the brain. We found one metal piece lodged inside the skull and removed it, but it's possible the brain stem has been damaged too—we have no way of knowing with our current tests, and we can't just go in and dig."

"Will he ... walk?"

She nodded. "I think so. But don't get your hopes up about much else."

Bret paled. "Talk?"

The doctor looked at him with a muted professional sadness in her eyes. "I really can't tell. Given the area, you can expect it to affect his coordination and dexterity, possibly vision too. There may also be Post-Traumatic Epilepsy, so you'll have to keep an eye on him."

Maddy looked at her son, tears in her eyes. "Does he ... recognize us? Can he ... uh...?"

"His cognitive functions have been seriously impaired. In instances like this, the body reverts to basic functions only." Seeing Maddy's shock, she added, "But as with stroke victims, some faculties can sometimes return. *Sometimes.* The wiring of the brain is flexible, up to a point. It's hard to say how much he'll recover."

Bret swallowed with difficulty. "So he'll be in a wheelchair?"

"Just for a while, until he learns to walk again. The orderly's getting you one now. His balance may always be a little off. Until he's walking you'll have to watch for sores. He'll be especially vulnerable to infections. He'll have to be changed for a while, I expect."

Maddy thought back to when Jackson was a baby, impossibly small. It didn't seem all that long ago. Changing him then had been easy. Now...

The doctor continued, "I want you to bring him in once a month, at least for the first year, until we see how he's getting along. After that..."

After that, more of the same until he dies. All the color drained from Maddy's surroundings and she felt dizzy. She worried that her strength as a mother would not be enough. How could anyone—?

"You'll manage," the doctor reassured her, touching her shoulder. "We all do, somehow."

For a moment Maddy wondered if death might have been better than this kind of injury, this half-life, but she pushed away the thought.

— · —

Gilligan, once they arrived home, rushed to the van and barked happily. When Jackson was wheeled out he ran around in circles, expecting the boy to get up and play. When he didn't, the dog watched, puzzled, as they pushed Jackson inside and into the bathroom to be cleaned up.

Gilligan waited, and when Jackson was brought out again forty minutes later, he put his muzzle on the boy's knee.

The dog wouldn't eat, and when Charity took him outside and threw the Frisbee he wouldn't even look at it, let alone run to catch it in his teeth, as he used to.

Maddy finally took her aside. "Charity, he's Jackson's dog. He knows something's wrong."

A woodpecker attacked a nearby tree. Jackson flinched.

"I'll build some ramps for the wheelchair," Bret said. "Robbie can help."

Robbie looked miserable. "I'm due back at the camp tomorrow." He waited until his brother was in bed, still silent, before slipping away and lighting one of Jackson's cigarettes in his room. He couldn't smoke dope, much as he wanted to get wasted, and he couldn't even drink a beer since he was legally underage. His brother's condition made him yearn to get stoned to forget about it, but they tested for drugs at the camp, and if caught he would get an extended sentence. He wept for a while, and stayed awake thinking far more than he wanted to. There was nothing to dull his mind, and it chattered on into the night, reminding him of every stupid thing he had ever said and done.

— · —

Maddy fussed around Jackson's bed. "How do we know when he's hungry? How do we know when he needs the bathroom? What can he eat?"

"Mom," Sundown said, "It'll take a while to get it all sorted out. We can't do it all at once."

"We?"

"I'm staying home. To help."

Maddy smiled briefly in appreciation. "I'll close the shop. It doesn't make enough money, and I can't be away from home much any more."

"I'll help," Charity said, "As much as I can."

"I know you will, hon. Thanks."

Bret looked at Maddy. "We should talk."

Maddy looked at the girls. "Stay with him for a while. I'll get a bell he can ring when he needs us. Until then..."

— · —

Bret and Maddy walked out to the deck and turned to each other. There was too much to convey for words, but not knowing what else to do they tried anyway.

"It's my fault," Bret muttered, not meeting his wife's eyes.

"How?"

"I should've forced him to stay out. Somehow."

"If you had, he'd have just resented you for it."

"Still..." he looked off to the horizon. "Think he'll ever improve?"

"Doctor said it was possible, but she didn't want us to hold out any false hopes."

"My son. A vegetable."

Maddy winced. "Don't ever let him hear you say that."

Bret's eyes brimmed with tears. "I'm sorry for everything."

Maddy nodded and took his hand. "So am I."

"Can we start over?"

"We'll have to."

He took a deep breath. "Hey—I need a drink. Want one?" He walked inside and returned with shot glasses, tequila, limes and salt.

Without saying much, they watched the sun going down behind the tree house and got thoroughly, wretchedly drunk. Charity had to put them both to bed.

— · —

> At the end of the year bright red berries come out in bundles all over the toyon bushes. Hollywoodland is said to have been named after them, since those who established the development thought the bushes on the hills above were holly. Later, of course, the "LAND" fell down, and we got Hollywood.

Charity put her journal away in a drawer. There didn't seem to be much point to it anymore.

— · —

Century City was possibly the newest city in the world, newer even than Brasilia. It was built on land that had been 20th Century Fox's back lot, sold off when the studio hit hard times. The Century Plaza hotel was a curved modernistic monolith, stark and clean-lined. The Amway conference inside, on the other hand, was descending into drunken chaos.

Sundown was dressed as a Lakers cheerleader in a purple and gold V-cut satin blouse and matching short skirt, along with eleven other girls. As far as they could tell they were there as ornaments, and to flirt with the mostly male executives of the corporation, who had converged on Century City from all parts of the country.

As the evening progressed, the flirting was being replaced by mauling and not-so-subtle innuendos. Many of the men, especially the overweight Midwesterners far from home, seemed to regard her as some kind of geisha, there to satisfy their extramarital fantasies.

By the fourth declining of a visit to a hotel room, Sundown was reevaluating her modeling career. She fought her way to the bar to get herself a stiff drink, and when she achieved her destination she found a familiar face.

"Frank! What—?"

"Buy you a drink?"

"Of course. A double. Anything."

"Do I have to have a badge to talk to you?"

"I'll get you one. Wait." Sundown plowed back into the throng and picked a man who looked befuddled with booze. It wasn't difficult. She gave him a big kiss and pocketed his name badge. She took it back to Frank. "Here."

He looked at it. "Jack Braunschweiger. Isn't that a sausage?"

She laughed. "But why are you here?"

"I wanted to talk to you."

"Frank—it's not going to work."

"I think it can. I'm going to get you a proper place to live … an apartment…"

"No, I—"

"Everything all right here, Miss Sobieski?"

Sundown looked up to see her supervisor for the event. "Yes, sir. I was just having a drink with Mr. Braunschweiger here."

"Your job is to circulate, Miss Sobieski. Mingle. Please get back to it."

"Yes, sir." She got up to leave.

Frank followed her. "I was thinking I'd get you your own place…"

"No, Frank—"

"You'll like it. It'll be a place away from Topanga. At the beach, maybe. I saw this place today in Ocean Park—"

"I'm moving back home."

"Back home? Why? I thought—"

She turned to face him. "It's Jackson. He's … hurt. I'm going back to help take care of him."

Her supervisor was back. "Miss Sobieski, I won't tell you again."

"Shove it."

"Pardon me?"

"Shove your job. Now leave me alone."

Frank followed her through the corridors of the hotel until she reached the room the cheerleaders used for changing. Sundown turned again to face him. "He needs his sister. 'Bye, Frank."

26

Jackson was only semi-aware for the first few days after his return home. He felt half-awake, disoriented, and dizzy, as if he had been beaten up. He disliked the wheelchair intensely and forced himself to recover the ability to walk, albeit with a rolling gait. He relearned using the bathroom without help, and to eat without too much mess. He remembered where the tree house was, and after some experimentation learned to climb its ladder again. He rediscovered the GTO, though he could no longer drive it nor read its manual. He knew what stairs were for, but his legs and feet had forgotten, and every step was a mountain to overcome.

Being around his healthy family members only served to remind him of his handicaps. It was as if everyone was waiting for him to return to "normal," and their expectant scrutiny was oppressive. Because of this he tended to keep to himself, aside from accepting the companionship of the always-eager Gilligan. Neighbors and friends stopped by to see him, but when he heard the crunch of a car on the gravel of the driveway he usually made himself scarce.

He recognized his family, but had trouble recalling the faces of outsiders. He could not read, even large-print books—the words were a tantalizing but meaningless cipher—nor could he speak beyond basic grunts. He understood simple gestures—*go here, sit, follow me*—but anything more complex was beyond him.

Half the contents of his room consisted of bewildering objects, of no meaning to him now. Even commonplace items confronted him with his new limitations—the toaster, the TV, the radio, the phone. It was as if his fingers no longer responded to commands, or if they did, too slowly and clumsily to be of any use. He vaguely wondered if this tactile reaction would speed up, but it soon became clear it would not, and he would have to get used to it. This pained him, made him feel useless, pointless, and futureless, only half-alive or less. Worse, it made him feel as if he was no longer a part of the family. They had sympathy for him, and concern, but he didn't want either.

Overall, there was nothing that gave him pleasure. Not food nor drink, not touch nor conversation, not reading nor writing. Everything had been snatched from him by the shell that went off behind him that day.

— · —

Though the Sobieski family members pretended that things were the same as before, they clearly weren't.

Everyone spoke to Jackson as they had in the past, before he was sent to Vietnam, as if he could talk back. But he couldn't. His speech centers were too damaged, though he could express grunts of pleasure or dissatisfaction. His personality, such as it was, was mostly mild, though he could lose his temper in tantrums that, considering his size and strength, were so far mercifully brief.

Bret at first took some time off work, but it didn't seem to help much. Doing so took a little pressure off Maddy, but increased her worry about income, and so he soon accepted as many assignments as before.

He didn't know how to deal with Jackson; even less so now than before he went to Vietnam. From his square, reactionary son the boy had become a toddler in a man's body.

Sundown was right—fucking war. Did the generals get exposed to mortars? Hell no. They were safe behind the lines in the officers' club. They were loose with young men's lives, unless it was one of their own sons, and then they would make sure he was held back in some soft posting away from the front.

But that was the trouble—there was no front in Vietnam. It wasn't that kind of war. Fighting went on anywhere, and the American boys couldn't tell who was who. This wasn't like the wars of the past, with clearly demarcated lines of conflict; this was fluid, guerilla warfare. An unwinnable war, and the Pentagon should have known better. They should have called it quits long ago, like the French, but instead they, and a series of presidents, were trying to save face by throwing more ordnance and more manpower at the problem.

Bret wanted to stay but wanted to go. He longed to leave all this behind and start again. Each day, it was all he could do not to pick up the phone and book a flight to New York. Or Montreal. Or Madrid. Anywhere.

"I'm gonna get you a specialist, Jacks," he told his son before he left on another shoot. "V.A. docs are no good. We'll get you back up and running, no prob. How you feeling today? I have to go on another shoot soon. Some John Wayne oater with a young girl—*Grit,* or something. Weird name. Not a big John Wayne fan.

"Hey, that reminds me—don't bother with *The Green Berets*—what a crock of shit. It must've been written by the Joint Chiefs of Staff. No offense, it's just a bad movie. Charity wants to take you to a Beatles flick—*Yellow Submarine.* It's animated. Lots o' fun. You'll like it. Your mom'll drop you two off, OK?"

— · —

Sundown felt guilty about going on a date or shopping down at the Plaza, as if it proved her a coward, but nevertheless found more and more reasons to be elsewhere. It was awkward to be around someone who didn't respond. Besides, Jackson's condition made her angry—angry that he had been so damaged for so little purpose—and her anger made her short-tempered and bitter.

When she was home she made an effort to connect with her brother in one-sided conversations, which didn't seem to reach him and left her frustrated and furious. "What was it like over there, Jacks? Pretty rough? I wish you hadn't gone. I begged you … Well, at least you came back. You'll feel better soon. The doctor thinks you'll … get better. I was living over in an apartment in L.A., but I missed you. Besides, the guy I was living with was a wimp. All guys are wimps … except you, of course.

"Hey—Len says we have to watch the next *Star Trek.* Captain Kirk's gonna kiss Lieutenant Uhuru. First interracial kiss on TV. Pretty amazing, huh? Len says he'll come by later, OK? Well, I have to go. Anything I can get you? A smoke? Ring the bell if you need anything."

Then she would take a drive, alone, and scream. Much later, she would return, hoarse, to a quiet house and creep to bed, where she would lie awake and remember what her big brother used to be.

— · —

Len stopped by the house as promised, though he had never known Jackson well. Sundown had asked him to look in on her brother once in a while, but she didn't have to; he was a loyal friend. Maddy directed him to the garage.

Bret had paid for the GTO's dented fender to be replaced and repainted, and the car sat in the garage for Jackson to tinker with.

"Cool wheels, man," Len said, admiring the Pontiac. Given the lack of chairs or stools, he opened a door and sat on one of the car's seats. He looked briefly at Jackson, noting the young man's vacant affect. "What kind of music you into these days, Jacks? You dig jazz? Soul? What about the stuff comin' outta England—the British Invasion? I like some of it. The Beatles are pretty creative, seems to me. Never know what those boys're gonna pull next."

He lit a Kool. "Want one? No? Don't know any white guys that like menthol. They got something over in Europe they call 'White Blues.' Kinda weird, hearin' Howlin' Wolf an' Robert Johnson come back to me like an echo, but with a Limey accent. What do you think? I mean, it's flatterin' to have the music honored like that, but the black musicians never got any respect here for it. Nor any bread. It has to be redone by white boys who've never had to sit at the back of the bus for the public to accept it. Kinda sad. Still, if it means the music lives on, then it's good, huh? I guess you could say music belongs to everyone. Once you write a song it's out there, like a gift to the world." He looked around the garage. "What was it like over there? Bad, huh? I don't get it, personally, but you know more about it than me, I guess. Least you don' have to go back now."

Jackson still said nothing. Gilligan, in a kind of canine acknowledgment, wagged his tail once.

Len gave Jackson a mock punch to the shoulder. "OK, man, I'll check back in soon."

— · —

Robbie was able to win the occasional pass for a weekend at home if he scored well on his schoolwork, which, to his disgust, continued unabated, though dumbed down for the overall low educational level of the inmates.

When home, he helped his brother polish the car, lit his Camels and talked. "Hey, Jacks, what's happenin'? Still working on the GTO, huh? I've been stuck in juvie, in Malibu Canyon, remember? Bunch of assholes. Prob'ly makes boot camp look like kindergarten. Makes Pali High look like a…" he fumbled for an analogy and gave up. "Well," he made an effort to put some kind of positive slant on his experience, "it's not as bad as County jail; at least it's open. Full o' scumbags, though. Never seen so many hoods. It's like camping with criminals."

He studied his brother's face. It was hard to tell if Jackson heard, and if he heard, understood. And if he understood, cared.

"I should thank you, Jacks. It's 'cos I have a famous vet brother that I get all these weekend passes. If it wasn't for you I'd be stuck in there for fuckin' ever."

But on his brief stays at Hophead Hills Robbie mostly listened to music in his room for hours on end, volunteered to go into town on any pretext, and generally contrived to disappear until it was time to be dropped back off in Malibu Canyon.

— · —

Charity responded to the situation by appointing herself Jackson's keeper. She took him his meals, or he forgot to eat. She sat and chatted with him as he puttered with his car—it could no longer really be called working on it—and sometimes led him by the hand on walks around the property or into the village.

"Here—I brought you some sage. Smells good, doesn't it?"

Some nights she read to him from the latest *Motor Trend* magazines, just as he used to read to her before bed, sometimes, when she was small. She couldn't tell if he was interested, but she did it anyway.

"Toyota is introducing a model called the Corolla to compete with the Beetle. It doesn't have enough headroom for tall people, but it's supposed to be a good deal for the money. Grandpa refuses to buy a Japanese car. He says the same factories that built planes that shot up his friends now make cars to sell to American suckers."

"Hey—the Car of the Year is the Pontiac GTO! The current model, not yours, but still…"

"The new Volkswagen Beetle is going to be fitted with an automatic transmission..."

Sometimes she took him to the beach, if she could get someone to drop them off and pick them up. She thought of these excursions as therapeutic, but it was hard to tell if Jackson enjoyed them. If led, he would paddle through the wavelets; otherwise he would sit playing with the sand with a disappointingly blank expression. She tried not to look at the scars on his neck and the back of his skull, where the hair grew back in patches.

Her eagerness to help him took the form of a monologue. "Hey—you found a shell. Isn't it funny—seashells are so beautiful when you pick them up on the beach, but if you try to make something out of them it always ends up ... tacky. You remember you told me about all the fossils that were dug up when Pierce College was built? Well, I look for fossils in the canyon, but I never find any. Don't you think that's strange? It's mostly sandstone; surely there'd be some shells, at least. Maybe it's the wrong era or something—we haven't studied any geology yet. Perhaps I'll be an archaeologist when I get older, digging up dinosaurs. That would be fun, huh? Then we could go to the Natural History Museum and see my finds on display. Want to go down there one day? They have a *Tyrannosaurus rex*—did you ever see it? I like to imagine dinosaurs tromping through Topanga. Perhaps I'll find a new species, and call it *Topangasaurus Sobieskii*. Or after you, *Jacksonii*."

One afternoon, as promised, their mother drove them down into Woodland Hills to see *Yellow Submarine*. Jackson seemed to enjoy it, but halfway through he needed the restroom. Charity had to wait at the door, and when he came back out she had to remind him, "Jacks—do up your zipper." He didn't respond. Charity wasn't sure what to do—she couldn't do up his fly with everyone watching, and she could hardly ask a passing man to do it without a long and awkward explanation. At least in the dark theater auditorium no one would notice, but Jackson seemed reluctant to go back in. "Follow me," she finally said, and walked slowly out to the street, hoping he was close behind her. Outside, they sat on the curb to wait for Maddy's return, watching the cars, and the disarray of his clothing couldn't be seen. "Did you like it, Jacks? I liked the Blue Meanies. They were funny."

— · —

Charity was telling herself that she and Jacks had built some kind of wordless rapport, but her mother was not so sure. Maddy was afraid her youngest was reading more into Jackson's minimal responses than were realistic, given the extent of his injuries. Dr. Conover had explained to Maddy that the brain could sometimes, after strokes, reassign functions to areas formerly used for other purposes. But there were limits. Jackson's injuries were extensive, and it was entirely possible his brain would never be able to overcome the damage. In which case, she had been warned, Jackson would remain thinking at the level of a five-year-old for the rest of his life.

— · —

Tess was, as usual, smoking a joint half-in and half-out of the Stitch Witches' back door. When Maddy walked in she licked her fingers and quickly pinched out the roach. "Oh, hi."

Maddy looked around, her proprietorial frown softening as she regarded the array of merchandise. She had been so proud of all this once. "Tess, I'm closing the shop."

Tess' face crumpled. "But … why? I know we don't sell a lot, but we sell enough, don't we?"

Maddy shook her head. "Not really. I'm barely breaking even. And now, with Jackson home, we need all the money we can get."

Tess nodded, her small mouth downturned into an almost comical pout. "When?"

"Saturday's the last day. We'll have a sale. If you could stay to help box what's left, I'll have Jacks … *Bret* take it to the house."

"Sure."

Maddy wandered the shelves, fingering a scarf here, a tie there. This had been her big dream, once. Now, she just wanted her old life back, when the kids were small and their needs simple. When she and Bret got along. When Jackson was … whole, and full of potential.

"How *is* Jacks?"

Maddy didn't answer at first, unnecessarily straightening the bracelets on their dowel. "He's … he's …" she looked at her assistant with pained eyes, "I don't know how he is. That's the trouble. I don't know. He can't talk."

Tess shook her head. "Poor guy. It's not fair. Maybe—"

"No. It's not going to get any better. I can't kid myself he'll get any better. Bret says he's improving, but I know. I'm his mother. He's just the same."

Tess, uncomfortable, turned away to assemble markers and paper to make the sale signs. "Have you heard from the Limey—Owen?"

"No. You heard he went back, right?"

Tess smiled. "Yeah. I gave him a little going-away party."

"A ... party?"

"Well, y'know," Tess grinned mischievously, "Just the two of us. He was sad to leave. But he left with a smile on his face."

— · —

Maddy did not want to believe Jackson's V.A. doctor's prognosis, but unlike her husband, who flatly rejected the whole possibility of permanent disability, she at least felt prepared to deal with it if it turned out to be true.

"He'll come around," Bret kept saying, and saying so often it only proved to Maddy that he was deluding himself. Was no one going to deal with the situation head-on? Could no one accept that Jackson was no longer Jackson? Or at best, had become a fraction of his former self? It would have been better if he had lost a limb than this monstrous truncation of his faculties.

Bret had been back and stewing for days. Everyone avoided him, knowing his fuse was short. Finally, while he and Maddy were trying to have lunch on the deck, he exploded.

"I want a second opinion! Those V.A. doctors don't know shit! They're just a conveyor belt to get injured kids through and out."

Maddy was measured in her response. "Dr. Conover seemed experienced to me. She said—"

"She said what the Army wants her to say! They want deniability! They want to downplay the injuries to save money! They want to reduce expectations! They—"

"Bret, this is not helping. Jacks is injured, and we have to—"

"I want a second opinion! I'm getting another doctor in."

Maddy threw up her hands. "OK. Fine."

— · —

Bret found a doctor recommendation through his union, and the man, dour-faced, sixtyish, showed up with a bulky bag.

Some of the doctor's tests were invasive and potentially alarming, and Maddy held Jackson's hand to keep him calm. He had Jackson walk the length of the living room, stand on one leg, touch his nose with his eyes closed, much like a police drunk-driving test. He drew blood, asked for a urine sample, and tested his reflexes. Jackson complied, reluctantly.

He asked Jackson questions, at first simple and straightforward ones that required only yes or no answers, and progressing through ones that required more mental processing to answer. "What is your name? Who is this woman? What was your unit? Do you know what day this is?"

Jackson was unable to answer any of them.

When he was done, he repacked his bag and stood, indicating that Bret and Maddy should come outside to talk.

Jackson followed and put his ear to the door.

Outside, the doctor regarded Maddy and Bret with indifferent eyes. "His coordination is about fifty percent. His awareness of what's going on around him is severely limited, but it's hard to quantify. I think it unlikely he'll speak again."

"Well," Maddy began, "how do we treat him?"

"Like a six-year-old."

Bret lost his temper. "Is that the best you can do? He's a young man! His life has just begun!"

The doctor spread his hands. "What do you want me to say? It could be worse."

Bret glared. "Oh really?"

Maddy squeezed his arm. "Can we expect any improvement? Can he … learn? Have … relationships?"

The doctor shook his head. "He will continue just the way he is."

Bret indicated his bag. "But you haven't got the results of the blood test yet. Won't—?"

"No."

Jackson stepped away from the door and made his way out and down to the tree house. He hauled himself up the ladder at a slothlike pace.

Gilligan sat below and looked up.

— · —

Maddy found excuses to look in on Jackson several times a day, visiting the garage during the daylight hours, and the tree house in the evening. She wasn't sure how to deal with him yet, but she wanted to make sure he understood she was available; that she loved him still. That was a mother's duty, after all. It couldn't be healthy for him to be stuck inside when the sun was shining outside, but at least she always knew where he was.

He really shouldn't be smoking and drinking so many Cokes, but when compared to his mental disabilities these were petty concerns. Besides, one day when she tried to take the third can of the morning out of his hand he lost his temper, and a six-year-old six-footer's anger was an alarming thing to witness.

Sometimes, when she felt he'd had enough of the gloomy garage, she took his hand and drew him slowly up the spiral staircase to the tower to keep her company. He sat and played with offcuts and pieces of ribbon while she worked, just as he had when he was a tot.

"I let the shop go, Jacks," she told him one day, as she sewed. "I'd rather stay here with you. Besides, Tess was a flake. I'm too busy these days with band outfits, anyway. This one's for Love. Not sure how long this'll last, though. Fashions change quickly, and bands are wearing uniforms less and less. Guys go on stage in just jeans and T-shirts now, though I suppose I can always decorate the T-shirts. Only so much you can do with jeans. Everything's leather these days, Jacks. I need to buy a more powerful sewing machine. You hungry? Shirley phoned. She wants to come and see you. Is that OK? She misses you. I tried to explain you were … recovering … but she still wants to come. Can I tell her tomorrow?"

— · —

Shirley visited, clutching flowers and some copies of *MAD* and a carton of Camels. She looked very young. Maddy and Bret left the two alone, but after only a few minutes Shirley hurried out of the living room with a wild look in her eyes. "I don't think he knows who I am!" she wailed.

— · —

Duke showed up, uncharacteristically quiet, with a six-pack of Miller and yet another carton of Camels.

Bret showed him to the garage, where Jackson was sitting motionless

[287]

behind the wheel of the GTO. "Jacks," he said, in the soft tone everyone now adopted when addressing Jackson, "Duke's here."

Duke slid in next to him and clapped him on the shoulder. "Hey, man," he said, wrenching his church key into two cans and handing over one. "Have a beer."

They sat, saying nothing, drinking from the cans. Duke lit two cigarettes, anticipating that Jackson might have trouble performing the actions required, and handed him one with a grin. "Like in the movies, huh? We goin' steady now?"

Jackson did not respond.

"I hafta go back soon," Duke explained. "Only home for a coupla days. Tough stuff they've got us doin'. Took a bit o' getting used to. I was in the *tunnels,* man. It's creepy down there. These people," he waved an arm, indicating the outside world, "don't know what it's like. But we do, huh? Anyway, I wanted to see how you're doin'."

He turned the ignition key to the *on* position so they could listen to the radio, and found a news station.

"*...earlier this year that 128 Viet Cong and 22 civilians were killed in the Vietnamese village of Mai Lai during a 'fierce firefight' have been called false by witnesses. Soldiers in a company led by Second Lieutenant William Calley are reporting what they call a 'massacre' of unarmed civilians. Congress has called for an inquiry, and the Secretary of the Army has appointed Lieutenant General William R. Peers to conduct a thorough review of—*"

Duke flicked it off. "Rough out there, huh?"

— · —

Now, when any strange car pulled into the driveway, each of the Sobieskis experienced a frisson of dread. Was this even worse news? Was this another invasion by the courts, or the city, the medical establishment, the military? Almost everyone was unwelcome now, and friends were discouraged from just dropping in, like before. Even if not actively against them, visitors still rubbed their faces in the situation they were working hard to deny.

This time it was a battered old Hudson, and its driver was a young man in fatigues.

Once he was seated in the living room he sat on a chair awkwardly, drinking the coffee Maddy had brought him. He looked as if he hadn't slept for days.

"I'm Mike. I was a side gunner on a Huey," he explained. "Not the pilot, you understand—I didn't fly. Anyway, a bunch o' Hueys dropped off the grunts in the LZ. All of a sudden the NVA opened up from the trees and f— uh ... *damaged* two of the ships. So we had to leave 'em there. The Hueys, I mean.

"Jackson offered to help, so we flew him an' another guy out next morning real early. Took tools and parts an' everything. Gunships had gone in first an' wasted the area first. He was just finishin' when mortars opened up. And ... well..."

He took a gulp of coffee. "We got him out as soon as we could, o' course. Average time to get a guy from the LZ to the aid station is only thirty-five minutes. The doc saw him straightaway. But he took a lot o' shrapnel to the head." He paused, a pained expression on his face. "Everyone loved Jackson. He was ... *is* ... a great guy. I wanted to come and tell you what he ... meant to us all."

Maddy smiled and touched his hand. "Thanks, Mike. We appreciate you coming out here to tell us."

"Can I ... can I see him?"

Maddy glanced at Bret. "I guess. He's out working on his car. This way..."

They led Mike out to the garage, where Jackson was wiping a spark plug on a rag.

"Jacks!" Mike said, pushing forward into the gloom. "Good to see you, man!" He held out his hand.

Jackson looked at it.

Bret stepped forward. "This is Mike, Jacks. From 'Nam. Remember? He's come to see how you're doing."

Jackson returned to wiping the spark plug.

Mike dropped his hand. "Oh, OK. Sure." He glanced at Bret. "I just wanted to say hi." Turning back to Jackson, he said softly, "The guys send their regards. Anything you need, man, you just let me know, y'hear?" He gestured at the car. "At least this don't have rotors, hey?"

Bret guided Mike back out into the sunshine. "Thanks for coming out. It was good of you. Jackson is ... it's going to take a while, the doc said. You understand."

"Sure, sure."

"Would you like to spend the night before going back down? We could—"

"No, no thanks. Gotta be getting back. Well, look..." he held out a card. "Here's my number. You give me a call if there's..."

Bret nodded.

— · —

Nights took Jackson by surprise, so that his body was often unprepared for sleep and left him awake when everyone else was in bed. This was a benefit of sorts—he didn't have to suffer through people's looks of discomfort or pretend to understand what they said to him, and he could do whatever he liked.

The trouble was, he couldn't do much. He would wander to the tree house, climb up and sit, watching for the dawn, which sometimes seemed to take so long to arrive that he wondered if it ever would again. When the sun finally did rise in the sky, it soon became too bright for him, leaving him scurrying for shade, usually in the garage with his car. But the Pontiac seemed to reproach him for not driving it. Occasionally his dad, if home, would take him out in it, but Jackson was unable to ask for this, and had to wait until it occurred to Bret to take him. So he would slink from place to place, always uncomfortable, always wondering what it was that he was supposed be doing. His one overwhelming emotion was a sense of great loss. He couldn't quite remember what it was that he had lost, since it was gone, but he could tell he was less than he once had been.

The thought of thousands more days and nights like this, smearing into a bland and featureless future, was enough to bring him to tears, a bodily function that still appeared available to him. Would things never change? Would his brother and sisters grow up around him, leaving him a baby in a man's body, an oaf? The thought was unbearable.

As he did so often at night, Jackson wandered through the house, alone. Everyone else was asleep. The only sound was the hum of the refrigerator and the chirping of a late cricket that had been caught inside. He opened his little brother's door, but the room was empty. Robbie lived somewhere else now—he couldn't remember where.

He opened the refrigerator, but the light alarmed him and he closed it quickly. He considered drinking a can of beer, but decided against it in case his father disapproved. Instead, he lit a cigarette and walked out to the garage.

In the dark, the GTO looked about to pounce. He couldn't recall what it was like to actually drive it. He would never be allowed to drive it again. He would always need taking care of. He would never be able to live on his own, work a job, have a girlfriend. He was no longer a man.

The keys were here somewhere … here, on a hook. He took them and pressed the garage door opener button. The door made a grinding rattle as it slid back. He slid in behind the wheel and started the engine. That made a lot of noise, too. He slid it into gear and after some experimentation managed to turn on the lights, throwing everything ahead into stark relief. The car rumbled off, chased for a little way by Gilligan, who eventually gave up and stopped, panting, in the middle of the road.

He had thought his old driving skills would come back to him, but his arms wouldn't do what he wanted. The car swerved a lot, as he tried to keep it straight and overcompensated. He crunched the gears. Surely he never used to do that. Luckily there was nobody about.

In the mirror he saw the lights in the house turn on. But then they winked out as he rounded a bend. Topanga Village was dark; only the cat's eyes in the street stood out in a hypnotic row of red dots, marking his course.

The car's engine sent vibrations though him. He used to love this, didn't he? Wasn't this important to him once? He didn't feel anything any more, except stupid.

The road began to dip as it descended toward the coast, and twisted away out of sight. How did the brights turn on? He couldn't remember.

The big car slewed around, crossing and recrossing the yellow line. He couldn't see the road ahead. Everything was so dark.

27

Bret ran out half-dressed and stopped the tow truck from bringing back the crushed Pontiac. "Take it to the junkyard," he told the driver.

The man was confused. "But I'll need the pink slip."

"I'll bring it down later."

"But—"

Bret handed over a twenty-dollar bill. "Turn around *now*. No one's gonna see this."

Unwilling to go back into the house and deal with his family, Bret wandered downhill. Before he knew what he had done he was at the foot of the tree house ladder. He stopped and looked up. Under the eave hung the remains of a bird's nest from the spring, and dusty spiders' webs decorated the rest. Paint was already starting to peel off the south-facing side.

His hands reached automatically for the ladder, but his feet refused to climb the rungs. The tree house was where Robbie had watched him smoke dope, and had started on it himself—a habit that had ruined his prospects at school and possibly arrested some of his mental development. The tree house was where Charity liked to read her Bible, until he had bluntly told her there was no God. The tree house was where he had stupidly chosen to make love with that school bus girl, Freedom. On his family's property. And the tree house was where Jackson used to hang out before...

Bret turned away.

— · —

Corpus Christi church in Pacific Palisades represented the new look of churches: one side red brick, one side glass. Maddy sat in its office with the engagements secretary. She looked from the small Christmas tree to the wood and silver crucifix on the wall. *Look after him, Jesus.*

"Mrs. Sobieski? Morning or afternoon?"

"Afternoon, please."

"Name of deceased?"

At first, though her jaw moved, no sound came out of Maddy's mouth. She tried again. "Jackson Sobieski."

"Of this parish?"

"Yes."

The secretary consulted a thick register. "There's a note here that says 'suicide.' In that case—"

Maddy reddened. "Suicide? He had a car accident!"

"Church policy is that we may not allow a service if—"

"The coroner's report says 'death by misadventure.' That means accident!"

"All right."

Maddy stood and leaned over the desk menacingly. "Change ... your ... register!"

"I'll have the registrar take care of it, Mrs. Sobieski."

— · —

After solemnly promising to check in regularly with his probation officer, Robbie again obtained leave from the camp, though as the gates swung closed behind him he felt no satisfaction or excitement and being unconstrained. This state of freedom he had craved, dreamed about, was tainted by the reason for it. He would cheerfully accept more incarceration if it came with the return of his brother, alive.

The first thing he did when he got home was to hit up his father for some money. Then, with a crisp new hundred-dollar bill in his pocket he walked to the end of the street, made the "peace" sign with two fingers, and almost immediately got a ride down to Topanga Plaza. There, he wandered about feeling out of place, and bought an inexpensive black suit and a chocolate shake with the change.

As he was about to hitch back he glimpsed an old stoner buddy of his, and hid behind a pillar until the kid had gone. He didn't want to have to explain where he had been for the last couple of months, why he had been jailed in the first place, or why he had a suit in his bag. His old friends belonged to his old life, and that was impossible to resurrect until he had served his sentence and regained his freedom.

Early on the day of the funeral Robbie got quickly and determinedly drunk before anyone stirred. He had been craving intoxication all the time he'd been shut away, but once he'd achieved it the exhilaration quickly palled. Getting high had different connotations now, its fun and rebellious qualities scoured away by events. All it brought now was painful memories of lost times and lost opportunities.

I'm the man of the family now, he thought to himself, as he helped prepare the house for visitors, finding and putting out the photos of Jackson for his mother, since she couldn't bear to touch them. I thought I'd always be in Jackson's shadow, but instead I'm in his place.

As the day wore on, he became progressively straighter. By evening he was soberest of all.

— · —

At 2 p.m. a thunder of motorcycles reverberated around the church's interior, and bikers filed in and found seats.

Maddy took Charity aside. "Want to take care of the flowers, honey? Put them up front."

Charity met the florists at the front doors and carried their deliveries to the area in front of the altar. As she did so, she read the cards.

> With deepest sympathy as you remember Jackson. *Lance Bowman, The Bowman Agency.*
>
> With our deepest and heartfelt condolences. *The faculty, staff and students of Pierce College.*
>
> May these flowers in some small way express the sympathy and sadness we feel for you during this difficult time. With deepest sympathy, *The United States Army.*
>
> Jackson, you are in our thoughts and prayers. *Duke and Edward Samson.*
>
> God saw you getting weary, so He did what He thought best,

He put his arms around you and whispered come and rest. *John "J.J." Jameson.*

Shine on, Jackson. Love & Peace. *Tess.*

Please know that we are thinking of you and your family during this time of sorrow. *From the members of IATSE Local 728.*

I hope these flowers express what my words never can. *Frank Westerby, Westerby & Gloster.*

Vaya con Dios. *Cueball & Bonnie.*

There is one star in the sky tonight brighter than all the rest combined. *Len Williams.*

You're leaving there too soon...

"Dad?"

Bret was seated at the front pew looking down, which from behind made him look as if he was praying. In fact he was staring at the funeral program with unfocused eyes, having become tired of shaking hands and listening to guests' halting commiserations. No one seemed to know what to say, and he no longer knew what to reply. "What is it, hon?"

"This wreath..."

"Oh yeah? Who's it from?"

"Neil Young."

— · —

The previous night Charity had not slept, and spent hours on a prayer binge. At dawn she felt in a state of grace, beyond sadness, though she suspected it was only temporary. Before the sun burned off the dew, she gathered wildflowers and placed them in jelly jars around the house. Around the largest jar she draped Jackson's Purple Heart. Gilligan followed her around, trusting she knew more about what was going on than he, though he didn't particularly like getting his paws wet.

Then, recalling the season, Charity looked for mistletoe in the trees and soon found some to pull down and take indoors. It occurred to her that she had not written about mistletoe in her book, and was about to mentally compose a chapter when she abandoned the idea. The book was pointless, a waste of time, stupid. Nothing was worthwhile any more.

Now, as it came close to the time for the wake and cars started to line up along the fence, she placed herself at the front door as greeter, thanking everyone for coming. When the arrivals thinned, she made herself useful ensuring glasses stayed filled, since that was what her mother had always done at parties.

She saw Rain, and sat beside her on the couch. "What happens when we die?" Charity asked.

Rain touched her cheek. "No one's ever come back to tell us. But physicists say matter is never destroyed, and so those atoms that were Jackson are now a million other things in the universe. Maybe one day they'll come back together as another human being."

Charity considered this for a moment. "And then I'll see him again?"

Rain shrugged. "I don't know. I hope so."

"But how will I recognize him?"

"Oh, you'll recognize him."

Maddy brought Charity a handful of envelopes. "Here, hon—could you open these cards and put them on the mantelpiece?"

Charity took the stack and began opening them. All were condolences, except for one—it was expensive paper with an engraved WHITE HOUSE, WASHINGTON in its corner, and it was addressed to her. She tore it open.

> *Dear Miss Sobieski,*
>
> *Thank you for your letter requesting my help in ending the war. As of today, I am president-elect and unable to influence our country's policies, but as soon as I am president I assure you I shall seek to achieve a just and enduring peace with honor in Vietnam. I will actively seek to legislate a deadline for American involvement in Indochina, while maintaining our commitment to our brave fighting men like your brother.*
>
> *Sincerely,*
>
> *Richard M. Nixon*

— · —

Choosing what music to play at the wake at the house was a problem for them all to agree on. Robbie took charge, playing Jackson's favorite soul albums back to back—Wilson Pickett, Otis Redding, and Percy Sledge. As they played, he tried to tune out the pang in his heart at the thought that his brother would never again hear them.

Sundown wore rather more makeup than usual to hide the dark circles under her eyes that she couldn't seem to escape recently. She helped her mother with all the refreshments, saying little to anyone because everything that came out of her mouth tended to be sharp-edged.

Her friend Len came, and later in the evening took her aside and tried to talk her out of her anger. "Jackson wouldn't have wanted it."

"Jackson wouldn't have wanted to be dead," she snapped back.

"No. But he is, and there ain't no changin' it."

Sundown's face softened for the first time in weeks. "What am I going to do, Len? I can't bear it. I'll never get over it."

"You will. It's gonna take time, but you will."

— · —

A couple of men from Jackson's company somehow managed to get leave and find the house. With their close-cropped hair and their style of speech—all acronyms and cussing—they appeared to be some other kind of creature. They drank heavily from the moment they arrived, and after an hour and a half one had passed out and the other was glassy-eyed and incoherent. Maddy could only hope someone was picking them up, but mid-evening they careened off in an old Post Office jeep.

At least a dozen bikers showed up, not just Cueball and Bonnie. They paid their respects to Maddy and Bret, drank everything they could get their hands on, and left to ride through town trailing a huge American flag as tribute.

Bret's best boy Doug showed up and immediately hit on Shirley, who arrived at the same time. Shirley was already in a state of shock, and Doug's attentions—kept up for an entire hour—just flustered her. Eventually she apologized to Maddy and ran out to her car.

"Boy," Doug complained to Bret, "she's high-strung."

Bret guided him emphatically out the front door. "That was Jackson's girlfriend. Time to go."

— · —

Robbie felt a hand on his shoulder and looked up to see Cindy, his mother's friend. Her eyes were soft and concerned.

"How you doing?" she asked.

He shrugged. "Oh ... y'know."

"I wish there was something I could do to help."

At this point Robbie was just trying to endure an event he never dreamed he would have to. "That's OK."

"Last time ... at the party in the summer ... you invited me up to the tree house."

Robbie's face colored. The whole evening was a blur. A *blurred* blur. "Oh yeah. Uh ... sorry."

"No, no. It was sweet. We could ... go up there now, if you like."

Robbie blinked, afraid he had misunderstood. Then, when he understood, he couldn't imagine making love in his current state of mind. It was the last thing on earth he felt capable of. He would probably kick himself for eternity, but... "Thanks. I'm not feeling ... uh..."

Cindy stroked his cheek. "I understand."

— · —

Charity and Robbie collected ashtrays and wineglasses and stacked them in the kitchen, where Maddy and Sundown rinsed everything without speaking. Bret straightened furniture, picked up programs from the church service. Gilligan lay, head on front paws, watching.

When they were done, Charity said to Robbie, "Tree house?"

Robbie looked around the house interior. For Hophead Hills the silence was unnatural, oppressive. "Yeah."

The flowers at the foot of the tree house ladder had wilted.

Once inside, Charity lit candles. "Do ... do you think Jackson's in heaven now?"

Robbie looked uncomfortable. "I guess so. Yeah, of course."

"What if there's no heaven?"

"Then ... then he's in some other place where he's happy."

Sundown's voice came from outside. "Who's up there?"

Charity peered down. "Me an' Robbie."

Sundown climbed up and joined them, but once she was seated inside no one knew what to say. After a few minutes, Sundown looked at her brother. Her only brother, now. "You're not going," she stated, flatly. "Vietnam."

"No, I'm not going. I'd rather stay in jail."

— · —

Gilligan waited for a while at the foot of the tree house ladder. Then he retreated indoors and lay down outside Jackson's door. He knew his master was no longer inside, but he chose to wait there anyway.

2000

Sundown touched the faded Madras. "Whatever happened to Jackson's friend Duke?"

"Died in Vietnam," Robbie said. "Last coupla months of the war."

"And that English guy? What was his name—Owen?"

Charity shook her head, sadly. "I looked him up. Seems he got into heroin in the eighties and overdosed."

Both women looked at Robbie.

"What? You thought I was just a fucked-up druggie too, didn't you? Both of you! Admit it! Even you, Charity, who's supposed to be nonjudgmental. But *I* was the one who was here all the time. When dad hurt his back and had to stop work, when mom lost her contract with Butterick. Who visited all the time—you? No, *I* was the one up here."

Sundown said, "But you were the closest."

He brushed her hand away. "Bullshit! You were only ten miles further out—"

Charity touched his shoulder solicitously. "Sorry."

"Anyway," Robbie continued in a calmer voice, "After Jackson died they were never the same. They went through the motions, pretended everything was as it always had been, but of course it wasn't. Then when Gilligan died ... well, it was if Hophead Hills died too."

The three looked at each other. They were done here. It was time to go. They wouldn't be back.

One by one they climbed down the tree house ladder, clutching whatever they wanted to save—Charity Jackson's dog tags, Robbie the roach clip, and Sundown the GTO manual. At the foot of the ladder they stood on the grass, looking up.

Sundown asked, "Why do you think Jackson did it?"

Robbie looked briefly at her. "He just wanted to be able to drive again. He didn't believe he couldn't do it any more."

Sundown shook her head. "I don't know. He didn't want to spend the rest of his life handicapped."

They both turned to Charity.

Charity shook her head gently. "I think it was a gift to us."

"Huh?" Robbie said. This was not what he had expected to hear. "A gift?"

"He knew we would have to take care of him the rest of his life, otherwise."

They were silent for a long moment. A bird chirped briefly.

"They shouldn't have it," Robbie said.

Sundown frowned. "Who shouldn't have what?"

"The new owners. They shouldn't have the tree house. They haven't *earned* it."

"It's true," Charity said. "They'll just fill it with yuppie stuff."

Sundown put her hands on her hips. "We should burn it."

"But it'll spread," Charity said. "The fire—it'll set off a brushfire."

"No it won't," Robbie assured her. "It's been raining recently."

"But the trees'll catch fire."

"The trees are dying. They won't last another year. The new people shouldn't have them either."

"Yeah. It's symbolic, like a Viking funeral. Dad would've liked it."

"Mom too."

"And Gilligan." Robbie looked over to the small cross he and Charity had made for the dog's grave. He took his brother's Zippo out of his jeans pocket. "Everybody got everything out they want to keep?" When neither answered, he climbed back up, leaned in and lit the corner of the old curtain. It burst into flame with a shocking suddenness, and the fire spread rapidly to the dry wooden ceiling, and from there to the walls. Pushed by the hot air, Robbie scurried back down the ladder.

They watched the flames, fascinated, and after a couple of minutes moved back away from the intensifying heat. Robbie rolled a fat joint and handed it around.

"I thought you were in a twelve-step program," Sundown said.

"I am. But this is important."

— · —

In fifteen minutes a Topanga fire truck pulled up, accompanied by an EMT ambulance, their blue lights strobing across the meadow. Charity walked up to let them through the gate.

They were too late. The trees were now blackened stumps, the tree house a mass of charred planks that had fallen to the ground in a smoking pile.

"What happened?" the fire chief asked, as his men hooked their hoses up to the truck's tanks and hosed it down anyway.

"Don't know," Robbie told him. "Spark, maybe."

"Spontaneous combustion," said Charity.

"Meteorite?" Sundown said. "A piece of falling satellite?"

The fire chief regarded them all with distaste. "My dad told me about you. You're the hippie kids."

Robbie put his arms around his sisters and smiled. "That's right. We're the hippie kids."

— END —

ACKNOWLEDGMENTS

I'd like to thank Brian Anderson, Dwayne Bertram, Giles Bignold, Annette and Zac Collier, Norma Grier, the Hollerin' Hills crowd for letting me plagiarize their name, Brandon Lukacsko, Bill Nail, dahinda meda, Charlie O'Hanlon of Charlie's Place (Glendale), Barry Robin, John Rock, Larry Safady, Georgia Westwood, Angelique Weygand, Matt Wiedlin and Alan Zaslove, some of whom shared their expertise in specific areas, some of whose stories I have appropriated, and especially Terry Green, Dr. Beverly Kimpel, and Barry Rubin for their extra efforts on the story's behalf.

DAW

Also by David Andrew Westwood

Available as paperbacks and for Kindle
Read sample chapters at *www.davidandrewwestwood.com*

The World War One Series

BELMÉDON, 1914

DENDERBECK, 1915

OTTERBROOK, 1916

VATERLAND, 1917

CHARENTIN, 1918

The World War Two Series

EMMERSPITZ, 1938

DEAUVENOY, 1939

KELSMEATH, 1940

TULLYKILLANE, 1941

KOPERSUND, 1942

VALDINATO, 1943

MOSSINGDENE, 1944

ONISHIWAN, 1945